DEATH, DIAMONDS, AND DECEPTION

Books by Rosemary Simpson

WHAT THE DEAD LEAVE BEHIND

LIES THAT COMFORT AND BETRAY

LET THE DEAD KEEP THEIR SECRETS

DEATH BRINGS A SHADOW

DEATH, DIAMONDS, AND DECEPTOIN

Published by Kensington Publishing Corporation

DEATH, DIAMONDS, AND DECEPTION

ROSEMARY SIMPSON

KENSINGTON BOOKS
www.kensingtonbooks.com

KENSINGTON BOOKS are published by

Kensington Publishing Corp.
119 West 40th Street
New York, NY 10018

All Kensington titles, imprints, and distributed lines are available at special quantity discounts for bulk purchases for sales promotion, premiums, fund-raising, educational, or institutional use. Special book excerpts or customized printings can also be created to fit specific needs. For details, write or phone the office of the Kensington Special Sales Manager: Attn. Special Sales Department. Kensington Publishing Corp, 119 West 40th Street, New York, NY 10018. Phone: 1-800-221-2647.

Kensington and the K logo Reg. U.S. Pat. & TM Off.

Library of Congress Card Catalogue Number: 2020939650

ISBN-13: 978-1-4967-2212-6
ISBN-10: 1-4967-2212-4
First Kensington Hardcover Edition: December 2020

ISBN-13: 978-1-4967-2214-0 (e-book)
ISBN-10: 1-4967-2214-0 (e-book)

10 9 8 7 6 5 4 3 2 1

Printed in the United States of America

There are many sham diamonds in this life which pass
for real, and vice versa.
—William Makepeace Thackeray

DEATH,
DIAMONDS,
AND DECEPTION

CHAPTER 1

"Oh, Miss Prudence, it's the most beautiful dress I've ever seen!"

"It's House of Worth," Prudence MacKenzie said, which should have been sufficient explanation had Colleen Riordan been a properly trained lady's maid. Which she was not.

Most lady's maids were hired through exclusive employment agencies that demanded impeccable references and proof of extensive experience before referring them to their clients. But the late Judge MacKenzie's daughter wasn't like most society employers. She'd simply asked Colleen one day if she thought she would like to become her personal maid, and when the startled Irish parlor maid nodded yes, informed the housekeeper of the change. That was it.

She'd had to learn the fine points of cleaning and polishing jewelry, especially pearls, but her mother had taught Colleen early on how to sew a fine seam and press the wrinkles out of delicate fabrics without burning them. She could lace a corset tight enough to ensure it wouldn't come loose no matter how long her lady wore it, and she had a natural talent when it came to doing hair. Prudence thought she never looked as fine as when Colleen Riordan arranged her light brown hair into gleaming coils that accentuated the slender length of her mistress's neck.

Most important to her employer was Colleen's proven loyalty during one of the most difficult periods of Prudence's life. Judge MacKenzie had taught his only child that every human being was worthy of respect and should be rewarded for services rendered. In choosing to raise Colleen's status within the household, his daughter had both honored the judge's memory and paid a moral debt.

Prudence smiled as the still self-conscious and overawed maid ran a white-cotton-gloved hand over the shimmering fall of ivory satin hanging from the mirrored wardrobe. Its tight, V-shaped bodice shone with hundreds of tiny, pearlescent beads stitched in intricate swirling shapes that danced in the flickering gaslight before spiraling down into the bias cut skirt and looped train. Every stitch had been done by hand in Paris, where the gown had its own velvet-covered wooden mannequin sized to match exactly the proportions of the fortunate young woman who would wear it.

As Prudence had explained to a wide-eyed Colleen, the Paris fashion house of Charles Frederick Worth had clothed the likes of the French Empress Eugénie and the Empress Elizabeth of Austria. More to the point, Lillie Langtry, onetime mistress of the Prince of Wales and known the world over as the Jersey Lily, would wear nothing but Worth creations. New York City's own redoubtable Alice Vanderbilt had stunned society with the master couturier's electric light dress created for her never-to-be forgotten fancy-dress ball six years before. Prudence herself had been whisked to the French capital last year to be measured in Monsieur Worth's salon during a memorable visit to her titled and formidable British aunt. Lady Rotherton had decreed that it was inconceivable for her niece to appear socially in anything but the latest Worth sensation.

"I suppose I can't put it off any longer," Prudence sighed. She hated wearing the whale-boned corset that reduced her waist to an absurdly unnatural size and made it impossible to take a deep breath. But tonight was the first Assembly Ball of the New York season, and the elegant Worth gown had been sized for the fashionable wasp-waist silhouette that could only be achieved by cruelly constricted lacing. "You might as well get started, Colleen."

"Yes, miss."

Colleen removed the cotton gloves she'd put on to ensure that no trace of human skin oil or perspiration marred the perfection of the Worth evening gown, then helped Miss Prudence step into the garment that would reshape the natural curves of her already slightly built figure.

"Hold your breath, Miss Prudence."

"I'll be lucky if I can breathe at all," Prudence complained.

She'd tossed her corset onto the floor of her wardrobe and dared to ride astride during a recent and ill-fated trip to one of Georgia's beautiful and deadly coastal islands, but such conduct in staid New York would not be tolerated. Society condemned as unbecomingly careless and indiscreet any such relaxation on the part of its young women, especially those who were as yet unmarried.

"Breathing is highly overrated. I haven't breathed naturally except in my bed for more than twenty years," announced the dowager Viscountess Rotherton, former American socialite and heiress Gillian Vandergrift, from the doorway of her niece's bedroom. She wore a midnight-blue silk Worth evening gown studded lavishly with clusters of tiny diamonds. A diamond and sapphire tiara was anchored firmly atop high-piled hair unmarred by a single strand of gray. More diamonds and sapphires dripped from her ears and cascaded down a beautifully rounded bosom. "Get on with it, girl. We haven't got all night."

"Yes, my lady." Colleen gave an involuntarily hard jerk to

her mistress's laces, whispering an apology under her breath as Prudence took a small, stumbling step backward. Lady Rotherton frightened Colleen to death. Except for Mr. Cameron, the butler, every servant in the Fifth Avenue mansion was firmly under Her Ladyship's exacting thumb, cowed into impeccable service and not a whisper of complaint except in the safe confines of the servants' hall or an attic bedroom.

The dowager viscountess had been in New York for only two months, but Prudence's aunt had picked up the reins of her niece's everyday life the moment she walked through her late brother-in-law's front door. And never for a moment slackened her hold. Lady Rotherton had sailed from London and endured seven days of rough Atlantic seas to chaperone her unmarried niece through a New York social season, and chaperone she would. The matter of finding a suitable husband for her sister's only child was never far from her mind, although Prudence was proving to be annoyingly uncooperative.

"You can't wear diamonds until you're married, of course, but your mother's pearls will do very nicely," Lady Rotherton continued, running one slender forefinger over the earrings and necklace that Sarah Vandergrift MacKenzie had worn at her debut many years ago. The sisters had been so close in age and looks that people often mistook them for twins, but Gillian had been ambitious for a title and far more adventuresome than the quiet Sarah. She'd been one of the first American dollar princesses, as the tabloid press called them. So eager to see the world and experience life that she'd jumped without a second thought into a loveless, childless union that was fortunately both brief and, thanks to her father's deft and farseeing hand with the marriage contract, lucrative.

In her more introspective and occasionally tender moments, Gillian wanted something better for Prudence. But for tonight's ball, the devilishly handsome and wholly inappropriate Geoffrey Hunter would have to do. Prudence had refused to consider any other escort, and although Lady Rotherton was far from approving her niece's choice, she had deemed it a battle not worth fighting. The main thing was to get Prudence back into society again.

Lady Rotherton didn't doubt that Hunter would dance like a prince; men like him always did. Which, if nothing else, would draw all eyes to the vision of Prudence whirling across the ballroom floor in her devastatingly gorgeous Worth gown.

Catching her aunt's approving nod, Prudence realized that she hardly recognized the sedate and serenely beautiful young woman looking back at her from the long, wood-framed cheval mirror. The Worth gown shimmered in the pale yellow gaslight and the pearls Colleen had fastened into Prudence's ears and around her neck shone like dappled beams of moonlight. Pale gray eyes that usually flashed piercingly intelligent defiance looked back at her with wistful softness. The everyday Prudence she was accustomed to seeing had fled elsewhere for this one night.

That young woman had determinedly forged a new existence for herself during the past year and a half. She had gradually replaced the black dresses and heavy veils of mourning with plainly cut dark gowns and businesslike suits more suited for a secretary than a wealthy heiress. But it had always been for a purpose: to achieve something of the individual independence society denied a woman of her social standing but her father's ambitious tutoring had taught her to yearn for and seek to attain.

With Lady Rotherton's arrival, Prudence had been forced to balance on a tightrope where the footing was anything but sure and familiar. Nothing had brought it home to her as convincingly as seeing the exquisitely gowned and bejeweled figure in her bedroom mirror. Definitely Lady Rotherton's Prudence. Unequivocally not the woman Judge MacKenzie's daughter had been working so hard to become.

It was probably past time that aunt and niece had the potentially combative marriage discussion Prudence had been avoiding.

Tomorrow. Once the first Assembly Ball was over. It was too late now to back out of one of the premier social events of the season.

About one thing, Prudence had been adamant. The expensive Worth gown would remain in the wardrobe, unseen, unappreciated, unworn, unless Geoffrey agreed to be her escort. And if he didn't, she would personally call down Lady Rotherton's wrath on his handsome head.

He had bowed over her hand with all the innate gallantry of his Southern gentleman's soul and vowed he would not want to be anywhere else except at her side on the night of the first Assembly Ball.

"I know it's not an event to your liking," she'd told him. "But I don't think I could stand all the vapid conversations and the insincere flirtations if I didn't have someone with whom I could occasionally exchange a few choice words. Or a growl."

"Growl all you want, Prudence. I'll inveigle Ned Hayes into coming with us. He rarely replies to the invitations that come his way, but his name still shows up on all the best guest lists. He'll drive Lady Rotherton into teeth-grinding fury, but with so much charm that she won't be able to do a thing about it."

"That's very much her style also."

Although he would never admit it to his endearing and always fascinating business partner, ex-Pinkerton Geoffrey Hunter was a far more social being than he chose to let on. Mastering chivalrous manners with effortless ease had been an important part of growing up a gentleman in the South, even after the war ravaged so much of what had once been hauntingly beautiful and undeniably cruel.

Over the years, even as Geoffrey rejected slavery and the world it had created, he came to treasure the remembered moments of grace, the sway of women's skirts in candlelit ballrooms, the light touch of a lace-gloved hand on his arm. Even more contradictory, he understood the convoluted reasoning behind Bible-sanctioned ownership of fellow human beings, and while he repudiated it for himself, he could not hate the men whose way of life it once was. They were his people. Since his conscience would not allow him to join them, he had had to leave. The life he carved out for himself in exile in the North would always be marked by pangs of loss.

Tonight, though, he would put aside everything but pleasing Prudence. And for the first time, he would be able to hold her in his arms. As they danced.

"I don't know how I let you talk me into this," Ned Hayes said, leaning forward to peer out the side window of the carriage that was about to make the turn onto Fifth Avenue to the front entrance of the MacKenzie mansion. "I haven't had a pair of dancing shoes on since college days."

"I know for a fact that isn't true," Geoffrey said.

He caught a glimpse of Ned's face as they passed a gas streetlight. His friend looked good, better than he had in years. Thoroughly dried out, off the white powder, bulked up with the food his man Tyrus cajoled him to eat and daily boxing sessions in an improvised basement gym where a coal furnace drove away the damp of a New York winter.

Ned had survived scandal, the two worst addictions to which a man could fall victim, and the police department that had made him its scapegoat and nearly destroyed him. At one time, not so very long ago, fellow cops who had known him and newspaper reporters who'd followed his story had been taking bets on how long Ned would last. No more. He'd outfoxed them all and crawled his way back from the brink.

Like Geoffrey, Ned was a reluctant Southerner. His Rebel mother had coerced him into the Confederate Army at the age of sixteen, carrying him off with her when she fled her Yankee husband and returned to the plantation she'd never ceased to regret leaving. For love. Which hadn't lasted.

Ned had fought because he'd had to. He hadn't been given a choice, and more than once he'd prayed for death rather than the dishonor of what he was doing or the deeper shame of deserting. Damned if he did, damned if he didn't. He lived alone now in the home his mother had created as a bride, amid his dead father's books and her memories. With Tyrus, the ex-slave into whose arms she'd placed him as a newborn.

"Tell me again about Prudence's aunt," he said.

"What more do you need to know?" Geoffrey asked. "She's a widow, the dowager Viscountess Rotherton, elder sister to Prudence's late mother by two years, and a member of the Prince of Wales's Marlborough House Set."

"What made her decide to come back to America?"

"She wants Prudence to make a suitable marriage."

"Which means someone with an impeccable family background and a fortune too enormous to calculate. Too bad there won't be a title if the groom is American. What does Prudence say about it?"

"She's been remarkably silent on the subject."

And that's what worried Geoffrey. It wasn't like Prudence to keep her opinions to herself. If anything, they'd talked more frankly to one another during the journey back from Georgia than ever before. He'd felt hidden places within himself that hadn't seen light in years beginning to open again. The expression in Prudence's gray eyes had often seemed speculative, as though she were looking at him with fresh awareness of who he was now and who he had once been. He had felt her edging closer to where he wanted her to be when he posed the question whose answer he had to be sure of before he asked it.

Then Lady Rotherton had swept down the gangplank of RMS *Teutonic*, the White Star Line's newest, most luxurious, and fastest Atlantic steamship. And everything changed.

"At least she inveigled the old bat into allowing you to be her escort tonight," Ned said. "That's something."

"I doubt you'll think of Lady Rotherton as an old bat once you've met her," Geoffrey said.

The sight of her took his breath away.

And as Ned Hayes bent over her gloved hand, he wondered why Geoffrey hadn't thought to tell him that Lady Gillian Rotherton, dollar princess and imposing dowager countess, was also one of the most beautiful women on either side of the Atlantic.

CHAPTER 2

Crowds of curious onlookers gathered outside Delmonico's Restaurant to watch the three hundred attendees at the first Assembly Ball of the season descend from their carriages. Bursts of enthusiastic applause greeted faces made familiar on the society pages of weekly magazines and the tabloid press.

The women's jewels flashed under bright arc lamps that had replaced the soft yellow glow of gaslights along Fifth Avenue. Furred cloaks parted to provide a glimpse of embroidered silk and satin gowns costing more than a working man could earn in a lifetime. The city's most powerful entrepreneurs, dressed uniformly in white tie and tails, millionaires all, occasionally tipped a top hat or flashed a brief mustachioed smile.

The Delmonico's staff had laid a broad stretch of red carpet across the wet sidewalk and an army of small boys equipped with short-handled brooms darted along the cobbled street, sweeping away steaming piles of dung as soon as they fell.

Each time the restaurant's door opened to admit a new arrival, the shivering crowd outside was washed with warm, scented air and the tantalizing smells of a dinner menu whose delicacies were unpronounceable except by those who regularly traveled abroad. *Consommé de volaille. Filets de boeuf aux champignons farcis. Pâté de foie gras en croûte. Salade de homard. Marrons glacés. Petits fours.* And enough imported champagne to ensure that no guest ever held an empty glass.

Tomorrow's newspapers would wax rhapsodic about the flowers, the music, the dancing, the food, the names of the great and near great who had graced the event with their presence. The Four Hundred saw each other several times a week during the three-month winter season, from the opening galas of the New York Horse Show through obligatory Friday nights at the opera, the debutantes' introduction to society in December, Mrs. Astor's annual January ball, and countless dinner parties, cotillions, teas, and *at homes.* Their exclusivity marked them as an elite breed set well apart from anyone less wealthy, less well connected, less fortunate than they.

Though she belonged to this select tribe by virtue of her mother's Knickerbocker ancestry and her late father's wealth, their arrogant snobbery and absurd rules of behavior annoyed Prudence MacKenzie no end. Yet it was the denizens of that world who ruled New York City, the financial and social capital of the country. The wheels of commerce and industry turned at their command, banks and stocks flourished or crashed at their bidding. Their investments in the dazzling array of new inventions transformed daily life for millions of their fellow citizens. The wives of the moguls, led by an Astor and a Vanderbilt, dictated habits of dress and behavior that were slavishly followed by anyone with pretentions of belonging.

The Worth gown and suffocating stays Prudence was wearing tonight, for example.

She sighed.

"Almost there," Geoffrey said quietly as the carriage inched forward toward the busy entrance to Delmonico's.

He might have reached for Prudence's hand had her aunt not been sitting stiffly upright beside her, radiating disapproval. She had made it clear as soon as Geoffrey extended his arm to

Prudence as they left the MacKenzie home that he was there on sufferance only. He would be permitted one dance with Prudence, perhaps two. Under no circumstances was he to monopolize her time and attention.

Geoffrey had no intention of acceding to Lady Rotherton's wishes.

Ned Hayes cleared his throat as if to speak, but the dowager viscountess fixed him with a glare that dried up every drop of saliva in his mouth.

As they climbed the curved stairway to the ballroom on Delmonico's second floor, Prudence dug her gloved fingers into Geoffrey's arm. *Stay with me. Don't leave my side.* Her dance card and a tiny gold pencil dangled from one wrist. A girl had to be careful not to allow it to be filled in too quickly and never to bestow too many dances on a casual acquaintance.

Though she hadn't appeared at a major social event in more than a year, Prudence knew she would attract would-be suitors as soon as her presence and the end of her mourning period became known. The MacKenzie name, family background, and fortune made her an attractive prize despite the reputation she'd acquired for eccentricity. *She needs a firm hand*, everyone had thought when she'd gone into partnership with Geoffrey in Hunter and MacKenzie, Investigative Law. No doubt there were at least a dozen eligible bachelors who thought they could provide just that.

Lady Rotherton led the way toward where Mrs. Astor stood in regal black velvet and diamond-bedecked splendor beside her devoted shadow, Mr. Ward MacAlister. Between them, they dictated who was in society, and who was not. Who received coveted invitations to the season's most important functions, and who was forced to pretend illness or a sudden need to leave the city. Who was allowed to approach the acknowledged queen of the Four Hundred and who was condemned to remain on the fringes of the entourage that eddied around her wherever she went.

Lady Rotherton, proud possessor of an English title, albeit through marriage, could boast antecedents as correct in every way as the former Caroline Webster Schermerhorn. Though twelve years Mrs. Astor's junior, Gillian Vandergrift had dared to outshine her during a brief debut season before setting sail for England and her future. Now Gillian was back, a dowager peeress and favored intimate of the Prince of Wales. With an unmarried niece to launch. As she had told Prudence, any titled guest was a feather in the cap of a New York hostess. Wives of the American upper classes were besotted with the British aristocracy.

"Now's our chance," Geoffrey whispered as Mrs. Astor stepped forward to greet Lady Rotherton amid a fluttering chorus of welcoming twitters from a bevy of ladies closing in on the distinguished visitor.

"Quick, before she turns around," Prudence agreed, eyes twinkling with the mischief of escaping her aunt's notice.

"Shall we dance?" he asked, lips twitching with the effort not to smile too broadly.

Seconds later they were twirling across the ballroom floor, Geoffrey's arm lightly but securely around Prudence's waist, their gloved hands intertwined, his eyes never leaving her face as pure pleasure made her eyelids quiver and sent a pink flush over her cheeks.

"You waltz divinely, Miss MacKenzie," he murmured.

"As do you, Mr. Hunter."

Prudence raised her face to his and nearly missed a step. There was a look in his dark eyes that she had never seen before, a kind of naked hunger that caused a tremor to run up her spine and a wave of heat to singe her lips.

Then it was gone. Before she could be certain it had been there at all, the look vanished and Geoffrey was himself again. Shuttered against inquisitiveness and impeccably well-mannered. Not quite aloof, but definitely and conventionally correct.

Prudence concentrated on the rhythm of the waltz, willing

the bright spots on her cheeks to fade before anyone remarked that Miss MacKenzie certainly did look a bit odd tonight.

William De Vries caught sight of Lady Rotherton and her niece as soon as the ripple of interest in the American-born member of Britain's nobility made her arrival impossible to ignore. The moment she began to shake herself free of Mrs. Astor and her court, he steered a course in her direction, majestically bejeweled Lena on his arm. He glanced at his wife, a frown forming between heavy gray eyebrows.

"Are you quite well, my dear?" he asked. She looked pale and distracted, as though her mind were somewhere else.

"Quite well, William," Lena answered. "It's just that the heat takes some getting used to. After the cold of the drive over."

Three hundred formally dressed men and women crowded into Delmonico's ballroom where stands of green and red poinsettias and banks of scented candles had banished any trace of fresh air. New York's most famous restaurant was newly electrified, but nothing flattered a lady's skin like candlelight.

Waves of French perfume and the redolent odor of the men's Macassar oil hung over the dancers' heads, beads of perspiration ran down women's backs to their corseted waists, and more than one gentleman quaffed iced champagne like water. All along the walls, mothers and chaperones fanned themselves while keeping eagle eyes on the young ladies whose value on the marriage market must not be sullied by indecorous behavior.

"My dear Lady Rotherton." William De Vries bowed over the dowager viscountess's hand. "Please allow me to present my wife, Lena."

Lena De Vries smiled and inclined her head ever so slightly, not quite a bow because she was, after all, the citizen of a country that had chosen not to burden itself with an aristocracy.

"I am so delighted to finally meet you, Mrs. De Vries. Every

time your husband has come to London I've chastised him for
not bringing you with him."

"The only thing that takes me to London is business, as you
very well know," William chided.

"I venture half of New York's Four Hundred come for our
spring season," Lady Rotherton continued. "We're quite inun-
dated by them." She thought Lena De Vries looked very odd,
as though she were about to faint, and wondered if her maid
had remembered to put the tiny vial of smelling salts into her
reticule. She herself never succumbed to the vapors, but a
swiftly extended vial of smelling salts was often the tool that
pried open a cache of interesting and scandalous secrets.

William nodded toward a passing Delmonico waiter, who
immediately extended a silver salver of champagne glasses. Lena
sipped delicately at the bubbly golden liquid. Lady Rotherton
reached for a second flute before either of the two people
standing before her realized she'd downed the first with a well-
practiced hand.

"And where is our precious Prudence?" William asked, his
banker's calculating gaze sweeping over the dance floor.

"Dancing with that dangerous-looking Mr. Hunter," Lady
Rotherton said. "What is it that makes young girls want to slip
away from their chaperone's notice? They always think they're
having us on, but of course they're not."

Lena De Vries's spectacular diamond waterfall necklace and
matching pendant earrings flashed translucent lightning in the
reflected candle flames, attracting more than one jealously appraising glance. Lady Rotherton thought that not even Mrs.
Astor's much celebrated diamonds could match Lena's display
tonight and wondered idly what revenge the queen of New
York society would exact for being eclipsed.

The conversation eddied around the former Gillian Vandergrift while she nodded regally from time to time, dragging out
one of her stock phrases that meant absolutely nothing but

could safely be used to comment on any number of subjects. The only person who ever merited her full attention was the Prince of Wales. He had too well-developed an ear for sycophantic fawning ever to be fooled by anything less than sincerity. Dear Bertie. So desperately unhappy, so shut out of real power in his long wait to be king.

The diamonds around Lena De Vries's neck caught Lady Rotherton's eye again. There was something about them. What was it William had confided on one of those trips to London? Loose stones once owned by Marie Antoinette and destined to grace the guillotined French queen's lovely décolleté had recently fallen under the auction hammer and been carted off to the New World. Where William had commissioned Tiffany to create a necklace for his wife that would be the envy of every woman who saw it.

There were the usual rumors of blood curses, of course. If anyone were foolish enough to believe in that sort of thing, no lady would wear anything but lace to frame her face. And what a bore that would be!

"Aunt Gillian has her eye on us, Geoffrey," Prudence said as the music stopped and couples stepped away from each other in expectation of new partners. "I don't think we fooled her for a moment. She'll ask to see my dance card. I'll have to lose it before the night's over."

"Who is that she's talking to?"

"William De Vries and his wife, Lena. He was a friend of Father's; they went to school together."

"Like Charles and I?" Geoffrey never forgot that it had been his old schoolmate's death that had brought him into Prudence's orbit.

"Exactly. He used to say that there were only a few decent and socially acceptable schools to attend, so it was inevitable you'd wind up knowing the same people your whole life long. Lena is Mr. De Vries's second wife."

"I thought the current Mrs. De Vries looked considerably younger than he," Geoffrey remarked.

"By at least twenty years," Prudence said. "She was a widow with a young son when they married. I met him when we were both children. The son, I mean. His name is Morgan."

As the orchestra broke into another waltz, all thoughts of the De Vries family faded from Prudence's mind. Geoffrey's gloved hand holding her own, his strong right arm firmly encircling her waist, and the sandalwood aroma of the exotic cologne he favored transported her to a magical world within Delmonico's ballroom where everything and everyone surrounding her swirled past in a mesmerizing whirl. Even the music faded into the thrum of the blood racing through her veins.

Feelings she had been denying for who knew how long surged past Prudence's defenses. She told herself she would examine them later, in the quiet privacy of her bed. But then a flood of red stained her cheeks as she pictured herself, not alone, in the four-poster where she had slept since childhood.

I won't give in to this, whatever it is, she decided, fiercely denying herself the pleasure of wallowing in a sea of blind emotion. Her aunt wouldn't persuade her into the prison of marriage, and neither would the tide of ungovernable feelings that ruled the lives of so many foolish young women. No man, not even the fascinatingly seductive Geoffrey, would snatch away the independence Prudence was determined to secure for herself.

She wouldn't surrender to weakness. She just wouldn't.

Chapter 3

"The appraiser at Tiffany says it's definitely the work of a skilled professional." William De Vries spoke in the furiously aggrieved tone of a successful banker and investor who suddenly discovers he's been swindled.

The magnificent triple-strand waterfall diamond necklace his wife Lena had worn to the Assembly Ball lay on Geoffrey Hunter's desk, flashes of light nestled in a black velvet case.

"How many stones were taken?" Geoffrey asked.

"Almost half of the larger diamonds and many of the smaller ones. I asked the appraiser to mark the counterfeits with a spot of black ink, then return them to their settings."

Josiah Gregory's secretarial pencil hung suspended over his Gregg shorthand pad. Mouth agape and then quickly shut, he rapidly sketched the piece of jewelry said to rival anything in Mrs. Astor's private vault. Following William De Vries's disdainful finger, he marked the bogus stones on his drawing, counting and recounting to make sure he got them right.

"They're sure about this?" Prudence asked. Try as she might, she couldn't tell the difference between the diamonds believed to have been originally destined for Marie Antoinette's slender neck and the fake crystals.

"There's no doubt," De Vries assured her. "Tiffany bought a large lot of loose stones at the French government auction two years ago. Jewelers know their precious gems the way ordinary people recognize their children. I don't understand how they do it, but they claim it's true, and I have no reason to doubt them."

"Do they or you have any idea when the substitutions took place?" Geoffrey asked. He glanced at Josiah, who was scribbling away industriously.

"There's no way to be sure whether it was done all at once or piecemeal." De Vries fingered his gold cigar case, but out of deference to Prudence, he did not open it. "What they did tell me was that whoever took the original stones from their settings did so with great care and skill. Only one or two tiny scratches were found, probably where the tool being used slipped for a moment or whoever was wielding it had to use extra force. The necklace was a gift to my wife last Christmas, so the thefts had to have occurred within the past twelve months."

Possibly while we were on Bradford Island, off the coast of Georgia, Prudence thought. She liked to anchor events in time and place.

"And you're sure that what you gave Mrs. De Vries was the original necklace, that all of the stones were genuine, I mean?"

"A bonded representative from Tiffany delivered the necklace to my office, Mr. Hunter. There can be no doubt about it."

"Mr. De Vries, may I ask what made you suspicious? What impelled you to take the necklace to be reappraised in the first place?" Prudence asked. She still couldn't distinguish between one of the inked stones and the genuine diamond next to it.

"It was something your aunt did at the Assembly Ball on Thursday night. Lena was looking faint. I had remarked on it earlier but she assured me it was just the heat in the room. Lady

Rotherton was having none of that. You know how she is, Prudence. Before Lena could object, she was holding a vial of smelling salts under my wife's nose. By the time Lena managed to breathe normally and lift her head again, some of the stones in the necklace were fogged over."

"And Lady Rotherton could tell which stones were true and which were not by how quickly they cleared."

"Very good, Mr. Hunter. But then I understand you were a Pinkerton at one time. I had no idea until Lady Rotherton explained it to me. She was the one who insisted I bring the necklace back to Tiffany. In fact, she accompanied me during what was a very difficult meeting with their chief appraiser. You know the rest."

"She never mentioned any of this to me," Prudence said.

"I asked her not to," De Vries confessed. "It was important to be certain before I involved you and Mr. Hunter in the whole sorry business. As it turns out, I needn't have bothered. In all the years we've been friends, I've never known Gillian to be wrong about anything."

"How is Mrs. De Vries taking it?" Prudence asked.

"She's devastated. I've seldom seen her so upset. She blames herself, which is pointless. I know how careful she is with all of her jewelry. Lena has a safe in her dressing room to which only she and I have access. I insisted from the beginning that the combination not be written down anywhere her lady's maid might come across it. Lena herself removes and replaces whatever items she has decided to wear."

"Still, jewelry has to be cleaned," Prudence said, remembering how Colleen had had to be taught to work with mild soap, a soft brush, and polishing cloths. It was a painstakingly slow process that could not be rushed.

"We made provisions for that," De Vries assured her. "Lena's jewelry is never taken to any of the servants' workrooms downstairs. Her maid sees to everything right there in my wife's dressing room."

"And you're determined not to report this to the police?" Geoffrey asked.

"I am," De Vries replied. "The New York City Police Department is famously corrupt. I'm not telling you anything we don't all know. Patrolmen regularly take bribes and sell information to the press. If the newspapers get hold of this story, I'll be made a laughingstock. Who would want to trust his money to a man who can't protect his own home from burglary or thievery by dishonest servants? The facts of this case make me look the fool, Mr. Hunter. No man of business can afford to be a figure of fun."

"I assume the necklace is insured," Prudence said.

"All of Lena's important jewels are insured," De Vries said. "I haven't put in a claim yet, but I've begun an inventory to see if anything else is missing, and I've retained the services of Tiffany's appraisers to make a confidential check of Lena's other major pieces. The firm does not disclose their clients' transactions, but I can't be sure the insurance company will be as principled where a large amount of money is involved. For the moment, I prefer to keep them in the dark."

Prudence was stunned. What her father's old friend was implying was acceptance of a loss she couldn't even begin to calculate. For the sake of preserving his reputation. Appearances.

"What good is insurance if you won't claim reimbursement?" she murmured.

"Again, Prudence, it's a question of discretion," De Vries insisted. "Clients will begin to question my ability to safeguard their assets the moment a newspaper breaks the story that my home could not be protected from the predations of a common thief. I've seen it happen before. A weakness in one area implies weaknesses in others. And who knows how long the thievery has been going on? I wouldn't want to do business with someone like that myself. How could I expect anyone else to feel differently?"

"It makes the investigation more difficult if we can't reveal what it is we're doing," Geoffrey said. He'd had to do that kind of work many times when he was a Pinkerton, and he was good at it, but he'd never liked the constraints it placed on the detective. People were far less likely to answer your questions if they had no idea why information was being sought. When you could provide just enough facts to whet their interest, they suddenly saw themselves as allies in a crusade against crime and criminals. The only problem then became separating what was useful and true from all the other bits of gossip the informant considered pertinent.

"Will you take the case?" De Vries asked.

"Why us?" Prudence asked softly.

"Your father and I were friends. I've known you since you were born. You're family, and Mr. Hunter comes highly recommended by a former client who was willing to share a portion of his experience with me. That's another thing a successful business runs on, my dear. Information. Without good sources you might as well be a blind mole snuffling in an underground burrow. You'll never see the light of day." He paused to finger his cigar case again. "It's no secret that you've stepped outside the boundaries of what is considered proper behavior for a young lady of your background. But I trusted Judge Thomas MacKenzie; I trust his daughter."

And there isn't anywhere else you can turn. A glance at Geoffrey's nearly inscrutable face told Prudence that he shared her thought.

"We'll let you know, Mr. De Vries," Geoffrey said, rising to his feet, shaking the prospective client's hand, signaling Josiah to show him out.

Prudence waited until she heard the outer office door open and close again.

"Why not accept the case on the spot?" she asked.

"It has to be an inside job. Someone with ties to the family or a member of the household staff. Even though he's loathe to admit the possibility, someone working for Tiffany. Once De

Vries begins thinking deeply about how the theft could have occurred, he's bound to have his own suspicions. We can expect him to act on them. His kind of man would never stay on the sidelines of anything remotely affecting him. So whatever we do, wherever we turn in the investigation, he'll be in our way. And when we do discover who the culprit is, De Vries will want to take matters into his own hands. It could become very messy, Prudence. You need to be sure you realize what we might be getting into."

Josiah knocked perfunctorily on Geoffrey's door, new client folder in his hand.

"I am sure, Geoffrey. I agree that it could become acrimonious. But at least it's not murder. What may be more to the point is that Aunt Gillian seems to have been the first to suspect something was wrong with Lena's necklace. I can't believe a reaction to smelling salts would cause the kind of fogging over Mr. De Vries described."

Geoffrey waited, an intrigued Josiah beside him, still clutching the newly inked file folder.

"I think she deliberately breathed on the necklace, Geoffrey. When she held the smelling salts under Lena's nose, Aunt Gillian must have leaned in solicitously and breathed on the diamonds. It's not as obvious a test as scratching on glass, but for someone who's worn a king's ransom of them nearly every day for twenty years, it's apparently just as reliable."

Josiah whispered something that sounded like *Dear God in Heaven.*

"You haven't met her because she hasn't been to the office yet, Josiah," Prudence told him. "But it's only a matter of time. She has to have something to occupy her, and my marriage prospects are out of the picture. At least for the moment."

"You had the conversation?" Geoffrey asked.

"I did. Yesterday in fact. Over tea. It seemed the safest time."

"And how did she react?"

"Not as indignantly as I'd expected. I can't figure her out,

Geoffrey. She's American, but she's not. She looks and sounds like a born member of the British aristocracy she married into, but she has a sharpness about her that's at odds with an inherited title. Did I tell you that my father said she more than tripled her personal fortune after her husband's death?"

"How did she manage that?"

"Shrewd investments, apparently. He said she got in the habit of reading the financial news every day and took no one's advice but her own. A very keen mind and nerves of steel."

I might say the same about you, my dear Prudence, Geoffrey thought.

"We don't want her interfering, especially not if you're right about Mr. De Vries getting in our way," Prudence mused.

"So we're taking the case? You're sure?"

"I think we have to," Prudence said. "Don't you want to find out who had the nerve to steal Marie Antoinette's diamonds from right around Lena De Vries's neck? I certainly do. Josiah can telephone William's office to let him know our decision."

Josiah laid the client folder containing an information sheet on William De Vries and the sketch he'd made of what he was privately calling the Marie Antoinette necklace on Geoffrey's desk. He'd transcribe his shorthand notes this afternoon and perhaps make another try at using the Remington Standard No. 2 typewriter currently taking up an inordinate amount of desk space in the outer office.

"I think the first thing we have to do is locate the fence who handled the stones," Geoffrey said. "We need Ned Hayes for that, but it's going to be difficult with Billy McGlory temporarily out of the picture. He was Ned's pipeline to everything shady going on in the city."

"What's McGlory doing?" Prudence asked.

"Nothing, at the moment. Lying low. Plotting and planning, I suppose. He sold the Armory after it was finally closed down.

Ned says he thinks Billy's looking for another property to buy, one that won't be as ready a target for the do-gooders."

"That's a strange relationship, an ex-detective and New York City's most notorious saloon keeper."

"McGlory owes his life to Ned Hayes. Saving him was what got Ned cashiered, though it was only the last straw in the department's case against him."

"All we need to get started is a name," Prudence said.

Three hours later they had one.

"Word on the street is that a gem cutter named James Carpenter recently came into a cache of diamonds whose provenance is murky enough to be suspicious." Ned Hayes settled himself comfortably into the client chair in front of Geoffrey's massive oak desk. He wasn't an official partner or even an employee of Hunter and MacKenzie, Investigative Law, but only because he wanted it that way. He was well aware of the baggage his name carried.

"What exactly does a gem cutter do?" Prudence asked.

"He's the master craftsman who cuts, shapes, and polishes the stones that go into the creations you dear ladies love so much. Most of them work in the design studios of a famous jeweler like Tiffany or Dreicer & Son, but there are smaller firms, also. Sometimes it's just one man working alone."

"They can straddle the line between legitimate craftsmen and receivers of stolen goods," Geoffrey said. "The temptation to work with really fine stones is strong. And it's lucrative if all the gem cutter has to do is cut up or refacet a purloined stone that would be recognizable."

"This James Carpenter is well known in the trade," Ned went on. "He started out as a cutter, then a few years ago he opened a small jewelry store on Eighteenth Street just off Fifth Avenue."

"It's a good location," Prudence commented. "He must have

attracted a substantial clientele to afford a building in that area."

"My source says he's particularly adept when it comes to getting the best out of a stone. He has a way of shaping the facets that captures more light than most of the other New York cutters have been able to manage," Ned said.

"What went wrong?" Geoffrey asked.

"My guess is that he got greedy. He had his own store where he was creating his own designs, and he still contracted with the big jewelers on special commissions, so that should have been enough. But it wasn't. My source said he couldn't be clear on the first few times Carpenter picked up something from a fence, but when he didn't get caught, he let it be known that he might be interested in quality stones that couldn't be sold elsewhere."

"Where are the police in all this?" Prudence asked.

"Where they always are. Standing in the doorway with their hands out. It's a victimless crime, so they wink at it."

"Victimless how?" Prudence demanded. It always astounded her that the police could be so dismissive of any but the most horrific and bloodiest of crimes.

"The owner of the stolen property gets reimbursed by his insurance company, then turns around and buys another piece of jewelry for his wife or mistress or daughter. If the thief was clever and lucky, he was in and out of wherever the jewelry was being kept without anyone noticing him. He jimmied a lock or found a door or window a careless servant had left open, so there wasn't even evidence of a break-in. Nobody got hurt. Nobody got killed. As I said, a victimless crime."

"Back to James Carpenter," Geoffrey said. "How widely known is it that he's open to purchasing stolen gems?"

"If I made it sound like every thief in Manhattan is aware of his under-the-counter business, I need to correct that impression," Ned explained. "My source says Carpenter is still a well-kept secret. He's dealing with three or four fences at most, and he rarely buys directly from whoever lifted the jewelry. He's greedy, like I said, but so far he's managed to control the risk. What's going to do him in is when he tries to pass some loose stones on to a larger retailer and an appraiser recognizes one."

"But I thought you said he recut them," Prudence interrupted.

"He does. But cutting is a long, laborious process if it's done right. He'll get impatient for a quicker turnover eventually. They all do."

"How much do we owe your source?" Geoffrey asked. No point asking for a name. "Let Josiah know and he'll get the money for you." Cash. No check. No paper trail. "It's time to pay a visit to this James Carpenter."

"I'm coming with you," Prudence said. "He's less likely to be suspicious if you seem to be picking out a gift for your fancy woman."

"Ned?"

"I don't think I ever ran into Carpenter when I was working for the police department, but it's better not to take a chance. So I won't go, but I don't think there's any danger at this stage of the game. The Ladies' Mile has some of the safest blocks in the city."

"I've been to unsafe places before," Prudence snapped. She hated it when Geoffrey or Ned or anyone else implied that she couldn't do a job because she was female.

"My apologies. Of course you have," Ned said. He raised one hand in a languorous salute. And smiled.

CHAPTER 4

"I'll let you out here on the corner," Danny Dennis called down to the two passengers in his hansom cab. "Something's happening on Eighteenth Street. It looks like there's a crowd in front of the address you gave me. I can see a morgue wagon blocking the way and uniformed policemen on the sidewalk." He reined in Mr. Washington, a big white horse with enormous teeth, recognized on sight by every cabbie in the city.

Geoffrey Hunter hopped out of the hansom, turning to extend a hand to Prudence.

"Can you stay in the area, Danny?" Geoffrey asked. "I don't know how long this will take, but I have a feeling we'll be needing you."

"Mr. Washington and I will go as far as Twenty-Third Street in front of the Fifth Avenue Hotel, then double back," Dennis decided. "As long as we're not standing still the coppers stay happy and leave us alone." He flicked the heavy reins over his horse's back and moved up Fifth Avenue, threading his way expertly through foot traffic, horse drawn carriages, hansom cabs, and delivery wagons. Being on retainer to Hunter and

MacKenzie, Investigative Law, meant studiously ignoring the angrily waving arms of would-be passengers who frequently yelled colorful invectives after his empty cab. The trade-off was steady pay and as much adventure as a hardened survivor of imprisonment in Dublin's infamous Kilmainham Gaol could wish for.

"I don't like this," Geoffrey said as he guided Prudence onto the sidewalk, carefully stepping around piles of fresh horse dung and torn sheets of newspaper. It was mid-December, so the street stench wasn't too bad, but even with cold weather and a brisk wind off the river, it could never be described as pleasant.

"Do you think it's Carpenter's shop?" Prudence asked.

"Let's find out."

Geoffrey made his way steadily through the throng of on-lookers who were clearly waiting for something to happen. A body to be carried out and loaded into the morgue wagon? A man in handcuffs thrown into the Black Maria pulled up beside it?

Prudence kept her ears open for bits of conversation that might answer some of their unspoken questions, but it didn't appear that the curious bystanders knew any more than she did.

A newspaper reporter pushed rudely past them, pencil and notepad clutched in one fist, the other hand propelling him through the crowd. In his wake followed one of the sketch artists who sold lurid drawings of bloody gore and slashed body parts to the sensationalist weekly magazines printed on cheap, flimsy paper. New Yorkers loved the vulgarity of yellow journalism, never more than when it invaded the enclaves of the wealthy denizens of Fifth Avenue.

By the time Geoffrey and Prudence reached James Carpenter's jewelry store, policemen had formed a cordon to keep back the crowd. Nightsticks at the ready, they cleared the sidewalk in front of the store, maintaining open passage to the morgue wagon and the Black Maria.

"Do you see anyone you know?" Prudence asked, teetering on heels that were not meant for the free-for-all shoving of a crowd.

"Isn't that Mick McGuire over there?" Geoffrey nodded toward a handsome, blue-eyed, burly cop guarding the shop's open door.

"I thought he'd been made to resign after being accused of murder last year," Prudence said. "He doesn't look much the worse for wear, despite the third degree they put him through."

"He was one tough Mick when things were going badly, right up until he was exonerated," Geoffrey said. "He probably bought his way back into the good graces of the higher-ups by keeping his mouth shut about the beatings at police headquarters."

"I remember Ned saying that everybody knew about them and nobody cared."

"That's only because no reform do-gooder has taken up the cause," Geoffrey said. Taller than almost every other man around him, he raised one arm in McGuire's direction until Mick noticed him, then nodded toward the shop.

"Do you think he'll let us go in?" Prudence asked.

"He owes us. If we hadn't solved the case, he might have been railroaded to the gallows or up the river to Sing Sing. Let's see if he's bright enough to know it's in his best interests to pay back the debt."

Apparently he did, because a few minutes later Prudence and Geoffrey were escorted into what remained of James Carpenter's jewelry shop.

Glass littered the floor and crunched under their shoes. Every display case had been smashed, the valuable contents taken. Here and there cheaper pieces of jewelry lay broken on the floor where they'd been flung. Paintings had been torn off the walls, as though the thief had searched for small safes hidden behind them. A man's trousered legs stuck out from behind the central display counter, rivulets of bright red blood congealing under the fabric. Recent, then. The theft and the killing had occurred within the last few hours.

"What are you two doing here?" barked Steven Phelan, one of a select group of detectives assigned to investigate crimes in what was supposed to be a part of the city where no crook dared ply his craft. "Who let you in? I'll have his badge for this."

"We have a client, Detective Phelan," Geoffrey said, his voice confident and smooth as silk.

"You always have a client," Phelan rasped. He'd had run-ins with Hunter and MacKenzie, Investigative Law, before, but he'd been reminded more than once that it was in the department's best political interests not to shut them out of an open case when they were already involved. He followed orders begrudgingly, even though there was nothing about the elite private inquiry agents that he liked. He especially didn't relish the idea of a woman butting into men's business. He'd tried before and failed to rattle the society girl's calm demeanor, but he wasn't above having another go at her. "You can take a look at him, if you've got the stomach for it. According to the shopkeeper next door, it's James Carpenter, the owner of the store, but we don't have an identification from next of kin yet. We're going on the theory that it was probably a burglary and our victim unwisely tried to stop it. Took a bullet in the belly for all the good it did him."

Prudence stepped forward and to one side, careful to avoid the pools and streams of blood that already bore the careless footprints of policemen conducting anything but a well-organized and careful search. Her throat tightened and her stomach threatened to surge up against her teeth when she saw what had been done to James Carpenter. White feathers lay all

over and beside his body, a damaged display pillow tossed to
the floor where it floated in a puddle of red. He hadn't died
right away. That was obvious from the anguished expression on
his face and his hands clutching the gaping wound from which
coils of intestine spilled out.

"Looks like he was doing his damnedest to stuff his guts
back in his belly," Phelan said, never taking his eyes off Prudence. "I make it out that the gunman shoved a pillow up against
him and shot right through it. Deadened the sound, and there's
enough noise out on the street so nobody heard it."

"Any idea when it happened?" Geoffrey asked, rounding the
corner of the display case to stand beside his partner. Prudence
was pale but steady. He would have given anything to have
been able to put an arm around her, but Phelan was waiting for
just that type of gesture. He'd read it as a sign of feminine
weakness. And Prudence herself would bristle at the implication that her partner thought she needed shoring up.

"I'll leave that to the medical examiner," Phelan answered.
"The body is flaccid, so either rigor hasn't started yet or it's
passed off."

"It doesn't look as if any jewelry has been removed from the
window displays," Prudence said, turning her back on the late
Mr. Carpenter's remains. She noticed a space where a small pillow might have cushioned a garnet necklace and matching earrings that lay slightly askew in the window. She wondered if
Phelan would point out the obvious.

"The killer gained himself some time. Locked the door when
he left and pulled down the shades so a casual passerby wouldn't
glance in and notice anything wrong."

"Then who found him?" Geoffrey asked.

"A customer who had an appointment to pick up something
he was having repaired. When he couldn't get the door open
and nobody answered his knock, he reported the problem to a
beat cop."

"It doesn't look as though Mr. Carpenter put anything in his windows that was of exceptional value," Prudence remarked. "Semiprecious stones at best, silver instead of gold."

"It's about time you told me about this client of yours," Phelan said. Hunter and MacKenzie took on cases for some of the city's biggest names. Their political connections were the only reason the chief insisted his detectives had to play nice with the ex-Pinkerton and the late judge's daughter. You never knew whose foot you might trod on if you weren't careful, and what the repercussions might be.

"You know we can't do that," Geoffrey told him.

"If you won't give me a name, at least tell me what the case is about," Phelan insisted. "You're here for a reason. I want to know what it is."

"I'd like to take a look at Carpenter's workshop," Geoffrey said, ignoring Phelan's demand. "I assume it's a room in the back." Without waiting for permission, he walked toward the open door connecting the display area and the rearmost part of the store where the jeweler worked on his clients' commissions.

Nodding at Phelan, Prudence followed.

There were no glass-fronted cases in the workroom, but every delicate tool on the workbench had been swept to the floor, the loupes and large magnifying glasses smashed, furniture overturned, and gas lamps broken. Just as in the outer room, it looked as though the killer had determined to leave nothing behind him that was untouched or undamaged. Not a single expensive piece of jewelry or valuable unset gemstone remained.

Bloody boot prints tracked across the floor. From the size of them, Prudence decided they had most likely been made by the police. She heard Geoffrey sigh, and knew he was deploring what passed for good investigative work.

"Unless Carpenter had an assistant, he would have had to close the shop every time he needed to work on a piece of jewelry or made a delivery," Prudence said speculatively. "I don't imagine he'd leave the sales area empty for anyone to walk into."

"From what Ned was able to find out from his source, our man wasn't depending on the casual buyer coming in off the street."

"But he did go to the trouble of displaying a number of items in the front windows," Prudence insisted stubbornly. "I'll go ask Detective Phelan."

"He had someone, according to the shopkeeper next door who identified him," Phelan answered her question. "Young fellow with yellow hair and a squint. He hasn't been seen around for a while, so either Carpenter let him go or he quit on his own. We don't have a name yet."

The morgue attendants had placed the jeweler's body on a stretcher and covered it with a sheet of stained canvas. One of them lit a cheroot against the smell of ruptured intestines, waving the smoke around as he waited for instructions.

A wooden crate stood by the door to the street. Prudence watched as a policeman showed a black apron to Phelan, then threw it haphazardly onto a small pile of other items collected in the box. According to what Geoffrey had taught her, every piece of what might be evidence should be tagged with the time and precise location it was found. It looked to her as if whatever might prove useful in building a case was being randomly tossed into a container that could easily be misplaced itself.

She drifted over to the door, waiting until no one was looking her way before stooping down to rifle quickly through the contents of the box. No accounts book that might contain a record of clients and transactions, perhaps the name and amount of money paid to the missing assistant. Not even any loose receipts.

Why would a burglar bother to take casual paperwork or Carpenter's accounts book? Unless Phelan's men had already found it. Or it was lying in some hiding place in the workroom, safe from prying eyes. She could hear the sound of breaking wood. If an accounts book existed, and Prudence was sure there had to be one somewhere, Detective Phelan's men were obviously looking for it, too.

Geoffrey came out of the workroom and stood for a moment watching as the morgue attendants carried James Carpenter's body out of the store. Sawdust was being sprinkled over the blood to keep it contained, and planks of wood had been leaned against the door frame. The shelves of the Eighteenth Street display windows had been emptied, the contents presumably carted off to police headquarters. As soon as Phelan gave the word, his men would nail the rough wood planks across the front door whose lock the beat cop had broken to gain entry. And if there was a back door into the alley that couldn't be secured, that would be nailed shut also. Eventually whoever owned the premises would rent it out to another retailer. James Carpenter and his jewelry shop would be as forgotten as the hundreds of other victims of unsolved crimes. New York City moved on.

"Our client will appreciate your cooperation, Detective Phelan," Geoffrey said, extending his hand. *Don't burn any bridges behind you*, had been a Pinkerton watchword. Phelan might not be a very good cop by Pinkerton standards, and he was certainly deep in the graft that permeated the police department to its core, but he was the face of officialdom for this murder. *Don't burn your bridges behind you.*

Prudence had taken out a lace-edged handkerchief and lightly pressed it to her face. The odor of death was strong, despite the overlay of cheap cigar smoke. The handkerchief suddenly fluttered to the floor, and before either Geoffrey or Phelan could retrieve it for her, Prudence had bent and picked it up with an odd, scooping motion as though she'd almost lost her balance and had to brace herself before being able to rise again.

"Are you all right?" Geoffrey asked, reaching out to support her.

"Perhaps some fresh air?" Prudence murmured, clutching the handkerchief as she fumbled to open her reticule. Every lady carried a small vial of smelling salts wherever she went, and many of them couldn't brave the city streets without a calming dose of laudanum as well. The handkerchief disappeared inside.

Phelan touched the brim of his hat as they made their way toward the door, but he didn't trouble to hide the smirk that passed as a farewell smile.

Once outside on the sidewalk, leaning on Geoffrey's arm as he steered her toward Fifth Avenue, Prudence's steps steadied. "Is he watching us?" she whispered without turning around.

"Who? Phelan?"

"Is he watching?" she hissed.

"No, he's still inside the shop," Geoffrey said, after a quick look over his shoulder. "What is it, Prudence? What's wrong?"

"Just get me to Danny's hansom cab," she said, leaning more heavily on his arm.

Mr. Washington stood on the corner, stolid, placid, and immovable as other cabs edged their way past him. The big white horse had been known to take a bite out of lesser beasts who challenged his right to plant his hooves wherever he chose. High above, Danny Dennis perched at the rear of the cab, hat raised to signal his whereabouts, whip at the ready.

With Geoffrey's help, Prudence climbed into the hansom. She leaned back into the concealing shadows of the cab, waited until he had settled himself beside her, then opened her reticule and took out the handkerchief she'd dropped onto the filthy floor of the ruined jewelry shop. She held out a fisted hand and slowly opened it. Nestled in the folds of the lace-trimmed square of fine linen lay a diamond.

"Tiffany," Geoffrey ordered through the trapdoor above them. "As fast as you can get us there."

"It's definitely a diamond from the French Crown jewels lot," the appraiser told them. "And I'm equally certain it's one we set in the necklace Mr. De Vries commissioned for Mrs. De Vries."

"How can you be sure?" Prudence asked.

The appraiser took the jeweler's loupe from his eye and set it down on the counter where the sparkling gem lay on a flat velvet cushion. It was impossible to explain to an amateur how distinctive one precious stone was from all the others that looked exactly the same to the unschooled eye. "I'm afraid you'll just have to take my word for it, madam," he said. "Shall I inform Mr. De Vries of what we've found, Mr. Hunter?"

"I'd rather tell him myself," Geoffrey said, cocking one dark eyebrow at the *we*. "I'd prefer you say nothing at all for the moment. Circumstances being what they are."

The Tiffany appraiser had no idea what circumstances the gentleman meant, but one didn't question one's clients too closely, and especially not when confidentiality had already been invoked. Mr. De Vries had informed Tiffany that Mr. Hunter was to be given every cooperation, by which the appraiser inferred that a private investigation was underway. It would be worth his job and his skin if anything leaked out, especially to the press. He reached for the diamond, intending to place it with the rest of the De Vries jewels that were being studied, but a tapered female finger nudged his hand aside.

"We'll take it with us," Prudence said, rolling the diamond into the stained handkerchief from which she had presented it, dropping the small bundle into the embroidered reticule hanging from her wrist.

The appraiser blinked and then sighed. At least this ladies' purse had a clasp. Some of them had nothing but drawstrings to hold them closed.

"Do you remember what you said when we were talking about whether or not to take the case after De Vries left the office?" Geoffrey asked as they climbed into Danny Dennis's hansom cab again.

"I was wrong," Prudence said. "Now it's definitely murder. And you were absolutely right. It's going to get very, very messy."

Chapter 5

The plan was for Prudence to question Lena De Vries while Geoffrey tracked down the missing shop assistant.

"Do you think he was involved in planning the burglary?" Prudence asked. The description of a young fellow with yellow hair and a squint didn't fit her notion of what a man who could commit such a vicious murder would look like.

"Possibly. Or he might have been paid to supply information and then panicked when he realized what he'd done. If he didn't have the sense to run, he could be as dead as James Carpenter." Geoffrey shrugged. "Nevertheless, I've got to try to find him."

"You'll need Danny's cab tomorrow, especially if you're going into the tenements. I'll use my carriage to visit Lena," Prudence decided. "It will look as though I'm paying a social call in case anyone is curious."

"Be careful," Geoffrey warned.

"You're the one who will need to watch out for himself," she admonished, smiling.

"I'll go armed," he promised. "And if Ned is free, I'll take him along with me. There's something about the look of a city cop that marks them forever, at least as far as the criminal element is concerned. If I need a little extra persuasion, Ned will supply it just by being there."

"You can't possibly be paying a call at this time of the morning," Lady Rotherton said. She poured another cup of coffee from the imported French pot she'd insisted was the only remedy for the weak American brew that was unfit for drinking.

"It's not exactly a call," Prudence hedged. She'd hoped to be out of the house before her aunt came downstairs, but Lady Rotherton had been waiting in the breakfast room for her, the first time Prudence had known her to be up and dressed before eleven o'clock. "Then Josiah is expecting me at the office."

"Have I met him?"

"No, Aunt Gillian. Josiah is our secretary, though he has helped out occasionally when an extra operative was needed." *And was nearly killed for it in the underground works of the Central Park merry-go-round.* She didn't think it wise to elaborate on the details of that case. Geoffrey's advice on how to endure Lady Rotherton's chaperonage had been to smile, smile, smile. And say as little as possible.

"You're dressed for paying calls."

Once Lady Rotherton took hold of something, she didn't let go until she was satisfied she'd bested it.

"Will there be more decorators coming today?" Prudence asked brightly. "I think you've already done wonders with Victoria's rooms." Victoria was her deceased father's unlamented second wife and the source of some of the most difficult moments in Prudence's young life. Victoria had favored pink satin and heavy perfumes. Lady Rotherton's taste ran more to pale French furniture upholstered in cream and blue.

"The last delivery was made yesterday. If you'd been home where you should have been, you would have known that."

"I do have to be on my way, Aunt. I'll try to be back in time for tea."

"Not to bother. I'm coming with you."

"But you don't know where I'm going."

"All the more reason. You're not yet twenty-one, Prudence. And we both know that for some unfathomable reason you're determined to avoid even the slightest brush with any eligible suitor. In my opinion, that makes it doubly important that you be properly chaperoned at all times."

"Does this have anything to do with Lena De Vries's diamonds?" Prudence asked. She might as well get straight to the point. So far, Aunt Gillian had been remarkably immune to attempts to dissuade her from pursuing a quarry right into the ground.

"I assume Tiffany agreed with me that her necklace had been tampered with?"

"William De Vries has hired us to get to the bottom of the theft." There didn't seem to be much point keeping that bit of information secret. Prudence suspected that Lady Rotherton had been behind their new client's visit in the first place.

"I told William he needed to have the rest of her jewelry reappraised as well. I presume you and Mr. Hunter recommended likewise?"

"Tiffany will submit a report as soon as all of the pieces have been examined."

"Well, that's settled then."

Prudence reached for the gloves and reticule she had set on the table beside the morning edition of the *New York Times*. There was a short story about the burglary of James Carpenter's jewelry shop yesterday and the tragic death of its owner, but nothing to connect it to the De Vries name. Detective Steven Phelan assured the reporter that the crime would soon be resolved and the guilty party locked away behind bars.

"You never did tell me what made you think there was something wrong with Mrs. De Vries's necklace in the first place," Prudence said as they settled themselves into the MacKenzie carriage. It was a short ride up Fifth Avenue to the

De Vries mansion, but chauffeur James Kincaid had provided warm bricks wrapped in flannel for the comfort of his passengers. Like so many of Prudence's servants, he'd been hired by her father when she was a child; fiercely loyal, he sometimes thought of her as the daughter he never had.

"I'd heard about the damn thing, of course," Lady Rotherton began, scorning to notice her niece's quick turn of the head at the word *damn*. One of the British habits she most liked and had immediately and permanently espoused was the occasional use of strong language where a polite euphemism was like tepid milk in the mouth. "With all the to-ing and fro-ing across the Atlantic you'd sometimes think London and New York were the same city. Except for the weather, which in London is usually filthy at this time of year."

"The necklace, Aunt Gillian."

"William told me he planned to commission something from Tiffany that would put Mrs. Astor's diamonds to shame," Lady Rotherton went on as smoothly as though she hadn't been interrupted. "I believe he fixed on the idea as soon as the French government announced the auction. There's something compelling about owning royal jewels that a decidedly unroyal man of business can't resist. The more he talks democracy, the more he yearns for a king. It's one of the great dichotomies of our supposedly egalitarian society." She made an odd, dismissive sound at the vagaries of human nature. "We all understand that Mrs. Astor is your uncrowned American queen, so this rivalry to best or unseat her is rather fun to watch. From a distance." No one would dream of upstaging Queen Victoria, the long-widowed monarch who two years before had celebrated the Diamond Jubilee of her accession.

"I'm afraid I don't know very much about diamonds," Prudence confessed.

"It's about time you learned," Lady Rotherton snapped decidedly. "Your mother had some beautiful pieces that you'll no doubt want to wear as soon as you're married."

Best not to inform her aunt that her father's second wife had sold many of Sarah MacKenzie's jewels or had them reset to suit her more garish tastes. According to a story the late judge had once told her, Lady Rotherton was capable of stupendous rages that could last for days.

"The first thing you must do is be able to distinguish a genuine stone from one that is not. Unfortunately, as some old family fortunes have declined, it has become rather commonplace for imitations to be commissioned. It sometimes takes a good eye to tell the difference." She didn't bother to explain to Prudence why it was vital to discern which of the two a woman wore around her neck or on her fingers.

"So you knew immediately that something was wrong with the necklace Lena De Vries was wearing?" Prudence asked.

"I could spot the difference between the stones from halfway across the room," Lady Rotherton declared unequivocally. "I don't know why no one else saw it before now. All I had to do to confirm what I already suspected was breathe on them. Diamonds clear almost instantaneously while fakes do not. It's really quite simple. I assume William explained all this to you?"

"You managed it beautifully," Prudence said. "I don't imagine even Lena realized what you were doing until much later."

"Of course she did," Lady Rotherton retorted. "If it hadn't been for the smelling salts I was holding beneath her nose, she would have collapsed at my feet. Believe me, Prudence, she was well aware of the fraud she was perpetrating. And terrified that William would learn of it. That's why she was looking so pale and unsettled. It had nothing to do with the heat of the room."

"We're here," Prudence said as the carriage rolled to a halt before a mansion that rivaled anything the Vanderbilts had constructed along Fifth Avenue. She thought she understood now why Lady Rotherton had insisted on coming with her this morning, and also why she'd remained silent on the subject of the De Vries diamonds until now. The way her aunt spoke William De Vries's name told her that the friendship dating back to before Gillian Vandergrift left America to marry a title had developed over the years and his many London visits into something considerably warmer.

She wondered if Lady Rotherton knew how much of herself she gave away to the niece trained by a master litigator and judge to read through the layers of deception with which people protected the secrets they most wanted to hide.

Geoffrey began with the merchants on either side of James Carpenter's jewelry shop. Its front door and display windows had been crisscrossed with rough wood planks, nailed firmly in place to discourage looters. The few early morning shoppers on Eighteenth Street gave it a wide berth, hurrying past with a sidelong glance as if they expected the door to open and a river of blood to flow out over their shoes. The *Times* had buried the story on its back pages, but the city's other newspapers had supplied all the gory details of the murder and added speculation about the motive, none of it based on anything more factual than the reporters' fertile imaginations.

"Carpenter kept to himself," the haberdasher who had first identified the body said, folding and refolding a brightly patterned silk waistcoat. "I don't mean he was standoffish, because he was friendly enough, but he didn't have much to say for himself and he never talked about his clients."

"You told the police that he employed a young man to help him in the shop," Geoffrey said.

"We've been getting more street traffic the past year or so," the gentleman's outfitter volunteered. "Especially after Thanksgiving. People shopping for Christmas gifts, you know."

"So the young man he hired to clerk for him was only here for a very short time? Didn't you tell the detective that you hadn't seen him in a while?" There were inherent contradictions in what the haberdasher was claiming. Pointing them out was one way of getting to the truth of the matter.

"Well, he worked odd hours and not all the time. I wouldn't

see him for a few days and then he'd show up again. There wasn't any pattern to it." Now he rearranged a stack of already perfectly aligned cravats. "Actually what I thought was that Mr. Carpenter was giving occasional employment to a nephew or perhaps a cousin's son. Maybe the lad was looking for something permanent, but in the meanwhile was helping out behind the counter and running errands when needed."

"The lad? How old would you say he was, this nephew or cousin's son?"

"Early twenties would be my best guess. I only saw him from a distance."

"But close enough so you remember he had yellow hair and a squint."

"I did step outside one day as he was arriving. He doffed his hat and said good morning. Very polite."

"And his name?"

"We weren't introduced. And I don't recall Mr. Carpenter ever mentioning it."

"So when was the first time you remember seeing this anonymous young man with the yellow hair?"

The haberdasher had to think about it. "Six or eight months ago, perhaps? It was in early summer, I believe. I remember thinking that he didn't look very much like a customer."

"How so?"

"His suit was a bit shabby and his boots weren't polished. Not the kind of person you'd expect to see going into a jeweler's shop in this part of the city."

"Unless he was casing it," Geoffrey said.

"That did occur to me. But then he came back. Very irregularly, as I said, but he soon became a familiar figure and I got used to seeing him."

"When was the last time he was in Carpenter's store?"

"Two weeks ago. I didn't remark it much until the police asked if I'd seen anyone suspicious hanging around. I hadn't. But then I got to thinking that the young fellow who'd been helping out there hadn't shown up in a while. I suppose he could have found other work."

But from the tone of the merchant's voice, Geoffrey could tell he doubted it.

The other shopkeepers on the street had nothing to add to what the haberdasher recalled. They seemed more interested in what kind of enterprise would be moving into the now empty store and when it would reopen than in getting to the bottom of James Carpenter's sudden demise.

The one clue to the missing shop assistant's identity came not from Carpenter's neighboring storekeepers on Eighteenth Street, but from Danny Dennis.

"The sweepers who work this area all remember him. He had a smile and sometimes a penny or two for them," Dennis told Geoffrey, adjusting the feed bag of oats and cracked corn into which he'd fitted Mr. Washington's broad, white muzzle. "They get to know the regulars pretty quickly. No names, of course, but faces and whether or not they're good for a touch." Sweeping up the piles of manure that littered the streets was a tough and dirty job; without the gangs of street boys wielding brushes and shovels, the city's roadways would very soon become nearly impassable.

"Did any of them see what direction he came from?"

"Not on a regular basis, but one of the sweeper boys claims to have seen him down around the Five Points where the Italians are moving in on the Irish gangs. He thinks he lives there and came up here whenever Carpenter sent word he needed him."

"Does he have proof of any of that?"

"You know how these boys are, Mr. Hunter. They keep their eyes open and their hands out, but most of what they sell is speculation. A lot of them are biding their time until they're old enough and tough enough to get into one of the gangs. It's not an easy life, but for the orphan sweepers sleeping in the streets, it's more attractive that what they've got; they're desperate to belong somewhere."

"I've seen Jacob Riis's photographs."

"He's only touching the surface. For every tenement room shared by three families, there are dozens of others far worse."

"Are you up to going down to Five Points, Danny?"

"I am. But I think we'd be wise to take Mr. Ned Hayes with us, if he's available. Everybody in the city knows the police department fired him for saving Billy McGlory's life. That's enough to keep knives in their sheaths and pistols in their holsters—for a while, at least."

"McGlory's out of the picture, or so Ned says."

"For the moment. But he's not forgotten. He's still a power to be reckoned with. And nobody believes he'll move out to Long Island to cultivate vegetables. He'll be back. And when he does resurface, anyone who used to deal with him will want to be on his good side. Stepping on Mr. Hayes wouldn't be the way to do that. He's like an insurance policy that pays off more than once."

Danny ran a lightly oiled rag over the long driver's whip, as lethal as a bullet in the right hands. He uncoupled Mr. Washington's feed bag, waited for Geoffrey to seat himself in the cab, then eased out into the midmorning traffic, a loaded revolver tucked into his belt and another hidden beneath his footboard. A razor sharp knife was strapped to his right ankle.

It was best not to take any chances in the Five Points.

CHAPTER 6

The De Vries mansion was darkly opulent and affluently silent, furnished from floor to ceiling with imported antique tables, chairs, and sofas in varying styles of pre-Revolution French courts. English landscape paintings adorned the walls, enormous Chinese vases lurked in all the corners, the windows were draped in heavy velvet, and Turkish carpets in faded jewel tones muffled footsteps and stray voices. It was, Prudence thought, as gloomy as a lily-drenched funeral parlor, without the corpse.

Lady Rotherton had informed the butler that Mrs. De Vries, despite the early hour, would indeed receive them. Trained in England, he took one look at Her Ladyship and was immediately convinced that contradiction or argument would not be tolerated. Nor would they do a bit of good. Bowing deeply, he ushered Prudence and her aunt to the morning parlor, offered coffee in case their wait should be longer than a few minutes, and left to deliver the news of their unexpected arrival.

"Remind me again how well you know Lena De Vries, Prudence," Lady Rotherton said as soon as the butler had departed and an aproned parlor maid delivered the coffee tray.

"Not well at all. William De Vries was a frequent visitor to the house when I was very young, but he and my father always closeted themselves in the library together. I was sometimes paraded in from the nursery to say a brief hello and drop a curtsy, but hardly more than that. After Father married Victoria he met his men friends at one or the other of his clubs. No one came to the house anymore. Even Father stayed away as much as he could. I mainly remember Lena as another of the ladies in big hats and veils who leaned over to say something I didn't understand after church on Sundays."

"William spoke very little of her when he came to London," Lady Rotherton volunteered. "Not entirely unexpected, under the circumstances. I introduced him to the Marlborough House Set; he and His Royal Highness get along very well. They have cards, horses, and women in common."

It seemed to Prudence a strange conversation to be having in the lady's own parlor, but her aunt's instinct for rents in the fabric of polite society had already proved to be exceptionally acute. And as she had learned from Geoffrey, no bit of information was too insignificant to be ignored, especially during the early days of an investigation.

Lady Rotherton contended that Lena was aware that some of the stones she had worn to the Assembly Ball were fake. It would be up to Prudence to persuade Lena to confirm or disprove that allegation. She intended to question William De Vries's wife until she was satisfied Lena had told them everything she could. As politely as possible, Prudence would have to convince her aunt that she knew what she was doing.

"I think it would be best if you were to leave most of the questioning to me, Aunt," Prudence began.

"You're not a Pinkerton, my dear, no matter how well Mr. Hunter has trained you in their methods," Lady Rotherton declared, peering disapprovingly into the silver coffeepot.

"But I have had considerable experience getting to the bottom of things," Prudence insisted.

"I doubt Mrs. De Vries will take kindly to being asked personal questions by someone young enough to be her daughter. It's simply not done, Prudence."

"Nevertheless, Aunt . . ." Prudence was on the point of saying something she later thought she would have regretted when the parlor door opened to a very pale and exhausted-looking Lena De Vries.

"I do hope you'll forgive my having kept you waiting," she said, gliding warily across the room, one hand lightly touching the back of every piece of furniture she passed, as if seeking reassurances of support.

"I regret that my visit had to be on such short notice," Prudence said. *My* visit.

"William told me to expect either you or Mr. Hunter." Lena seated herself opposite Lady Rotherton, nodding politely at each of her guests in turn.

"Then you know why I'm here," Prudence continued smoothly.

"I do. But I'm not sure I can be of help." Lena folded her hands neatly in her lap. The fingers twitched as though desperate to twist themselves into knots. "I was as surprised as you, Lady Rotherton, to learn that some of the diamonds in my necklace were not what they appeared to be."

"I rather doubt that, Lena," Lady Rotherton said. "I hope I may call you Lena, my dear. Your husband and I have been on first-name terms for many years. I should so like it if we, too, were to dispense with formality."

"Will you tell us the story of the necklace, from the beginning?" Prudence said before Lady Rotherton could get another word in, before their hostess realized that one of her guests had just implied she'd deliberately lied to them.

"It was a gift," Lena began.

"And a very splendid one, I must say," Lady Rotherton commented. "But then, William is the soul of gentlemanly generosity."

What on earth is she doing? Prudence wondered how she would deflect her aunt's remark. No wife could miss the obvious implication. "I'm sure it must have been a delightful surprise."

"The design is not a Tiffany original," Lena continued. "It seems there was a drawing of what was to have been created for Queen Marie Antoinette to celebrate the birth of the Dauphin in 1781. No one knows why the king changed his mind, but the necklace was never made. The stones that had been selected for it were still in the royal coffers at the time of the Revolution, and they were included in the auction. William commissioned Tiffany to replicate it, and they agreed."

"What a lovely story," Lady Rotherton purred.

"Where is the necklace usually kept?" Prudence asked.

"William leases a vault at Tiffany for the most valuable family pieces," Lena said.

"Is all your jewelry kept in the vault?"

"Just the items he judges irreplaceable. Most of what I wear every day and to all but the most exclusive balls is here in the house. I have a safe in my dressing room, and there's another one in the library. But, really, Miss MacKenzie, it's not something we've ever worried about. Our servants are well-trained and loyal. Many of them have been with us for years."

"I'm sure my niece would not object to your calling her by her first name, as you undoubtedly did when she was a child," Lady Rotherton interrupted smoothly.

Lena nodded. "You and Morgan played so sweetly together," she murmured nostalgically.

"Can you take us back through the day of the Assembly Ball?" Prudence asked, borrowing a leaf from Geoffrey's book about never allowing a witness to direct or deflect an interrogation. "Begin with whoever was to retrieve the necklace from Tiffany's vault. I assume it wasn't done any earlier than that Thursday."

"Actually it was the day before," Lena said. "And that was a last-minute change of plans no one could have known about in advance."

"May I take it that one of Tiffany's bonded messengers delivered the necklace directly to you, and that you signed for it?" Prudence went on.

"I wasn't here," Lena stammered.

Lady Rotherton's eyebrows shot up. She set down her coffee cup with exaggerated care, then fixed a gimlet-eyed stare on William's wife. A generation younger than her husband. And yes, Lena De Vries was every bit as beautiful as gossip had reported her being. Pale, porcelain skin; deeply violet eyes; midnight black hair without a thread of silver to hint that she had passed her fortieth birthday. No wonder William had been smitten by the wealthy young widow who at the time he met her was mother to a six-year-old boy. The first Mrs. De Vries had never conceived. He must have expected his world to change when he took Lena Whitley to wife. But it hadn't. He'd remained a childless husband, desperate for a son to succeed him in the banking and investment businesses that had made him one of America's wealthiest men.

"I don't understand," Prudence said, reading quick condemnation in her aunt's eyes. "Surely the necklace wouldn't have been turned over to anyone but you or Mr. De Vries."

"I didn't know William had made the arrangements he did." Lena hesitated, then explained, all in a rush. "He assumed I would be home, but by the time he telephoned to inform me that the Tiffany representative was on his way, I had already left. He was furious because it meant he had to leave his office. The necklace had to be put into a safe, and there was no one here who knew the combinations."

"I'm not sure I'm hearing this correctly," Lady Rotherton interrupted. "On the day of the Assembly Ball you were out paying calls?"

"The day before," Prudence corrected.

"That's nearly as bad," Lady Rotherton snapped. A lady devoted the utmost care to her appearance at all times, but never so meticulously as when she appeared at an important social function. It could and often did take days to complete all the preparations. To gad about in wintry New York weather the day before an Assembly Ball was nothing short of foolhardy.

"I wasn't exactly paying calls, Lady Rotherton." Lena De Vries seemed to be acquiring a bit of backbone. "Had I known William intended that the necklace be delivered a day early, of course I would have made sure I was here to receive it. Since I did not know of his plans, I see no reason why I should have to explain my absence."

"So I suppose that you inspected the necklace sometime that evening?" Prudence asked. She knew it was on the tip of her aunt's tongue to ask just where Lena De Vries had spent that important afternoon, and why her husband had not known where she was, but Prudence wasn't ready to risk antagonizing William's wife yet. Where she had gone wasn't as important as who had handled the necklace between the time it left Tiffany's vault and Lena's appearance at the ball.

"William had placed it in the library safe. He gave it to me before dinner and I handed it over to Taylor, my lady's maid."

"You didn't open the case and look at it?"

"William and I both did. In the library. Neither of us noticed that anything was wrong."

"So Taylor cleaned the stones and the settings. And she didn't suspect anything either?"

"She told me before I went to bed that she'd only had to give it a light polish. I don't wear it very often. But no, she didn't remark anything out of the ordinary. And it was locked in the safe in my dressing room that night."

"Was there anyone in the house the day of the ball who was not a member of your regular staff?" Prudence asked.

"No. I spent most of the day resting. Reading, writing letters. Getting ready."

"Why don't you wear it very often, Lena?" Lady Rotherton asked before Prudence could stop her. "It isn't every woman who can boast of owning a necklace literally made for a queen."

Lena flushed a pale shade of pink with two red spots high on her cheekbones, the only sign that Lady Rotherton's remark had touched a nerve. Her hands remained in her lap and her fixed smile never wavered.

"Is it because the original necklace was to have been crafted to celebrate the birth of a royal son?" Lady Rotherton spoke so softly that Prudence wasn't sure she had heard her correctly.

"I have a son," Lena De Vries whispered.

"But William doesn't," Lady Rotherton said.

"It's been a while since I've been down here," Ned Hayes told Geoffrey as Danny Dennis's hansom cab inched its way along the muddy, unpaved streets of Lower Manhattan. This dangerous, gang-ridden section of the city held a peculiar fascination for the former Confederate officer and once star detective of the New York City Police Department. During his deeply drug and alcohol addicted years, when fellow officers and newspaper reporters who watched his every move were betting on how long he would last before one of his twin loves killed him, the Five Points had given him both anonymity and as much morphine and cheap booze as he could consume. That he'd survived at all was only because after he'd saved Billy McGlory's life, the saloonkeeper had put the word out on the street. Ned Hayes wasn't to be touched, and the white powder he bought wasn't to be cut with rat poison or anything else that would leave him convulsing in the gutter.

They had a sketch of the yellow-haired young man with a squint, a likeness the haberdasher had sworn was close enough to what he remembered of James Carpenter's assistant to make him recognizable. The sweeper boy who claimed to have seen him in the Five Points verified the resemblance and thought the sighting had been on Mulberry Street, right where it curved into the area known as Mulberry Bend. "He was walking along with his hands in his pockets, like he was thinking real hard about something and not paying attention to who was coming up behind him," the sweeper had recalled. "I'm sure it was him because I saw him turn the corner off Fifth Avenue and go toward Carpenter's the very next day."

Geoffrey gave him a nickel for his trouble.

"We'll start on Mulberry Street," Ned directed Danny. "It's the only clue we've got."

Danny parked Mr. Washington in front of a saloon whose bouncers he knew by sight and a previous adventure best not mentioned. The big white horse bared his teeth and the bouncers nodded an okay. If Danny chose to step down from his high driver's perch at the rear of the hansom cab, he'd be in no danger. Neither would his property. They'd keep a weather eye out and ensure that the denizens of Mulberry Bend took as wide a detour around Mr. Washington as the crowded roadway and deeply pocked sidewalk allowed. Neither of the bouncers recognized the fellow Danny and his toffs were looking for.

An hour later Geoffrey and Ned had completed a circuit of the block where the sweeper boy claimed to have spotted their quarry. No one would admit to having seen him. And, as one of the shopkeepers pointed out, with the Five Points being heavily Italian and Irish now, a thatch of Nordic blond hair would have stood out like a sore thumb.

"There's one more possibility," Ned decided. "I should have thought of it before we started slogging through the mud." He shook heavy clods off the boots his manservant Tyrus had polished to a bright gleam that morning. "I'll owe him a poker night for this," he said disgustedly. The octogenarian ex-slave who had been his childhood guardian and body servant during the war considered it his bounden duty to keep Young Master in check by regularly humbling him at cards.

"What's that?" Geoffrey asked, continuing to scan the crowds pushing their way along the busy road. Mostly men. The streets of the Five Points were dangerous for women except in the open-air markets where vegetables that weren't good enough for uptown tables were sold at deep discounts. The more rotten they were, the cheaper the price.

"Mama Oshia. If she's still here," Ned said.

Mama Oshia was the voodoo healer who had nursed Billy McGlory back to health in a tiny tenement room hung with dried animal parts, strong-smelling roots, and faceless dolls waiting for a spell to animate them. How she got from Louisiana to New York City was a mystery she'd never revealed, but she'd recognized a kindred spirit in Ned Hayes when he'd declined to arrest her for hexing an especially vicious pimp. They'd shared whiskey, white powder, the hallucinogenic nightmares of a particularly nasty angel's trumpet and, occasionally, a bed. She was old enough to be Ned's grandmother, but that hadn't mattered to either of them.

Mama Oshia was reputed to know everything that went on in the Five Points and everyone who lived there. On both sides of the law.

Geoffrey had never met her and Danny Dennis refused to take Mr. Washington to the street where Ned Hayes had last visited her.

"He wouldn't be safe there," Danny said, choosing not to elaborate. "We'll wait for you here."

He made the sign of the cross as the two men disappeared down the street.

CHAPTER 7

"Perhaps you have questions for my maid," Lena De Vries managed after several moments of painful, emotion-charged silence. "She'll be able to supply you with the dates when the necklace was worn. There's really nothing more I can tell you."

Without waiting for Prudence to reply, Lena summoned the butler and gave him instructions. "Ask Taylor to come to the parlor. She's to bring my wardrobe record with her." She glanced at the clock on the mantelpiece. "You may tell Cook that luncheon will be delayed."

"I'm sure there's no need for that," Prudence said.

"It's no trouble," Lena assured her. "Our midday meal is taken *en famille*, as it were. William often lunches with colleagues or clients."

"And your son?" Lady Rotherton asked.

Prudence wondered where she got the gall to mention him again.

"En famille, as I said." Lena's cheeks flushed red, but she kept her composure and volunteered no further information. She smiled at Prudence, but when her eyes met Lady Rotherton's, a gleam of something strong and stubborn shone in them and the smile grew taut and fixed.

Taylor was a small, thin woman of uncertain age, dressed entirely in modest, unrelieved black, as was required of a lady's maid. Her hair was pulled back unfashionably tight into a low bun from which no stray locks escaped, and the only jewelry she wore was a pair of jet earrings. Spectacles dangled from a hook on her corseted bodice. In her right hand she carried a leather-covered ledger, pencil neatly tucked into the binding.

"I brought what you asked for, Mrs. De Vries," she said, holding out the book. Her voice trembled.

"Miss MacKenzie is helping with the investigation into how the Marie Antoinette necklace could have been tampered with," Lena explained. Introductions would have been improper, so none were made.

"Specifically, I would like the dates when the necklace was worn," Prudence began. "When it arrived at the house, who brought it, and who signed for it. Whether it was put into a safe, and if so, which one. At what time it was removed from the safe for Mrs. De Vries to wear, and when it was locked up again. It goes without saying that I shall require the type of event to which it was worn."

"And whether Tiffany cleaned the diamonds or you did," Lady Rotherton put in sharply.

"I've always been the one to clean them, madam," Taylor stuttered. "I use only the gentlest soap and the softest polish cloths. Sometimes jewelers employ a cleaning paste that can leave a residue and a bit of an odor. It's usually a job that's left to an apprentice to do. They're not always as careful as they should be."

"And how do you know that?" Lady Rotherton demanded.

"My father was a jeweler," Taylor answered. "He crafted settings into which the designer's stones were placed."

"And he taught you how to work with diamonds?"

"He did." Taylor's eyes gleamed brightly. Her father had

died too young, sight clouded and back bent by years of close work over a jeweler's table.

"May I see the wardrobe record?" Prudence asked. She paged through the book, noting as she did so that every entry was dated, neatly inscribed, and followed by the initials *A.T.* Included were the details of what Lena De Vries had worn in the morning, at luncheon, for afternoon calls, for tea, for dinner, to the opera, the theater, and the balls that were the high points of every social season. Notes were made of cleaning and repairs made to each garment and pair of shoes or boots. At the beginning of every inscription was the most recent preceding date on which the garment had been worn. It was possible to leaf backward through the record and reconstruct the life of every item in her boudoir. When it was purchased, from which couturier, the occasions on which it was worn, when it was finally discarded. Prudence wondered whether she could expect Colleen to adhere to such a system, then swiftly discarded the idea. The life she was fashioning for herself was not that of a society icon whose every outfit was subject to intense scrutiny and imitation.

"The initials *A.T.* are yours?" she asked.

"Yes, miss."

Prudence waited.

"My first name is Amelia," Taylor said, glancing at her mistress.

Lena De Vries nodded, as if to indicate that she hadn't forgotten Taylor's Christian name, though it was never used when referring to her.

"Is there no separate list kept of when Mrs. De Vries's jewelry was taken out of the Tiffany vault?" Lady Rotherton asked. She had scanned the wardrobe record pages as Prudence turned them, and generally approved Taylor's method of keeping track of her mistress's possessions. Improvements could be made, however; that was always true.

"No, my lady," Taylor answered.

"I wonder why not."

"I didn't think it necessary," Lena said. "I've found Taylor's records quite sufficient for my purposes." Which she didn't need to emphasize were essentially to ensure that she didn't appear in the same gown at functions where it was likely to be recognized as having been worn before.

"I don't need to take this record with me," Prudence said. "But it would help a great deal if you could extract from it the specific information I've asked for. Most important is a list of the dates on which the Marie Antoinette necklace was removed from the vault and the events to which it was worn." Prudence returned the wardrobe record to the woman who had compiled it. All of the other details of how Lena dressed on a daily basis muddied the water. They were overwhelming in their detailed precision.

"You may get right to work on that, Taylor," Lena instructed. "I'll have it sent to your office, shall I, Prudence?"

It was as obvious a dismissal as a polite hostess could make.

The building in which Mama Oshia had nursed Billy Mc-Glory back to health after the gunshot wounds that should have finished him off was a five-story brick tenement that appeared to be better maintained than its neighbors. There were no broken windows on the ground floor and the front stoop had been recently swept. The garbage bins were chained together outside the door to the basement, lids secured so the contents wouldn't be strewn across the sidewalk.

"You see this every now and then in the Five Points," Ned Hayes said. "It usually means someone of importance to the neighborhood lives there." He opened the front door and stepped into a dark hallway. Geoffrey followed, his coat unbuttoned for quick access to the revolver holstered under his shoulder.

An elderly woman bundled in several layers of ancient sweaters, head swathed in a black kerchief, was moving a broom across the floor with unsteady, though determined strokes. When she turned to face them, her milky eyes registered no change as the shaft of light from the doorway lit up a small pile of dusty debris nestled atop a sheet of newsprint.

"I'm looking for Mama Oshia," Ned called out. The blind sweeper was likely to be deaf also. A lifetime of hard manual labor and near starvation took its toll on men and women alike. Few of them lived into old age, and those who did were usually severely handicapped.

"She's up where she always is," the woman replied. "Top floor at the front. Been living in that window apartment for as long as I can remember."

There were no windows along the sides of tenement buildings. Except for the two apartments on each floor that faced front and back, the rooms were as dark as midnight and smelled of poverty, cabbage, urine, no ventilation, and too many people packed into too small quarters.

Mama Oshia's door opened as they climbed to the top of the narrow wooden staircase on the fifth floor. She stepped out onto the landing, fists on ample hips, a broad smile creasing her fleshy face.

"I knew you was comin' today, Mr. Ned. All the leaves fell off my tea plant yesterday."

"That doesn't sound very good, Mama." Ned stood to one side. "This gentleman with me is Mr. Geoffrey Hunter. He was a Pinkerton at one time."

"I won't hold that against him," she said, running deep-set black eyes over the two men. She flashed a white-toothed smile that lit up her dark face. "You'd best come inside where we can talk about the bidness that brung you here." It went without saying that as soon as Ned had turned in her direction one of her street boys had come running with the news. She already knew the name of the person he was looking for.

Walking into Mama Oshia's apartment was like being transported back to Bradford Island off the coast of Georgia, where

Geoffrey and Prudence had sailed in May to a wedding that became a murder. Where two wise women named Aunt Jessa and Queen Lula had built log cabins hidden deep in live oak groves. Where the walls and ceilings of those one-room shacks sprouted dried herbs and dangling corn husk dolls waiting for spells to be cast and lives changed. The sights and smells were the same, as were the dozens of candles covering every surface, the gilded images of the Virgin, and the darker faces of a pantheon of voodoo saints. It was a blood part of the old-time South that Geoffrey would never be able to wash from his veins.

Mama Oshia lit a black candle in front of a miniature altar on which stood one of the faceless corn husk dolls.

"Is that him?" Ned asked. "Yellow hair and a squint?"

"It might well be," Mama Oshia answered.

Ned laid a stack of silver coins before the altar, hesitated a moment, then added a Liberty Head half eagle five-dollar gold piece. A king's ransom in the tenements.

"I reckon that's him all right," Mama Oshia said.

"What can you tell us?" Ned took a small leather notepad out of his jacket pocket and licked the tip of a sharpened pencil. Habits learned when he was a policeman died hard.

"Showed up around here about a year ago. Thought too much of himself to turn a hand to the heavy work down at the docks or in the slaughterhouses. Knew how to read and write, pick a lock and a pocket. Not slow with a knife, but he didn't have a good head for the kind of liquor he could afford to buy, so he ended up on the wrong end of bar fights. Disappeared for a while. When he came back, he had cash money, enough to rent a room and buy a woman. He'd come and go, and rumor had it he was working the streets up around the Ladies' Mile. That's off limits. Police headquarters sent the word out. Anybody caught lifting anything up there can say his prayers because the third degree will be too good for him. No negotiating. Strictly off limits."

"What name did he give?" Geoffrey asked.

"Vincent Reynolds. He didn't look like a Vincent, and he wasn't no Reynolds neither."

"How do you know?"

"Only Swede boys has that kind of yellow hair. Thick like summer hay. Blue eyes, too. I reckon he took him a walk through a graveyard and picked a name he liked off a tombstone."

"What else can you tell us, Mama?" Ned scribbled in his notebook.

"He's in Bellevue, stretched out naked on a slab."

The pencil he was writing with fell out of Ned's hand onto the floor.

"They hauled him out of the river a couple of days ago. Head all smashed in and enough knife holes to make him look like a pincushion. So I was told."

"Who did it?" Ned knew there was always speculation on the street. And if the victim had been stupid enough to venture onto gang territory, the body would be marked.

"Nobody knows," Mama Oshia said. "He's going into a pauper's trench on Hart Island, so nobody much cares." She blew out the black candle she'd lit before the small altar and handed Ned the corn husk doll propped up there. "Cain't use 'em but once."

"Did you ever hear Reynolds's name linked to an uptown jewelry store?" Geoffrey asked. With someone like Mama Oshia, unless you came up with exactly the right questions, the information you were looking for stayed locked away forever.

"They's a sweeper boy claims to have seen Reynolds up around Eighteenth Street," Mama Oshia said.

"Is that all?"

"Rumor has it the boy was keeping an eye on him for the Broken Fingers Gang. Your Mister Reynolds had a debt to work off."

"Will they talk to us?" Geoffrey asked.

"Not unless you want a knife in the gullet." Ned Hayes cut off Mama Oshia before she could answer.

"You got that right," she said. "Whatever he was into, your dead man was at the bottom of the heap. Not making enough to carry him out of the Five Points, and with that squint, he wasn't never goin' to make it. Too easy to recognize. It didn't take you long to find out about him, did it?"

"Nobody on Mulberry Street would own up to knowing him," Geoffrey said.

"Wouldn't expect them to. Not in daylight. Sooner or later somebody would have slipped you a word, but not while there was anybody around to hear it."

"When are you going home, Mama?" Ned asked. It was a question he'd been raising for years.

"Not till I find my girl," she answered. "I didn't come all this far and stay as long as I have to go back empty-handed."

"She might not be where you can get at her," Ned said gently. Meaning that the grieving voodoo woman's daughter was more likely dead than alive.

"I know that, Mister Ned. But it don't make no difference. Like I said, I ain't going home without her. One way or the other."

Danny Dennis collared the sweeper boy as soon as he ran full tilt around the corner and nearly into Mr. Washington's broad hindquarters. Grabbing him by the back of his jacket, he slung him against the hansom cab's tall spoked wheel and held him there until the boy gave up and ceased struggling.

"I didn't do nothing, Mister Dennis," he protested.

"You followed us down here," Danny said. "Don't try to deny it."

"I just wanted to find out why you was asking about the yellow-haired fellow with the squint."

That was a bald-faced lie. He already knew. "Talk to me, boy. You don't want Mr. Washington here stepping on you."

The boy took one horrified look at the size of the white horse's steel shoes and began blubbering. He squirmed and hiccupped and blurted out everything he knew until Danny Dennis was satisfied he'd get no more out of him. "Next time I see you, it better be with a broom in your hands."

"Yessir. I promise. Yessir."

"He didn't know much more than he'd already told me," Danny told Geoffrey and Ned. He would have given a lot to have been able to follow them to Mama Oshia's, but the danger to Mr. Washington had been too great. The deeper you got into the Five Points, the less likely it was you'd come out alive. And healthy horse meat was too tempting for a determined gang of starving street urchins to resist. "He knows Reynolds went back and forth from this area to Carpenter's store and that he must have been working there. Odd hours, nothing regular. But that's all he could figure out. I did the best I could with him, but I think the chances are good he was telling the truth."

"He didn't seem to know the man is dead?" Geoffrey asked.

"Dead?"

"Mama Oshia says he's lying on a table in the Bellevue morgue."

"Timmy is the sweeper boy's name. I'd lay odds he had no idea."

"Our dead man went by the name of Vincent Reynolds," Ned said. "Not his real name, of course."

Danny Dennis unfastened Mr. Washington's feed bag. He knew where Mr. Hunter would tell him to go next.

CHAPTER 8

Vincent Reynolds's body waited to be released from the Bellevue morgue and loaded aboard a barge that carried deceased indigents to the Potter's Field burial pits of Hart Island.

"Day after tomorrow," the morgue assistant told Geoffrey and Ned. "Friday."

"Is that a regular run?" Geoffrey asked. He realized he'd never given much thought to where the bodies of those who couldn't pay for burial plots in cemeteries ended up. Potter's Field, yes, but he guessed that most New Yorkers knew nothing about the mechanics of getting them there. And couldn't have cared less.

"Regular as clockwork. They pile up, you know, and we're always strapped for space."

"We'd like to see the body." Ned Hayes slipped a generous bribe into the attendant's outstretched hand. He'd learned long ago that coins were more persuasive than arguments. On the force or off it, money greased the wheels that made the system run.

Vincent Reynolds had been in the debris-choked water of the East River for at least a day and a night before being pulled out. His skin was pallid with death, leached of blood, and puckered into fine wrinkles by the long soak. The fish had gotten to what remained of his face after a heavy, blunt object shattered and rearranged the bones into a horror mask facsimile of human features. They could just make out the heavy droop of one eyelid—the squint everyone who described him had mentioned. The other eye was missing. But the thick yellow hair was undamaged, matted with tiny bits of debris, stiff and straight as a board.

"The body hasn't been washed," Geoffrey commented.

"Enough so's the doc could certify the cause of death," the attendant said, pointing to crimped slashes on the torso where river mud had been scrubbed off. "Eleven stab wounds. Count 'em, if you want to." Ned's generosity had put him in an expansive mood.

"Do you still have the clothes he was wearing?" Ned asked.

The hand came out again. Ned complied.

"They usually sell the clothes for whatever they can get unless there's family to notice and object," Ned told Geoffrey as the attendant disappeared into another room.

Geoffrey handed over the loose bills he kept in his pocket. "This should be enough."

"Someone went to a lot of trouble to try to make him unrecognizable." Ned added more bills to what Geoffrey had given him. "And I don't think our killer expected the corpse to be found as soon as it was." He'd seen many a body pulled out of New York City's rivers that a layman would be hard pressed to identify as a fellow human being.

"A blow to the back of the head to bring him to his knees," Geoffrey said, pointing to abraded skin that looked like a deeper wound than the fish-nibbled layers around it. "He went down on rough pavement of some kind. And to rub that much skin off his knees, he must have tried to crawl away before he passed out or died."

"So the killer hit him from behind, then came around to beat him on the face."

"Kicked him in the chest to lay him out on the ground." Geoffrey nodded toward a midchest bruise that could have been made by a heavy boot. "Finished the job with a knife."

"Eleven stab wounds," Ned mused. "He was either an amateur wanting to be sure he'd gotten the job done or unable to control himself once he started."

"Not crazy, though. We're not dealing with a madman here. These are stab wounds, not frenzied slashes. And if Reynolds was already dead when most of them were made, there wouldn't have been much blood."

"In an alleyway? That would account for the knees and the fact that nobody interrupted what was happening. Plenty of places like that down by the river."

Eyes assessing every feature of the body lying exposed before them, Geoffrey and Ned waited for the attendant to return with the clothes they were purchasing for many times what they were worth. No autopsy had been performed on the dead man because the cause of death was obvious. No point taking up more of the medical examiner's time than necessary. There were always more corpses to be examined than the city's badly stretched resources could cover. Bodies like this one were shunted aside as soon as possible. Nobody cared.

They took the bundle the attendant gave them. Wrapped in brown paper and tied with butcher's string, it was heavy enough to contain water-soaked boots. "Is this everything?" Ned asked as he handed over the bills he and Geoffrey had fished out of their pockets.

The attendant shrugged. If the stiff had been wearing a watch or ring, that would have been stolen by the stretcher bearers. They weren't his responsibility. He only claimed a cut of whatever arrived at the morgue. "You've got what he was wearing when we laid him on the table." He pulled up the spotted sheet that covered Bellevue corpses until they were stitched into their canvas burial shrouds.

Time to go.

Josiah laid a protective oilcloth on the polished surface of the long oak conference table. Mr. Hunter and Miss MacKenzie didn't usually bring back evidence as dirty and smelly as the clothes tumbled in a damp heap atop stained brown paper, but Josiah believed in being prepared for all eventualities. And he'd learned from past experience that when Mr. Ned Hayes was involved in a case, anything was liable to happen.

Geoffrey sorted belt, pants, socks, and underwear from jacket, shirt, and cravat. The leather boots were cracked and scuffed. There wasn't a cap or a hat. No handkerchief, either. "What do you think, Josiah? Would you like to make a guess about the quality of the clothes our dead man was wearing?"

Josiah's black suit was always impeccably pressed, his shirt starched and gleaming white, shoes buffed to a mirror shine. The Hunter and MacKenzie secretary was both vain and secretly addicted to the men's fashion magazines he kept hidden in one of his desk drawers. If anyone could deduce a man's character or financial state from what he wore, it was Josiah.

"They're all secondhand," he sniffed, waving a dismissive hand over the garments worn by the man who called himself Vincent Reynolds. "But the socks are silk and the shirt is definitely bespoke."

"How can you tell?" Ned asked. Josiah's quirks fascinated him.

"By the stitching," Josiah said, running a manicured finger along the seams of what was hardly recognizable as a gentleman's custom sewn garment. "The owner's initials are often embroidered along the hem if he doesn't want them displayed on the pocket or one of the cuffs. That's especially important for the laundresses if there are several gentlemen in the house.

When a shirt like this one is given to the gentleman's valet, the initials are picked out before the valet sells it." He bent over the mud and bloodstained piece of clothing that had been pierced by violent thrusts of a single-bladed knife. "Here. You can just make out the marks where the threads were cut and pulled out."

"Can you tell what the initials were?" Geoffrey asked, leaning over the shirt to see for himself what Josiah was pointing to.

"The shirt was worn too many times after the valet sold it to be able to tell. There's no clear track left, just enough needle marks to be sure something was there at one time."

"How long ago?" Ned asked.

Josiah shrugged. "Months, at least. The thing is, a shirt of this quality wouldn't sit very long in a secondhand store before somebody bought it. The same for the socks. It looks like they're a mix of cashmere and silk. Very expensive. Probably imported from England."

"But you don't think the rest of the clothes are of that same quality?" Geoffrey hefted the thick tweed jacket and matching pants.

"Bulky, cheaply woven, and sewn on a machine with a too thick needle to reduce the incidence of breakage," Josiah pronounced. "The suit may or may not be secondhand, but it's not anything a gentleman would wear. It's a workingman's Sunday best, perhaps, but that doesn't make it any the less objectionable." He smoothed the fine wool of his own bespoke suit. The money left him in his late employer's will had made Josiah a rich man. It was purely by choice that he had opted to continue running the renamed firm that the former Senator Roscoe Conkling had bequeathed to Geoffrey Hunter.

Neither Prudence nor Geoffrey could imagine the office without him.

"I thought for a moment you'd brought a corpse back from the Five Points," Prudence said from the doorway. Her cheeks were red from the December cold and she carried a large white envelope in her gloved hands.

"Tea, Miss MacKenzie?" Josiah asked, turning from the debris on the table.

"As hot as you can make it," she answered. "I sent Aunt Gillian back to the house in the carriage while I followed a hunch and then caught a hansom down here. The leather curtains wouldn't stay closed, so my face feels like it's been bombarded with ice pellets." She rubbed more red into her cheeks. "What is that mess you're looking at? And what is that smell?"

"It's Vincent Reynolds's clothes," Ned told her. "We bought them at Bellevue."

"Bought them?"

"Better not to ask," Geoffrey said, slipping off her gloves and taking both her hands in his own to knead some warmth back into them. The soft skin against his palms sent fiery sparks up his spine. How much longer would he have to wait?

"That's enough," Prudence said briskly, snatching her hands away and reaching for the envelope she'd dropped on the table. "I do have some information that might be of use." She ran one finger under the flap of the envelope and withdrew a sheet of paper covered with what appeared to be a neatly inscribed list of names.

"Lena De Vries uses the Wentworth Domestic Employment Agency to staff her household," she explained. "Coincidentally, so do I. The MacKenzies have been clients for years." There was a ring of triumph in her voice. "I thought it would help at this stage of the investigation to know the names and employment histories of everyone working for the De Vries family during the period of time when the stones might have been pried from their settings." Geoffrey hadn't pointed her in that direction; she'd decided entirely on her own to do more than ask Lena the obvious questions about her staff.

"Bravo, Prudence!" Ned Hayes clapped lightly and executed a fanciful bow in her direction.

"I've only glanced at it," she began, "but what's interesting is that there appears to be more recent turnover among the younger female staff that I would have expected to see." She didn't have to say anything more explicit. There was only one reason why maids voluntarily left positions that were hard to come by and offered regular wages. Whether the molestation came from the master of the house, his sons, or senior male servants, it only ended badly for the girls who had been violated. Pregnancy meant instant dismissal without a reference or an agonizing death at the hands of an abortionist.

"Anyone in particular?" Geoffrey asked.

"No," Prudence answered, gratefully accepting the cup of tea Josiah had brewed and poured. "Just a general pattern. But it tells me that there is someone in that house whose moral compass is not pointing true north."

"The obvious one is your client, William De Vries," Ned decided. "That kind of man is a law unto himself. As a banker and investor he answers to no one. He inherited a fortune and he's increased it many times over. He's more than twenty years older than his wife, which means he may be choosing to meet his needs with partners who don't dare refuse him or suggest that they find his performance lacking in any way." It was a remarkably frank statement to make, but Ned frequently paid Prudence the compliment of ignoring the social niceties of female exclusion from the realities of daily life.

Prudence sipped her tea as she pictured the William De Vries she'd seen at the Assembly Ball and sitting here in the Hunter and MacKenzie office. Of average height. Portly, as were most wealthy men of his age. Exquisitely clothed and groomed to conceal a belly devoted to the pleasures of the table and rivers of imported wine and liquor consumed in a nearly constant haze of cigar smoke.

William was, she recalled, the same age her father would have been, had Judge MacKenzie lived. Well past sixty. His hair had silvered, pouched wrinkles sprouted beneath his cold blue eyes, his skin had developed the reddish hue of someone whose doctor repeatedly counseled moderation and exercise without much hope of convincing his patient to change his ways.

De Vries must have been handsome in his younger years, Prudence decided, but as an older man he was both compelling and attractive in ways that had little or nothing to do with the physical attributes of a man in the springtime of his life. Perhaps it was the aura of power that hung about him like an expensive opera cloak.

"Prudence?"

"Sorry, I must have drifted off for a moment. What was it you were asking, Geoffrey?" She wondered if Josiah had slipped a tot of whiskey into her tea to make her thoughts wander away like that. She put teacup and saucer on the table in front of her and willed herself to pay attention. Geoffrey was reading down the list of De Vries's household staff. When had he picked it up?

"Twenty-five servants," he said. "How many are in your household, Prudence?"

"Half that number. But mine is a very modest establishment."

"Ned thinks the shirt and socks our occasional shop assistant wore when he was murdered came from the kind of secondhand store that specializes in buying used clothing from men in the upper echelons of society. Their valets sell the items as one of the perks of the job."

"I remember my father passing on some of his suits, but I believe he earmarked them for charitable donations," Prudence said. "Though now that I think about it, some things he might have just given to whoever was dressing him that season."

"Do you have the name of William De Vries's valet?" Geoffrey asked.

"Connections?" Ned asked.

"Someone in that house had to have been involved," Geoffrey said. "I don't know who or how yet, but I have a gut feeling that one connection will lead to another. They usually do."

"Carpenter and the diamonds," Ned summarized. "Connected by the stone Prudence so cleverly found. A man calling himself Vincent Reynolds and Carpenter again. Connected by Jimmy the sweeper boy and Mama Oshia. And Carpenter and Reynolds themselves, connected by violent deaths within days of each other."

"Someone is very worried," Geoffrey theorized. "And doing whatever he can to eliminate anyone who could point the finger at him."

"There are two names listed here as valets," Prudence said. "I wasn't expecting that. Both of them still apparently employed in the De Vries household." She held out the agency list from which she was reading. "There's always a notation when a servant leaves or changes his post."

"That's odd," Ned commented, but he didn't suggest that Prudence might have made a mistake. She never did.

"Lena De Vries has a son by her first marriage," Prudence said, pulling from her skirt pocket the small notebook in which she jotted down items she wanted to remember. "Aunt Gillian made a rather embarrassing reference to him while we were there this morning. I remember Lena telling the butler to inform the cook that her luncheon would be delayed, and then when I began to apologize for disrupting the routine of her staff, she said it wasn't important because the midday meal was usually taken en famille. William apparently often dines at a restaurant with clients." She paged rapidly through the most recent pages. "Here it is. I don't know why I wrote it down, but I did. *En famille* implies more than one person in an informal setting. My French governess insisted on using the right expression to define every situation."

"Go on." Geoffrey knew where this thread was leading, but he would give Prudence the pleasure and reward of following it to its end.

"If he lives in the house with William and Lena, the second

valet could be his. Which would give us two servants selling their master's old clothes."

"What can you tell us about this son?" Ned asked.

"Obviously not enough," Prudence replied. "We knew one another as children, but I saw very little of him once he went away to Harvard. Whitley was Lena's surname when she was widowed, so unless William adopted him, it wouldn't have been changed when she remarried. His first name is Morgan."

The recently installed telephone in the outer office rang, still such an unexpected noise that all heads turned to glare at the interruption.

"That was Mr. De Vries's secretary. The police have been called," Josiah announced a few moments later. "De Vries wants you to meet him at his home."

"What's happened?" Geoffrey asked, reaching for a key to lock the door of the conference room behind them as they decamped. He'd leave Vincent Reynolds's clothing on the table, but it was better not to tempt Josiah into tidying up the evidence.

"Someone is dead. That's all he was told." Josiah's hand tightened around the telephone receiver. He'd broken the connection, but hadn't been able to pry his fingers from the instrument.

"Messy," Prudence said. "You said it was going to be messy, Geoffrey."

"This is one time I wish I hadn't been right."

CHAPTER 9

The police hadn't bothered trying to conceal their presence outside the De Vries mansion on Fifth Avenue. A mortuary van was already pulled up at the curb, its team of horses patiently waiting for their burden to be loaded. Unlike most animals, they weren't spooked by the smell of death; over the years they'd grown inured to it. A pair of uniformed patrolmen paced on the sidewalk to keep would-be onlookers moving along, and another pair guarded the front door. Every now and then a face appeared at one of the basement windows as a servant looked outside to see what, if anything, was going on. So far, nothing.

Everyone was waiting for Mr. William De Vries's arrival and the firestorm that was certain to erupt when he walked into his home and found policemen had invaded his privacy.

"I hired you to find out what happened to my wife's diamonds," stormed De Vries. "How in the name of all that's holy could you have allowed something like this to happen?" He tore the cashmere scarf from around his neck and hurled bowler hat, overcoat, and gloves onto the floor before the butler could help him out of them. Face reddened by fury and the cold December air, he stalked toward the closed parlor door without waiting for an answer.

"Detective Phelan is upstairs, waiting for the medical examiner," Geoffrey said calmly. He and Prudence had arrived only minutes before their client, but it had been time enough to speak quietly to the butler. "Shall we join them? Miss MacKenzie has gone to see if there is anything she can do for Mrs. De Vries."

"How could you have allowed this to happen?" De Vries repeated, turning around to confront Geoffrey again. "Did you see the fools gathering on the sidewalk outside? It will be in all the papers this afternoon."

"That can't be helped. The New York newspapers are a world of their own."

"Don't be ridiculous. Everyone has his price." Over a lifetime of accumulating enormous wealth, William had bought influence and anonymity too many times to believe he was now going to be flung without recourse into the court of public scrutiny and opinion. "Damn the man!"

"His name is Leonard Abbott," the butler told Geoffrey in answer to his low-voiced question. "He started as a footman, then added valet to his duties, though I didn't consider him fully trained yet."

"And he hanged himself in the attic?"

"One of the maids found him when the housekeeper sent her up to look for more blankets for the staff bedrooms." He didn't have to add that the tiny servant rooms directly under the roof were frigid in the winter, uncomfortably hot in summer.

"I'm going up," Geoffrey said. "Whether you come with me is your affair, Mr. De Vries, but as the man's employer, you will almost certainly be called upon to make an identification of the body."

Geoffrey kept his face carefully neutral. In the last few minutes he had decided that his client was inherently unlikable. This William De Vries bore little resemblance to the one who had sat in the Hunter and MacKenzie offices less than a week ago, recalling his past friendship with Prudence's father and proclaiming his trust in the judge's daughter and her partner. Definitely not the same concerned husband who had expressed dismay at his wife's assumption of guilt over circumstances beyond her control. *Damn the man,* he had said. No compassion for a servant so demonstrably unhappy that he had taken his own life.

Entry to the storage attics was along a narrow passageway at one end of the fourth-floor hallway where the servants' bedrooms were located. Geoffrey heard voices and sounds of movement as he approached, William De Vries lumbering irately in his wake. They hadn't passed a single member of the household staff on the way up. Likely they were all gathered in the servants' hall in the basement, cups of tea or coffee clutched in their hands as they tried to make sense out of a death none of them could understand or have anticipated.

Leonard Abbott's body hadn't been cut down yet from the beam over which he'd slung the rope that choked him to death. An oval window in the end wall of the attic flooded the space with gray, wintry light. Enough so that no detail was lost on the men examining the scene and the two men who came to an abrupt halt in the doorway. De Vries would have pushed his way in, but Geoffrey's outstretched arm blocked his way.

Detective Steven Phelan and two uniformed officers stood in a half circle staring at the still figure whose feet dangled above an overturned three-legged stool. One of the man's hands clutched at his throat, fingers caught in the circle of rope around his neck. The other hand flopped uselessly by his side. A stench of loosened bowels filled the air and a puddle of urine stained the floorboards. He was dressed in a cheap brown tweed suit, not the livery worn by a servant on duty. Most household staff, except on their afternoons off, wore livery or a uniform from the time they got up until they went to bed.

"So the client you were at such pains to conceal is William De Vries," Phelan said, spotting Geoffrey in the doorway. "You'll have to tell me what he's hired you for, you know, and what brought you and your partner to Carpenter's jewelry store. This changes everything." He gestured at the corpse, setting it to swinging slowly as one hand brushed against a leg.

"Whatever you have to say can be addressed directly to me, Detective," De Vries barked. He pushed past Geoffrey, well into the attic. "Get the body out of my house. I don't want the maids seeing it."

"Would you be so kind as to identify the deceased, sir?" Phelan touched his hat, but did not remove it.

"You know perfectly well who he is. The butler's already told you."

"Nevertheless. We need a formal identification from next of kin or someone in authority."

"His name is Leonard Abbott. He was hired as a footman two years ago." De Vries's tone of voice was peremptory and dismissive.

"I understand he was also doing the duties of a valet," Geoffrey said.

"Temporarily. Filling in, so to speak, until a suitably trained valet could be found."

"Did you find his services inadequate then?" Geoffrey asked. He could well imagine what the dead man might have said about his employer.

"I wouldn't have put up with the likes of him. My valet has been with me for ten years or more. Trained in England."

And every time he threatens to leave, you raise his salary.

There were men in society whose valets made many times what anyone else on their staffs did. Blackmail for putting up with foulmouthed outbursts of temper and the keeping of marital and extramarital secrets.

"I'll require a complete list of family members living in the house," Detective Phelan said. He nodded toward one of the policemen, who immediately took out his notebook and a pencil stub.

"I fail to see that it's any of your business," De Vries snarled. "This is a servant who's chosen the coward's way out of whatever difficulty he found himself in. It has nothing to do with the family."

"We'll need to speak to everyone the dead man might have come in contact with," Phelan insisted. "Upstairs as well as below." He took a knife out of his pocket and flicked open the blade. "Sometimes a valet and his master share secrets they'd rather no one else know. Or so I'm told."

"Abbott saw to my stepson and my nephew," De Vries conceded. "But I doubt if either of them can tell you anything useful."

"And why would that be?"

"We're not in the habit of consorting with our servants, Detective." De Vries was making it obvious that an unbreachable gulf existed between the police and New York City's upper class, one Phelan would do well to consider before attempting to push his way into an arena where he did not belong. "Now get this wretched creature out of my house!" He turned on his heel, shoved Geoffrey out of the way, and stormed off down the corridor.

They heard his heavy footsteps on the uncarpeted stairs leading to the servants' quarters, then the muffled thud of his descent into the opulent family rooms. He left behind the scent of expensive imported English cologne and the sour residue of his anger. De Vries was not a man who would be trifled with, especially not in his own house.

"Do you know these two young men he mentioned?" Phelan asked.

Geoffrey shrugged. He wasn't about to give away any information, even when he didn't have much to begin with. The New York City Police Department was like a sieve. And he was still working for William De Vries. Both of them had signed a contract.

The policeman who had been taking notes joined his partner beside the corpse. They held it by legs and torso while Phelan stretched to cut the rope. Leonard Abbott had been a slight fellow; his thin body was easily lowered to the floor.

"The doc should have been here by now," Phelan said, twisting the dead man's head from left to right. "But he doesn't always show up. And I don't think we need him to tell us what happened here." He rifled through the valet's trouser pockets, removing a dirty handkerchief, a few coins, a small black comb, a package of W. Duke Sons & Co. cigarettes, and an expensive-looking gold and tortoiseshell snuffbox.

"This didn't belong to him," Phelan said, opening the snuffbox. He sniffed a pinch of the white powder it contained. "Good stuff. Not cut by much. He shouldn't have been able to afford a snuffbox like that on what he was being paid." He shoved it into his jacket pocket without offering it to Geoffrey to examine. "But maybe that's why you showed up at Eighteenth Street. Was Abbott fencing the odd bit of jewelry he could lift from his mistress's boudoir? Is that why De Vries hired you?"

Geoffrey turned away without answering. Phelan was edging uncomfortably close to his case.

Two attendants from the mortuary van appeared with a canvas sling on which to carry the body down the three flights to the ground floor. They conferred briefly with Detective Phelan, complaining that the uncarpeted staircases used by the servants were slippery and too narrow to accommodate them and their burden without the serious possibility of dropping the corpse to tumble its way unceremoniously toward the waiting wagon. Phelan told them to take it through the family rooms and hallways. One of the policemen went ahead to make sure they were empty while Leonard Abbott was trundled through the house and out across the busy Fifth Avenue sidewalk.

Phelan watched them go with a grim smile on his face. He hadn't missed the condescension in William De Vries's voice and attitude. There was nothing he could do about it except continue the investigation as fully and annoyingly as he could.

"The bedrooms have name cards on the doors," he muttered, gesturing to the remaining uniformed officer to find the one where the dead man had slept. He nudged the three-legged stool with his booted foot, then stood for a moment looking speculatively at the death scene. As if imagining the victim entering the attic, rope in hand, locating something to stand on, securing the noose around his neck, hesitating, weeping perhaps with the inevitability of what he had come to do. Kicking himself off into eternal damnation.

Geoffrey watched, not saying a word, counting on the possibility that Phelan would allow De Vries's private investigator into the case to aggravate the man. And because he sensed a connection between Abbott and Carpenter, but couldn't yet prove it.

He ticked off the facts he'd repeat to Prudence as soon as she was free to leave Lena De Vries. There was no doubt in his mind that the case was escalating at an alarmingly fast rate. The challenge would lie in maneuvering behind the scenes, milking Phelan for every bit of information he was worth, and tracking down some of the most famous diamonds in the world while concealing from the police detective and New York City's shrewd reporters what he and Prudence were really doing.

He expected Phelan to want to keep the suicide and the valet's implied guilt of other crimes alive in the press. De Vries had insulted and demeaned him, never a wise thing to do when you had the kind of newspaper contacts every cop cultivated.

"I've located his room, sir. Third on the left. Nothing much to see."

The policeman had left the dead man's door cracked open. Inside was a narrow metal cot made up with worn sheets and thin blankets. A candle stood on a battered bedside table, an equally scarred chest of drawers against one wall. A row of hooks took the place of a wardrobe, a faded rag rug lay beside the bed, and a single chair held a neatly folded nightshirt. A small round window beneath the eaves let in light and a wintry draft. What looked like a scrap of old toweling had been tacked over the window against the cold, then allowed to fall loosely against the wall.

It was as dreary and unwelcoming a room as Geoffrey had ever seen. Cold, barren, devoid of the warmth of a happy human presence. He wondered if all the servants' rooms were this bleak.

Phelan pulled open the drawers of the chest, tossing the contents onto the floor, doing the same with the sheets and blankets of the bed and the few garments hanging from the wall hooks. He overturned the mattress, beckoning to Geoffrey when a brown envelope fell onto the springs. "I'd like to hear your client explain this," he chortled, shaking out a small snowstorm of what appeared to be betting slips and IOUs. "No name on any of these." He rifled quickly through the bits of paper. "Not even initials."

"It's enough that they've been marked by the bookie," Geoffrey commented, turning one of them over, noting that the odds and amount of the bet had been written in ink, not pencil.

"There's too many bets here for someone barely earning enough walking around money to make his days off worthwhile," Phelan said.

Abbott may have aspired to be a valet, but he was still learning, still being paid the low wage of a footman. Shelter and decent meals were the chief attractions of a servant's life, that and the knowledge that unless he was stupid enough to be caught for thievery or demonstrated unacceptable laziness, the job was better proof against firing than anything he could find on the docks, in the slaughterhouses, or on a factory floor. And you were less likely to lose a foot or a hand in service than working where safety was of no consideration when measured against profit.

"So you think he was running bets for somebody in the family?" Geoffrey asked, unobtrusively pocketing the betting slip he'd been examining.

"Had to have been," Phelan agreed. "And probably for quite some time." He swept up the flurry of paper and stuffed the slips back into the envelope. "We'll check the dates, but I think some of these will go back at least six months."

The real question, Geoffrey knew, was whether Leonard Abbott had been persuaded to place bets under his own name in order to conceal the identity of whichever De Vries man or men were using him as a go-between. It was a layer of protection that might have cost him dearly, especially if losses had mounted up and gone unpaid.

Bookies seldom served as their own enforcers; they didn't have to. Lives were cheap in New York's underworld. Limbs could be broken or severed for less than the price of a new hat, and there were more than enough knifers eager to prove their worth. Dozens of ex-boxers stood ready to beat and kick what he owed out of a man. Suicide might have seemed the only alternative to the kind of maiming that would have left the aspiring valet an unemployable cripple for life. Unless he gave up a name. But who would believe him without proof?

"You'll have to pick your side, Hunter," Phelan said. "I

think your client is about to find himself in a very uncomfortable spot. And I'm not the one he'll blame for putting him
there." He dragged a small ring box in distinctive Tiffany blue
from the far depths of the single drawer of the bedside table,
snapped it open, held it out for Geoffrey to see.

It was empty.

CHAPTER 10

Phelan carried the empty Tiffany ring box and the envelope containing the betting slips downstairs where, according to the butler, Mr. De Vries would be pleased to speak with him in the parlor before he left the house. Phelan didn't bother telling him he had no intention of vacating the premises until he damn well felt like it. And he'd yet to decide how much longer he was going to allow Geoffrey Hunter to shadow him. The private investigator hadn't interfered, but Phelan didn't like providing information while getting nothing in return.

Phelan's partner, Detective Patrick Corcoran, bustled through the front door as the mortuary men edged their way out. Late as usual. He had a broad Irish smile, piercing blue eyes, and no sense of time. As bent as everyone else on the force, he was also as good a cop as could be expected and better than some. Affable rather than short-tempered, he tried to avoid physically abusing suspects, preferring to bore them into confessing with seemingly unrelated queries and yarns that took forever to tell and went nowhere. Phelan considered him one of the best interrogators there was for the kind of job that needed to be done here.

"Pat," he said, "the staff is downstairs in the servants' hall. Would you run them through the usual questions? We'll want to know what contact they had with the dead man and anything they can tell us about the kind of valet he was. Also whether he seemed to have more money recently than could be accounted for by his wages." He lowered his voice and half covered his mouth with one hand. "Dig up whatever dirt you can. And don't spare the family."

"Do I ever?" Corcoran asked, touching his hat in Geoffrey's direction. He usually ended up knowing more about a suspect's background or a victim's family than even the city prosecutor could ask for.

Phelan watched as Corcoran and the butler disappeared through the green baize-covered door to the basement. He nodded to Geoffrey to follow him, then barged his way into the mansion's main parlor without knocking.

Whatever conversation the occupants of the room had been having stopped abruptly. As one, they turned to stare at the interloper who had thrust himself unceremoniously into their midst.

The first thing Geoffrey took note of was Prudence's presence beside Lena De Vries. Both women sat with straight-back perfect posture on a pale green Louis XV love seat, Lena's hands lightly and comfortingly clasped in Prudence's. From the swift upward motion of their heads, Geoffrey knew they had been conversing in whispers so the two men standing before the fireplace wouldn't overhear what they said.

William De Vries was the first to break the silence. It was his house.

"Has what I requested you to remove been taken away, Detective?" he asked, eyes glancing meaningfully at the ladies.

"It has, sir."

"Then I bid you good day. My butler will see you out." De Vries turned back to the fire, extending his hands toward the warmth of the flames.

"I'm afraid we have more business to conduct, sir." Phelan strode across the room as if he owned it. "There's questions that need to be asked and answered. And explanations to be given."

"Explanations?" De Vries turned around sharply, as if not believing what his ears had heard. A man of his standing did not explain anything to anyone.

"It would probably be best to take care of these matters here, Mr. De Vries," Phelan continued smoothly, "rather than down at the station."

"Perhaps we should hear him out, Uncle." The younger man standing beside William laid a placating hand on De Vries's arm, as if to urge him to bear with this buffoon for as long as it took to get rid of him.

"And your name, sir?" Phelan asked.

"I'm Everett Rinehart," the young man said. "My late mother was Mr. De Vries's sister. That makes me his nephew." He extended a hand and smiled winningly, as though the police detective were a welcome guest.

Geoffrey introduced himself, noting that Rinehart's grip was that of a gentleman, neither too weak nor too strong, his palm warm and dry. He was dressed for business, in the kind of sober, dark suit meant to inspire confidence in his financial judgment. A solid gold watch chain stretched across his gray waistcoat, no doubt attached to an equally fine pocket watch, and he wore a gold signet ring on the little finger of his left hand.

Geoffrey judged him to be in his late twenties, as handsome as any husband-seeking girl could wish for. Regular features, smooth dark blond hair cut conservatively, blue-eyed, clean-shaven except for a modest mustache, every facial feature sculpted and unblemished. Too perfect to be real. Glancing at Prudence, he saw that she had read his mind and was amused at what he was thinking.

"We'll need your address, Mr. Rinehart," Phelan instructed. "And where to contact you during the business day."

"My nephew works in my office and lives here," De Vries interrupted. "Though I see no reason why he should be subjected to your inquiries."

"In that case, I believe the deceased Leonard Abbott may have been serving as your personal valet, Mr. Rinehart. Is that correct?" Phelan flipped up the tail of his long coat and ensconced himself in a comfortable upholstered chair opposite Lena and Prudence, smiling politely at them. No one had asked him to sit down. He took his police notebook out of his pocket, uncapped one of the modern pens that carried its own ink, and poised it over an open page. "Is that correct?" he repeated.

Lena seemed to study her husband's nephew, waiting for his answer, though she certainly could have replied for him. The housekeeper informed her of everything to do with the indoor staff, including her assessment of their personal and presumably private conduct.

"Leonard was learning on the job, so to speak," Everett said, using the dead man's first name as though he had never risen above the status of footman. "I had no real complaints against the young man. His performance was far from perfect, but he did seem to be trying his best. I cannot think why he would have done what he did."

"Are you a betting man, Mr. Rinehart?" Phelan asked. He watched De Vries trim a cigar, roll the cut end in his mouth, and set the tobacco afire with a gold lighter. He hadn't asked his wife's permission to smoke, and he seemed oblivious to the lack of common courtesy.

"Only at my clubs," Everett replied. "And rarely on anything more risky than a hand of cards." He moved away from the mantel, gesturing to Geoffrey to be seated. "I'm afraid I'm not much of a one for sowing wild oats."

That was an interesting remark to make, Geoffrey thought.

It put him squarely in the category of well-to-do young men who could be considered relatively harmless to that season's debutantes. Every mother's dream, if his personal fortune was big enough. Prudence, he noticed, smiled at Everett in what Geoffrey reluctantly decided was a coquettish simper. Surely she didn't believe a word of what he had said?

"I would not have welcomed Everett into the firm had I not trusted him unreservedly," De Vries added.

Phelan nodded. "Do you recognize this, Mr. Rinehart?" In the palm of his outstretched hand the gold and tortoiseshell snuffbox gleamed in the reflected light of the fire. "Is it perhaps yours?"

"I'm not partial to snuff, Detective. It's a beautiful piece, but it's not mine. More's the pity."

"Mr. De Vries?"

William took the box from Phelan and flicked back the lid with one practiced fingernail. He raised it to his nose, but carefully. "It's not snuff," he said.

"Cocaine," Phelan told him. "Very pure. And very dangerous."

"And you thought this belonged to one of us?" Restrained fury burned across De Vries's cheeks. "How dare you?"

"I had to ask, Mr. De Vries," Phelan replied laconically. "We found it in the dead man's trouser pocket."

"Then that's your answer. He wasn't in his right mind when he put the noose around his neck. Crazy mad with this drug! It's a wonder he didn't kill us all in our beds!"

Lena let out an anguished cry, clutching Prudence's hands so tightly her fingernails made red crescents in the skin.

"Go up to your room, Lena," De Vries ordered, reaching for the bellpull to summon her maid. "This is no conversation for a lady to hear."

No apology. No expression of remorse or concern for how he spoke to his wife in front of a vulgar policeman and a man he had hired to solve a mystery he didn't want made public.

"I'll stay, William," Lena said. She released Prudence's fingers and folded her hands tightly in her lap. "I have a right to know what's happening in my own home."

"I'd prefer you leave, Lena." De Vries's hand gripped the bellpull, but he hadn't tugged on it yet. "I'm sure the events of the day have been both disturbing and fatiguing."

"I'll stay," she insisted. Two red spots burned in her cheeks. It was obvious that despite the effort it took to do so, she was determined to get her own way, even if it meant defying her husband. And probably not for the first time.

The tension between William and Lena stretched like the taut string of a violin until it finally broke with an almost audible twang.

"Suit yourself. But don't complain later that I didn't warn you." De Vries let his hand drop and turned his attention back to Detective Phelan. The confrontation with his wife might never have happened. "Abbott would have been shown the door without a character reference had I known about this." He set the snuffbox down as though it were dirtying his fingers. "It's a filthy habit."

"I'm afraid that's not all your footman or valet was up to," Phelan said, taking a handful of betting slips out of the envelope in which they had been concealed.

"There are no names on any of these." De Vries passed some of them to his nephew, both men searching front and back for identifying initials.

"Bookies don't use them on the slips," Phelan explained. "It's safer all round."

"Then how do they get redeemed if the bet is won?" Everett asked.

"The slip is as good as cash money," Phelan told him. "And the bookie has his own records. Which, I might add, he keeps hidden where no one else can find them. If he knows what's good for him."

"It's another world," De Vries pronounced. "One I have no wish to be a part of."

"Nor I," Rinehart said, handing the slips he had been looking at back to Phelan. "Banking interests and the stock market provide all the excitement a gentleman could ask for."

Prudence glanced at Geoffrey, sitting as silent and motionless as a statue. He made a miniscule movement of his head, enough to let her know that this was Phelan's game and he was content to let him conduct it however he chose. Observing the byplay between De Vries and his nephew, between De Vries and Phelan, was giving him insights into their characters he would put to good use later on. Geoffrey was nothing if not patient. It was sometimes all Prudence could do not to jump in and snatch the reins of conversation into her own capable hands.

"He didn't place all these bets for himself," Phelan said. He fixed an accusatory glare on William De Vries, then on his nephew. "Someone else in this house was paying him to run them and hold the slips, someone who was afraid his weakness would be discovered."

Neither man said a word. Each returned Phelan's stare with the perfect aplomb of a gentleman of means whose reputation is above reproach.

"And then there's this." Phelan held out the robin-egg blue Tiffany ring box.

Lena De Vries slid to the floor in a dead faint.

In the flurry of activity that followed Lena's loss of consciousness, William De Vries managed to get rid of Detective Phelan and his partner. Like most men, they did their utmost to avoid being confronted with a woman's weaknesses.

"We'll be back at a more opportune time, Mr. De Vries," Phelan promised as he and his fellow detective were ushered toward the front door. Pat Corcoran had surged up from the basement with the servants summoned by their master's repeated yanks on the bellpull that rang in the staff dining room where he had been questioning them.

A cluster of chattering maids poked their heads around the baize-covered door to spy out what was going on that had made such a disturbance. All they saw were the backs of two plainclothes policemen disappearing out onto the street where a few passersby craned their necks past the uniformed officers urging them on their way. The morgue wagon had already left for Bellevue.

Lena's lady's maid and the housekeeper fluttered around their mistress with smelling salts and brandy, chaffing her hands, covering her legs with a warm knitted throw, calling her name repeatedly. Her eyelids fluttered, opened, closed again.

Prudence slipped her fingers onto one of Lena's wrists, feeling for the pulse she had been taught to find when her father's heart condition had worsened and he needed constant nursing. *Strong and steady*, she communicated silently to Geoffrey. Prudence had no illusions about the ways in which women evaded distressing moments. Whether this was a true faint or a ruse to avoid unpleasantness, the Tiffany-blue ring box was at the root of it.

"Is she coming around?" William De Vries asked brusquely. He'd instructed the butler to serve whiskey to the gentlemen and ordered sherry poured for Prudence. There only remained the problem of getting his wife onto her feet and up the stairs to the chaise longue in her boudoir.

The ring box at which they had all been staring when Lena slipped to the floor was nowhere in sight. He assumed Detective Phelan had taken it with him. Evidence that Leonard Abbott had been a thief as well as a gambler and a self-killer.

Good riddance to him, William De Vries decided.

"She's definitely hiding something, Geoffrey," Prudence said as they walked arm in arm down Fifth Avenue toward their offices near Trinity Church. The gloomy winter clouds had lifted and the sky was a clear, bright blue. Snow crunched beneath their feet and bells tinkled on the harnesses of some of the horses pulling hansom cabs for hire. It was close to Christmas; the city was putting on its best face for the shoppers along the Ladies' Mile.

"Was it a real faint?" he asked. Gentleman though he was, his investigative instincts made him wary of convenient swoons.

"Maybe," Prudence said, reflectively. "But if she wanted to divert attention away from the Tiffany ring box, she certainly succeeded."

A flash of robin-egg blue showed against the black leather of one of Geoffrey's gloved hands.

"You stole it!" Prudence exclaimed, skipping two quick steps in gleeful recognition of his criminality. "How on earth did you manage it?"

"No one was paying attention to me, thanks to Lena De Vries and her vapors," he said, smiling broadly. He handed the small box to Prudence, who opened and closed the lid several times and pulled sharply at the velvet lining.

"Nothing," she said, handing it back to him.

"What did you expect to find?"

"I don't know. Something that would reveal to whom it belonged?"

"I think Lena told us that."

"You think she recognized it?"

"A tiny piece of the blue leather has been chipped off the corner. As though it was roughly handled at one time. You could see it quite clearly when Phelan held the box in his hand. She might have recognized it and realized in that instant that she had to do something drastic to avoid having to answer questions."

"Aunt Gillian has been right all along. Lena knew that some of the diamonds she was wearing the night of the ball were fake."

"I'm not sure I'd go that far. Not yet. Your aunt has a tendency to jump to conclusions without any proof to back them up."

"But Lena *is* the only one in the house likely to possess a ring purchased at Tiffany. Yet it wasn't in the box. Where was it? And why was she afraid to admit that it was gone?"

"And how did the empty box end up in the bedside table of a footman with aspirations to become a valet? Who put it there?"

Prudence stopped so suddenly that a woman walking behind nearly bumped into her. "You don't think it was Leonard Abbott himself, do you, Geoffrey?"

"I think someone wants us to believe it was," he replied enigmatically.

"A third murder?"

"The jeweler who probably bought some, if not all of the diamonds; the assistant he hired to run dubious errands in and out of the Five Points; and now a servant who worked in the house where the theft had to have occurred. It's too neat, Prudence. As though names on a list were being ticked off, item by item. I don't like it."

"Is William De Vries still our client?"

"For the time being."

"Until he becomes a suspect?"

"Or the next victim." Geoffrey tightened his hold on Prudence's arm and scanned the street for an empty hansom cab. The sooner they got back to the office the better.

CHAPTER 11

"It's time to shift our focus." Geoffrey aligned the items on his desk into a precise row, tapping each one decisively as he placed it in the straight line he was creating. "We know almost nothing about Everett Rinehart and Lena's son, yet both young men are living in the house where we presume the necklace was tampered with."

Prudence watched, fascinated and amused, as he ordered his thoughts. "Lena's son is Morgan Whitley," she volunteered. "His mother rarely if ever mentions him in conversation. She's either being very protective or she's indifferent to him."

Josiah, taking notes, approved Geoffrey's straight rank of pen, pencil, inkstand, and paperweight. "Unconcerned about her own son?"

"Possibly. We don't have enough information to decide whether she's silent about him because she's doting or uncaring," Geoffrey said.

"Are we moving away from concentrating on how the theft itself was managed?" Prudence asked.

"From what we know at the moment, the substitutions most

likely took place either at Tiffany or the De Vries mansion," Geoffrey began, ticking off the steps of his reasoning. "If we eliminate Tiffany, the tampering had to have been initiated by someone at the De Vries home."

"Has there ever been a theft of this magnitude committed by a Tiffany employee?" Josiah asked, fascinated as always by the unraveling of a case in progress.

"Two employees were caught and convicted after a series of minor thefts from the workrooms was discovered about twelve or thirteen years ago," Geoffrey said. "It could have been an enormous blow to the Tiffany reputation, but they recovered quickly and put an elaborate system of anti-theft precautions in place. They started their own investigation the moment De Vries brought the necklace into the store for them to verify what Lady Rotherton had told him. We can count on Tiffany to be very thorough."

"Motive, means, and opportunity." Josiah made three columns on his stenographer's notepad.

"Let's leave motive and means aside for the moment," Prudence told him. "Opportunity definitely encompasses anyone living in the De Vries home."

"Which brings us back to staff and family," Geoffrey agreed.

Josiah was listing names as fast as he could scribble them in the incomprehensible Gregg shorthand he had recently mastered.

"We said that Lena was definitely hiding something," Prudence mused. "Could she possibly have stolen the diamonds from her own necklace?"

"There's no reason to exclude her," Geoffrey said. "It didn't require a great deal of strength to pry the stones loose from the prongs holding them in place."

"It would take skill and the right jeweler's tools to remove the diamonds without damaging the settings, and we know that the maid Taylor had been taught how to care for diamonds by her father. Could Lena and Taylor have been working together? For some reason we don't know if that speaks to motive?"

"Possibly. But could either or even both of them make a hanging look like suicide?" Geoffrey asked.

"We need more personal information about each one of the people in that house. Otherwise, we're just speculating." Prudence gestured toward their secretary. "And wasting Josiah's time and paper."

"I've got it all, Miss Prudence," Josiah said. He prided himself on not missing a word of the conversations he transcribed.

"Do you remember Russell Coughlin?" Geoffrey asked.

"Ned Hayes's reporter friend who works for the *Herald*?" Prudence recalled.

"He's not on the society beat, but he's always been able to discover the gossip that editors leave out of the stories they *do* print."

"Will he share it with us?"

"If we promise to give him an exclusive on a story every other reporter in town will be scrambling for, I think he'll cooperate. In fact, I know he will."

"We can't tell him about the theft of the diamonds without our client's permission," Prudence said. She didn't want to remind him aloud that it was a matter of ethics. "You didn't say a word to Detective Phelan about why De Vries hired us."

"If possible, that's the way we'll keep things. It won't be the first time. When the two murders we're sure of and the murder made to look like suicide do get solved, and if the guilty party leads back to the De Vries household, we won't have to compromise client confidentiality. The police and whoever confesses will do it for us. Coughlin will get details from an unidentified source that no other reporter has; inside stories are gold to newsmen." Geoffrey ran his hand over the items he'd arranged so carefully on his desk, sending them scattering. "It'll work. Trust me."

*   *   *

Russell Coughlin met them in one of the side dining rooms of the Astor House, just a few steps across Broadway from the *Herald* building.

"Very few people in society come here nowadays," he told Prudence, who had worn a veiled hat to conceal her face. "I don't think you have to worry about being recognized. Businessmen still come for lunch in the Rotunda, but they rarely stray off to the smaller rooms."

The Astor House had once been the most famous hotel in the country, but by now it had seen better days. Competition from newer hotels and the general move of Manhattanites northward toward Central Park and beyond had taken their toll. The fabric on Prudence's chair was a bit frayed and the carpeting beneath her feet worn to the nap in places. The white linen tablecloth had been washed and starched too many times, and even the silverware didn't gleam as brightly as it should.

Coughlin consulted his reporter's notebook as soon as the waiter had taken their orders and left the table.

"As far as our society page reporter knows, William De Vries is as staid and respectable as they get. In New York, at any rate. She says there's some talk among her British colleagues about what he gets up to when he's in England, but nothing she can confirm. He makes business trips to London and the continent at least once or twice a year, but he goes alone, doesn't take his wife with him. And while he's there, he frequents the Marlborough House Set. The Prince of Wales and his friends are notorious for what they get up to, and the queen stays angry at Bertie, as he's known in the family, all the time. But the newspapers are careful about what they print. They have to be."

"What about the nephew and the stepson?" Geoffrey asked. From what Prudence had told him of Lady Rotherton's comments about De Vries, he hadn't expected anything different.

"The nephew is considered one of the most eligible bachelors in the city," Coughlin said. "Up until about two years ago he lived with his widowed mother in a small town on the Hudson. Wickelton, population practically nothing. Went to Harvard, graduated with honors, received a small inheritance when he turned twenty-one. When his mother died, he sold the family home and came to live with his uncle, who took him into the banking and investment business. The story is that De Vries gave him an account to manage and challenged him to double its worth in one year. Which he somehow did. So the rumor is that De Vries will entrust him with more and more of the business until he becomes a full partner or takes it over entirely. That's what makes the mothers of marriageable daughters invite him to their soirées."

"That's it?"

"Everett Rinehart seems to be living an open and charmed life. My contact says he's a bore to cover. His only vice seems to be a love of sailing, but even there he's not over his head. He owns a small boat that he takes out into Long Island Sound or the East River several times a month with some friends from Harvard. Four or five of them. The boat won't hold any more than that. He hasn't joined an expensive yacht club yet, but that would be the logical next step if he wants to get into racing and eventually a bigger boat. Right now it seems more a hobby than anything else. He has been seeing one young woman rather more than any others, so there may be an engagement on the horizon."

"Do you have her name?"

"Lorinda Bouwmeester."

"It sounds Dutch," Geoffrey said. "Bouwmeester."

"One of the Knickerbocker families. They're as old–New York society as you can get. Old money, too." Coughlin flipped to the next page in his notebook.

"Do you know the name, Prudence?" Geoffrey asked.

"I think you'd do better to ask Aunt Gillian. She may have spent the last twenty some odd years in England, but there isn't much she doesn't know about who's who in New York. She would probably have married into that type of family if she hadn't succumbed to the lure of a title."

"I've saved the best for last," Coughlin said, signaling to the waiter that he'd take another stein of beer. Roast beef, sliced fried potatoes, and a small mountain of pureed root vegetables had disappeared as though he hadn't eaten in a month or more. And somehow the eating hadn't interrupted his narrative.

But he waited to begin until the waiter had removed their plates, brought coffee for Prudence and Geoffrey, and a brimming stein of frothy beer for himself.

"Are either of you familiar with the Keeley Cure?" he asked.

"I've never heard of it," Prudence said.

"According to Dr. Leslie Keeley, he's discovered the cure for excessive alcohol consumption," Geoffrey said, leaning back in his chair. "He claims drunkenness is a disease, and that's how his institute handles it. Somewhere in a small town outside Chicago. He treats other addictions, but the main one is drunkenness."

"That's right," Coughlin commented. "Are you acquainted with someone who's undergone the treatment?"

"I looked into it for a friend. But he took a different direction." Geoffrey didn't need to mention Ned Hayes by name. Until Tyrus had taken over and tied him to his bed where he sweated and shook out the devils he'd swallowed and injected over the years, Ned's condition had been the despair of everyone who cared for him. Most of the so-called cures for alcoholism were eventually proved to be quackery, but desperate cases called for desperate measures.

"A lot has been written about it in the Chicago papers," Coughlin continued. "And there's talk that Keeley will eventually open a branch of the institute in New York. But for now, anyone who wants to take the Gold Cure has to go to Dwight, Illinois."

"Why is it called the Gold Cure?" Prudence asked. She had a

reason for asking that far outweighed anything to do with the De Vries case. Deep in the most hidden recesses of her worst fears, Prudence had a horror of falling victim once again to the soothing, addictive balm of laudanum. She collected reports of treatments that promised to break the cycle of dependency the way other women accumulated bits of jewelry. Not even Geoffrey knew how often she awoke in the night sweating from a nightmare in which one swallow of the bitter-tasting liquid opium turned into a river of poison.

"The main treatment is daily injections of bichloride of gold," Coughlin explained. "The formula is a well-guarded secret, but patients come to the institute and line up like trained monkeys four times a day to be jabbed in the arm with a needle by doctors who pass them along as fast as they can. Hundreds at a time. They're also required to drink specially prepared tonics every few hours. Another secret recipe. And while they're undergoing the treatment, they have to live in hotels and boardinghouses in Dwight because the only place they can get the injections is at the institute."

"Women too?" Prudence shuddered. She had a sudden vision of herself in a long line of withered female addicts.

"The women receive the injections in their boardinghouses or hotel rooms. The institute cooperates to conceal their identities."

"How long does the treatment last?"

"Four to six weeks, Miss MacKenzie. At the end of that time, Keeley declares the patient cured."

"What about relapses? Surely not everyone is successfully treated." Prudence knew that the majority of laudanum users drifted through what remained of their lives in a state of permanent reliance on the drug to get them through each day.

"Keeley says his cure is absolute, and if one of his patients begins drinking again it's through choice and not need. As long as a patient keeps to the regimen, the doctor doesn't admit to the possibility of failure."

"And this is where Morgan Whitley comes in?" Geoffrey asked.

"No one boasts of taking the Keeley Cure," Coughlin said. "But if a register of clients were ever made available, I'm told you'd recognize many of the names. Some of the nation's most public figures, male and female both. Drunkenness isn't reserved for the down and out, but it costs money to subscribe to a cure."

"And Lena's son has done that? Gone to Dwight, Illinois, for his bichloride of gold injections?" Prudence asked.

"Six months ago De Vries apparently gave him an ultimatum. *Get cured or get out.* And my source assumes that meant out of the house as well as the business. Something precipitated the situation, but my source doesn't know what that was. Only that Morgan has been a fairly public drunk since his Harvard days. His stepfather took him into the investment firm when he graduated. It wasn't until Morgan proved himself unable to make sound decisions that De Vries started leaning heavily on his nephew. What's interesting is that the two young men appear to be friends. You'd think there would be animosity between them, some sort of cutthroat competitiveness at least. But there isn't. Or if there is, it's so well hidden no one has detected it yet."

"It must be agony for Lena that her son is skating so close to the edge of ruin," Prudence said. "That might be the reason she never willingly speaks of him. She knows his weakness could easily prove to be his undoing. As it has for so many others." She felt a familiar tingle of apprehension travel up her spine.

"Morgan has until the end of the year to prove himself. I should point out that this isn't the only ultimatum his stepfather has pronounced. There have been a number of them over the years. But Mrs. De Vries has apparently managed to talk her husband out of turning his back on her son all those other times. My source says it won't happen again. Morgan isn't a blood relative to De Vries; the nephew is. And De Vries doesn't need

Morgan now that Everett is turning out to be so much like his uncle."

"The son Lena was unable to give him," Geoffrey said. He knew firsthand about the crushing expectations fathers laid upon their male children.

"Mrs. De Vries is something of an enigma," Coughlin added. "She was a Bergen before her marriage to Jacob Whitley. Two Knickerbocker families. Old names, old money. It wasn't a love match, but the arrangement seemed to suit both of them. She's related to Mrs. Astor through one of those complex cousin strands that takes a genealogical chart to unravel. When Whitley died, Lena was left to raise Morgan alone. No other children. She was expected to remarry and she did, again staying within the social milieu in which she's always lived. De Vries is a much wealthier man than her first husband and perhaps that was one of his attractions. She must have thought he would eventually adopt Morgan, who might have been a difficult child from an early age. I'm just guessing now." Coughlin put away the reporter's notebook he'd been consulting from time to time.

"I'll let Ned know we met," Geoffrey said, rising to shake Coughlin's hand. "He was hoping to be able to join us."

"I haven't seen him in a few months. Is he still dry?"

"Tyrus keeps him on a tight leash," Prudence contributed.

"I'd hate like hell for anything to happen to him," Coughlin said. "He's one of the good ones."

"So is he," Geoffrey commented as Coughlin wove his way through the tables toward the crowded Rotunda. "One of the good ones. For a reporter."

"What next, Geoffrey?"

"We go back to the office and write a report for Josiah's files."

"And then what?"

"We contrive a meeting with Morgan and evaluate him for

ourselves. Right now he's the only member of the De Vries family we haven't spoken to directly."

"From what Coughlin said, he doesn't seem to be accepted as a member of William De Vries's family. Not if he has to prove himself or be thrown out into the street."

"Lena won't let that happen," Geoffrey predicted. "She'll move heaven and earth to make sure it doesn't."

"To protect her reputation and keep scandal from attaching itself to the family name?" Prudence asked. "Or because she loves him enough to force her husband into choosing between them if that's the only leverage she has?"

"That's what we don't know," Geoffrey said. "And what we'll have to find out."

CHAPTER 12

"Your Mr. Whitley is apparently not showing up at the De Vries offices with any kind of regularity," Josiah reported. "I've telephoned several times for an appointment and they keep putting me off."

"Do you think he's drinking again?" Prudence asked. She'd been both fascinated and appalled by Russell Coughlin's description of the Keeley Cure. Despite the doctor's claim that his institute's patients were restored to health and sobriety by the treatment, she knew from her own experience that the craving for laudanum was never entirely eliminated. She presumed it was the same for alcohol.

"If he's gambling and losing, he's probably drinking, too," Geoffrey said. "The racetracks are closed for the winter, but gaming parlors are open for business year round."

"I've never been to one," Prudence declared, "nor to a race-track, either."

It was immediately clear to both Josiah and Geoffrey that she was announcing her intention to remedy that situation as soon as possible. Ladies often occupied the upper boxes of Jerome Park where the Belmont Stakes were run, and in good weather picnicked with their escorts on the track's manicured lawns. But they rarely if ever frequented gaming parlors and casinos. Except for a certain type of woman, who wasn't a lady at all.

Once Prudence made up her mind, it would only make matters worse to try to stop her. Better to deflect her attention elsewhere and hope she didn't realize what he was doing.

"We can put someone on Morgan's tail when he leaves the De Vries mansion tomorrow morning," Geoffrey decided.

Among the men the firm employed for this kind of work were a number of ex-Pinkertons, all of them expert trackers. The trackers, in turn, used street urchins vouched for by Danny Dennis to relay their information back to the office. Often ragged and barefoot even in the icy slush of winter, they ran through crowds of pedestrians like fish slipping through water weeds. Josiah, who had a soft spot for them, kept a box of boots and jackets in the supply closet.

"In the meantime, we'll find out all we can about Leonard Abbott."

"I'll go to the employment agency," Prudence volunteered. "They'll have the most complete records there. We should be able to trace him, if he didn't lie on his application."

Despite the fact that the MacKenzie household was a long-standing client of the Wentworth Domestic Employment Agency, the firm's owner was reluctant to open her files.

"We do promise both our clients and our applicants a degree of confidentiality," Claudia Wentworth explained. "There are certain types of information that do not have a direct impact on conditions of employment." She wore a pince-nez securely anchored on the bridge of her nose. When she twitched or wrinkled her nostrils, it slipped neatly down to dangle from a black silk ribbon attached to her formidable bodice by a discreet gold brooch.

"The list you've already provided has proved to be very

helpful," Prudence told her, trying to pull her eyes from the dancing pince-nez. "But we need details about Leonard Abbott's background. I'm sure you understand why I can't supply any more information than that, but I wouldn't trouble you if it weren't vitally important. Without exaggeration, Miss Wentworth, it's a matter of life and death."

"The young man gave us no indication he was the type of individual who would take his own life," she said, vigorously rubbing the lenses of her pince-nez before repositioning it.

"I can assure you that Mrs. De Vries attaches no blame to the agency for what happened," Prudence said, wondering who had informed the Wentworth Domestic Employment Agency about the suicide before reporters broke the story. Probably the police, she decided. Detective Phelan would have requested the same information she was seeking to obtain.

"We have already spoken to the police," Claudia Wentworth confirmed.

"And so you should have," Prudence agreed. "Once a tragedy like this has occurred, there are no more secrets. I'm sure you understand that the De Vries family would not be probing into their late footman's private life were it not for a wish to assure themselves that his despair, and also the habits leading to his wretchedness, have not infected other members of the staff. Particularly the younger, more impressionable servants. There is also a most Christian concern on their part to be certain that the wages owed to Leonard, and perhaps a little something extra, be paid to his surviving family."

In the end it was the purely human weakness of curiosity that compelled the Wentworth Agency's owner to order the information on Leonard Abbott's employment application be replicated. It was no secret that Miss MacKenzie was blotting the copybook of her perfect society credentials by partnering with an ex-Pinkerton operative in what was essentially a private inquiry firm. The attempt to imbue it with respectability by adding the word *law* to the company letterhead fooled no one. As they sat chatting, drinking tea, and waiting for the pertinent facts to be copied, Claudia Wentworth did her experienced best to pick Prudence's brain.

"The police were not very forthcoming about the details of young Mr. Abbott's death," she began.

"All I can tell you is that he was found in the attic of the De Vries home with a rope around his neck," Prudence told her, not revealing anything more than what she knew was already appearing in the newspapers.

"And apparently there is some indication that he was involved in what can only be termed shady operations? Detective Phelan mentioned betting slips that had been found and certain indications of possible theft."

Prudence nodded her head sadly, but said nothing.

"We do our best to ferret out character flaws and weaknesses in the individuals who come to us seeking employment," Miss Wentworth went on. "As you may imagine, Miss MacKenzie, it requires a certain amount of delicacy and not a little perseverance to ascertain the truth. However, I may say with some degree of pride that we rarely fail in our quest to provide only the best candidates for our clients to interview."

"My father was always satisfied with the applicants supplied by the Wentworth Agency," Prudence said. "As I also have been."

"That's very kind of you to say, Miss MacKenzie. Especially under the circumstances."

Neither woman was giving much away. In that respect, they were a matched pair.

The neatly inscribed report on Leonard Abbott was not as informative as Prudence had hoped it would be.

"He appears to have no living relatives," she said, skimming the page that had been handed to her.

"Which is perhaps a blessing in this case," Miss Wentworth commented. "Those who take their own lives bring shame and great sorrow to their families. And of course they cannot be buried in consecrated ground." The pince-nez tumbled from her nose again.

"A former employer is listed."

Miss Wentworth would have to have a word with the clerk who hadn't had the sense to omit that particular detail from the copy he'd made of the dead man's file. Employers did not relish having to remember servants who had left their service. For whatever reason. Now she would have to decide whether to forewarn Abbott's former mistress or hope that Miss MacKenzie would decide not to pursue the matter.

"I don't see anything here that need cause Mrs. De Vries disquiet," Prudence said, readying herself to leave. "As I believe I mentioned, she was chiefly concerned that if the late Mr. Abbott had family, any wages owed to him would be paid."

"Very generous of her," Miss Wentworth agreed. And decided that she probably did not need to contact his former employer after all.

"The reference he provided for the Wentworth Agency was a forgery," Prudence reported. "The name and address of his supposed former employer were entirely made up."

"How did you find that out, Miss Prudence?" Josiah asked.

"I went to the address he had supplied. It was a boardinghouse. My guess is that he'd decided he could claim it had been a private home at one time and that the change to paying guests occurred after he left. But apparently whoever was supposed to check his references at the agency fell down on the job. Or was slipped something under the table not to investigate them."

"It makes you wonder how many times that happens," Josiah said.

"Did you say Mr. Hunter has gone out?" Prudence asked.

"One of his ex-Pinkertons came by right after you left. Amos Lang. He had given him the assignment to keep an eye on Morgan Whitley, and I guess Lang struck pay dirt right away. He sent one of Danny Dennis's boys to the office with a message just a little while ago. Mr. Hunter grabbed his hat and coat and was out the door without telling me where he was going." Josiah was plainly miffed at being excluded from what could prove to be a significant development in the case.

So was Prudence. She'd planned to insist that Geoffrey allow her to accompany him to whichever gambling palace Lena's son frequented. Now she had no idea which one it was.

"Do you still have the note the messenger brought?"

"No note. Just a verbal message."

"But you heard it?"

Josiah shook his head. "The boy shot past me like a rat toward cheese when Mr. Hunter opened his office door. I couldn't hear what he said, but I'd lay odds Lang located Morgan Whitley in a gambling hall somewhere."

"He's almost certainly gone to the Mint," said a voice from the doorway.

Josiah shot to his feet.

"Aunt Gillian," Prudence said. "What on earth are you doing here?"

"I don't like being pushed aside as though I have neither the brains nor the stamina to keep up with this investigation. Do I have to remind you that if it weren't for me, Hunter and MacKenzie wouldn't have a case at all? And William De Vries would be well on his way to being the laughing stock of New York society. Imagine a man who can't tell the difference between diamonds and glass!" She hadn't spared so much as a glance for the meticulously attired man who couldn't take his eyes off her.

"Aunt Gillian, this is our secretary, Josiah Gregory. Josiah, my aunt, Lady Rotherton."

He executed something between a bow and the opening steps of a jig, and may have inquired if he could serve her a cup of tea. Neither Prudence nor Lady Rotherton understood a word of what he said.

"What is the Mint?" Prudence finally asked.

"The most exclusive gambling parlor in Manhattan," Lady Rotherton replied. "It's located within easy walking distance of William's office and just off Fifth Avenue. Not everyone who seeks admittance is allowed in. It's very select. You have to be prepared to lose a great deal of money in a very short amount of time."

"How do you know about it?"

"If you're going to keep up with your precious ex-Pinkerton partner, Prudence, you have to ask the right questions of the right people."

Prudence felt her face flush. She turned away and walked toward the window out of which she could glimpse the spire of Trinity Church. She was *not* going to lose her temper. No matter how unreasonable her aunt proved to be, and she hadn't been anything but difficult to deal with since the moment she'd arrived on American soil, Prudence was determined not to forget for a moment that Her Ladyship was her beloved and much mourned mother's only sister.

"It's barely past midafternoon," Lady Rotherton declared. "The habitual gamblers are well into it and the evening sports are hours away from dressing for dinner and a turn at the roulette wheels."

"What does that mean?" Prudence asked. Her cheeks had cooled and the slender elegance of Trinity's steeple against the blue of the sky had calmed her.

"It means that we don't have to dress. We can go the way we are. But if you wait around here and do nothing for another hour or two, it will be too late."

"I didn't think ladies were welcome in the gambling halls."

"They are in this one. A very special type of woman is always welcome, as long as she's on the arm of a millionaire."

"Which we wouldn't be," Prudence pointed out.

"A title is as good as a fortune," Lady Rotherton said. "Better. It's one of the first lessons you learn when you marry into the aristocracy. You can be as poor as a church mouse and as ugly as a bulldog, but if you're a lord or a lady, you're welcome everywhere. In fact, no one would dare refuse you admittance."

"This isn't England, Aunt."

"So much the better. Americans worship the ground blue bloods walk on and can't tell the difference between a duke and an earl. They have no idea how to address us, and even less notion why it matters. Are you coming?"

The Mint looked like an ordinary office building except that it was windowless and the front door was made of two immense plates of studded steel. A thick-shouldered man stood at the foot of the four steps rising from the pavement and an even thicker-shouldered individual waited by the door. Prudence was sure they both wore revolvers in shoulder holsters. Geoffrey had taught her to read the peculiar bulge in a man's jacket that meant he was armed.

Lady Rotherton swept past the first man without hesitation, thrust a calling card at the second man, and tapped her foot impatiently as he read it. Prudence glimpsed a signature scrawled in bold black ink on the back of the card. Without a word or a challenge, the security guard tapped a code knock on the door and stood aside as it swung open. He handed the card to the frock-coated greeter, touched a hand to his hat, and turned back to study the street.

The Mint might have looked businesslike from the outside, but its interior was as plush as anything the Vanderbilts had been able to commission for their Fifth Avenue mansions. The entrance hall into which Prudence and Lady Rotherton stepped was a vaulted foyer of crimson, gold leaf, and black marble. Tall potted palms flanked a wide hall down which could be glimpsed the dark, exotic wood paneling of an opulent ground floor bar and the white linen of a glass-doored dining room. Its gas chandeliers had been dimmed to a flattering glow that made it possible to avoid recognizing anyone a guest might wish to avoid.

"Roulette," Lady Rotherton said. Just the one word.

Prudence was about to correct her, about to say that American men preferred poker. But there wasn't time. Her aunt's skirts swished across the royal red carpet as they were ushered toward a black marble staircase leading to the building's upper stories. The roulette tables, they were told, were on the second floor.

Lady Rotherton dismissed the greeter with a cutting wave of her hand. He had disappeared before Prudence reached the first landing. Whatever else she was, her aunt never appeared less than commanding. As they walked down a wide, mirrored corridor toward the sound of roulette tables, Prudence realized that Aunt Gillian had correctly assessed the situation before stepping foot inside the Mint.

All around them were the soft, regular sounds of bets being made, cards being shuffled, dealt, and laid out on felt-covered tables. The men they caught sight of in the dim parlors they passed were all clothed in the daytime uniform of the wealthy dilettante who could afford to absent himself from the office out of which his fortune flowed. Bespoke suit exquisitely tailored to minimize belly and beefy shoulders, diamond stickpin securing a silk cravat, heavy gold watch and fob catching the light across the dark expanse of tightly buttoned waistcoat, rings that flashed on fingers whose nails were buffed and manicured to a fare-thee-well. Later in the evening would appear the white tie and tails of evening dress and, she supposed, the female creatures for whom her aunt had disdained to use the word *ladies*.

But for the moment, Prudence and Lady Rotherton, distinguished by their ramrod-straight posture, swayless gait, and discreetly elegant winter tweeds beneath fur-lined coats, blended right in. The Mint catered to anyone with a grand name and deep pockets. As long as they remained circumspect and inconspicuous, it appeared that respectable members of the fairer sex were welcome. At least until it was time for their less reputable sisters to make their appearances.

The roulette room was worthy of the European elite who had first popularized the game. Its chandeliers were imported crystal, the spittoons polished brass, the whiskey glasses heavy-bottomed and the exact right size for a gentleman's hand. The wheels themselves had been constructed of rare and expensive woods, the numbers painted with exquisitely delicate curlicues, the all-important ball of polished ivory. Unlike the card rooms, where a hush as thick as cigar smoke hung over the tables, the clicks of the bouncing balls and the soft whir of the wheels were as hypnotic as a pirouette.

Positioned beside her aunt just inside the wide, arched doorway, Prudence scanned the dimness for a familiar face and tall figure. Just when she was beginning to think that Lady Rotherton might for once be wrong, she saw him. Standing not far from a dark-haired young man whose skeletal thinness and once handsome, now ravaged face reminded her of Ned Hayes during his worst days. When no one who saw the ex-detective thought he would last out the year.

Morgan Whitley. Impossible for it to be anyone else.

And when Geoffrey turned his head and glimpsed her looking back at him across the roulette parlor of a gambling casino, Prudence knew she was right.

Her partner was furious.

CHAPTER 13

From across the expanse of the roulette room Geoffrey's eyes bored mercilessly into Prudence's. They skipped briefly to rest on the imperious figure standing beside her, then flicked away as if the high-handed Lady Rotherton were of no importance at all. It was Prudence he cared for, and Prudence who had heedlessly thrust herself into a situation where no unmarried lady of her social standing should ever find herself. He was well aware of the risks she ran whenever she stepped beyond the bounds of propriety, but this was edging precariously close to the edge of what society would tolerate.

And then Geoffrey reminded himself that he had no right to dictate to his partner what she should or should not do. Prudence had made it clear from the beginning that she was determined to be her own mistress, that the position of subservient female was not one she would endure without putting up a fight. She'd already stepped farther outside the bounds of what was suitable and fitting than almost every other young woman he had known. This latest act was simply the next in what he feared would be a long string of challenges. He had no license to be angry with her. And he wasn't even sure what to call the violent emotion that had surged through him when he first saw her across the roulette tables. Something other than fury, but just as devastating.

Morgan Whitley gave no sign that he was aware of being watched. He drifted from one roulette table to another, betting wheel after wheel in search of the one that would bring him luck and a return of the money he had already lost that afternoon. But he seemed plagued by the ill will of the fickle goddesses of fate. The stack of chips in his left hand grew steadily smaller until, finally, he tossed and lost the last one.

It was at that moment that Prudence appeared at his side, though she had been several steps behind him for nearly an hour. Unnoticed as he concentrated single-mindedly on the game whose willing dupe he had become.

"Morgan, is that really you?" she asked, slipping one hand through the crook of his arm. "It's been so long I wasn't sure."

He stared at her for a moment, struggling to come back from the world of swirling numbers that repeatedly hurled him with dizzying speed from hope to despair. Pale brown hair, fair skin, regular features blossoming into beauty when she smiled. Gray eyes of a compelling clarity that drew you into their mesmerizing light. He'd only ever met one person with eyes like that. "Prudence! Prudence MacKenzie!" He looked around him, panicked; he'd spoken her name too loudly in the clickety-clack hush.

"Not to worry, Morgan. It's perfectly respectable for a lady to accompany her elderly British aunt on an afternoon expedition to see the famous sights of New York City." She gestured toward a regal woman of a certain age who was studying the single-zero European layout on one of the roulette tables.

Morgan paled. "Is she . . . ?"

Drat. Prudence hadn't thought to allow for the fact that Lena had almost certainly told her son about the missing diamonds and how the theft came to be discovered. Everett Rinehart, during the initial police investigation of the valet's suicide, hadn't seemed to connect the death with anything but the betting slips and snuffbox Detective Phelan had shown them.

"My aunt Gillian. Lady Rotherton. Yes, she's the one who first noticed that some of your mother's diamonds had been replaced by paste. I didn't realize you knew."

"I don't think William meant for me to be told. But Mother and I have no secrets from one another."

Prudence laid her other hand on Morgan's arm, steering him from the roulette tables toward a curtained alcove containing a cushioned banquette and table. Within moments of their reaching it, a white-gloved waiter asked what he could serve them.

"Whiskey," Morgan said. "A double."

"Sherry," Prudence ordered. "Amontillado, if you have it." It was the only sherry she could think of, having read "The Cask of Amontillado" numerous times in her father's 1874 edition of *The Works of Edgar Allan Poe*. She'd always wondered what that particular sherry tasted like.

"I'm sorry for your loss, Prudence," Morgan mumbled awkwardly, not knowing what else to say. It had been two years since Judge MacKenzie's death, but they had been difficult ones for him, periodically marked with blackouts as he lost himself deeper and deeper in drink.

Morgan vaguely recalled attending the judge's funeral, bending over Prudence's hand, murmuring the polite phrases of condolence. The coldness with which his stepfather had spoken to his late friend's widow. There had been a moment when he and Prudence had spoken privately, a few words only, but enough to rekindle the childhood understanding that had once connected them. When she raised her mourning veil, the beautiful gray eyes looking up at him had been lost and drifting in the drugged solace of laudanum. It had been a cold, sobering shock to recognize a mutual dependency.

"We both lost a parent when we were young," Prudence said, as if reading his thoughts, willing them out of the depths of a bereavement that only another bereft child could fathom. "You're fortunate to have your mother."

"I remember the lawns on Staten Island," Morgan said wistfully. "From when Mother and William visited there. Do you still have the house?"

"My father couldn't bring himself to sell it," Prudence said. "And neither could I."

"Of course."

"We'd already returned to Manhattan that fall, but as my mother felt herself weaken she asked to be taken back to Staten Island. My father could deny her nothing. When Mother begged to be carried out onto the porch so she could look at the water, Father bundled her in blankets and had the servants put warm bricks under her feet and tuck hot water bottles all around her. I'll never forget the sight of them sitting together like that for hours, hand in hand."

"Remind me of how old you were when she died."

"Six. I was six."

"My father had been dead for two years by then. I remember telling you that I had begun to forget what he looked like, and how terrible that made me feel. I meant it to be a comfort, but I don't think it was."

"Your mother had recently married William."

"He was kind to me, but I always knew he wanted a son of his own."

"That must have been hard for you."

"Harder on Mother. She wept a lot during those early years of the marriage. Looking back I think it must have been every time she had to face the fact that a child had not been conceived." He reddened and twirled the glass of whiskey from which he had not drunk. "I beg your pardon, Prudence. That was indelicate of me."

"I'm sorry we drifted apart, Morgan."

He shrugged. "It was to be expected. All we had in common as children was that both of us had lost a parent. I went off to school, as boys do, and I'm sure you had governesses. By the time of your coming out, I had begun to avoid balls and dinner parties. For the obvious reason." Tales of his drunkenness had made the rounds of every parlor in town. There were few secrets in the enclosed world of New York society.

"I never came out, not officially." Judge MacKenzie had died between Christmas and New Year's, of an illness that had plagued him for weeks before his heart failed. The debutantes ball was traditionally held in December. Prudence's white dress had hung unworn in her armoire until her stepmother ordered it burned. "After the year of mourning was over, I decided there wasn't any point to it. I hope you're not too shocked."

"My mother told me that William hired Hunter and MacKenzie, Investigative Law, to solve the mystery of her missing diamonds. And that you're the MacKenzie."

"I am."

"You haven't let life overwhelm you, Prudence."

"I have a weakness that I go to great pains to conceal. I'm not proud of it. Every day is a battle."

"If anyone can understand that, I can." Morgan's hand tightened around the glass of whiskey he still hadn't raised to his lips. "We were told at the Keeley Institute that the treatment would cure us and that if we fell into drunkenness again, it was because we chose that path, not because our body craved the drink too strongly for us to resist. The injections of bichloride of gold would make us physically sound. The tonics we drank and the meals we ate would restore us to health, as though we had never been debilitated by demon rum. The promise was that Doctor Keeley could work a miracle on us."

"And did he?" Prudence asked.

"You tell me. Do I look like someone who's been touched by the miraculous?"

He looked, Prudence thought, like a man on the brink of falling off a cliff. Far too thin, so pale the veins throbbing in his temples were as blue as the rivers bracketing Manhattan Island.

The ringless fingers holding his glass of whiskey were almost skeletal, elongated, the brittle nails gnawed and cracked. She read despondency in Morgan Whitley's eyes, in the furrows that lined his face, in the dark circles that testified to nights without sleep. He was far from being in good health. But was he desperate enough to have robbed his own mother? Was he even physically and mentally capable of concocting what had to have been a complex and dangerous scheme? She shook her head.

"That's what I think when I see myself in the mirror," Morgan said. "I wonder what a miracle is supposed to look like. The only thing I know for certain is that it doesn't look like me."

"Perhaps it takes time," Prudence said, deciding to change the subject. "Tell me about William's nephew. You're about the same age. Does he understand the demons you're battling?"

"I don't think I would have lasted this long if it hadn't been for Everett. We're as close as brothers, though there aren't any blood ties between us and he's everything I'm not. My mother's husband thinks Everett can do no wrong, and if you were to compare his successes to my failures, you'd come to the same conclusion. And to answer the question you're too kind to ask, no, I'm not jealous or resentful of him. I said we were as close as brothers, and that's true, but we're also the best of friends."

"Both of you work in the De Vries banking and investment offices," Prudence prodded.

"That's a long story that I'd rather not get into," Morgan said, shifting the whiskey glass from right to left and right again, imitating the roulette ball's search for a winning number. "I don't go to the offices very often now. There doesn't seem much reason for it."

There was no point asking how he managed to cover his gambling losses. Prudence imagined that what he had inherited from his father had long ago trickled through his fingers. Lena must be financing him. She wondered if William knew. Surely his stepfather suspected.

"We sail together," Morgan continued. "Everett has a boat. Nothing grand yet, but he'll be a yachtsman to reckon with some day. For the time being, we sail on the East River and in Long Island Sound whenever the wind is steady."

"Just the two of you?"

"No. There's a whole crew from when we were undergraduates at Harvard. Four or five of us can always manage to show up. We're sailing tomorrow morning, as a matter of fact."

"Won't it be too cold?" Prudence asked. She shivered, imagining the chill of being out on the water in a December wind.

"That's the challenge of sailing in wintertime." A flush of enthusiasm animated Morgan's face. "It's cold, but bracing. As long as you don't fall overboard. And everybody brings a flask, so there's plenty of whiskey to keep the blood flowing."

"Would I know any of these friends of yours? Anyone crazy enough to enjoy nearly freezing to death?" Prudence asked, more to keep Morgan talking about something he obviously enjoyed than because she was interested in the antics of college classmates who hadn't quite grown up.

"I doubt it. Though you might recognize the surnames."

Again that acknowledgment of how small and inbred was the pool of New York society's acceptable families. Prudence thought that if you went to the trouble of tracing their lineages, you'd find they were all distant cousins of one sort or another. New money and new blood married into the old, but the end result was the same.

Prudence caught Geoffrey's eye across the room. She had the answers she'd come here to find. Time to leave Morgan to his own devices and rejoin her erstwhile chaperone. Who had piled up an impressive array of chips at the single-zero roulette table.

"I'm so glad to have run into you, Morgan," she said, sipping the last dregs of her amontillado and gathering her gloves and reticule.

"Would you say it was fortuitous?" he asked, following her

look. "I see your Mister Hunter over there. He's kept his distance while we talked."

Geoffrey and the ex-Pinkerton Amos Lang had nearly disappeared into the mirrored hallway outside the roulette room.

"I suppose I should congratulate you, Prudence. But I would have answered your questions without this elaborate stratagem." Morgan stood, bowed correctly, and then bent over to kiss her cheek lightly.

In the moment before she moved away, she saw him lift the double shot of whiskey to his lips and drain the glass dry.

"He figured it out, Geoffrey," Prudence said. She'd had last night and most of the morning to go over her conversation with Morgan Whitley.

"He must have been in the house somewhere and seen us arrive. I don't recall having been introduced to him."

"Morgan may not be as impaired as he would have you believe," Lady Rotherton observed. She had settled comfortably into the Hunter and MacKenzie conference room, a steaming cup of imported English tea in front of her. Made according to precise directions she had written out and deposited on Josiah's desk.

"It felt as though no time at all had passed since we were children together," Prudence mused. "I can't explain why exactly, but that was the feeling I had. And I remember now that he came to my father's funeral." *Laudanum allows you to forget so much.*

"He's lost a great deal of money at the Mint," Geoffrey said. "Amos managed to get hold of a copy of his account there. Morgan pays off just enough to be allowed to continue to gamble. Never the whole tab. And I suspect he's in arrears in other places, as well."

"The boy's a drunkard," Lady Rotherton said without the slightest suggestion of pity. "He'll ruin himself and whoever is foolish enough to believe he can change. He can't. None of them can."

"He's taken the Keeley Cure," Prudence reminded her.

"Quackery," Lady Rotherton snapped.

"Do we know enough to exclude him from a list of suspects?" It was always Geoffrey who brought their conversations back on track. "Josiah? And speak American, please."

Josiah cleared his throat with a great sigh of put-upon affliction. "He has motive."

"Of course he does," Lady Rotherton interrupted. "Morgan needs capital. Funds. A bankroll. We all know that."

"And he certainly had opportunity if the thefts took place in the De Vries house." Josiah was not going to be scoffed at, even by Her Ladyship.

"What about means?" Prudence asked, struggling with the idea that someone who had been a childhood playmate could have become a thief.

"We can't discount the lady's maid, Taylor," said Geoffrey. "I imagine it would be the work of a few minutes for her to make the substitutions. And they probably weren't all done at the same time."

"The first theft must have been the hardest," Prudence said, following his line of thought. "He needs money, but can't or won't ask his mother to give him any more than she already has. So he exerts his not inconsiderable charm on her maid. Who strikes me as a very frightened and emotionally vulnerable woman."

"With skills he doesn't hesitate to exploit," Lady Rotherton put in. "Young men have no moral scruples at all when they want something from a woman."

"Instead of taking the necklace to Carpenter, he takes the stones," Prudence continued.

"Cleaner and more efficient. If he's caught, he can always say he bought the lot from a wholesaler and was taking them to be worked into a gift for a lady. And he'd probably be believed," Geoffrey added.

"He spent six weeks at the Keeley Institute outside Chicago," Prudence reminded them. "We need those dates."

"Prudence?" Lady Rotherton's use of her niece's name was more command than question.

"He'll tell me if I ask him."

"Send a note," Lady Rotherton instructed her. "It might be useful to have a sample of his handwriting."

Josiah stared at her. He wondered how many men had penned love letters to the enchanting American turned British aristocrat. And what use she had made of them.

The same barefoot urchin who had brought Amos Lang's urgent message to Geoffrey the day before scooted into the conference room. His nose dribbled beads of moisture and his hands were blue with cold, but he had on the boots and jacket Josiah had given him.

He handed Geoffrey a grubby piece of paper, then hopped from foot to foot as he waited for a reply.

"There's been an accident," Geoffrey said, tossing the note on the table. "Josiah, get word to Danny Dennis that we need him right away."

"What's happened?" Prudence asked, reaching for the coat she had laid on the chair beside her.

"Morgan has followed his valet's example and taken the easy way out," predicted Lady Rotherton, taking a last sip from her teacup.

"Two men went overboard from Everett Rinehart's boat. Into the East River," Geoffrey said, shoving his hands into his coat sleeves.

"Are they dead?" Prudence asked, wondering why she bothered. Of course they were. No one could survive the river's icy waters at this time of year.

"Amos doesn't say. He saw them being pulled out onto the

dock and driven off in a hansom cab. Someone shouted to take them to Bellevue."

"They're dead then," Lady Rotherton said, settling the matter. "That's where your city morgue is located." She wondered if Josiah had made enough tea for her to have a second cup.

"It's also the hospital closest to the East River," Geoffrey reminded everyone. "It may be the infirmary for indigent cases, but it has an emergency pavilion as well. If anyone can save them, it's the doctors and staff at Bellevue. They see injuries no one else does."

Prudence picked up the note Geoffrey had let drop.

"I tell you he's dead," Lady Rotherton said, watching her niece's face. "No use hoping for anything else."

But Prudence whispered a quick, guilty prayer, begging to be assured that her conversation with Morgan at the Mint had not tipped him over the edge. The image of him tossing the contents of the whiskey glass into his mouth seared itself into her brain.

Please, God. Please don't let him have taken a flask with him this morning. Not onto the slippery deck of a sailboat pitching through the waters of the East River. Please, God. No.

Amos Lang's note had not mentioned Morgan by name.

CHAPTER 14

By the time Prudence and Geoffrey reached Bellevue, the two men who had been pulled out of the East River had been released from the Emergency Pavilion. Miraculously, one of them had rallied from his immersion in the freezing, contaminated water. The other was dying.

"We could do nothing further for him," a doctor told them. He was a young man, sad faced and plainly exhausted by the succession of hopeless cases that poured through the hospital's doors every day. "We've put him in a curtained alcove on one of the wards for the time being. The parents are arranging to take him home where he'll be attended by private nurses and his family physician."

"And the other man?"

"His friend is sitting by his bedside. He refused to leave him."

"Can you direct us to the ward he's on?"

"No visitors," the doctor said. "Family members only." He'd already balked at giving out the patients' names.

Geoffrey handed over a business card.

"Investigative Law?" questioned the doctor. "I didn't think this was a police matter. We were told it was an accident."

"Nevertheless." Geoffrey glanced around the Emergency Pavilion's waiting area. There was usually at least one reporter hanging about, waiting for a story that might fill a few lines of copy. With fresh editions of the city's newspapers being hawked throughout the day, the hunger for news was insatiable. If he couldn't get the names he wanted one way, he'd try another.

But the waiting area was empty of newshounds. He glanced at his pocket watch. Close to deadline for the afternoon editions.

"I'll ask one of the nurses," Prudence said quietly when the doctor turned away to attend to another case. She was soon back with the information they needed. "Morgan Whitley and Aubrey Canfield," she said, reading from a scrap of paper. "Canfield is the one who's in a bad way. The staff has been paid not to reveal his name."

Geoffrey didn't bother asking how much she'd had to hand over to overpay the Canfield family bribe.

"He's on the floor above this one."

Another horse-drawn ambulance had pulled up to the Emergency Pavilion entrance. In the rush to unload the bloody losers of the latest Five Points bar fight, no one noticed the well-dressed lady and her tall companion disappear up the staircase to the second-floor wards.

They found Morgan Whitley seated beside Aubrey Canfield's narrow iron cot. White curtains strung on a ceiling rail had been drawn around three sides of the bed for privacy. Someone had wrapped a blanket around Morgan's shoulders and another one over his legs. A pierced-cover pot of charcoal burned at his feet. River-wet clothing had been draped over a chair. Even before Prudence reached out a comforting hand, she could tell that his whole body was quivering relentlessly.

"It's all right, Prudence," he said, looking up at her, unable to stand. "They tell me I'm no worse off than if I'd caught a bad chill in the ordinary way. This must be that miracle cure we were talking about yesterday."

"Can I call the nurse to bring you something hot to drink?" she asked.

"I've had enough tea and beef broth to last the rest of my life," he said. He nodded in Geoffrey's direction. "Don't bother with an introduction. I know who Mr. Hunter is."

"What happened, Mr. Whitley?" Geoffrey wasn't sure how much time they would have before someone, perhaps the tired young doctor from the Emergency Pavilion, realized where they'd gone and decided to do something about it.

"I'm not sure I know. Everything seems jumbled together. I can't make sense of it."

"Morgan jumped into the river to save Aubrey's life. That's what happened." Everett Rinehart closed the white curtains behind him and set a small suitcase on the floor. He held out a hand to Geoffrey and tipped his hat to Prudence. "I've brought clean, dry clothes," he said, leaning briefly over the unconscious man in the bed, then turning his attention to Morgan. "We can't have you walking out of here in whatever the hospital was able to scare up. Aunt Lena wrote a note. She wanted to come, but Uncle William very wisely wouldn't allow it. They're both waiting for you at home."

"I'm not leaving him," Morgan said. "I told you that, Everett."

"I won't insist. And neither do they. But you do need to get some decent clothes on if you're going with him when the Canfields have gotten the arrangements made. That could be any time now. There's a linen storeroom at the end of the ward you can use to get dressed in. I've already cleared it with the floor nurse." He helped Morgan to his feet.

Geoffrey picked up the suitcase.

"Someone he knows has to be here. In case he comes to," Morgan said.

"I'll stay," Everett promised. He placed a chair for Prudence next to the bed, then indicated he would take the seat Morgan had vacated.

Suitcase in one hand, the other clasped firmly around Morgan's right arm, Geoffrey led the still shivering man out of the curtained cubicle. Their slow footsteps faded down the length of the ward.

"He won't regain consciousness, will he?" Prudence said. She spoke in a low voice, but there was no indication that Aubrey Canfield was aware of anything that was going on around him. Nothing except the slight rise and fall of his chest testified to evidence of life.

"No," Everett said. "Aubrey's parents are taking him home to die. There's no hope of recovery. I don't know a lot about medical matters, but even I could understand that much. He was under water too long for his brain to remain undamaged. If that weren't bad enough, he inhaled and swallowed huge gulps of the river. The doctor said his lungs will never recover."

"Pneumonia?"

"That and a host of other things I don't remember and can't pronounce. Having to do with contamination and toxic poisons. The East River is apparently as filthy as a sewer."

"It looks so beautiful with the sun sparkling on it," Prudence said.

"Beautiful, deadly, and full of shipping. We usually go out into the Sound."

"But not today?"

"This was going to be a short sail. No more than two hours on the water from start to finish. Our last outing before the New Year. And who knew when we'd get another day like today? The winter weather can turn on you without warning."

"What did you mean when you said Morgan jumped into the river to save Aubrey's life?" Prudence asked, studying the patient in the bed as she spoke. If a man did not react to the sound of his own name, then he was well and truly beyond reach.

"That's what happened, though I don't think any of us actually saw Aubrey go in. We were tacking northward. . . . Do you know what tacking is, Miss MacKenzie?" Everett asked.

"It means you were going from one side of the river to the other. On a diagonal," she answered, recalling her father's explanation of nautical maneuvers when they watched small pleasure boats racing each other in the Hudson River off Staten Island.

"Because you can't sail directly into the wind," Everett confirmed. "We were on a broad reach, which means the boom was nearly at a right angle to the hull of the boat."

"How long is your boat, Mr. Rinehart?"

"It's a thirty footer, built narrow for racing."

"Go on."

"So when you tack, the boom swings across the boat to the other side."

"I understand."

"We had a ten- to twelve-knot wind, good and steady. I called out 'Ready about,' somebody shouted back 'Ready,' and I swung the wheel into the tack. As I said, none of us saw it happen, but Aubrey must have been struck and knocked over by the boom when it swung from port to starboard. That's the only way to explain it. He was lying out on the deck, looking up at the sky. It was beautiful, Miss MacKenzie, bright blue and crystal clear the way it only gets in winter. He didn't hear me or he raised his head at exactly the wrong moment. I'd glanced over at the shoreline for a second. The next thing I knew, people were shouting 'Man overboard.' I never even heard the splash."

"And that's when you said Morgan jumped in?"

"Not right away. But the wind had caught the sail and we all realized pretty quickly that we wouldn't be able to get back to Aubrey in time if he went under. Which we saw him do. That's when Morgan went in. I don't think he stopped to think about what the consequences could be. For him, I mean. When we came about and got close enough to pick them up, he was holding Aubrey's head above water, but it was pretty clear that neither one of them could last much longer."

"Such a brave thing to do," Prudence said.

"And foolhardy," Everett said. "Aubrey will die anyway. And who knows what may happen to Morgan in the weeks ahead. We could lose both of them."

Still no sign that the friend Morgan had risked his life to save had heard anything of the conversation taking place so close to him. It wasn't difficult to believe that he would never speak or open his eyes again.

"Mr. Canfield's private ambulance is here," a nurse announced. "We'll need to get him ready to be transported." She held the white curtain open for them to leave.

"I think you have one additional patient to see to," Prudence told her.

Followed closely by Geoffrey, Morgan Whitley was making his way down the ward toward Aubrey's bed. He looked frail and still blue around the mouth, but Prudence thought he was shivering less. Lena had sent a thick overcoat, wool scarf, and heavy gloves, all of which hung off Morgan's thin frame like hand-me-downs on a scarecrow. But he was walking steadily and had a determined set to his jaw. Nothing and no one was going to stop him from sitting with his friend until the end.

Aubrey's room in the Canfield mansion was darkened and hushed. His mother and younger sister sat on one side of the bed, Morgan on the other. Mr. Canfield stood at the foot, one hand on the gold watch he frequently withdrew from its waistcoat pocket. Time was racing by and standing still.

Morgan had managed to make it up the outside steps of the Canfields' home, but two footmen had had to half carry him to the upstairs bedroom where the ambulance stretcher bearers had deposited his dying friend. And there Morgan collapsed into the chair where he had now been sitting for more than three hours. With Prudence beside him.

Geoffrey had gone to find Danny Dennis's waiting hansom cab while Aubrey was being loaded into the ambulance at Bellevue. When one of the attendants held out his hand to assist Prudence into the specially equipped vehicle, she took it and climbed in. "He assumed Morgan was Aubrey's brother and I was a wife or sister," she told her partner later. "I decided not to inform him otherwise."

The Canfields, seeing how Morgan clung to Prudence, and knowing that he had nearly given his life to save their son, welcomed her. Custom dictated that Death should not be met alone.

From time to time a maid brought a tray of tea and small sandwiches into the room. Only the tea was touched. The family doctor stayed until his services were urgently required elsewhere. Death was no stranger to anyone; it would come when it would come. He gave a few instructions and a small brown bottle of laudanum to the housekeeper, urging her to persuade Mrs. Canfield not to begrudge herself a decent dose when the moment of her son's passing arrived.

Which it did, inevitably, and as everyone gathered around Aubrey's bed had known it would.

He opened his eyes, seemed to recognize Morgan, and motioned for him to lean in closer. Then he sighed or perhaps said something to his friend on one of his last breaths.

Sought and found his mother's gaze. His father's. Smiled.

"I am content to go," he whispered. "This life has been so very hard."

Morgan Whitley fell ill the evening Aubrey Canfield died.

"Will you go in my place?" he begged Prudence when it became obvious that he was far too sick to attend his friend's funeral.

"Of course I will," she promised.

Then told Geoffrey that the situation had become impossible.

"I used our childhood acquaintance to pry information out of him." Prudence tried to keep the anguish she was feeling out of her voice, the misery of betrayal from her eyes. "I do feel very sorry for his pain and the mess he's made of life, and I can't even begin to imagine the courage it took to jump into the East River after Aubrey. But I can't allow personal feelings to get in the way of the investigation. Someone in that household played a part in stealing Lena's diamonds, and it could very well have been Morgan." She gratefully accepted the cup of tea Josiah had brewed for her. Always tea. Rarely coffee since the arrival of Lady Rotherton. The evidence of Josiah's partiality toward her aunt brought a rueful smile to Prudence's lips. Even now. "We've been over it so many times," she sighed.

"Shall I come with you to the Canfield boy's memorial service?" Geoffrey offered.

"It's tomorrow afternoon at Trinity Church. Can you spare the time?"

Geoffrey thought it an odd question to ask. Anything and anyone associated with the De Vries household was part and parcel of the inquiry they had been hired to conduct. Morgan and the friends with whom he shared his pastimes certainly qualified.

On a hunch, Geoffrey had sent Amos Lang back to the Mint, to the same easily bribed employee who had supplied him with Morgan's gambling tab. Aubrey Canfield had run up a staggering debt since graduating from Harvard and returning to live in his parents' home on Fifth Avenue. There had been talk of using muscle to collect it. And then it had been paid off in its entirety. Not all at once, but in several considerable installments that mirrored the way Morgan had discharged the bulk of his debt. The dead man hadn't remained free and clear, however. Starting a few months previously, the arrears had begun mounting again. At the time of his plunge into the East River, Aubrey owed several thousands of dollars. Amos had been told that someone from the Mint would be visiting the elder Mr. Canfield. After the funeral. They weren't, after all, barbarians.

The memorial service was surprisingly brief and ill attended. No *in memoriam* cards had been sent out and no announcement placed in the *Times*. The Canfields did not receive mourners at home and the closed casket went directly from a mortuary parlor to the church and then to entombment in the family vault.

It was, Prudence decided, the oddest obsequies she had ever observed.

"What do you think it means, Geoffrey?" she asked as they left the church.

"The family is anxious to hide something. This son obviously didn't live up to their expectations."

"The gambling?" Prudence had begun to wonder if every young man of wealth concealed profligate spending and indebtedness he was at pains to pay off.

"More than that, I think."

"They'll never tell us. I imagine Mr. Canfield has bought off the newspapers in the same way he tried to conceal that his son had been admitted to Bellevue."

"Which in itself is odd," Geoffrey speculated. "It made sense to take Morgan and Aubrey there for immediate treatment. It's the closest hospital to where the boat docked, and even though it's largely a charity institution, it has a reputation for knowing how to deal with emergencies. I think they didn't want some nosy newspaper reporter to start digging into his past. Or his present, for that matter."

"For fear of what would be found?"

"Scandal, a stain on the Canfield name. Past misdeeds that had been hushed up. Payoffs to keep young Aubrey out of trouble."

"The more we learn, the more complicated and confusing

this case gets," Prudence said, taking Geoffrey's arm for the short walk up Wall Street to their offices. The hearse and family carriage had already moved off; the sidewalk was nearly empty. "And the wider we seem to need to cast our net."

"We go back to the beginning," Geoffrey declared. "We go over every clue, every incident, every person with any connection to the De Vries family and home."

"Have we missed something?" Prudence asked.

"The pieces are always there," Geoffrey reminded her. "It's just a matter of finding them and then putting the puzzle together so it makes sense. We've never failed before. And we won't this time, either."

She wished she felt as confident as he wanted her to believe he was.

CHAPTER 15

"Aubrey Canfield's father knew about the wagering long before any of his son's creditors came to collect from him," William De Vries told Prudence and Geoffrey.

He'd surprised them by appearing in their offices without any forewarning. It wasn't the type of thing they'd expected from him.

"How much are we talking about?" Geoffrey asked.

"He didn't give me a precise figure and I didn't press. But it was far above the boy's ability to pay, especially since he'd already squandered the inheritance he'd come into from his grandfather."

"On his twenty-first birthday?" Prudence remarked. That was the usual age at which legacies were bestowed.

"Aubrey's grandfather should have stipulated age twenty-five or thirty," De Vries declared. "But I suppose he had no way of knowing when the trust was set up that his grandson would turn out to be both a drunkard and a spectacularly bad gambler. I'm assuming that's what drew him and Morgan together. *Birds of a feather . . .*"

"How is Morgan?" Prudence had sent a note asking if she could stop by, to which Lena had replied that on the advice of his doctor, Morgan was not to receive visitors.

"What I'm about to tell you is going to break his mother's heart," William said, "but I don't see any way out of it. Which is why I'm here." He glanced toward the door of Geoffrey's office, checking to be sure it was tightly closed. "This must remain strictly between us."

"Of course," Geoffrey agreed.

"I don't want any notes of today's meeting put into the files I know you keep." William had already demanded that Josiah and his Gregg shorthand notebook be excluded from what he had to say.

"Confidentiality is very much a part of what we do," Prudence assured him.

"Your father was a great one for knowing how to keep a secret." De Vries almost reached out to touch her hand, then thought better of it. "It made him a judge even his political opponents respected."

Geoffrey said nothing, waiting for his client to begin. He knew from past experience that once the first words were spoken, the floodgates would open.

"Morgan is the one who stole his mother's diamonds. I don't know how he managed it, but he's guilty. There's no doubt in my mind. None at all."

Again, Geoffrey waited.

"He dragged Aubrey into the scheme with him. They both needed money, and I suppose Morgan thought no one would notice if he only pilfered some of the stones. Or maybe he believed Lena would cover for him if she discovered what was going on. He threatened or blackmailed his valet and Lena's maid into helping him. Leonard Abbott committed suicide rather than be sent to prison, and I expect to wake up tomorrow morning and find out that Taylor has packed her bag and left during the night."

"If you're right about this, Lena will be devastated," Prudence said. William's theory created such a neat, self-contained package that it made her uneasy. If the police were kept out of it, there was no need for Morgan's part in the crime to be made public. The whole distasteful episode would be swept under the carpet.

But three men were dead.

"Are you asking us to find the proof of what you're alleging?" Geoffrey was often blunt and to the point when something annoyed him.

"Yes."

"What will you do with it?"

"I think it's obvious that Morgan cannot be allowed a position of trust in either the banking or investment areas of my business. Not for some years and never without supervision. He failed the Keeley Cure and began drinking again. But there is a new morphine treatment being administered in a clinic in Switzerland. It may be the last resort in the handling of dipsomania. Morgan has to admit his fall from sobriety and repent of his theft. If he does that, I could be persuaded to make it possible for him to be admitted to the Swiss clinic as a patient and to remain there for as long as the doctors deem necessary."

"That's very generous of you," Prudence murmured, shocked and horrified at the idea that injections of morphine would be used to combat a thirst for alcohol. Substitute one mind-altering substance for another? The premise seemed ludicrous. How could anyone seriously believe it would work? And then she remembered how much private clinics charged to hide their patients from the outside world. How easily they duped rich clients into believing that the more something cost, the higher its quality. And how easily Morgan could be made to disappear until even the New York City newspapers forgot about him.

"What we find may not indicate that Morgan is your thief," Geoffrey said.

"He is. I'm certain of it," De Vries repeated.

"Is there anything you're not telling us?" Geoffrey asked. "Something you're holding back?"

"Lena said that Taylor has already confessed to being the daughter of a jeweler."

"I'd hardly call it a confession," Prudence commented, trying to keep their client from leaping to yet another dubious conclusion. "She simply told us that her father trained her in the art of cleaning and caring for diamonds and other precious stones. That doesn't make her guilty of tampering with Mrs. De Vries's necklace."

"I want this matter settled. I want it dealt with quickly and quietly."

"The police will continue to investigate your valet's death," Geoffrey reminded him.

"That can be seen to," De Vries declared.

So, added to the enormous cost of a clinic in Switzerland to get Morgan out of the way, his stepfather was prepared to bribe a New York City detective to conclude that Leonard Abbott's death was a suicide. Once again, Prudence thought, the power of money would twist truth and conceal facts.

"We'll continue the investigation," Geoffrey said. "But I can't guarantee you'll be satisfied with what we find."

"We need to know who bought the diamonds," Prudence said, starting yet another list in her notebook. Josiah's organizational habits were rubbing off on her.

"I set Ned Hayes to working on that." Geoffrey spun the stone that Prudence had found on the floor of Carpenter's jewelry shop. It glittered like a teardrop and shot out fragments of light. "Without an accounts book, he says it's probably a lost cause."

"Is there a chance the book could still be there?" Prudence asked. "Hidden somewhere the police haven't looked?"

"I doubt Detective Phelan would tell us if they'd found it."

"But we have our sources within the police department. Josiah pays them regularly and complains about it just as often."

"The book hasn't turned up," Geoffrey said. "We would have heard right away."

"I hope you're right."

"The police searched the shop and then turned his apartment upside down. Nothing there either. No wife, no children, not even a cat to keep the rats under control."

"Where was he living?"

"About eight or nine blocks from the store. On a back street that's mainly rooming houses and a few larger buildings that aren't quite tenements, but nothing you'd want to live in any longer than you had to."

"I don't understand. He was dealing in stolen diamonds," Prudence said. "Surely he could have afforded something better."

"Probably. But my guess is he had to spend a lot on rent for the store off Fifth Avenue. I think Carpenter was new at the game he was playing. He hadn't graduated to the big time yet, so he wasn't getting top dollar for the stones he was selling. He was a trained jeweler; there's no doubt about that. But I wouldn't be surprised if he'd also been a fence at one time."

"Is that all?" Prudence asked.

Geoffrey shrugged. "I think we can close the book on Mr. James Carpenter. For the time being, at least. His body will be in Potter's Field in a few days, if it's not there already, and his landlord has undoubtedly got new tenants in the rooms he was renting. The only way we're going to find out who killed him is if whoever stole the diamonds confesses to the murder as well. And we're a long way from being able to name a suspect."

"I wish we could take another look around the jewelry store."

"Shops don't stay empty longer than a few days in that area, Prudence. A week at the most."

"But don't the police have to release the scene of a crime before it can become *business as usual* again?"

Geoffrey rubbed the thumb and first two fingers of his right hand together.

"I always forget that bribery is the oil that greases the city's wheels," Prudence said ruefully.

"Carpenter was occupying a valuable piece of property."

"Humor me. Just this once. Danny Dennis could have us up there in no time."

"What do you think you'll see?"

"I don't know. But if we don't go, I'll always wonder."

What they saw outside the shop on Eighteenth Street was a pair of rubbish bins waiting to be picked up by one of the private companies that serviced the area. The eight-year-old Department of Street Cleaning wasn't functioning much better as an independent city administration than it had when it was attached to the police department. No one depended on it to haul away their trash.

Danny Dennis pulled Mr. Washington as close to the curb as he could. Geoffrey handed Prudence out, steering her away from the puddles of horse urine and piles of manure that the street urchins hadn't swept away.

"It looks like the next tenant is already moving in," Geoffrey said once Prudence was safely out of the street and on the sidewalk.

"As long as we're here . . ."

"You're stubborn enough to become either a great detective or a first-class nag. You do realize that, don't you?" But Geoffrey smiled as he said it, and he kept hold of Prudence's hand.

"Just for a moment."

"He won't thank you for getting in his way."

"The customer is always right, Geoffrey. And that's what I am. A potential customer."

"You don't even know what's going to be sold here."

"Does it matter?"

The man who was dragging another, smaller rubbish bin out of the storefront paused when he saw a handsomely dressed couple looking inquisitively at his newly rented property.

"We won't be open for business until next week," he said, wiping his hands on a gray canvas apron that covered his clothing from chest to knees. "Manfred Gruner, at your service, sir. Madam. Watchmaker extraordinaire."

"Watchmaker. How wonderful," Prudence said. "My late father's gold watch hasn't run properly since the day he died."

"I'd be proud to have you as my initial customer," Mr. Gruner said. "I can promise it will be the first item I work on."

"That's very kind of you." Prudence glanced down at the debris in the rubbish bin. She could have sworn some of the broken tools looked like the ones that had been strewn around Carpenter's workroom. "Such a shame, what happened to Mr. Carpenter," she said.

"Did you know him?"

"He had some lovely pieces. Nothing terribly expensive, but the workmanship was good and the designs very new and fresh."

"I wouldn't know about that, miss, never having met the man." Gruner suddenly waved his arms over his head. "Here now, get that horse away from my bins," he called out. "I don't want him pulling that stuff out all over the street. They'll charge me extra for whatever's not in the container."

Danny Dennis took hold of Mr. Washington's bridle and eased the great white head toward the street.

"I didn't get his feed bag on fast enough," Dennis explained when he handed Geoffrey a damp, slightly chewed accounts book. "Careful now. Something smelly and rotten has soaked into the cover. That's what he was after. He does like a soft apple or a head of lettuce now and then."

Prudence refrained from saying *I told you so.*

But only just.

The accounts book told them almost nothing about James Carpenter's illicit business of buying and reselling precious stones of dubious provenance.

"This is why he crossed the line into dealing in stolen goods," Geoffrey said, pointing to a set of figures at the bottom of one of the pages. "He wasn't making enough to be able to continue renting his shop for very much longer. He appears to have lost some commissions from the larger jewelry houses and wasn't able to make up the difference."

He turned several pages and found a much larger sum at the bottom of a long column of figures. "Here we are. I'd guess that this is the first result of his foray into a life of crime."

"But there's nothing identifying either the gem, who brought it to him, or to whom he sold it," Prudence said. The line on which the transaction was recorded contained only a monetary amount, in stark contrast to the entries on the rest of the page. "He was being very cautious."

"But he couldn't resist putting his profit in writing where he'd have the pleasure of looking at it whenever he wanted. It wouldn't mean anything to anyone else, but to James Carpenter it shouted success."

"There is a date," Prudence said. "That should tell us something."

"I'll have Josiah go through the book from front to back and copy out all of the dates and sums where an entry is otherwise blank," Geoffrey said. He rifled the pages. "There doesn't appear to be too many of them. That would support the idea that he was new to the scam and hadn't been involved in it for very long."

"Nothing we've seen here connects him either to Lena's maid, Taylor, or to the valet who hanged himself." Though she hadn't seen the body dangling from the rafters, Prudence's mind had created a vivid mental picture that made her shudder every time she thought of it. "I know I shouldn't jump to conclusions, but William De Vries has done exactly that, and I can't seem to shake off his assumptions."

"Morgan is an obvious suspect," Geoffrey agreed.

"I doubt William has ever really warmed to him. Every time he looked at Morgan he had to be reminded that he didn't have a son of his own. That Lena failed him. And now he must know it's too late unless he gets himself a younger wife."

"He'll be looking for an excuse to free himself from Lena if that's the way his thoughts are turning." Geoffrey had seen it happen so often that it no longer surprised him when men who married more than once chose new partners half their age.

"Geoffrey. Think about this for a moment," Prudence urged. "All of the maids who left the De Vries household over the past few years were provided with a good reference, according to what I found out at the Wentworth Agency. Which means none of them could have been dismissed because of pregnancy."

"Perhaps they left before the condition was discovered."

"Not likely," Prudence said. "Maids who find themselves in the family way hang on for as long as they can, hoping they'll miscarry naturally or trying home remedies to make them lose the baby. Housekeepers keep a sharp eye on their waists. They know who's stepping out and whether one of the gentlemen of the family is in the habit of taking advantage of his position."

"What are you saying?"

"It might not be Lena's fault that William doesn't have a son by her. Isn't that possible?"

"I'm not a doctor, Prudence."

"If it's true," she said, ignoring his protestation of ignorance, "and William suspects that it might be, his resentment of Morgan would have grown over time. He'd be quite willing to get him out of the house where he wouldn't have to see him every day across the dinner table. Hence the Swiss clinic."

"And the eagerness to find him guilty of the theft of the diamonds."

"Without any kind of proof at all. Not even any circumstantial evidence. Just the fact of his excessive drinking and gambling. He needed money, so he must have stolen his mother's diamonds. *Q.E.D.*" Would Geoffrey agree? "*Quod erat demonstrandum,*" she added for good measure.

"William didn't bat an eye when I told him that our investigation might not prove Morgan guilty."

"He's too good a businessman to admit of an outcome he can't control," Prudence said. "And my father often told me that a lawyer who was worth his salt never let the idea of absolute truth enter into his pleadings. Truth becomes whatever version of reality can be proved."

"I think you're becoming more cynical with every case we work on," Geoffrey said. "Not that I'm objecting. I just find it interesting."

"The only one who can tell us how William has treated his stepson over the years is Lena," Prudence continued.

"She won't reveal anything that might paint an unfavorable portrait of her son," Geoffrey argued.

"Do we take William's resentment of Morgan for granted?"

"I think we have to. He sees himself as protecting her son for his wife's sake," Geoffrey hypothesized. "That and the bitterness he must feel toward Morgan blind him to any possibility other than the one he's put forth. So we're up against a wall of suspicion and antagonism that we may not be able to breach."

"Much as I hate to admit it, we can't ignore the fact that William could be right. Morgan might very well be the guilty party."

"We need to move on, Prudence."

It seemed to her that with every new discovery, they stepped backward. Could you build a case out of negatives?

CHAPTER 16

Prudence stared at the four lists she had laid out on the conference room table.

One, in Amelia Taylor's neatly cramped, lady's maid handwriting, itemized every occasion on which Lena De Vries had worn the Marie Antoinette diamond necklace. In each instance except the most recent one, Lena herself had signed for the delivery from Tiffany's vault.

Josiah had put together the second list from the accounts book Mr. Washington had pulled from the rubbish bin outside the late James Carpenter's jewelry shop. It had lain for a full day beneath the globe of a gas lamp, emitting a faint stench of rotted vegetation as the pages dried out.

Amos Lang had brought the third list, along with a notation of the bribes he had been paying a cooperative clerk in the Mint's accounting department. Aubrey Canfield's gambling debts, sporadic payments, and frequent episodes of monumentally bad luck at the tables were depressing testimony to the waste of what should have been a full and promising young life.

From the same susceptible clerk, Amos had obtained a

record of Morgan Whitley's time at the Mint. Not as extensive as his friend Aubrey's, it was nevertheless another dismal witness to the damage that could be done by an addiction to wagering on cards and an ivory roulette ball.

"The thing is," Amos told Geoffrey while Prudence stared in horror at the amounts that had been squandered on a few hours of excitement ending in disappointment. "It's likely that both Canfield and Whitley gambled at other casino parlors that would let them run up a tab when they didn't have cash money to bet. There aren't many of them, because the only ones who extend credit cater exclusively to gentlemen, but it will help if you can get Whitley to tell you where else he played. And I should warn you that the bribes are expensive."

"Our client has very deep pockets," Geoffrey told his operative. "But hold off for the moment. Let's see what we learn from the information we've got so far."

A small man who faded unnoticed into crowds and was so nondescript in appearance that no one ever remembered what he looked like, Amos was a few years older than Geoffrey. Nicknamed "the ferret" by Allan Pinkerton himself, he had been the famous detective's first choice when the challenge was to discover information that someone had gone to great lengths to conceal. Amos never spoke of why he left the Pinkerton National Detective Agency, but Geoffrey had once told Prudence that rumor hinted at involvement with a woman.

"Do you think Whitley did it?" Amos asked.

"I don't want to believe it was Morgan," Prudence said, "but that's because I knew him when we were both children trying to survive the loss of a parent."

"Facts are facts, Miss Prudence," Amos said. He'd had mixed feelings about working for a woman when Geoffrey had first tapped him for a job with Hunter and MacKenzie, but he'd come to respect and admire the tenacity with which the judge's daughter pursued a case and fought her private demons.

Amos Lang carried a small brown bottle of laudanum in his coat pocket and kept a needle and a vial of cocaine in his bedside table.

"He's an odd one," Prudence commented after Amos had left. "There are times I can't be sure I've actually talked to him when my notes tell me that I have."

"He's one of the best in the business," Geoffrey told her. "But don't try to figure him out. It won't work."

He bent over the table, shuffling the lists like a card shark practicing the layout of a hand. "I see parallels, but there are also instances when Lena wore the necklace and it seems not to have been tampered with. If we're looking at Carpenter's notations and Canfield's debt payoffs to provide the clues we want."

"Why don't I put it all on a single calendar?" Josiah suggested. He firmly believed that compiling information in the correct format was the real secret to good detection. He'd lately begun constructing elaborate calendars with entries made in various colors of ink. The firm's appointment book had become a multihued wonder.

"If you think that will help," Prudence agreed. "Lena has finally consented to let me visit with Morgan. I'm on my way there now. She won't object if you come, too, Geoffrey."

"Are you sure? I don't want to get in your way."

"If I sense that Morgan doesn't want to talk about his bad habits in front of me, I'll excuse myself so you can continue the conversation alone with him. He may feel more comfortable if a man asks that type of question. I can use the time to encourage Lena to tell me about how her son and his stepfather have gotten along all these years. It's another piece of that puzzle you're always talking about putting together."

They heard Josiah humming contently behind them as they left the office.

Morgan looked better than he had at Aubrey's bedside, but no one could mistake him for anything but an invalid. His skin had the thin, flaccid look of a very old man, his eyes were bloodshot, and his hands and lips trembled spasmodically. Lena had seen to it that her son was propped up in a pillowed armchair because it wouldn't do for him to receive a female visitor while he lay in his bed. A fire blazed in the hearth and heavy drapes had been drawn across the windows. The room was as hot and stifling as a New York summer.

Prudence had written a note after Aubrey's funeral, doing her best to remember details of the service that might have comforted Morgan. He hadn't answered, and now she knew why. No way in the world those quivering fingers could clasp a pen firmly enough to form the letters of a comprehensible sentence.

The tricky part about this visit would be conveying William's offer of treatment at the Swiss clinic. And its terms. Morgan would have to confess guilt and the humiliation of admitting that he could no longer control his own actions. Drunkenness. Cards and roulette. A spectacular failure at the much lauded Keeley Institute. And perhaps persuading his vulnerable friend into criminal activity. Prudence wondered whether any small, valuable, easily pawned items had gone missing from the Canfield household.

"I didn't do it," Morgan said, without preamble. "I know William thinks I did, and he's tried to convince Mother that I might be guilty, but I'm not and I didn't." Exhausted by the vehemence of his denial, he sank back against the pillows, panting like a dog after a run.

"No one is accusing you," Prudence said, though she and Geoffrey had discussed the possibility. Echoes of the arguments against Morgan's innocence still rang in her head.

"We have the records of your wins and losses at the Mint," Geoffrey said.

"I thought those were confidential," Morgan protested.

"Anything can be bought. You should know that. It's how investors get the tips that make them overnight millionaires."

"My stepfather will tell you I'm as bad at managing money as I am at gambling." Morgan bit his lower lip until a drop of blood appeared.

"You didn't always lose," Prudence reminded him. "You paid off substantial sums from time to time. The funds had to come from somewhere." She was hoping he would recount a tale of triumph on the Stock Exchange or a winning bet he hadn't then immediately wagered away, but he said nothing. "We do need to know if you and Aubrey gambled anywhere but at the Mint."

"Not recently. Neither one of us could play without being able to run a tab. I can't speak for Aubrey, but the only reason I was welcome at the Mint was because I had a history of paying off my losses there. I can't say the same for the other casinos."

"Morgan, do you still owe money around town?" Prudence asked.

"I told you I didn't take those diamonds. There's no *still* about it. I haven't been completely out of debt since my second year at Harvard."

"What happened after you came back from the Keeley Institute?" Geoffrey asked.

Prudence looked at him gratefully. She could feel tears tickling at the back of her throat. Morgan's hopelessness was the saddest thing she had ever encountered.

"I was cured," Morgan said. "That's what I was told, and I believed it."

"Until . . . ?"

"Until I took that first drink to celebrate my new sobriety."

"Surely you knew what would happen?" Prudence asked. She was fast progressing from compassionate sorrow to frustrated anger.

"We were told never to drink again. But I thought that if I was cured, it meant I was like everybody else. I could partake or not, as I chose. It turned out I was wrong. There is no choice for people like me. And there is no cure, either. I already told you that, Prudence."

"I don't believe it," she said. "There has to be something you can do, some regimen you can follow." Was now the moment to bring up the clinic in Switzerland?

"Abstinence," Geoffrey said, cutting her off before she could mention William's plan for his stepson. "That's the only way. Have you thought about going back to the Keeley Institute for a second course of treatment?"

"Aubrey did that. Took the bichloride of gold shots again. Drank the tonics. Gained twenty pounds and started feeling like the athlete he used to be. It didn't last once he was back in New York. He was a lush with an unquenchable thirst. So am I. The most I can hope for is that it kills me quickly."

"William has always been kind to Morgan," Lena told Prudence over the inevitable cups of tea that were all ladies were permitted to drink in the afternoon.

Prudence hadn't been able to remain any longer in Morgan's room. She'd left it to Geoffrey to continue questioning him, patted away the dampness in her eyes as she descended the curved staircase to the ground floor, and joined Lena in the parlor.

"Has your husband talked to you about a Swiss clinic?" she asked.

"Morgan won't go," Lena replied. "Not if he has to confess to something he didn't do. He doesn't lie. He never has. Not even as a child. He's as candid and forthright as they come."

She was blind, Prudence thought. Deliberately blind. Her son drank himself into stupors and gambled away money he didn't have. That didn't happen without a belly full of lies and half-truths.

"I can attest to that," Everett Rinehart said as he bent over Lena to kiss her lightly on the cheek. He'd come in so quietly that neither of the women had heard him open the parlor door. "I was hoping I wouldn't be too late to catch you, Miss MacKenzie. Morgan told me this morning you would be coming by."

"Is William with you?" Lena asked. She touched the spot on her cheek where Everett's lips had brushed her skin.

To Prudence it looked as though she were wiping away an annoying stain.

"He's still at the office. I've finished the real work for the day. Just a few things left that can easily be done tomorrow morning."

"It's not like you to leave this early."

He smiled briefly at his uncle's wife, then turned his attention to Prudence.

"I wanted you to know that I intend to try to persuade Morgan to accept my uncle's offer," Everett said, checking the time on his gold pocket watch before sitting down. "It might be just the thing to set his feet on the road to recovery. Far enough away so he won't have the kind of visitors who would undermine his healing. It also makes sense for his sojourn there to be long enough to do some real good."

"What harmful visitors did you have in mind, Mr. Rinehart?" Prudence asked.

"Not to speak ill of the dead, but Aubrey Canfield was the type of person Morgan should have been avoiding."

"I had the impression the late Mr. Canfield was a mutual friend."

"He was, although closer to Morgan than to me. Our connection was a shared love of sailing. Aubrey and Morgan had much more than that in common." Everett stopped just shy of naming them both degenerate wastrels and partners in crime.

"Are you aware that your uncle's Swiss clinic comes with conditions?" Prudence asked, glancing at Lena to judge her reaction.

"I am. I don't find them unreasonable."

"He says he didn't take the diamonds, Everett," Lena blurted, those two red spots Prudence had seen before blossoming on her cheeks. "I believe him."

"Drunkards have blackouts, Aunt Lena," Everett said soothingly. "He may not remember some or even much of what he's done in the past few months."

"I'll never believe he would steal from his own mother," Lena said firmly. "Never. No matter what proof you think you've dug up, Prudence. I know my son. He doesn't lie and he's not a thief."

"Perhaps it would be enough if he were to admit that he *might* have taken the diamonds during one of his blackouts. He doesn't have to remember the details of how and when. Maybe Uncle William would be satisfied with that. I can talk to him, if you like," Everett offered.

Prudence watched as Lena weighed what must have seemed to her like a contradiction of the innocence she was so staunchly declaring. If Morgan admitted that he *might* have tampered with his mother's necklace, but couldn't actually remember doing so, wasn't that a de facto acceptance of guilt? And if she urged him to make that statement, wasn't she acknowledging lack of belief in the basic honesty she'd sworn had been a part of his character since childhood?

Possibility has a way of turning into probability when logic takes a crooked turn. Prudence's father had often said that on the nights they'd discussed case law together after dinner. When, against all evidence to the contrary, they'd both allowed themselves to believe that Prudence might one day find herself arguing at the bar. Perhaps even in the courtroom over which he presided. She had the feeling that Lena had been arguing Morgan's case before the jury of a mother's heart and soul.

"You can speak to your uncle William if you think it will do any good," Lena finally said. "But I won't advise Morgan to use the notion of blackouts as a pretext to concede guilt for something I know he is incapable of doing."

She looked exhausted, Prudence thought, as though she'd wrestled with the devil himself.

"I'll go back to the office," Everett said, bowing to both ladies. "Sometimes Uncle William is more amenable to persuasion there than he is at home."

"What did he mean by that?" Prudence asked, when the parlor door had closed behind her client's nephew. "I thought you told me that William has always been kind to Morgan. In fact, I think those were your very words."

"There have been some problems," Lena admitted reluctantly.

"Will you tell me about them?"

"Before Morgan went to Chicago, to the Keeley Institute, he made some mistakes at work. Neglected to follow some clients' instructions regarding the sale of stocks when they reached a particular high. As a result, when the stocks went down again, the clients had lost the chance to make a sizable profit. William covered the losses with his own money and the clients were none the wiser. But he was furious at Morgan. That's when he gave him the ultimatum. He had to turn his life around or William would expel him from the firm."

"And out of this house?"

Lena nodded. "He hasn't said it in so many words, but the implication is clear. If Morgan isn't welcome in William's business, he shouldn't expect to make his home with him."

"What was Morgan's reaction after the confrontation? I assume words were exchanged," Prudence said.

"You could hear the shouting all the way upstairs in my bedroom." Lena raised a hand to one ear as if the acrimonious voices still reverberated there. "He seemed to pull himself together for a while. Left as soon as he could for the Keeley Institute. The house was so quiet after he'd gone. He came home looking better than I'd seen him in years. None of that awful yellow pallor or the sounds of retching in the night. He renewed his subscription at the athletic club where Everett is also a member. They boxed together. But it wasn't more than a month or so before it all fell apart. The drinking. Staying out late. Not showing up at the office until after lunchtime."

"Morgan says he thinks he's incurable."

"I can't allow myself to believe that," Lena said. "It would be the loss of all hope."

"Tell me about Morgan and his stepfather in the years after you first married," Prudence urged.

Lena's face brightened. "They were good times. The best, I suppose. We anticipated adding to our family. William thought of Morgan as the first of many children we would have together."

"Yet he didn't formally adopt him."

"No, he didn't. In the beginning he said it was because he wanted Morgan to retain his father's name, as a way of not forgetting him. That made sense to me, and I was grateful for the honor William was paying my first husband."

"And then?"

"As time passed and I did not conceive, it became more important to me that William accept Morgan as his true son. Not merely someone I had brought with me into his life and for whom he was obliged to show affection and consideration."

"Were you afraid, Lena?" It was the question that lay at the heart of the De Vries marriage. "Did you think William would find some pretext for divorcing you if you failed to give him a child?"

The tiny cry that forced its way through Lena's tightly clamped lips was like the jolt of an arrow shot through her heart. "I knew why he married me, you see. I've never blinded myself to that."

"Because you had already proved your ability to carry a child?"

"There was mutual attraction, even love, but I was always aware that my greatest value lay in not being an unknown quantity."

"I'm so sorry," Prudence said. It was a side to marriage and womanhood that was rarely spoken of, this devaluation of the female of the species who could not bear young. Barren, she was called. A word that connoted cold, empty, windswept ground where nothing would grow.

"I didn't mind so much for myself," Lena said, "but for my son it was devastating. He adored William, you see. And he didn't understand when his stepfather began to draw away from him, when the silences between them increased and lengthened. Every time William looked at Morgan, a frown creased his forehead and he seemed plainly disappointed that this creature was the only child he would ever be able to claim. Sometimes a new acquaintance would assume that Morgan's last name was De Vries. Whenever that happened William made a point of correcting the mistake. By the time he left for Harvard, Morgan was in no doubt that he had been tried and found wanting." Lena's voice trembled and tears stood in her eyes. "That's when the drinking really began."

"What gave him away?"

"Bay rum cologne never quite manages to mask the lingering odor of alcohol," Lena explained. "The moment Morgan leaned over to kiss me hello after those first few months in Cambridge, I knew what it was. My brother had struggled with drink; he died young, of a pneumonia he might have survived had his body been strong enough to combat the fever."

"Does William know? About your brother's affliction?" There was probably no scientific proof, but it was widely believed that tendencies to madness and drunkenness ran in families, making their presence known generation after generation.

"It was something we didn't talk about, a hidden shame I was foolish enough to believe had perished with my brother. I should have known better."

"But the animosity between William and Morgan never broke out into real quarreling," Prudence continued, pressing as hard as she dared.

"Only recently, after the incident I told you about. And then again when Morgan failed the Keeley Cure. My husband has come to the end of his rope. He will cut Morgan off, and this time I won't be able to do anything about it."

"There was mention of an inheritance he received from his father," Prudence said.

"I don't know how much is left," Lena said. "It was a substantial amount to begin with, but I fear it's been much depleted."

"Enough to drive Morgan into penury if William disowns him?"

"I doubt things have gone to that extreme." Lena's certainty was the confidence born of never having had to question how a lavish lifestyle was maintained or whether it might someday be in jeopardy.

Money was a topic too vulgar to be discussed in a lady's parlor.

Lena rose to her feet as Geoffrey was shown into the room.

No one commented on whether Morgan was doing better. On his prospects for the future.

Nobody wanted to admit that he might not have one.

CHAPTER 17

"If we accept Morgan's claim that he and Aubrey rarely gambled anywhere but the Mint during the past year or so, we should be able to find out what we need to know from these four lists alone," Prudence said. She had unobtrusively pushed aside Josiah's colorful calendar. The miniscule handwriting in four different shades of ink made her eyes ache when she tried to decipher it.

"Start with last season's Assembly Balls," Geoffrey instructed.

"I'm sure you'll think I'm a bluestocking for this, Geoffrey," Prudence said, as she picked up Amelia Taylor's list, "but I'm delighted not to attend all of these balls and cotillions and dinner parties. I'm very happy not to have to worry about ball gowns and jewels and whether my head will ever stop aching from all the pins holding my hair up."

"To qualify as a bluestocking you have to pontificate on literary topics of no interest to anyone but other bluestockings. With the occasional obscure political argument thrown in from time to time. I don't see you ever doing that, Prudence."

"I'll take that as a compliment to my good sense."

"Last season's initial Assembly Ball?" Geoffrey repeated.

"William and Lena attended, of course," Prudence said, one finger on the relevant entry. "No one in society who receives an invitation ever refuses. I think we can assume that Morgan and Aubrey were also there. It's the first occasion of the season on which the debutantes are seen en masse as it were. Eligible bachelors are as necessary to the evening's success as flowers and champagne. Taylor has written that the necklace arrived at the house on Tuesday, December fourth. The ball took place that Thursday evening."

"Giving time for Taylor to clean and polish the stones."

"There's no note to that effect, and she's otherwise very detailed. It went back to the vault the following week, after the first Patriarchs Ball."

"All right, let me look at the other three lists," Geoffrey said, using crystal paperweights to mark the entries he wanted. He, too, had found Josiah's calendar beyond comprehension. "Aubrey pays down his debt two days after Christmas, as does Morgan."

"Working backward then," Prudence began. "If stones were removed from the necklace during the week it was out of the Tiffany vault, they could have been sold to Carpenter very soon thereafter."

"I doubt he would have paid Aubrey and Morgan the full sum right away," Geoffrey said.

"You're jumping to an unsupported conclusion. We don't know yet who was working with Carpenter."

"You're right, of course," Geoffrey conceded. "But just for the sake of argument and to make the best use of these lists, let's say for the moment that Aubrey and Morgan are likely suspects. Would you agree to that premise?"

"Reluctantly," Prudence said.

"Good enough. I doubt Carpenter had sufficient ready cash to pay anything near what the diamonds would fetch from a fence, even if we're only talking about a very few stones. He would have to sell them elsewhere to get the money to pay our thieves. And that would take us logically from the beginning to the end of December."

"Which was when Morgan and Aubrey suddenly had enough to satisfy the Mint. At least temporarily."

"It's also possible that both young men received gifts of cash for Christmas that year," Geoffrey said, blowing apart his own argument.

"I wonder why De Vries continued sending his wife's necklace back and forth to Tiffany's vault so many times during the season. He has two safes in his home. Why not simply store it there from December until the beginning of Lent when most of the important social occasions are over? Wouldn't it be safer not to be transporting it through the streets like that?"

"A determined professional thief would very soon catch on to what was being done. We may be dealing with a second-story man, Prudence."

"What is a second-story man?"

"It's a very skilled burglar whose specialty is entering a building through a window above the ground floor. Usually at night, almost always when a business is empty or the occupants of a home are asleep or away. If he's really adept, his entry and exit go unnoticed until someone realizes that a theft has occurred. And that's usually not until the item in question is missed and no one can find it."

"He'd have to make his way into Lena's dressing room or the safe in William's library downstairs. Could he do that?"

"I seem to remember a very adroit young woman who went through a suspect's desk drawers in a supposedly safely locked room in the dead of night before disappearing from the house the next morning. She wasn't caught, either," Geoffrey said, reminding Prudence that her midnight escapade had provided important clues in their investigation of a wife murderer.

"Of course he could," she agreed. "I have to keep reminding myself that no matter how difficult or impossible a task may seem, someone is bound to attempt it. And eventually succeed."

"If a second-story man *was* used, he needn't have been working on his own," Geoffrey said.

"The more people you bring into an operation, the greater the likelihood of discovery. Isn't that what you always say?"

"And it's usually true. In this case, if either Taylor or Leonard Abbott was involved, a second-story man could have been used to bring the paste gems into the house and get the real diamonds out. Don't forget that many employers regularly search their servants' rooms and that days off can be canceled without warning. Hiding the diamonds after they were removed from the necklace and then getting them to Carpenter's shop would have been the riskiest parts of the heist. That's where timing would have been of primary importance."

"Do we know whether the young man calling himself Vincent Reynolds had the expertise to be a second-story man?" Prudence asked, remembering his frequent but unpredictable appearances at James Carpenter's jewelry shop.

"We can find out," Geoffrey said. "If he could make it up the side of a building without breaking his neck, it's another piece fitted into the puzzle."

"But we still won't know who hired him." Prudence tapped restlessly on the lists lying before her. "Do you think this type of crime has been committed here in New York City before, Geoffrey? I mean prying stones out of a necklace or bracelet instead of stealing the entire piece."

"If Lena's necklace had disappeared, there would have been an enormous hue and cry about it. The police, the insurance company, and probably even Tiffany's own investigators would have been on it right away. Someone would have suggested calling in the Pinkertons. Which would have made it much more difficult to dispose of the stones. The thief or thieves might have had to wait for as long as a year or two before being able to move them. Even if they'd broken up the necklace themselves, there would have been warnings and watches out for the sudden appearance of quality diamonds without provenance."

"Aunt Gillian spoke of impoverished aristocrats wearing paste because they'd surreptitiously sold the family jewels bit by bit. It doesn't seem outlandish under those circumstances to let go of a stone or two in dire circumstances."

"I agree. I don't think it's at all unheard of. But what happened in the De Vries household is very different. Unless we hypothesize that Lena is the guilty party, that she has been secretly bailing Morgan out of his many financial holes, obviously without her husband's knowledge or consent. She could easily have persuaded Taylor to help her. And Abbott, possibly to make the initial contact with Carpenter."

"She couldn't have done it without Morgan's knowledge. And he gave no hint of suspecting his mother of such duplicity."

"Lena has a settlement from her first marriage," Geoffrey reminded her. "That could be the source of the money that's been keeping Morgan afloat."

"William would have control of it. I doubt he would let anyone in the firm except family manage his wife's fortune."

"Which means Morgan or Everett, if not William himself."

"And that brings us right back to Lena's dilemma," Prudence said. "Unless she can go through Morgan, and he will say nothing to William, she has no direct access to anything but the funds her husband gives her to manage the daily running of the household. Which she couldn't possibly stretch to cover her son's indiscretions."

"Ask who manages her money," Geoffrey said, seeing Prudence write in the notebook she kept in her skirt pocket.

"I will. And there's something else I want to know."

"What's that?"

"Where she was the day the necklace was delivered, when William had to come home from his office to sign for it and lock it away in one of the safes. She's never explained that to my satisfaction."

"Are you thinking of her as a suspect, Prudence?"

"I'm thinking that Lena De Vries, the former widow Whitley, may be a much more mercenary character than I've believed her to be. She'll do anything for her son, that I don't doubt, but she also had a care for her own well-being when she married William. And I also believe that he'd go so far as to divorce her if he thought she was stealing from him. He may have gifted her the necklace, but it shouts to the world that he's a man of enormous wealth and influence. It's as much his possession as she is."

"But did she commit a crime? Technically, a woman's jewels are usually considered to belong to her, rather like a dowry that assures she won't be impoverished if her husband dies without making specific provision for her in his will."

"It's a nicety that a man like our client would fight tooth and nail in a court of law if he thought his wife had betrayed him," Prudence said. "And in William's case, it would be the swiftest road to a younger and presumably more fertile wife. Whatever happened to those stones, Lena De Vries has been in desperate straits from the moment she realized her son was an inebriate."

"And she began to believe she was the only person in the world who could keep him from an ignominious death as a drunkard and a pauper," Geoffrey agreed.

"God help her."

CHAPTER 18

Morgan returned to the world of banking and investments a week after his friend Aubrey's funeral. He had spent that interim time probing deeply into his battered and bruised psyche, wrestling with the remnants of what he remembered of who he had once been. Long, empty days in the company of fellow sufferers at the Keeley Institute had introduced him to introspection, though the Gold Cure relied more on its regimen of injections and tonics than forays into the inner man. But for Morgan, alone in a bedroom of his stepfather's home, there was no place else to go.

William cautiously welcomed him back, the Swiss clinic lurking as a temporarily shelved threat. Or beacon of hope. Morgan was sober again—his eyes clear and focused, skin showing a modicum of winter ruddiness, hands steady, posture erect, clothing appropriately somber. He drank coffee at breakfast, hot tea at lunch, water at dinner.

Beside him from morning to late afternoon, though for fewer hours as each successful day followed another, Everett Rinehart played the role of caretaker, much as the white-coated attendants at the Keeley Institute monitored the behavior of sometimes recalcitrant patients. The friendship between the two young men grew deeper as Morgan's trust in his stepfather's nephew escalated to something close to the confidence he had in his mother. Everett kept a weather eye on his calculations and smoothed the way back to active management of client portfolios. Morgan was far from being allowed to work unsupervised, but his personal minder was solicitous and encouraging. He had never known what it was to have a brother; Everett was teaching him what that relationship could be.

Morgan was healing.

"I no longer require you to find proof of Morgan's guilt," William De Vries said, removing a blank printed check from his wallet. "I've decided to end this farce here and now. What happens inside my home and my place of business is no longer your concern, though I appreciate the unobtrusive way the investigation has been conducted. Worthy of Allan Pinkerton himself."

"Has Morgan confessed to you?" Prudence asked. He'd been so adamant in declaring his innocence that she couldn't imagine the abrupt about-face his stepfather's presence at the Hunter and MacKenzie offices seemed to indicate. She ignored Geoffrey's signal to stop asking questions. "Did he agree to begin treatment at the clinic in Switzerland?"

"Neither, if you must know, Prudence." William uncapped one of the new gold-nibbed fountain pens that had lately grown popular for their convenience and cachet. "His mother and my nephew have pleaded eloquently for his rehabilitation, and he himself is showing signs of having turned over a new leaf. I don't think it an exaggeration to say that the death of his friend Aubrey Canfield shook him to the core. It happens that way sometimes. A man obstinately refuses to see the truth until it stares him in the face and delivers a blow to his viscera. He's never the same afterward."

"I doubt you'll be able to claim compensation from your insurance company unless they can be satisfied that a thorough investigation has been conducted," Geoffrey said. "It's not uncommon for Pinkertons to be called in when their own people can't crack a case."

"No insurance claim will be made," William said. "I'm sure I indicated when I first came to you that such a possibility was to be considered."

"You did," Geoffrey agreed. He spoke into the tube connecting him to Josiah's desk in the outer office. A few moments later the secretary appeared with the De Vries case folder and a neatly written statement of the amount owed to date. "I trust this will be satisfactory."

De Vries glanced at the figure, asked no questions, and did not open the folder to peruse the reports written by Prudence, Geoffrey, and Amos Lang. He seemed anxious to put the episode behind him, unwilling to find out exactly how much of his private and business life had been subjected to scrutiny.

"My wife is eager to lay the matter to rest," William said, waving the filled-in check in the air to dry the ink. He handed over the last document of their arrangement with an unmistakable sigh of relief. "I regret you had to learn the sad truth about someone you considered a childhood friend, Prudence," he said.

"We all have our weaknesses and dark moments," she answered. "No one is exempt. That's one of the first things I learned after Father died."

"We all miss him. The judge was an honorable and principled gentleman. You can be proud to call yourself his daughter, my dear."

William softened for a moment, his facial features slackening into something resembling a blurred facsimile of the hard-edged man of business he presented to the world. Prudence wondered if this was the side of her husband that Lena saw. Then, as quickly as it had appeared, the gentleness was gone.

"It's over," Geoffrey said when their client had left. Josiah would take the check to the bank later in the morning and place the De Vries file in the cabinet reserved for cases that had been marked *Closed*. "It didn't turn out the way I wanted, but I told you when we first got involved with him that William would be a difficult client. I said he would want to interfere, and he did. It was like working with someone pulling on your coattails every step of the way."

Unusually for him, Geoffrey was showing signs of anger and frustration. He'd warned Prudence long ago that not every case ended well for its investigators, and that she would have to learn to let go when holding on was no longer feasible. He seemed to be having trouble practicing what he preached.

"It's not a satisfactory conclusion," she said. She'd already voiced her opinion about William's decision not to inform either his insurance company or the police about the missing diamonds. The only thing that remained was to decide what, if anything, they could do on their own to tie up the loose ends that would continue to beat at their professional pride for months, perhaps years to come. It was a discussion that promised to be as bleak and unrewarding as the nonresolution of the case itself.

"I'll tell Josiah he can open the appointment book again," Geoffrey said. "We need to put Morgan Whitley and Lena De Vries behind us. Guilty or not, we can't live their lives for them."

"Aunt Gillian will probably agree with you. She's a very pragmatic woman. But I suspect she'll step up the number of calls she's been making and urging me to make with her. Society's greatest gift to its members is the sharp-tongued gossip of its ladies. It's also a scourge to the one being talked about. A trip to Europe or a retreat to the country is sometimes the only answer. We'll see which one Lena chooses."

"Has she said how long she plans to stay in New York?" Geoffrey asked.

"Aunt Gillian? I think she misses London more than she likes to admit. The only thing keeping her here may be the im-

propriety of leaving me alone without proper chaperonage."
Prudence made a sound that was not quite a laugh, not quite a
snort of exasperation. "And no, Geoffrey, I am not considering
marriage to any of the fatuous young men who might be anxious to ask for my hand. Aunt Gillian may be irritating to live
with, but I'm not that desperate. Not yet, at any rate. Marriage
in general is not on my immediate horizon."

Josiah appeared with a laden tea tray, so she failed to see the
wash of disheartened gloom that coursed over Geoffrey's face.

But Josiah did. And wondered when Miss Prudence would
stop torturing the poor man.

"The Homestake is proving to be the richest strike in the history of American gold mining," Travis Collins told Morgan
Whitley over lunch at the Astor House. "I don't need to tell
you that it was the first mine ever listed on the New York Stock
Exchange, and it's still there ten years later, making a fortune
for everyone who had the foresight to buy into it." He signaled
the waiter to pour more wine even though the man he was trying to interest in his proposition hadn't touched the pale golden
liquid in his glass. Maybe he preferred red? Two open bottles
nestled in silver wine chillers beside the table.

"Everything else in the Black Hills is played out," Morgan
said. "And whatever claims were worth working were bought
up by Homestake. They've got a monopoly on that entire
area." He'd researched the Black Hills gold rush before agreeing to meet with Collins, and almost canceled the lunch when
Everett backed out at the last moment.

But Everett had urged him to at least listen to what the man
had to say. The South African gold rush that had erupted three
years before was still attracting thousands of miners from every
country in the world, but getting in on the ground floor of
mine ownership was a thing of the past. And the Brits and
Boers were monopolizing the South African finds. Some peo-

ple predicted there would eventually be war over the disputed territories. That kind of development could lose you the cash you'd risked. Better to stay within the United States, Everett contended, where the government could be counted on to keep the Western savages under control and their lands open for business.

"The stake I'm talking about isn't owned by the Homestake Mining Company. It's considerably south of Deadwood, in a region that's only been lightly prospected. But I'm of the conviction that there's as much gold in the southern Black Hills as there is up north. And it's not placer gold, either. It's deep in the rock, Mr. Whitley, very deep. But so was the original Homestake mine. They figured out how to get the gold out, and so can we. It'll take capital, engineers, equipment, and guts. I can hire the engineers, buy the machinery, and supply the on-site grit. What I need from you—or somebody else if you don't want to be richer than Commodore Vanderbilt—is the cash money to bankroll the operation."

Collins placed a dark gray rock on the white tablecloth. About the size of a child's fist, it was stippled with streaks of gold that gleamed in the dining room's gaslights. It looked, Morgan thought, like a piece torn from one of his mother's gold-embroidered satin gowns from House of Worth. Folded and molded around a heavy weight. He traced a thread of bright yellow with a hesitant forefinger, forgetting the beef growing cold on his plate. This was magic.

"How much money are we talking about, Mr. Collins?" Tiny grains of the precious yellow metal attached themselves to his skin, like a dusting of fine powder.

The sum his luncheon companion named was staggering, but not entirely out of Morgan's reach. If he cashed in the securities he managed in his mother's name, he could just make it. All of the issues were solid, income-producing stocks originally purchased by William with his new wife's legacy from her first husband. Largely untouched for years—until very recently—the principal had quietly mushroomed from a respectable to an enviable fortune.

Somewhat depleted, it was true, to meet Morgan's debts before the shame of them surfaced, but still an amount not to be despised. The problem was in selling them off without attracting the attention of any of the brokers in the firm who had a habit of looking over one another's shoulders, especially his stepfather. Under the circumstances, he thought it better not to involve Everett in any phase of the deal. Wiser to tell him that he'd found Mr. Collins's offer an undesirable risk. As busy as Everett was, he'd soon turn his attention elsewhere, forget that he'd ever been interested in what the South Dakota gold miner had to sell in the first place. That he'd ever arranged this lunch meeting he hadn't been able to attend.

"I'll need to see more proof than this," Morgan said, though the ore sample was both mesmerizing and convincing.

"I have maps," Collins replied, "assay reports, engineering specs, projections for how much tonnage we can expect to remove and process the first year, the second, and so on. It's a sure thing, Mr. Whitley. You won't be sorry you decided to come in with me."

"I suppose you should call me by my Christian name," Morgan said, extending his hand across the table, "since we're about to become partners if the paperwork checks out."

"You won't regret it, Morgan," Collins repeated, retrieving the scintillating bit of mineral that had proved captivating and irresistible.

"I know I won't. When can you have the contracts drawn up?"

"Just as soon as you're ready to fulfill your end of the bargain."

"I'll have the cash money available by the end of the week," Morgan promised.

"And I'll open a bank account for you to deposit it in," Collins said. He raised his glass to toast the new working relationship, noting as he did so that his latest business associate drank their mutual health and wealth in water.

Collins figured Morgan Whitley would soon be needing something a lot stronger.

It took a full ten days before Morgan realized he'd been had. Scammed. Swindled. Bamboozled. Robbed blind.

Almost more than he dreaded having to tell his mother what he had done, he was terrified of what William's reaction would be. So panicked by the inevitability of repudiation that he didn't dare allow himself to consider the specifics. Except to remember that his stepfather had already put him on a six-month leash. He had been promised the direst of consequences if he failed to meet William's demands. And fail he had. Spectacularly.

Except that he was still sober.

Which he proceeded to remedy. Quickly and disastrously.

An early January snow mixed with sleet had begun falling when Morgan tumbled out of a hansom cab in front of the De Vries mansion well after midnight. This stretch of Fifth Avenue was deserted, but candles and gaslight glowed behind curtained and draped windows, casting pale rectangles onto the icy sidewalks. The absence of carriages wheeling down the cobblestoned street meant that the second Assembly Ball of the season was still in full swing at Delmonico's. He could almost taste the extravagant late supper of lobster and champagne, smell the flowers and the greenery. He and Aubrey had whirled whiteclad debutantes across that same dance floor at the first Assembly Ball only a month ago.

So much had happened since then. Nothing would ever be the same.

He had only the vaguest idea what time it was, but he knew the empty street meant he could avoid for a few more hours having to explain himself to his mother and stepfather.

He'd lost his overcoat sometime during the night. And his hat and gloves. The butler was sure to remark on that, and by morning every servant in the house would know that Mrs. De Vries's son had come home in a disreputable and disheveled state. Morgan fumbled in his pockets, which he'd emptied of coins to pay the cab driver. No wallet, no handkerchief, no key to the front door. The gold watch and chain that usually hung across his waistcoat were gone. He couldn't remember much of the early evening and nothing of the frantically desperate hours that followed.

He'd had blackouts before. Gotten used to them. Shrugged them off as easily as he'd absorbed the useless bichloride of gold that had been shot into his veins four times a day when he'd still had hope of saving himself. What a joke. What a horrible, dispiriting, depressing, painfully useless experience that had been.

Never again. No second chance at the Keeley Institute. No Swiss clinic.

He'd take the scathing rebuke William was sure to deliver and then get on with things. Go out west somewhere. San Francisco maybe. Consign New York and its humiliating memories to a past he'd spend the rest of his life forgetting. Why not the gold fields after all? He pictured himself clad in heavy canvas pants and rubber boots, swishing a flat tin plate around in the icy waters of a mountain stream. Surrounded by a host of other desperate men, hard drinkers and reckless gamblers all of them. And each one with a story of how he'd been cheated out of a mine that would have made him rich. It might not be a long life, but at least it would be one of his own choosing.

Morgan climbed the four steps of the De Vries mansion. His leather-soled shoes slipped on the accumulating ice; he gripped the iron railing so as not to fall. A dim light showed faintly through the row of small windows that ran horizontally across the top of the front door. The butler, his father's valet, and his mother's lady's maid would be drinking tea in the servants' hall, waiting to attend to their employers' every need before sinking into their own attic beds.

Leonard Abbott used to perform those same services for him on the many nights when he was so drunk he wasn't able to unbutton his shirt or remove his shoes. Poor Leonard. He'd disappeared. Or died. Morgan couldn't remember which. Something awful had happened.

He rang the bell, and when he didn't hear footsteps on the other side of the door, rang it again. It chimed in the foyer and in the servants' hall, so where was the damned butler? How long was he expected to wait outside like this, shivering as the snow and ice pellets melted on his hair and shoulders? Damn the man! He'd go around to the kitchen entrance and bang on that door, wake him up as he sat fast asleep by the fire. God, it was cold out here!

Morgan stumbled down the stairs to the narrow paved walkway that girdled the mansion below the level of the sidewalk. The windows that should have been throwing light onto his path were dark. One hand outstretched against the stone wall to keep him steady and upright, he fumbled his way slowly toward where he thought he remembered delivery men brought baskets of kitchen provisions. He'd seen them often enough when he'd chosen to alight from the family's carriage in the stables before trying to steal into the house unnoticed. He breathed a sigh of relief when his hands located wood and a doorknob. The breath came out of his lungs in streams of white vapor.

No one answered the bell. No light flickered when he beat on the door until his fists left bloody smudges on the painted wood. He couldn't see the blood, but he could feel the pain and the wetness. He howled a bellow of despair.

Damn his unfeeling, uncaring stepfather! Damn him to hell for all eternity! Before leaving with Lena for the Assembly Ball, William must have ordered the servants not to admit his wife's son to the residence that had been his home since he was six years old. Not to respond to the peal of doorbells or to frantic pounding. Somehow William had learned about the gold mine disaster, tried his stepson in absentia, and decreed the punishment he had many times threatened but never executed. Until tonight. Tomorrow every parlor in the city would be atwitter with speculation about why Morgan Whitley had not appeared at last night's ball. What had become of the once promising young man about town? He doubted anyone would guess the truth.

The stables. They were warm with the heat of horses' bodies and there was always clean hay in the stalls. He'd hidden there before, sneaking past early rising servants and into his bed at dawn with no one the wiser. He would sleep off this numbing cold and the liquor he had consumed, then face down his stepfather in the morning. Bid farewell to his mother, cash in what little remained of the inheritance he had once thought he would never run through, and be on his way. Knock the dust and dirt of New York off his shoes. Start over again. Show them what he could make of himself without the constant nagging and nit-picking.

But the stable doors were locked, too. And no lights went on in the grooms' quarters above when he kicked at the sliding wooden door until his shoe fell off and disappeared into the dark.

Inside the house, William De Vries stood without moving in the pitch black of the stairway that curved gracefully above the black and white marble tiles of the foyer. He listened to the peal of the doorbells, the pounding, the shambling footsteps as Morgan made his way toward the rear courtyard. More bells, more pounding, until at last all was silence.

Then he went up to his wife's bedroom, watched her for a moment as she breathed softly and dreamlessly from deep in a laudanum sleep. She hadn't wanted to go to the Assembly Ball without Morgan, but William had insisted. Had himself fastened the magnificent Marie Antoinette necklace around her slender neck. Not all of its diamonds could be traced back to the hoard of Crown jewels the French government had sold to Tiffany, but all of them were at least genuine again.

She had cut a magnificent figure at the ball, as she always did. His beautiful but barren Lena. And when he suggested that they leave before the cotillion and the supper, she had agreed without protest. Not until they were home had he explained to her what Morgan had done and what his punishment must be. That henceforth she would live a life devoid of his presence and without contact of any kind. Everett would become the son she should have given her husband. But didn't. When she had cried herself into hysteria, he held a glass of laudanum-laced sherry to her lips. She needed sleep, he'd told her, and she'd nodded, giving in the way she always did.

As William climbed into his bed that night, he thought he heard a whimpering from the darkness outside. It didn't last long and he was asleep before it ceased.

CHAPTER 19

Morgan Whitley's published obituary was a masterpiece of understatement. He was the son of the late Jacob Whitley and Lena Bergen Whitley De Vries and stepson of William De Vries, financier. He had attended Harvard University and was employed at the time of his death in the banking and investment field. The cause of death was pneumonia. Interment in the Whitley family plot of Trinity Church Cemetery in Washington Heights.

"This says nothing about who he really was," Prudence mourned, handing the clipping she had brought with her from home to Josiah. He, in turn, would file it in the folder where he had already placed all of the reports generated by William De Vries's original commission to investigate the theft of his wife's diamonds

"There's a viewing scheduled for tomorrow morning," Josiah noted, flipping through the firm's appointment book. They rarely scheduled client consultations on Saturdays, but Josiah insisted on documenting how the partners spent their time every day except Sunday.

"My aunt and I will be attending," Prudence said, watching him block off the hours she would be unavailable.

"Lady Rotherton?" Josiah exclaimed.

"She's known William since she was a debutante," Prudence informed him. "And while Morgan wasn't his son, he was the child of William's wife."

"Not to mention having lived in the De Vries household since he was six years old," Geoffrey added sharply. He'd been in an increasingly foul mood ever since he'd endorsed William's check and sent Josiah off to the bank to deposit it. Case closed.

But Prudence knew her partner had never truly halted the inquiry. She'd seen Amos Lang arrive at the office and closet himself with Geoffrey too many times in the past week and a half to believe Geoffrey had accepted a dismissal he would consider defeat. Though he often reminded Prudence that the work they did could not be taken personally, he was anything but detached from passionate involvement in every case they worked on.

He just hid it well.

"I don't suppose De Vries will object to our presence," Geoffrey said, instructing Josiah to add his name to Prudence's in the appointment book.

"As long as Ned Hayes and Amos Lang don't show up to scan the crowd of mourners for guilty faces," Prudence said.

"The case is closed. Officially and unofficially," Geoffrey insisted.

"What does that mean?"

"It means the police department is no longer interested in what's been going on at the De Vries home. Detective Phelan declared himself satisfied as soon as William's bribe fell into his pocket. And we were paid in full for our services."

He spoke with the caustic edge to his voice that Prudence had heard many times before. It usually signaled a renewed determination to get to the bottom of whatever secret someone was trying to hide from him.

Geoffrey had his own way of refusing to back down.

*   *   *

"You have my sincere condolences, William," Prudence heard Lady Rotherton say, her distinctively British accent cutting through the American voices all around her.

There was a stir of interest as the mourners realized that a dowager viscountess had appeared to pay her respects to the family of the late Morgan Whitley, a deeply disappointing son and stepson by any measure. Given the recent very private funeral of Aubrey Canfield, it was nothing short of extraordinary that a young man given to drink, gambling, and disgracing his lineage should be sent to his rest with all the ceremony usually reserved for a paragon of socially acceptable behavior.

Lena De Vries, standing deathly pale and soldier straight beside her son's open casket, stared down anyone who attempted to murmur a condolence laced with regret for the deplorable lifestyle that must have caused his mother so much pain. She was having none of that today. Her child was dead, and he would be remembered and buried with dignity. Beyond that she was choosing not to think.

"William tells me that Lena insisted on all of the usual formalities," Lady Rotherton told her niece, standing close enough so her words would not carry across the De Vries parlor. "He himself was very much against the idea of visitation and an open casket. He doesn't think she's strong enough to bear it."

"I doubt his reasons are quite so altruistic," Prudence said. And then she stopped, unsure how much of what she had picked up as she circulated through the room had also reached her aunt's ears. Nothing of what was being gossiped about had made it into the newspapers, but it was being treated as gospel truth nonetheless, though there were several unproved theories about where and by whom the body had been found.

One story had Morgan dead on the sidewalk in front of the De Vries mansion. Another insisted a milkman came across him in the alleyway. A third maintained that the body had been slumped against the door of the carriage house, sending the stable boy into a fit. The dead man's overcoat, hat, scarf, and gloves were missing. One shoe had turned up buried in a snowdrift. He had obviously been set upon when too far gone in drink to be able to defend himself.

The only thing on which the mourners saw eye to eye was that the dead man had been close enough to call for help had anyone been awake to hear him. And what was he doing wandering the streets when everyone else was dancing the night away at the second Assembly Ball of the season?

The scintilla of scandal had tongues wagging and nimble brains scrambling to dig up old bones of outrageous behavior that the De Vries family had been anxious to leave buried. But then Morgan wasn't really a De Vries, was he? Not even adopted, though he'd been a young child when his mother married his stepfather. Men who had seen him in the gambling casinos recalled his shockingly reckless betting behaviors, and women who had failed to interest him in their daughters clucked relievedly over their narrow escapes.

He looked healthier in death than he had in life, Prudence decided, staring down into the satin-lined black-walnut box in which Morgan would lie until he and it rotted into nothingness. She chided herself for so doleful a thought, but couldn't shake the feeling of angry melancholy that had put her in nearly as unpleasant a mood as Geoffrey.

Something wasn't right. And it couldn't be just the fact or circumstances of the death they had gathered to solemnize. She was positive Geoffrey felt it also. The two of them were like bloodhounds held back on a tight leash from the scent trail their every instinct told them to follow.

Her mind was spinning off in all directions. Time to anchor it in reality again. Time to find Geoffrey and withdraw with him into a private corner where they could confer without anyone overhearing them. Meaning Lady Rotherton, one of the most inquisitive individuals on the face of God's green earth.

"We need to talk," Prudence said when she finally located

her partner. Geoffrey had stationed himself in the alcove of a recessed window, eyes following as first one, then another respecter of the dead approached and spoke to William, moved on to Lena and the body in the coffin.

"I agree," he said, stepping into deeper dimness not illuminated by the discretely lowered gaslight. "It's past time."

"You're not satisfied that we know everything that happened." It wasn't a question, and he was still scanning the room.

"Are you?"

"I've never fully believed he stole his mother's diamonds," Prudence said.

"It was an elaborate scheme," Geoffrey agreed. "Far too complex for a habitual drunkard to manage. As far as I can tell, not a single mistake was made."

"If it hadn't been for my aunt's exceptionally acute eye for authenticity, Lena would never have known that half the diamonds she was wearing were paste."

"But no more," Geoffrey said. "Amos found out from one of the Tiffany jewelers that William had all of the phony stones replaced well before the second Assembly Ball. The few skilled artisans in the workroom who know the whole story have been sworn to silence."

"Threatened, more likely," Prudence said.

"The end result is the same. Lena wore her necklace Thursday night to the great admiration of every lady who hasn't anything half so fine."

"Aunt Gillian said nothing about it. She was there with us. She spoke to Lena and danced with William." Prudence had been as sumptuously dressed in yet another House of Worth creation as she had been at the first Assembly Ball. And just as reluctant to spend another evening in the company of people she found tedious. Except that there had been the promise of being in Geoffey's arms again. Dancing, of course. Which was perfectly acceptable.

"Did you notice the difference, Prudence?" Geoffrey prodded.

"I just assumed William told Lena she had to wear the necklace because if she didn't the whole town would be asking why. Remember that I was the one who couldn't tell the paste diamonds from the real ones," she said disgustedly. "Not even when they were pointed out to me."

"You'll make someone a very inexpensive wife one day."

"If that's your criterion for a spouse, I pity the woman who has to depend on you for an allowance to run a household," Prudence said. "Don't try to distract me. It won't work. I've seen Amos go into your office. I know what you're up to."

"And what would that be?"

"You're continuing the investigation on your own. Without a client to pay the expenses. That's something you've warned me against time and time again."

He didn't answer, but he looked away from Prudence out into the parlor. His eyes swept from left to right and back to the left. Scrutinizing, examining, storing away impressions until he could sort them out, make sense of them.

"I'm not criticizing you, Geoffrey. I'm just letting you know that I would have done the same thing if I'd thought any good would come of it."

"You give up too easily," he said softly, still not looking at her.

"You're not being fair." This wasn't the conversation she'd wanted to have with him. "Play by the rules."

"I didn't think we needed to have rules between us," he answered.

And now he did look down at her. And moved to block her view of the room. Or maybe he was blocking the room from viewing her. She could feel tears welling up in her eyes and knew they weren't for Morgan.

"I'm sorry, Prudence," he said, taking one of her gloved hands in his, lifting it to his lips. "I shouldn't have said what I did about giving up. You're one of the strongest women I've ever met. Certainly among the most stubborn."

That was Geoffrey all over again. One moment serious and almost tender, the next making a joke, coaxing her into a smile, wiping away a teardrop with the tip of his finger. It was maddening.

"I want to talk about the case."

"We will. I promise. Monday morning without fail. I'll arrange for Amos to come by the office. You can question him yourself about what he's discovered. But I have to warn you. It's not much more than we already knew."

"Or could guess."

"Hypothesize is the preferred word in detection circles," he said. "It sounds more professional." He let go Prudence's hand at the sound of Lady Rotherton's demanding voice speaking to his back.

"Turn around, Mr. Hunter, and tell me who that man is, the one who's looking down into the coffin."

"I've never seen him before," Geoffrey said. "Prudence?"

"I don't know him either, Aunt Gillian."

"I don't like the looks of him."

"Perhaps he's one of Morgan's drinking or gambling friends," Prudence offered.

"Too old. And he looks too cunning. That's the kind of man who only bets on a sure thing. Who's always coming up with a scheme to fleece anyone foolish enough to fall for some hairbrained notion or a dose of flattery. You see his type all the time in London. Usually younger sons of soon-to-be impoverished families out for a last ditch chance at catching the brass ring."

"What do you know about carousels, Aunt Gillian?" Prudence asked.

"I'm not talking about wooden horses," her aunt snapped. "I've as good an eye for a fraudster as I do for other phony business."

The man Lady Rotherton had called to their attention was probably in his midforties, Prudence guessed, handsome in a smooth, slightly oily way that made him oddly out of place in this gathering. He was dressed well, though on careful examination, not expensively. Of average height and build, he wore a mustache that concealed his upper lip and made it impossible to read whether it was strong or weak. Brown hair left to grow a little long, hazel eyes, ordinary features. Nothing special to remark or remember. Except that his skin was tanned, as though he'd come from one of the western prairies or the deck of an oceangoing ship. He didn't seem to know the other mourners, neither speaking to anyone nor trying to catch the eye of an acquaintance.

He glanced around, as though curious to see who might be watching him, then turned toward Lena. The word *sidle* crept into Prudence's brain. Whoever he was, there was something about this man's actions that put her in mind of furtiveness, of a sneak thief working his way through a crowd until he found a pocket to pick or a reticule string to cut.

Lady Rotherton and Geoffrey studied him with the intent concentration of hawks following a doomed prey.

For the first time since the viewing had begun, Lena stepped away from her son's embalmed body and rouged cheeks. She glanced at William, who was deep in conversation with a prosperous-looking gentleman of advanced years, then glided smoothly toward the bank of tall lilies rising up behind the casket. Before she vanished into the fragrant whiteness, Prudence saw her grip one hand in the other, tugging at her fingers as if to relieve the pain of an arthritic joint.

The man who had been staring into Morgan's coffin had also disappeared.

"Where did he go?" Prudence whispered.

"Behind the flowers," Geoffrey said. "He looked at Lena, nodded so slightly that I almost missed it, then stepped out of sight. She followed him a moment later."

"Now we wait." Lady Rotherton's tone was smug. Her smile was that of a gambler who sees his winning hand fanned out and face up on the table.

"It won't be long," Geoffrey predicted. "They can't risk being caught."

"Am I the only one who doesn't know what's going on?" Prudence asked.

"Lena wasn't here to sign for the first Tiffany delivery of her necklace," Lady Rotherton reminded her. "And she never explained why not. Not to my satisfaction. That was all I needed to know."

Her aunt's complacency was infuriating.

"There," Geoffrey said. "She's back."

Lena had appeared beside Morgan's coffin again. And no one seemed to have noticed that she hadn't been there all along.

"She's given him one of her rings," Lady Rotherton exclaimed. "The dark blue sapphire from her right hand. She's moved a black opal onto that finger. Very clever. And planned for in advance."

Prudence stared at her aunt. The woman never failed to astonish her.

"He's her lover," Lady Rotherton went on. "The one she was meeting when William arranged for the necklace to be delivered without telling her it was coming. And judging by the suit he's wearing, he's not in the best financial condition. Definitely not of her social class. Lena has stepped down in life. And now she has to pay for it."

"Where did he go?" Prudence asked, recovering her equilibrium.

"On his way out," Geoffrey said.

She caught a glimpse of the back of the man's head as he wound through the crowd toward the foyer.

"Will you follow him?" she asked, knowing that Geoffrey stood a better chance of not being observed than a young woman dressed in funereal black.

"Amos is outside," he said, moving to a front window. He waited a moment, then tweaked one of the lace curtains. "He's got him in his sights now."

"I presume this Amos is also an ex-Pinkerton," Lady Rotherton said.

"We keep him on retainer," Geoffrey answered.

"Like that Danny Dennis hansom cab driver person?"

"Exactly."

"I approve," Lady Rotherton declared. "Hire the best and pay them well. It's the only way to get good, reliable service." She took a pearl-encrusted gold snuffbox out of her reticule, flicked open the lid, and extracted a tiny smear of white powder onto one gloved hand. Sniffed. Sneezed delicately into a cobweb-thin lace handkerchief. Gave a little shiver of delight.

"Now," she said firmly, taking hold of Prudence's arm. "Let's go see how much information we can squeeze out of the very naughty and misbehaving Lena De Vries."

"She's in mourning, Aunt Gillian. She's standing next to the body of her son," Prudence protested.

"No better moment," Lady Rotherton asserted. "Or would you rather give the lady time to cover her tracks?"

Geoffrey wondered if the firm should put Prudence's aunt on retainer also.

CHAPTER 20

Lena De Vries blenched as Lady Rotherton approached, moving through the crowd of mourners with all the authority of years of titled privilege. Prudence trailed in her wake, torn between admiring her aunt's forthrightness and being appalled at her lack of sensitivity to a mother's loss. She thought the best she might do was soften the blow of the questions she was afraid her mother's sister planned to ask.

"Lena, my dear," Lady Rotherton began, reaching for the hand that had once sported an exquisite dark blue sapphire and now bore a rather ordinary black opal. She ran a thumb over the ring on Lena's finger, watching closely as Morgan's mother tried not to snatch her hand away. "How very admirable to have so many kindred souls to share your grief. It shows how much your dear son meant to them."

William turned to listen to what Lady Rotherton was saying to his wife, but his attention was quickly drawn away by the condolences of a banking colleague. It was difficult to hear with so many lowered voices expressing regrets and urging him to remember the good times rather than dwelling on the difficult.

With Morgan, there hadn't been many good moments once he began drinking his way through adulthood.

"Do tell me the name of the gentleman you were just speaking with," Lady Rotherton went on, holding Lena's hand tightly, digging the opal ring into her victim's finger. "Neither Prudence nor Mr. Hunter recognized him. Friend of the family?"

"I don't know who you mean," Lena stammered.

"Medium height, brown hair, mustache, tanned skin. A suit that's seen better days. And a very practiced way of ducking out of sight."

"I don't recall anyone matching that description," Lena whispered.

"Perhaps I should ask William," Lady Rotherton said. "You can't be expected to know all of his business acquaintances." She pursed her lips firmly.

"No. No, don't do that." Lena tried to pull her hand free from the grip that held it so tightly the opal ring had incised a white circle around her finger.

"Then who is he?" Lady Rotherton insisted.

Lena had the trapped look of a rabbit caught in a snare, desperate to break free. She looked pleadingly at Prudence, who hadn't said a word during this exchange.

"Was he a friend of Morgan's?" Prudence asked gently.

"Yes. Yes, he was," Lena agreed. "William would not be pleased if he knew this particular friend had come to the house." She paused to find the threads of the story she was making up on the spot. "They drank and gambled together, you see. And knew one another at the Keeley Institute. He was devastated to learn that Morgan's cure hadn't lasted."

"What is his name?" Lady Rotherton persisted. The tilt of her nose indicated that she wasn't buying a word of the tale Lena was concocting.

"I don't remember. I'm not sure he told me," Lena said. "It doesn't matter. He won't come here again."

"I think we can be quite sure of that," Lady Rotherton said.

"It's kind of you to take the time to comfort Lena." William stepped away from the couple he had been talking to. "I told her this might prove to be too much to bear, but she wouldn't listen."

"Sometimes it's best to say farewell with all the pomp and ceremony society urges on us," Lady Rotherton murmured, keeping a sharp eye on Lena's face as she seemed to shy away from the consoling hand her husband laid on her arm. "If one is tempted to deny the death, one remembers the face of the beloved deceased, and acceptance becomes inevitable."

"Please excuse me." Lena drifted toward the window where Geoffrey had spotted Amos Lang taking off after his prey. She stood there for a moment before twitching back the curtain to peer out into the street. When she let the drapery fall, it was with something like a sigh of despair or relief. Then a large-hipped older woman slid an arm around her waist and assured her that it was certainly not going to sleet again before they got Morgan safely to his final resting place.

William glanced into the casket and returned to his position near the condolence book, his eyes following his wife as the older woman guided her toward the dining room and a restorative cup of tea.

"That was not altogether satisfactory," Lady Rotherton complained. "I would have gotten the name out of her if William hadn't interrupted us."

"Amos will have it," Geoffrey predicted. "He'll stick with him until he's got the whole story. Or at least as much as observation and talking to neighbors will dig up."

"I think we should post a man on this house," Prudence said. "Around the clock."

"What would he be looking for?" Geoffrey asked.

"From what people are saying, when William refused to allow Morgan into the house he as good as signed his stepson's death warrant. It was well after midnight, pouring down sleet.

Who knows how long Morgan had been wandering the streets, how many times he'd already pounded on the door. He must have been hoping Lena would persuade William to let him spend at least one more night under his roof."

"William is the kind of man who doesn't bend when he's made up his mind," Lady Rotherton said. "He'd already given Morgan more chances than he probably deserved."

"This is January, Aunt Gillian, the coldest time of the year. And the weather was foul. If Kincaid hadn't put hot bricks in the carriage we would have had chilblains by the time we got home on Thursday night."

"I'm not saying he hoped Morgan would freeze to death," Lady Rotherton argued. "He probably thought the young man would have the sense to go to a friend's house or to one of the clubs where he wasn't in arrears on his membership dues. A hotel, perhaps. He wouldn't have been turned away. People in this town would have assumed his stepfather would pick up his bill just as he must have done in the past."

"He was too drunk," Geoffrey said. "When a man gets like that, he isn't capable of thinking."

Prudence stared at him for a moment. She'd never seen Geoffrey in anything but unimpaired possession of himself, but now she wondered if he spoke of drunkenness out of past experience. Laudanum eased you into oblivion after blunting both physical and mental pain. You reached a place where you simply didn't care anymore. Could alcohol have the same effect?

"I think Lena may decide to leave William," Prudence whispered, not daring to glance at the man who stood so correctly receiving expressions of sympathy on the untimely demise of his stepson. "Every time she looks at him she must remember that he wouldn't open the front door to her son. And that if anyone except himself is to blame for Morgan's death, it's her husband."

"She's considering it," Lady Rotherton agreed. "I don't know that she'll find the courage to leave all this." She waved her hand in a vague but expressive gesture. Money, pride of place, social position, a life of luxury. "Women have been known to put up with a great deal more, especially if they are considerably younger than their husbands."

"She won't decamp until after Morgan has been interred," Geoffrey said. "I'll leave Amos on our mysterious stranger's tail and pull in someone else to keep an eye on Lena."

"I think it's time for a cup of tea," Lady Rotherton declared. When she went into the dining room, Lena wasn't there.

"He's bolted," Geoffrey said, reading the note Amos Lang had had one of Danny Dennis's street urchins deliver.

It was late on the Monday afternoon following Morgan's viewing and interment on Saturday. According to Damien Rosarlo, staked out opposite the De Vries mansion, Lena had not left the house, not even pulled aside a curtain as far as he could tell.

A steady stream of sweeper boys ran messages back and forth between Geoffrey and his ex-Pinkertons. The street urchins were all wearing warm coats, sturdy boots, and woolen gloves and hats. Josiah ordered sandwiches from the bar on the corner every lunch hour, handing them out at the same time as he made sure the tough little runners were well protected against the elements.

The storm that had contributed to Morgan's death had passed, leaving behind freezing air and bright blue skies.

"Does Amos say where he thinks he's going?" Prudence asked.

"To the train station," Geoffrey replied. "Carrying a suitcase. Mr. Jasper Owens isn't coming back. We'll let him buy a ticket and get aboard, but he won't leave the depot. Amos will see to that."

"If Lena is to join him, she should be leaving the house any time now," Prudence said. "She can't take her own carriage and the trolleys are undependable. She'll have to hail a cab."

"Danny Dennis and Mr. Washington will be the first vehicle she'll see at the curb."

But although Geoffrey and Prudence paced their offices for another two hours, Lena De Vries remained shut up inside her husband's Fifth Avenue mansion.

Jasper Owens, with no evidence against him to prove he was part of the diamond theft, had to be allowed to take a late train out of the city.

"He bought a ticket to Chicago," Amos told them. "The man had money in his wallet."

"But no sapphire ring in his pocket," Prudence said.

"He sold it this morning," Amos confirmed. "I got a quick look at it when he made the transaction. It was a beautiful piece of jewelry. He got a lot for it. Enough to carry him to San Francisco if Chicago is too close for comfort."

"Maybe we were wrong," Prudence fretted. "Perhaps Lena never had any romantic connection to him. He could be a friend of Morgan's, as she said. Giving him the ring might have been a last homage to her son. She couldn't do any more for him, but she could help his crony."

When she confided that possibility to Lady Rotherton over dinner that night, Prudence's aunt scoffed.

"Don't call off the man you've got on Fifth Avenue," she advised. "Not yet."

Lena left the next morning, after William had departed for his office and hours before he could be expected home for lunch. If he wasn't dining out with clients that day.

She was dressed in mourning black and veiled hat, carrying one small suitcase and moving quickly down the steps and across the sidewalk. Danny Dennis secured the suitcase to the back of the hansom and mouthed the destination he'd been given to Damien Rosarlo, who immediately set out for the Hunter and MacKenzie offices. Mrs. De Vries would be unable to shake off Danny Dennis's runners inside the train station, and Mr. Washington could be depended upon to take his time getting there.

Lena bought her ticket and then went to the platform to wait. Passengers eddied around her as she stood alone in the crowd, suitcase at her feet, head swiveling anxiously as the train's scheduled departure time grew closer and closer.

No one joined her.

Conductors and porters wove their way along the track, urging passengers to board, loading luggage, helping ladies mount the car steps.

Gradually the mass of people thinned out. Friends and relatives of departing travelers backed away from the train and its billowing clouds of smoky steam, waving good-byes, calling out farewells.

Lena remained frozen in place.

"It's time to board, miss," a porter said. He reached for Lena's bag, but she waved him off.

Tears glittered in her eyes.

From where they stood behind a pillar, Geoffrey and Prudence watched as Lena slowly realized that she had been abandoned. Used and callously discarded as soon as her usefulness was over.

After the train had left the platform to begin its westward journey, Lena tore in half the ticket she had never relinquished and let the pieces flutter to her feet. She turned toward the station's massive waiting hall, leaving the suitcase in place behind her.

"I'll get it," Geoffrey said.

Prudence nodded, eyes fixed on the tragic figure moving blindly back toward the life she had thought to escape. When she reached Lena's side and touched her arm, the other woman gripped Prudence's hand convulsively, but did not speak.

What was there to say?

* * *

"We'll leave the suitcase in the cab," Geoffrey explained to Prudence. "After the butler has let us in, Danny Dennis will carry it up the steps. When I'm sure there's no one in the entry hall, I'll open the door. You'll have to be quick about it. Up the stairs to her bedroom and get it unpacked and put away as fast as you can. Are you certain no one saw you leave, Mrs. De Vries?"

"I'm positive. I planned it out very carefully. But I never thought I'd be returning." Lena no longer wore the stunned look of incredulity that Prudence had noted when she took her arm in Grand Central Depot. This was a woman who seemed able to weather the storms and disappointments of her life with remarkable resilience. She was pale but calm. Fatalistically controlled. Her son was dead; the lover she trusted had cruelly deceived her. "I'll instruct our butler that Taylor need not attend me until after my guests have departed. She won't interrupt us. She'll stay in the servants' hall until I ring for her."

"Are you expecting William home for luncheon?" Geoffrey asked.

"I didn't see him this morning, but he'll have left word with the butler. My instinct says that he'll want to avoid me for a few days. He knows I blame him for Morgan's death. But he thinks I'll forgive him."

"And will you?" Prudence asked. *How could you ever forgive a man whose heartless disregard for human frailty robbed his stepson of any chance to redeem his wasted life?*

Lena didn't answer.

"He had no resources of his own," Lena began. "I gave him pieces of jewelry to sell. Whatever I thought was insignificant enough so William wouldn't notice it was gone. The money was supposed to give us a start together in the West until we could find a lawyer who would initiate divorce proceedings.

We thought we'd try Denver. William would never think of looking for me there."

Prudence hadn't asked Lena to explain why she had carried a suitcase to Grand Central Depot that morning. Unaccompanied. They'd unpacked Lena's clothes, stowed the valise in her dressing room, and come down to the parlor where Geoffrey waited.

As soon as the parlor door closed behind them, the story had started pouring out of Lena as though she were powerless to stop it. She had to tell someone.

"People were saying at Morgan's funeral that he'd lost money that wasn't his own," Geoffrey said. "And that was why he drank himself into insensibility."

"They were right. William swore he'd fire whoever leaked the truth, but I told him not to bother. In the end, there are no secrets in society that someone doesn't uncover. He should know that."

"When did Mr. Owens learn that it was your money Morgan had lost, that you were virtually penniless?" Geoffrey was trying to spare Prudence the task of asking the hard questions. It would be enough if she could soften the blows he was dealing.

"I think he knew before he came to the viewing. I can't be sure, but I suspect he did because he asked me for more jewelry to pawn. Not asked, demanded. As if he reckoned that since he could no longer count on a fortune sometime in the future, he might as well get what he could right now."

"Was he behaving differently?" Prudence asked.

"Not so I noticed. And I was terrified that William would guess who he was. Pretending he was Morgan's friend was stretching things because Jasper is at least twenty years older than my son. That's why I came up with the idea that the two had met at the Keeley Institute. Men of all ages take the Gold Cure."

"I'm so sorry, Mrs. De Vries," Prudence said.

"You might as well call me Lena. You know all of my secrets." A wan smile curved across her lips, making her appear both frail and resolved.

"The sapphire ring was valuable," Geoffrey said. "Your husband is bound to ask why you've stopped wearing it."

"It's not fair to blame a crime on a dead man, but that's what I'll do. That ring and every other piece Jasper sold. I don't know how the Tiffany ring box ended up in Leonard Abbott's room, but in William's mind he's already a thief. I'll simply add to the number of things he allegedly stole. And if my husband questions me about not knowing they were missing, I can truthfully tell him that worry over Morgan had me so anxious and distracted that I didn't notice half of what was going on around me. He'll believe it."

Why did you come back? Why are you so determined to stay? Prudence wanted to ask.

But she did not dare. They were the kind of questions to which Aunt Gillian wouldn't hesitate to demand answers, but Prudence wasn't as unyielding as Lady Rotherton.

It was enough to witness the desolate sorrow on Lena's face and the fierce struggle she was waging to keep her back straight, tears from her eyes, and misery from carving furrows of agony on her cheeks.

CHAPTER 21

"I could have turned this over to the servants to accomplish," Lena De Vries said, standing woebegone and despondent in her son's room. She looked around as though unable to decide where to begin. "But I couldn't bear the thought of it."

"William really ordered you to get rid of everything?" Prudence asked.

"I'm not surprised." Lady Rotherton peeled off her gloves and unpinned her hat. "But it's not the kind of thing a mother should ever have to do alone. You were right to send for us."

"I didn't know what else to do."

"We could start with the clothes," Prudence suggested. She remembered from her father's death that disposing of the garments he had worn was by far the hardest thing to do; they were permeated with his familiar aroma of cigars and bay rum shaving lotion. Sorting through her friend Eleanor Dickson's trousseau had been almost equally difficult because that death, barely seven months ago, had been so senseless. If she'd learned anything from those two experiences, it was that it was best to tackle the worst of it first. Before energy flagged and emotions erupted into tears.

Lady Rotherton closed the bedroom door.

"We might need some help, Aunt Gillian," Prudence said. She was thinking of the boxes that would have to be labeled and hauled away.

"Later. After we've gone through everything. I think it's best that things remain private until then."

"There's nothing to be found that we don't already know about," Lena said. "William kept track of every detail of my son's transgressions. Morgan has no more secrets from me."

"Everyone has secrets," Lady Rotherton maintained. "Even the dead."

She opened the armoire door, scanned the row of suits hanging neatly from padded hangers, and took out a dark brown jacket and pants frayed around the cuffs. "The valet who was supposedly looking after him was not doing a very good job," she sniffed. "These pants should have been turned and mended before being hung back in the armoire ready to wear again. Better still, they should never have gone back at all."

"William didn't pay Morgan's tailor bill," Lena said, taking the trousers from Lady Rotherton and smoothing the worn cuffs with motherly affection.

"We haven't talked about Morgan's trust fund from his father." Prudence set a stack of starched and ironed shirts on the bed.

"It was more than adequate to begin with," Lena said. "Morgan could have lived on it quite comfortably for the rest of his life if he'd turned the management over to a competent investment consultant."

"Why didn't he?" Lady Rotherton asked. She herself had never trusted anyone else to oversee her fortune. She'd educated herself in the ways of finance and profited handsomely from what she'd learned, never gambling on anything but a sure bet. Which wasn't really speculating at all.

"He felt he had to prove himself to William," Lena explained. "If his stepfather was going to trust him with the firm's clients and assets, he had to show that he could double or triple his own holdings. It was a challenge he couldn't resist."

"But the drinking impaired his judgment, so the more he lost, the greater and more foolish the chances he took," Lady Rotherton said. She shook her head over the condition of the jacket pockets she was rifling through. "I've seen it before. Many times. London is full of second and third sons whose lack of prospects doesn't keep them from throwing good money after bad. They're a pitiful lot. The only hope is that their elder brothers will die or an heiress will become besotted and persuade her parents to make the match."

"It's not much different here, Aunt Gillian," Prudence said. "Except that everything doesn't automatically go to the eldest son. But a father can write a wastrel out of his will, if he wants. Or younger sons can contest the bequests. There are always hungry suitors angling for wealthy debutantes."

"What's this?" Lady Rotherton said, holding something compact and leather bound in her hand. "Is this Morgan's diary, Lena?"

"He had a larger appointment book for business. But I remember a smaller one he kept for personal notes. I think that must be it. May I see?"

Lady Rotherton passed it to Morgan's mother, staying close as Lena turned the pages. "Nothing," she concluded when Lena had finished. "An incomplete record of sums he's won and lost, and a few scribbles here and there."

Lena handed the book to Prudence, who sat down in Morgan's easy chair to go through it. Page by page. Slowly. Taking nothing for granted. The way a trained Pinkerton approached documents. "He's written Aubrey's name. With a question mark after it," she said. "Just once. Leonard Abbott's. And here's Everett's name. Again with a question mark. Toward the end of whatever record he was keeping. After all the numbers he's added up and scratched through. In fact the names are the last things he wrote, except for a page that's been torn out."

"Run a pencil across the next page," Lady Rotherton instructed. "That's how you discover who's careless enough to write love notes in the library at a house party. They often leave an impression on the blotter. Sometimes you can read the whole thing."

"Not this time, Aunt Gillian," Prudence said. When Lena nodded permission, she slipped the notebook into her reticule for Geoffrey to look at later.

Morgan's small personal items were inexpensive and limited. Two pairs of moderately priced cuff links, a cigar trimmer, a tarnished silver money clip. A pair of well-worn hairbrushes, an unused mustache trimmer, and a leather-handled shoehorn. Toothbrush in a glass, a tin of tooth powder beside it. Macassar oil for his hair, an almost empty bottle of the bay rum cologne worn by so many men.

"We buried him with his Harvard ring," Lena said, fingering the empty money clip.

"Is this all he had?" Lady Rotherton asked. "It's not much for a young man of his social standing."

"He must have sold his father's cuff links. They were solid gold. And there was a gold cigar case also." Lena straightened her shoulders. "He was desperate toward the end."

"This does not look like the lair of a diamond thief," Lady Rotherton declared. She'd emptied the armoire and piled the clothes onto the bed. "Everything I touched needed to be mended or discarded. Even his evening clothes were a disgrace."

"He didn't steal the diamonds," Lena said obstinately. "He told me he didn't, and I believe him."

"Of course he didn't," Lady Rotherton snapped. "No young man could resist the lure of new suits to entice the ladies into his net. If he'd taken the diamonds, we wouldn't be pawing through this miserable excuse for a decent wardrobe."

"Aunt Gillian!" Prudence exclaimed.

"Lena knows I'm right. Don't you, Lena?"

"Morgan took pride in dressing well when he was at Harvard."

"His tailor bills were probably huge," Lady Rotherton said.

"I helped him out sometimes." Lena smiled. "William never knew."

"And that was well before he'd lost the bulk of his trust fund, wasn't it?"

"They all spent as though there were no tomorrow," Lena said. "All of those boys. They were from wealthy families and they'd never had to question where their next dollar was coming from. Life after Harvard was a never-ending round of debutante balls, soirees, and appearances at the opera. Their greatest fear was boredom. They partied madly to avoid it."

"Surely they worked?" Prudence was horrified at the notion of a crowd of well-educated ne'er-do-wells squandering their lives and fortunes in the pursuit of pleasure.

"These are the heirs, Prudence," Lady Rotherton said. "Their fathers and grandfathers were the moguls. All these children have learned to do is spend."

"Not all of them, Lady Rotherton," Lena said. "I grant you that Morgan seemed determined to run with the worst of their type, but many of the friends he made at Harvard have taken on the responsibilities they were primed to accept. I know their families."

"You're talking about Everett Rinehart, aren't you?" Prudence asked.

"I suppose I am. Comparing him to Morgan became de rigueur in this household. My husband is proud of his sister's son. Deservedly so. He boasts that Everett takes after the De Vries side of the family. Blood to blood, as they say."

"The son he never had," Lady Rotherton declared.

"Shall we tell William that we're going to reopen the case?" Prudence asked. She felt as though she were carrying the weight of the world on her shoulders. "He'll take it better from you than from me."

"This development occurred after he ceased being our client," Geoffrey reminded her. "We were investigating on our own, tying up the loose ends William preferred to ignore."

"I wish you'd been able to go through Morgan's clothes the way Aunt Gillian and I did, Geoffrey. It was so obvious he'd spent little or no money on his wardrobe in a very long time. Almost everything he owned was worn and frayed. Not quite noticeable to the casual eye, but he soon would have been forced to incur considerable expense at a good tailor. A gentleman in banking can't afford to look shabby."

For once Josiah had nothing to add. He continued to take notes in his Gregg shorthand, amazed that any young swell would neglect his appearance.

"That's the point, isn't it?" Geoffrey commented. "He was on his way to being eased out of the banking and investment businesses, and he had to have known it. He continued playing the game to some extent, showing up at his stepfather's offices and managing a few portfolios, with Everett's help and always under his supervision, but he surely understood that his stepfather knew he hadn't the gift of making money. Nothing he touched turned to gold."

"Including the South Dakota mine whose ore samples were probably salted," Prudence said. William had not spared Lena the details of how Morgan lost the last of his fortune and all of his mother's.

"Back to the thorny issue of whether we tell De Vries that the investigation has to be reopened," Geoffrey said.

"He won't take it well," Prudence predicted. "It suits him to believe Morgan was the thief and that with his death, the whole incident can be put to rest."

"The jeweler to whom the stones were sold has been murdered, the runner who worked for that jeweler was beaten senseless before he died, and a servant in the De Vries house either committed suicide or his hanging was made to look as though he had taken his own life. Not one of those deaths has been satisfactorily resolved."

"Detective Phelan closed all three of the cases."

"Either he or his superiors were paid off. Probably both."

"He hasn't always been a bad cop. Or is it copper?" Prudence asked. She wasn't consistently sure about the slang Geoffrey used without thinking twice about it.

"Either one will do. And you're right, Phelan isn't as bad as I've made him out to be. If a bribe isn't involved he'll work a case as hard and honestly as he can. But nobody cares too much about ordinary crime in this city. And the casual killings of men whose bodies are likely to end up in the trenches of Hart Island are definitely ordinary by every definition of the term."

"I think we owe it to Morgan and especially to Lena to inform William that we are as convinced now of Morgan's innocence as we once were suspicious of his guilt. It will make Lena's life easier to bear if she can believe that someone is working to clear her son's name."

"Did she tell you why she went back?" Geoffrey asked. "Why she didn't get on that train and set off somewhere on her own?"

"We may have to wait a while for the answer to that question," Prudence said. "And we might never know."

"I'll make an appointment to see William at his office," Geoffrey said. He wasn't happy about it, but Prudence was right. If they were to work to exonerate Morgan postmortem, William deserved to know about it. He might decide not to cooperate, and he almost certainly would not underwrite their investigation, but going behind his back was sure to enrage him.

It was never a good idea to bait openly a man who was both wealthy and powerful.

The offices of the investment bank of De Vries & Co. were luxurious, dim, and silent. Thick carpeting muffled footsteps, capable receptionists and secretaries steered clients where they needed to go, and private consultations took place behind heavy mahogany doors. The building itself was five stories tall, and there were rumors that De Vries was considering installing one of the ascending rooms like that operating in the Lord & Taylor department store. It would be equipped with padded benches, a chandelier, and gold-framed mirrors on three walls. Elevators, they were being called now, though some doubted their safety and preferred a solid staircase. For that very reason, the firm's senior officers conducted their business on the first two floors. Older wealthy clients tended to be robustly rotund if they were male, tightly corseted and averse to anything re-sembling exercise if female.

Geoffrey did not make an appointment with William De Vries, reasoning that Lena's husband might, if given time to think about it, guess at the reason for his visit and refuse to see him. They had parted amicably when De Vries dispensed with the further services of Hunter and MacKenzie; Geoffrey's pres-ence would only bring up memories of the recent unpleasant-ness that were best forgotten. But at the same time, Geoffrey and William were both gentlemen, and no gentleman was ever deliberately ungracious toward another. Without cause.

William listened politely while Geoffrey laid out the reasons he and Prudence had decided that Morgan could not possibly have engineered and carried out the theft of Lena's Marie An-toinette diamonds. He ended his recital with a description of the clothing Prudence, Lady Rotherton, and Lena had meticu-lously prepared for donation to charity.

"They were quite certain that none of the garments was newly purchased," he concluded, "and that since Morgan had been somewhat of a dandy when he was at Harvard, he would not have allowed his wardrobe to fall out of fashion and even into disrepair for anything less than a seriously embarrassing shortage of funds."

"He gambled away every last penny he had," William said,

puffing furiously on the cigar clamped between his teeth. "Threw away his mother's fortune without a care for her welfare. A man like that is perfectly capable of losing thousands of dollars on the turn of a single card. He was as worthless as they come. Lena will never admit it, of course, but she's well rid of him."

"I hardly think any mother would feel that way about a dead child."

"I know what you've come for, Mr. Hunter, and I am astounded that you should think for a moment I would countenance any attempt at rehabilitating the reputation of a wastrel like Morgan Whitley. A wastrel, a scoundrel, a liar, a cheat, a drunkard—" William ran out of names to call his stepson. His face had flushed a deep red and the hand now holding his cigar trembled. "I won't have it. You are *not*, I repeat *not*, to involve my family in anything that will result in another smear on my name."

"I wasn't aware that had happened," Geoffrey said calmly.

"It was all over the papers when that valet chose to put a rope around his neck in the attic of my home. Reporters and gawkers milled around outside for days, and I can only describe the speculation in the newspapers as publicly injurious. I made sure Lena was not exposed to any of it."

"It's partly for your wife's sake that we're doing it," Geoffrey reasoned. The other rationale, which he forbore from mentioning, was the simple justice of clearing an innocent man of suspicion of a crime he had not committed.

"Leave her out of this. The sooner she forgets she ever gave birth to that miscreant the better."

"Surely you don't mean that."

"I never say what I don't mean," William stormed, rising from behind his desk. "No gentleman interferes in the personal life of another gentleman. Not if he wishes to remain in society's good graces."

"My profession would seem to exclude me from that august company," Geoffrey said. He stood, and for a moment won-

dered if William would commit the unpardonable affront of refusing to shake his hand. Decided not to push the financier that
far. "I regret to have to inform you, Mr. De Vries, that Hunter
and MacKenzie has decided to reopen the case and to continue
the investigation into the disappearance of your wife's diamonds and the three deaths that appear to be linked to that
crime. We will not rest until we have solved the theft and the
murders."

"I forbid it!" roared William De Vries.

"I'm afraid we will not be dissuaded."

Geoffrey was back out on Fifth Avenue before William's secretary knocked on his office door to inform him that his
nephew was requesting a few moments of his time.

And found his employer sprawled on the floor beside his
desk.

William's body shook with spasms and one side of his face
drooped into paralysis. His garbled speech was incomprehensible, he could not stand, and the fear in his eyes reflected knowledge of the horror that had descended upon him.

Any man of a certain age and girth could fall victim to an in-
capacitating weakness of heart or brain that ended his usefulness and his independence. There were no cures for the half-life
that stretched before him if he survived the first few hours or
days.

Now that nightmare had visited itself on one of the country's
wealthiest and most powerful entrepreneurs.

And there was nothing he could do about it.

CHAPTER 22

Lena turned William's bedroom into a sickroom, complete with twenty-four-hour nursing care and an array of nostrums that ranged from tincture of opium to quiet his spasmodic tremors to mustard plasters applied to the feet to draw excess blood from his damaged brain.

Three women clad in long, white nursing aprons saw to his needs in rotating four-hour shifts. Two of them had learned their skills during the late war, on the wards where wounded and dying men sometimes suffered for months before succumbing to their battlefield injuries or the contagions that raged through military hospitals. The third hoped to study at the New York Medical College and Hospital for Women as soon as she could persuade her outraged father to allow it. Or she turned twenty-one and no longer needed his permission.

The patient was unable to do anything for himself. Everything, from bathing and massaging his paralyzed limbs to cleaning the most intimate areas of his body, had to be done by someone else. William De Vries was as helpless as a newborn infant.

Except that deep in his eyes gleamed a spark of comprehension. He was conscious, aware of his surroundings, yet unable to speak or move. He could not even control the movements of his eyelids, which sometimes drooped like heavy curtains, and at other moments remained obstinately wide open as if touched by the rigor that comes to the body after death.

The nurses spoke in quiet, even tones, withdrawing into a corner of the large room or out into the hallway to discuss medical procedures and problems, even to exchange notes at the end of a shift. They understood that the mind of a paralyzed patient often absorbed what was being said and done around him. They had read horror and dismay in the eyes of mutilated soldiers unable to do more than lie on their backs and wait for death to release them from unanesthetized amputations, the sucking maws of greedy leeches, and the pitying condescension of healthy men. There was no reason to assume that the once masterful financier William De Vries was any less sentient than a farm boy drafted into the army against his will.

Lena sat by her husband for as many hours as she could tolerate the reek of the alcohol used to rub his legs and arms, the pervasive stench of loosened bowels that no amount of diaper changing could eliminate, and the acrid odor of the tonics spooned between his lips at regular intervals. Strong smells tortured Lena's always delicate stomach these days; she frequently had to flee the sickroom with a handkerchief pressed to her nose and mouth. The nurses could hear the sound of vomiting from her room and they shook their heads in commiseration at her distress. Some women were made that way; there wasn't anything they could do about it.

No matter how ill she had been, Lena always came back. Pale and trembling, but seemingly determined to do her duty. A wife's place was at her husband's bedside.

William had put severe restrictions on Geoffrey and Prudence, both before the footman's suicide and afterward. The more convinced he became that his stepson was the guilty party, the less he wanted the detectives he'd hired to pry into the private lives of the people living under his roof.

But William was no longer their client. Lena had assumed that role. She had authorized Hunter and MacKenzie to do whatever it took to prove her son's innocence, sealing the contract with a sizable advance against expenses and carte blanche to pursue any investigative thread that seemed promising.

They started with the servants they'd only spoken to briefly before William fired them.

"I make it out to be twenty-four total," Prudence said, studying the list the housekeeper had given her. "Leonard Abbott would have brought it to twenty-five."

"No one's been hired to replace him?" Geoffrey asked.

"Apparently William's valet is looking after Everett now. The nurses see to changing William's nightgowns and linens. Another laundress comes every other day to help with the extra washing. I've added her to the list, but she doesn't live in."

"What do we know about the butler?"

"He was hired when William and the first Mrs. De Vries set up their household shortly before their marriage. The house was a wedding gift from William's father, who also greatly expanded the banking and investment firm. The furnishings were supplied by Mrs. De Vries's family."

The butler's name was Terence Harris. He had begun his life in service as a twelve-year-old boot boy, becoming a footman as soon as height and good looks qualified him to serve at table during formal dinners. He had graduated to the office of butler at the very young age of thirty-two. It was the pinnacle of a career; he never looked back and the only two moves he made were to larger and more important households. Now in his midfifties, he had settled in to the confirmed bachelorhood required of a senior servant.

"The hiring of Leonard Abbott might have been a mistake," he admitted, "but it was Mr. Whitley who insisted that we take him on."

"Do you know why?" Geoffrey asked. They had decided that he would question the male servants while Prudence occupied herself with the female members of staff.

"Leonard came with good references. He looked the part of a footman and he was punctilious in the execution of his duties."

"That doesn't answer my question. Why was hiring him a mistake?"

"I believe I said that it *might* have been a mistake, Mr. Hunter." Harris deflected the question by looking around the comfortably furnished basement room from which he was accustomed to ordering his small kingdom. He wasn't used to someone else sitting behind the desk that was almost as massive as the one Mr. De Vries used in his library, himself relegated to a chair pulled away from its usual place against the wall. He hoped this intrusive investigation would soon be over; there were numerous adjustments to be made to accommodate Mr. De Vries's medical condition.

"Abbott hanged himself in the attic. A footman wanting to become a valet who was under your supervision. Something had gone very wrong in his life. I would call your ignorance of what it was a failure in observation and management. And that would definitely constitute an error in judgment. Wouldn't you agree, Mr. Harris?"

"Leonard had become increasingly unhappy in recent months," Harris conceded. "He started returning late from his half days off and requesting permission to absent himself from the house when his duties permitted it."

"Do you know where he went?"

"He never said. And if I asked, he didn't answer. Since he was something of a favorite with Mr. Whitley, I didn't press or pursue the case. These things usually work themselves out, especially when the servant in question is young."

"Abbott was twenty-three."

"And doing well for himself."

"So I ask you again, why was hiring him a mistake?"

"It didn't seem so at the time."

"Would you have taken him on without Mr. Whitley's insistence?" Geoffrey asked.

Harris didn't answer immediately, staring down at his perfectly groomed fingernails and aligning the crease in his trousers. "I don't believe I would have," he finally said.

Reluctantly, Geoffrey thought.

"You'll have to be more specific."

Harris sighed. "It was something about him that struck me the wrong way. I can't put my finger on it, but I know when a candidate presents himself for an interview and I sense right away that he isn't right for the job. It's a feeling you develop over time and with experience."

"But you hired him despite this feeling? Because Mr. Whitley asked you to?"

"He didn't come right out and insist. It was more that he expressed a strong preference."

"It was my impression that household staff were provided by the Wentworth Domestic Employment Agency."

"They are," Harris confirmed. "The agency sends us candidates they have already interviewed so that we may accept or reject them."

"Do you accept more frequently than you reject?"

"We almost never reject the candidate they've chosen for us. Miss Wentworth selects with an eye toward compatibility as well as competence, and since the agency has already supplied most if not all of the other servants in the household, she knows very well who will fit in and who won't."

"Yet in this case, your first instinct was to deny Abbott the post for which he was applying?"

"It was," Harris said, a frown creasing his forehead. "I'm not sure I thought about it as deeply as your questions are now forcing me to look into my reactions."

"Did he like other men?" Geoffrey asked bluntly.

"He got along very well with the male members of staff."

"You know that's not what I mean."

Harris went so pale that if he had been a woman, Geoffrey would have reached for the smelling salts.

"I'm sure I wouldn't know, Mr. Hunter," he finally said. "We've never been troubled by that type of situation in this household."

Not that you know of or will admit, Geoffrey thought.

Prudence and Mrs. Mitchell talked over cups of tea.

In the housekeeper's mind her time with Miss MacKenzie was less an interrogation than a conversation. As she explained to Prudence, she chose to rule her maids lightly and allowed Cook to make kitchen decisions without undue interference. For the most part, given that there could always be exceptions, she was a woman who believed that too domineering a personality made for bickering, unpleasantness, and conflict below stairs.

"As in other walks of life, I imagine," Prudence agreed.

"I'll do my best to answer whatever questions you have," Mrs. Mitchell promised. "But I can't guarantee that I'll always have an answer, and I prefer not to guess at something personal."

"We're trying to get a sense of Mr. Whitley. How he conducted himself here in the house, what his relationship was with his stepfather, his mother, and the footman who hanged himself. Whether there were any improprieties of which you were aware."

Mrs. Mitchell swirled the few sips of tea remaining in her cup, but there were no leaves in the bottom to hint at either the past or the future. "When he was sober, Mr. Whitley was a considerate gentleman," she said slowly. "Unfortunately, for most of the time I knew him, he was in the clutches of demon rum. I didn't assume the position of housekeeper here until after the previous housekeeper retired. That was only two years ago."

"So you never knew him as a child or a very young man?"

"He had already graduated from Harvard and gone to work for Mr. De Vries."

"Had Leonard Abbott been assigned to him as valet yet?" Prudence and Geoffrey had agreed that addressing the suicide would be the first thrust of their investigation.

"Mr. Harris tried out one or two of the other footmen before settling on Leonard. Not everyone is cut out to be a valet or a lady's maid. It takes special talents."

"Did Mr. Whitley express a preference for him?"

"That was a bit odd. Mr. Harris and I had several conversations about it. Even though the maids fall under my care and the male staff under Mr. Harris's supervision, we do consult with one another as frequently as necessary to keep a good balance going."

"What was odd about Abbott?"

"Mr. Harris was never very explicit, but I got the impression that Mr. Whitley put in a word on his behalf when the agency sent him over for an interview. He certainly encouraged his rise from footman to acting valet. Leonard became a great favorite with the young men Mr. Whitley entertained in his rooms. If Mr. Harris sent another footman up to wait on them, he always came back down saying Leonard was wanted. Asked for by name."

It was unusual for a visitor to the house to know the name of a footman. Even more strange that he should be singled out.

"Tell me about Mr. Whitley's friends. How often did he entertain them?"

"Usually two or three times a week. Almost always in the late afternoon or when dinner was over. They were going out together, you see, drinking and gambling or attending one of the debutante affairs, so they spent an hour or two getting ready."

"Lubricating themselves?"

"I haven't heard it described like that before, Miss MacKenzie, but yes, that's more or less what they were doing. Leonard served them whiskey in Mr. Whitley's suite of rooms, hardly ever more than two or three guests at a time. Whenever Mr. Canfield stayed over, he saw to him as well."

"Meaning he acted as Mr. Canfield's valet?"

Mrs. Mitchell nodded, but did not elaborate.

"I find it a bit peculiar that Mr. Canfield would spend the night here," Prudence said. "His own home can't be more than five or six blocks away."

"Mr. Canfield didn't get along very well with either of his parents," Mrs. Mitchell said, pursing her lips in disapproval. "He'd taken the Gold Cure, but he couldn't seem to make it work. Whenever he was too far gone to chance going head to head with his father, or his parents had gone to their country house, Mr. Whitley would invite him to stay here. There were always empty guest rooms in that wing of the house, and Mr. De Vries didn't seem to mind. I'm not even sure he was always aware of Mr. Canfield's presence. He would be up and gone for the day long before the young gentleman stirred. It wasn't my place or Mr. Harris's either to inform him if Mrs. De Vries chose not to let him know."

"Is it your impression that Mrs. De Vries kept a good many of these inebriated nights from her husband?"

"The judgment isn't mine to make, Miss MacKenzie."

"But if you had to guess, Mrs. Mitchell?"

"I would say that this is a household in which lives are lived separately." She paused and swirled the teacup again. "Not many questions are asked upstairs."

"I'm sure you and Mr. Harris talked about Leonard after the young man's unfortunate demise," Prudence said. She'd led Mrs. Mitchell down a meandering path to make the direct questions less obvious. "I wonder if Mr. Whitley's preferential treatment of Leonard led to the footman's taking advantage of the situation."

"I don't know what you mean."

"Did he, for example, ask for and expect to be given extra time off? Was he often late back from his half days and was he reprimanded for it?"

"Mr. Harris disciplines the male staff, as I think I may have mentioned."

"Yes, but you also led me to believe that you and Mr. Harris work in tandem, as it were. That you value each other's opinions."

"We do." The housekeeper paused, as if to think through how to phrase what she would say next. "I don't see what harm it will bring to tell you that we did talk about Leonard. More than once. And after he did what he did, we tried to puzzle out the why of it. Mr. Harris was especially hit hard. He wondered if there was something about Leonard that he should have noticed, something in the days leading up to when he took his life. I told him not to be concerned, that none of us had the slightest notion he was in such desperate straits."

"Was Leonard Abbott treated differently than the other servants?"

"I can't deny that he got away with a few things. He was Mr. Whitley's favorite. And whenever Mr. Canfield stayed over, he always asked for him."

"You know we found a Tiffany ring box in his bedroom? And an envelope full of betting slips?"

"And I heard there was a snuffbox in his trousers pocket, also."

Proving once and for all that servants always knew everything that happened in the house where they worked.

"Can you think of any reason why he'd have those items in his possession?"

Mrs. Mitchell poured hot water into the teapot, then waited for the leaves to steep. "The snuffbox was a gift," she said. "Everyone downstairs knew Mr. Canfield had given it to him. Leonard used to sit at the table in the servants' hall with the snuffbox out beside his hand so we could all see it. Then he'd take a pinch and sneeze into his handkerchief. I've always thought snuff was a dirty habit, myself."

"The snuffbox contained cocaine when he hanged himself, Mrs. Mitchell," Prudence said, watching closely for signs of surprise or shock.

"So Mr. Harris said. But I know snuff when I see and smell it, Miss MacKenzie. And it was snuff he put up his nose in the servants' hall."

"What about the betting slips?"

"Mr. Whitley bet on the horses all the time. So did the other young gentlemen. You'd see Leonard stuffing bits of paper into his pockets and slipping out the kitchen door when he had no business leaving the house. He'd come home all out of breath, like he'd run to the bookie on the corner and back. I never saw him with any money, but he was placing bets, that's for sure." She hesitated. "I've thought about that Tiffany ring box, but Mrs. De Vries never told me she was missing any of her jewelry. And she would have, so I could question the maids and search their rooms. It might be that he found it somewhere and picked it up for no good reason except it was from Tiffany. A girl could be fooled into thinking the gift she was getting was worth a lot more than it actually was if it came in a Tiffany-blue box."

"Was Abbott walking out with someone?"

Mrs. Mitchell suppressed a low-voiced laugh. "He wasn't much of a one for the ladies," she said.

"So he wouldn't put a cheap ring into a Tiffany box to buy a girl's affections?"

"He might have thought to sell it to one of the other footmen," Mrs. Mitchell ventured.

"Was he the kind of person to try a little blackmail if he thought he could get away with it?" Prudence asked.

The housekeeper's startled expression told her that blackmail had been the furthest thought from Mrs. Mitchell's assessment of the dead footman turned valet. It was obvious that she immediately began running rapidly through the household roster to determine who, if anyone, could be hiding a misdeed serious enough to warrant extortion. Had one of the maids stolen a piece of seldom worn jewelry and then tried to dispose of the box in which it had been stored? Been caught in the act by Leonard? But if he wasn't much for the ladies, what could the maid have offered in return for his silence?

Prudence knew the moment Mrs. Mitchell realized that Abbott's blackmail victim was possibly Mrs. De Vries herself. And she also intuited that the housekeeper must have suspected that her employer's wife was too secretive about some of her afternoon excursions for them to be entirely innocent. A lady with nothing to conceal was always open about her whereabouts, never met alone with a gentleman not of her immediate family, and did not return to her home after an outing looking flustered or with her hair slightly disarranged.

"We'll never know whether Leonard would take advantage of someone else's misfortune," Mrs. Mitchell said stiffly. She genuinely liked Lena De Vries, who was by far the most gracious mistress she'd ever worked for. "Will we?"

"I think we'll find out a great deal about him," Prudence answered. "He's left footprints."

CHAPTER 23

The unopened envelope inscribed to Leonard Abbott that Mrs. Mitchell handed over to Prudence bore a return address on Long Island, in a town Prudence had never heard of and had difficulty locating on a map.

"It must be very small," she told Josiah, who had found the office atlas and studied it with her.

"Probably not much bigger than a crossroads village," he said dubiously. "Not on the coast, so the chief means of livelihood is likely to be farming."

"The letter is from his sister," Prudence said, rereading it now with a mental picture of where the writer lived. "She tells him to take care of his throat this winter because he had snow coughs when he was a child. Whatever those are."

"I'm going to guess that as soon as the first bad snowfall isolates the farms out there, people start hacking and sneezing and don't stop until spring. Hence a snow cough."

"It's not a long letter," Prudence continued, smiling at Josiah's logical explanation.

"And not very well written," he added, pointing out the

awkwardly penned sentences and misspellings. "A sister of limited education."

"But caring," Prudence chided. "She writes that everyone is well, but doesn't mention any names. Presumably he knows whom she means. The dairy herd has grown by three cows and a flock of ducks has been added to the chickens they already raise. The family sounds moderately prosperous."

"Why didn't the housekeeper open it when it arrived?"

"She said he got a letter every other month or so. This one arrived after William had had his stroke. Mrs. Mitchell didn't open it right away because she didn't want to have to make the decision to write the parents about their son's death. Not so much that he *was* dead, but the manner of it."

"But she would have done so eventually?"

Prudence nodded. "Either she or Mr. Harris, the butler. Neither of them wanted to bother Lena with it, not when she had William's condition to deal with and wasn't well herself. But she would have had to be informed that they now had an address for Leonard's next of kin. There's a terrible stigma to suicide. I can't even imagine how a family in a small community would handle it."

"What will happen now?"

"Geoffrey has sent Amos out on the train. He'll give them the news in person and hand over Abbott's few effects. Lena insisted on paying a month's wages."

"I don't envy him, having to tell a family that one of its members took his own life."

"What seems strangest to me is that the police found no photographs of relatives when they searched Leonard's room. Neither did the maids who cleaned it. He'd apparently thrown away or burned whatever mail he received from them, and as far as the butler and the housekeeper knew, he never visited."

"The Brooklyn Bridge has been open for more than six years now."

"Exactly," Prudence said. "The trip to Brooklyn and then further out on the island isn't that difficult anymore."

"So Leonard Abbott was estranged from them?"

"That's my best guess right now. Somehow he got from small farm to big city household via one of the most dependable domestic employment agencies I know of."

"He had to have had good references," Josiah said. "Possibly genuine. Probably forged."

"Amos will have the whole story when he gets back." Prudence tumbled the Tiffany ring box in the palm of her hand, opening and closing it as if a woman's diamond or emerald ring would miraculously appear when she raised the lid.

She'd seen Lena give Jasper Owens one valuable piece of jewelry at Morgan's viewing; she didn't doubt that what was missing from this box had also found its way into Owens's pocket. And then to a fence or a jeweler who didn't ask questions. But even Tiffany's investigators wouldn't be able to tell her what the box had once contained. She'd examined it carefully; there was nothing like a serial number or anything else distinctive to differentiate it from hundreds of other robin-egg blue boxes exactly like it.

The only other clue they had to whatever secret Leonard Abbott had been concealing that was worth his life was the apparent link to Aubrey Canfield. A footman with aspirations to become a valet and the son of a wealthy and socially prominent New York family that could trace its proud lineage to the original Dutch settlers. One of them ascending the ladder of accomplishment, the other plunging downward. The Knickerbocker asking for the Long Island farm boy by name. Morgan Whitley making it easy for his friend Aubrey to cross a social divide he should never have attempted to leap.

Geoffrey had already confided his suspicions, but until Amos returned with supporting evidence, they could be no more than that. Intuitions of a proclivity and possible crime so abhorrent to society that a man tarred with the brush of innuendo might never emerge unscathed.

Aubrey had been an only son, the eldest of the two Canfield children to survive into adulthood. His sister had made her debut at the first Assembly Ball in mid-December, at the same event where Lady Rotherton breathed on Lena's diamond necklace and discovered that many of the stones were fakes.

For a moment, Prudence wondered what case she and Geoffrey would be investigating now had her aunt not produced that damning exhalation. Would the dead jeweler and his assistant still be alive? Leonard Abbott and Aubrey Canfield, whatever connection there was between them? Geoffrey often said it was a useless exercise to speculate on the *what ifs* of life, but sometimes it was impossible not to.

"I'm going out, Josiah," Prudence said, making up her mind before it got too late in the afternoon to pay a social call.

He waited, eyebrows raised, but she didn't choose to elucidate.

He'd have to question Danny Dennis when the hansom cab driver got back from taking her to wherever it was she was going.

"Mrs. Canfield and Miss Letisha are not receiving," the butler said, shocked that someone of Miss Prudence MacKenzie's social standing would think that ladies in a house of mourning would be welcoming callers in the ordinary way.

"Please inform Miss Letisha that I'm here," Prudence told him, stepping through the doorway as if he weren't standing there trying to bar her way. "You may make it clear to her that this is not a social call."

Ten minutes later he ushered her upstairs to the small parlor where Letisha Canfield wrote letters and read the inspirational books approved by her mother. As well as the novels she and other daring young women passed among themselves. Her debutante season had come to an abrupt end when her brother died, as had Prudence's when her father succumbed to a heart attack. They had that in common, as well as a basic stubbornness of character that translated into a yearning for independence.

"The butler said you insisted he tell me this was not a social call," Letisha said when they had settled themselves before the fire and she'd rung for tea. "I confess I'm intrigued."

"I'm sorry to intrude," Prudence began, "but it's important, Letisha."

"I knew Aubrey would die tragically. You can't be the sister of someone with all of his weaknesses and not fear what the future will bring."

Prudence had expressed her condolences at the funeral. Now she simply reached out one hand to briefly clasp Letisha's fingers. "I know you were close," she said, not adding that she couldn't remember the exact number of years separating the brother and sister.

"I was just putting my hair up when he graduated from Harvard." Letisha touched the perfect bun nestled at the nape of her neck, as though recalling the moment when she had changed her appearance from child to woman. "We grew apart while he was away. Perfectly natural, of course. Things changed when he moved back home. My brother was a very troubled soul, Prudence. He seemed determined not to burden me with his problems, but I knew he was suffering. Sometimes I'd wake up in the middle of the night and tiptoe into his bedroom just to reassure myself that he'd made it home alive. He'd be lying across his bed exactly the way he must have fallen into it, arms trailing to the floor, shoes still on, red-faced and snoring like an old man. I've known for a long time that the drink would kill him. I started mourning his death well before it happened."

"It was an unfortunate accident," Prudence said.

"He should never have gone out on that boat." Letisha's brows furrowed and her fingers clenched themselves into fists. "He began every morning with cognac or whiskey in his coffee, and he more or less drank throughout the day. Whiskey and wine at lunch; whiskey and beer in the afternoon; whiskey, wine, and brandy at dinner. He was steady enough on dry land, but the deck of a sailboat is no place for a man with that much alcohol in his blood."

"I understand the boom knocked him overboard."

"If it hadn't been that, it would have been something else. Sooner or later he was bound to end up in the water. His bad luck that it happened in December. Between the pneumonia and the filth he'd swallowed, he didn't stand a chance. I don't blame anyone but Aubrey himself for his death. Morgan nearly lost his own life going in after him, and Everett is a skilled sailor, not one to overload a boat or go out when there are gale warnings posted. Aubrey and I grew up sailing together in Newport," Letisha explained. "It drove my mother crazy because girls aren't supposed to know how to handle small boats."

"I learned to sail off Staten Island," Prudence confided. "With a fisherman's daughter and her brothers." She still missed Nora Kenney, obscenely killed two years before by a madman.

"Aubrey didn't have many friends," Letisha continued. "They began to drop away as the drinking got worse. Morgan hung on, probably because they were two of a kind. And Everett looked out for both of them whenever he could. The others on the boat that morning may have been the only companions he had left. I think my brother had become very lonely."

"The De Vries housekeeper said that Aubrey was a frequent guest." Prudence began to turn the conversation in the direction she wanted it to go.

"My father grew very hard on him," Letisha said. "He sent him twice to the Keeley Institute. Each time Aubrey came back, he declared himself cured. And perhaps for a few weeks or a couple of months, he'd stay sober. Then something would set him off, he'd take that first drink, and it was as though he'd never had the tonics and the injections of bichloride of gold.

Aubrey preferred staying with Morgan to being called a disgrace to the Canfield name and things much worse than that."

"He was well seen to there," Prudence said. "He even shared the footman turned valet who took care of Morgan and Everett."

Letisha's shoulders froze. The smile on her face hardened into a rigid mask.

"His name was Leonard Abbott," Prudence continued, as if she hadn't noticed Letisha's reaction. "He hanged himself in the attic. Perhaps Aubrey mentioned the incident."

"Why are you asking these questions, Prudence? What are you after?"

"Information. Answers to the same questions you must have asked yourself. Must still be asking. Your brother, his best friend, and a favored servant who waited on them are all dead. An accident, a tragic mishap, and a suicide. There has to be something linking them together, Letisha. Even coincidence doesn't explain the timing of their deaths."

"Aubrey was crushed by the footman's suicide," Letisha said. "He told me over and over again that he could not fathom what had driven him to do it. Morgan was bitter. He blamed himself because Leonard Abbott was part of his stepfather's household and he'd used him to cover up some of the activities he knew William wouldn't have approved of."

"Abbott placed bets for him? For Morgan's friends as well?"

"I suppose you'll find out anyway," Letisha said. "It can't matter very much now, can it? They all gambled, all of that set Morgan and Aubrey hung out with. Except Everett. He was probably the only voice of reason and restraint in the group. But he was rarely with them. Except for the sailing. Most of the time Everett was working or squiring Lorinda Bouwmeester around town. Everyone is expecting an engagement to be announced."

"Tell me about the betting."

"All I know is what Aubrey owned up to whenever he was desperate for money. I couldn't give him much, but I always had some pocket change that was better than nothing. The way he talked they mostly used Leonard Abbott to place bets on horses when they couldn't be at the track themselves. Aubrey rarely won, but when he did, he forgot about all the bad times. It was as if they'd never happened. Fortune had finally smiled in his direction. The Fates were on his side. Every bromide you can think of, Prudence. Then he'd lose. He drank to celebrate when he was victorious and he drank to console himself when he got trounced. It broke my heart."

"He consoled himself with Leonard Abbott." It was as loaded an assertion as Prudence could make, worthy of her aunt Gillian's frankness.

Letisha stared at her.

"It was never a secret below stairs at the De Vries house," Prudence said, stretching the truth as far as she dared.

"I don't know the words for it," Letisha whispered. "I don't even know how to talk about it. Aubrey was my brother, and whatever he did or didn't do had no bearing on the love we shared. We were the only two in this house who truly cared for one another. If being with another man made him happy, then so be it. The only thing I worried about was that Father would find out."

Letisha's erect carriage had melted like candle wax. She sat slumped in her chair as though years of inflexible training in ladylike posture had never taken place. "I don't need smelling salts," she said when she saw Prudence open her reticule. "I despise women who loll about with the vapors. I'm stronger than I look." Her voice was reed thin, but she didn't try to keep the rancor out of her tone. "Do you have what you came for?"

"I had to confirm what we suspected," Prudence said. "I hope you can understand that."

"When you say *we*, you mean you and Mr. Hunter?"

"Yes."

"Do you enjoy playing at being an inquiry agent, Prudence? Do you like prying into other people's lives?"

"That's not what it's about, Letisha."

"Then what is it? You made it possible for Morgan to remain at my brother's bedside when anyone could tell he hadn't the strength to do it alone. Then you presume on that moment to prey on my grief and dig around in Aubrey's private life for a secret he never meant anyone to discover. What next, Prudence?"

"No one will ever know, Letisha. Neither Geoffrey nor I will reveal what you've told me. I promise you. It won't appear in any report we write." She would have liked to leave it there, but she couldn't. Not if she intended to be honest with the young woman whose trust she had just abused. "But the relationship between Aubrey and Leonard Abbott speaks to motive. That's why I had to uncover it. You can see that, can't you?"

"Motive for what? A suicide and a drunken fall off the deck of a sailboat?"

"No, Letisha. Motive for murder."

CHAPTER 24

What Amos Lang discovered on his visit to the Abbott farm on Long Island confirmed what Prudence had learned from Letisha Canfield.

"Take your time, Amos," Geoffrey told the exhausted ex-Pinkerton who had come directly to the Hunter and MacKenzie offices from the train station.

Prudence summed up the profiles they were building of the three young men whose lives intertwined in the months before their deaths. Two scions of prominent families and the footman who might have been the lover of one of them.

Amos nodded in agreement as he wolfed down the German pastries and coffee Josiah set in front of him and warmed his feet against the pot of hot coals that normally glowed under the secretary's desk in the winter. The train had been freezing and he'd leaped aboard without time to buy sandwiches for the return journey.

"Sisters are more forgiving than other women," he said, wiping traces of cream and buttery crumbs from his lips. "And fathers can be the cruelest of men." He flipped open the narrow notebook that slid easily into a breast pocket. Like Geoffrey, he had been well trained in accuracy of recall by Allan Pinkerton. "Leonard's father disowned him over an incident his sister was reluctant to do more than mention."

"This is the sister whose letter we read?" Prudence asked.

"Sophie," Amos said. "Older than Leonard by a number of years. She seems to be the daughter chosen by her parents to remain unmarried and on the farm to care for them as they age."

"How sad for her." Prudence imagined a small woman, thin and cowed by a gaunt, domineering father and a heavyset, narrow-lipped mother.

"In this case, I believe it suits her," Amos said. "Once Sophie Abbott inherits, she'll be well situated and independent. She's careful not to rile either of her parents, but I think that's only because she has an eye to her future. There isn't any love on that farm. It's all duty and obedience to the father. Who, by the way, is not a man I'd want to claim as my progenitor."

"You're certain he's the reason his son left?" Josiah asked. He rarely did more than take notes during a debriefing, but this dead man's story seemed to touch him more than the dozens of others he'd heard.

"The father threw him out with the clothes on his back. Not much more than that. Told him never to darken his door again. Or words to that effect. Sophie didn't hear from Leonard for several years, not until he'd gone to work for the De Vries family. Then wrote to tell her he was happy for once, settled."

"The letter couldn't have been sent to the Abbott farm," Geoffrey commented.

"It went to General Delivery at the nearest village. The postmistress knew the family," Amos confirmed. "Sophie sells eggs and garden produce at the street market there every week. She was able to send and pick up communications without her parents being any the wiser. She and Leonard were cautious. They wrote each other no more frequently than once every couple of months. It was enough to exchange basic news and ensure they didn't lose touch. She never brought the letters back to the farm. She burned them before leaving her market stall." He touched the spot on his chest where his heart beat. "She told me she memorized each one of them before destroying it."

"How long did you have with her?" Prudence asked.

"Less than an hour. Leonard's father shut the farmhouse door in my face as soon as I'd told him his son was dead. He didn't want any details, not even where the body was buried. Sophie was waiting for me where the road leading to the Abbott farm joined the highway. We stood in the shade of a tree and talked. It was obvious from the first that she and Leonard had once been very close and remained so even after he'd been forced to leave."

"Everyone needs someone to love," Prudence remarked, thinking of Letisha and Aubrey Canfield.

"In the final letter Sophie received from him, Leonard told her that he'd found the one he was meant to spend his life with. *There are problems, but we mean to overcome them.* She quoted that to me, and asked if I knew what her brother could have meant when he wrote it. I didn't tell her anything but that we would probably never know. She seemed to accept it. My reading of Sophie Abbott is that she has no illusions about life."

"Could Aubrey and Leonard have stolen the diamonds together?" Prudence wondered. "Was that how they were planning to overcome the obstacles standing in their way?"

"They had opportunity," Geoffrey speculated. "Abbott as valet on the floor where the family bedrooms are located, Aubrey also there as a frequent overnight guest. If we're able to check the dates, we may find that some of them overlap with when Lena's necklace had been removed from the Tiffany vault."

"Letisha said that Morgan's friends often gathered in his suite of rooms before going to a ball or debutante soirée," Prudence reminded them.

"Yes, but I question whether Aubrey or Abbott had the expertise to extract a diamond from its setting and replace it with a fake," Geoffrey said. "It had to be done so carefully that there were no scratch marks and the prongs holding in the diamond didn't look as if they'd been reset."

"Amelia Taylor," Prudence said. "Lena's lady's maid, with the jeweler father who taught her how to care for precious stones."

"Means and opportunity," Josiah chimed in, scribbling away in his incomprehensible Gregg shorthand.

"Motive?" questioned Geoffrey.

"It had to be money," Prudence declared. "She would be aware of the special closeness between Aubrey and Leonard. It's possible she was ready to blackmail both of them if they didn't cut her in to what they were planning. Where else would they get the funds to surmount the problems Abbott wrote his sister about? I think they may have been intending to run away together. Stealing and selling Lena's diamonds was their way of amassing the funds to do it."

"Did Morgan know about it?" There were few things Geoffrey enjoyed as much as watching Prudence work through a case with the quick, incisive vitality of a well-trained legal mind.

"I'm not ready to pronounce on that yet," she answered. "I'd like to think he wasn't part of the scheme in any way, not even to ignoring what he might have suspected was going on. But the jury is still out on that point." She grinned as Geoffrey quietly applauded her conclusion.

"There's no one left to testify to his innocence," Geoffrey mused. "Except Lena. And I think she was too preoccupied with hiding the affair she was having with Jasper Owens to be very aware of what her son might or might not have been up to."

"Amelia Taylor could easily have concealed what she and her confederates were doing with the necklace, if that's what happened," Prudence said. "A lady's maid is usually the most trusted servant of any household. She's at her employer's side throughout the day, sharing her most intimate moments."

"Not all of them," Geoffrey reminded her, black eyes shining mischievously.

"You know what I mean," Prudence chided. "A lady has no secrets from her maid because the maid is in the bedroom and boudoir when the lady isn't there; she has ready access to her lady's writing desk and the daily journal she keeps."

"Does every lady keep a journal?" Josiah asked curiously.

"It's the first lesson a governess drills into her charges," Prudence answered. "Not until someone else comes along and reads what you've written do you realize how dangerous it can be to put your true feelings into words." She smiled to take the edge off what she'd said. "I didn't have any pesky brothers or sisters to invade my privacy, but I did have a stepmother."

"Then there's a possibility that Amelia Taylor could have been blackmailing Lena," Geoffrey said. "That Lena knew about the missing diamonds and was obliged to keep silent about the thefts or be exposed to her husband as an adulteress."

"Possible," Prudence admitted, "but too far-fetched, I think." She rarely contradicted Geoffrey, but in this instance she was relying on her woman's intuition. "Lena's crime has been to give away small pieces of jewelry that could be easily pawned or sold. It may not even be a crime if the jewelry could be proved to belong to her through gifting."

"So we take her off the list of suspects?" Josiah inquired, his pencil at the ready to strike through her name.

"Not yet," Geoffrey replied. "I'd rather have too many suspects than miss the one guilty party."

"Though in this case, we may have multiple crimes committed for different reasons by several guilty parties," Prudence said.

"All of them coming out of the woodwork because Lady Rotherton has an exceptionally good eye for an authentic stone," Geoffrey said. "Which reminds me, has she said anything more about going back to England?"

"She asked me the other day what I'd done with the Dakota

apartment my father bought for my late stepmother," Prudence said. "I told her it's been standing empty for over a year now, like the Staten Island house. She said she might make an appointment with the building manager to see it."

"If you had no objection?"

"Aunt Gillian doesn't consider whether anyone could object to whatever it is she intends to do," Prudence said. "I imagine she's looking out over Central Park right now, deciding whether Victoria's apartment would make a comfortable New York City pied-à-terre."

Geoffrey shuddered.

Josiah wondered if he should order more imported English teas.

"It's so far-fetched an idea," Lena said, fingers twitching at the folds of her black silk dress. "Taylor would never do something like that. She's devoted to me, and she hardly ever leaves the house."

"We're following every thread," Prudence explained. "Which is what you said you wanted us to do."

"I never thought it would lead you to my lady's maid."

"How close was she to Leonard Abbott?" Prudence asked before Lena could decide she didn't want to have this conversation.

"Not close at all, as far as I know. Taylor is senior staff and at least fifteen years older than Leonard was. Senior staff tend to keep to themselves. They have a preferred status in the servants' hall and they guard it jealously. Most of them have worked very hard to rise from the ranks. I can't imagine any of the five of them doing anything to jeopardize their positions."

"Who are the five?"

"Cook, of course. The housekeeper. Our butler. William's valet, who is now looking after Everett. And my lady's maid, Amelia Taylor. Actually, we should probably raise that number to six. The coachman is also senior staff, but not quite of the same status as the indoor servants. I know you and Mr. Hunter have spoken to all of them."

"We have. But that was during the period when Mr. De Vries limited our time with members of the household."

"I hadn't realized he'd done that until we were discussing the new investigation," Lena said. "Why William would hire your firm and then try to limit what he'd allow you to do doesn't make sense. It's throwing away good money, and my husband has always been a man whose business deals had to be profitable."

"At some point he made up his mind that Morgan was the thief, and there was no turning back. He never gave us the chance to prove his innocence."

"The doctors tell me William won't recover," Lena said. "He may seem to improve from time to time, but from what I understand, the gains will be slight and fleeting. Each time he falls back, he'll sink a little deeper into the affliction. Until finally he lapses into a coma. It's only a matter of time."

"I'm so sorry, Lena. I know the strain on you must be enormous," Prudence said.

"That's why I can't believe Taylor has had anything to do with stealing those wretched diamonds," Lena said. "She has a cup of tea at my elbow before I think to ask for it. I don't have to decide which black gown to put on in the morning; Taylor has the perfect choice laid out for me. When I sit by William's bedside, she brings her sewing to keep me company so the nurses can slip away for a few private moments. I know you think her father's expertise has somehow made her a suspect, but the man has been dead for years. He taught his daughter how to care for precious stones, not how to cut and set them."

It was on the tip of Prudence's tongue to assure Lena that as far as she was concerned, the lady's maid was no longer under suspicion. But that was singularly un-Pinkerton-like, an emotional response having nothing to do with the logic of the case.

She looked carefully at Morgan's mother, trying to decide what it was about her that seemed so different today.

Despite the hours at William's bedside and the everlasting grief over the manner of her son's death, Lena De Vries had not faded into a shadow of her former self the way so many bereft women did. Instead of draining all color from her skin, the black of her mourning dress emphasized her pale porcelain beauty, and there was even a hint of rose in her cheeks. Which were plump with health rather than sunken from tears and lack of sleep. *Taylor must be taking very good care of her indeed,* Prudence thought. If she didn't know better, she would say that Lena had recently returned from taking the mineral rich waters at one of the health and beauty spas that dotted the hills along the Hudson River. Her eyes were clear and sparkling, her fingernails smooth and buffed, her almost plump hands holding a second crustless ham and butter sandwich.

Very odd.

"I'd like to speak to Taylor, if that's convenient," Prudence requested, not exactly sure what questions she would ask.

"I'll send her in to you," Lena promised, popping the last of the sandwich into her mouth. "It's time for me to check on William. Do you mind seeing yourself out when you've finished, Prudence?"

"Not at all."

Prudence could have sworn that Lena had put on a few pounds since the last time she saw her.

By the time Amelia Taylor knocked softly at the parlor door and let herself in, Prudence had decided she couldn't come right out and ask the kind of probing questions that would antagonize the faithful lady's maid; she'd have to be subtle about it.

"I want you to know that we appreciate all the information you've already given us, Taylor," Prudence began. "You've been most helpful."

"I'm happy to do whatever Mrs. De Vries requests."

"Do sit down."

Plainly ill at ease at the informality, Taylor perched on the edge of a heavily cushioned Louis XV fauteuil. Like Lena, she was dressed head to toe in black, but the overall effect was one of sallow dyspepsia rather than good health. The lady's maid smelled of the peppermint drops she chewed to keep chronic indigestion at bay.

"I know your father has passed away," Prudence began, "but I wonder if your mother is still alive and if you are fortunate enough to have brothers and sisters."

"My mother died shortly after I went into service, and I was the only one of her babies to survive into adulthood."

"How lonely for you, Taylor."

"You're never lonely in a big house," she said. "There are always people around to talk to. It's very comforting."

"Yes, but they're not family," Prudence insisted.

"As good as," Taylor maintained.

"I gather Mrs. De Vries is very pleased with you."

"I do my best, miss."

"Rather more than that, from what I hear."

"She's a very gracious lady. Everyone below stairs says so."

"It's a terrible shame what happened to Leonard." Prudence abruptly switched gears, watching to see if Taylor would give herself away by a sudden wash of tears or the red flush of a guilty conscience.

"We none of us can figure it out," Taylor said, as calmly as though they were consulting on a hemline. "Mr. Harris has said it's past time to stop speculating. And I agree."

The De Vries butler might be trying to curb the staff's curiosity, but Prudence still had questions that needed answers. "Were you close to Leonard?" she asked. "Was he one of the staff who made it impossible to be lonely?"

"Leonard always kept to himself. Except when he was sitting

at the table in the servants' hall. He liked to be noticed when he was playing with his snuffbox."

"The one Mr. Canfield gave him?"

"We older women knew what it meant, but as long as Mr. Harris hadn't figured it out and come down hard on him, we let it go."

"How often did you handle the Marie Antoinette necklace, Taylor?"

The lady's maid seemed confused at the abrupt shift in questioning, as though for a moment she'd forgotten the theft that had begun it all. "Every time Mrs. De Vries wore it," she finally answered. "And whenever it needed cleaning."

"Did Leonard ever come into the room where you were working on it?"

"It always stayed in the dressing room or the boudoir," Taylor said. "It was too valuable a piece to be taken from room to room."

"I asked you if Leonard ever watched you cleaning the necklace."

It was as though the answer were being slowly and painfully torn from her throat. "Yes, he did. Many times, miss."

"That hardly strikes me as something a footman should be doing."

"He wasn't a footman by then. He was a valet, though Mr. Harris was refusing to name him as such until he had more experience at it. But he took care of Mr. Whitley and Mr. Rinehart, and the other gentleman, Mr. Canfield. Whenever he stayed the night as Mr. Whitley's guest."

"Is that what he was doing on the bedroom floor, seeing to the gentlemen and incidentally admiring Mrs. De Vries's jewelry?"

"Leonard liked elegant things. He often said he wasn't going to stay a servant all his life."

"What did you take that to mean, Taylor?"

Her cheeks flushed bright red and she fidgeted in her chair. "I'm sure I don't know, miss."

"I think you do. And I also think you'd better tell me if you want to avoid angering Mrs. De Vries. She's adamant that everyone in her household cooperate with the investigation. That means answering the questions I ask."

"He meant that he didn't want a future waiting on gentlemen. He wanted to be one himself. Be a gentleman, I mean."

"And how did he propose to accomplish that feat?"

"It fell into his lap, miss. The first time Mr. Canfield had had so much to drink that he couldn't go home. Leonard took care of him. After that, Mr. Canfield made sure to ask for him if Mr. Harris sent up a different footman."

"So Mr. Canfield became Leonard's way out of service?"

Taylor nodded, eyes fixed on the tips of her shoes peeping out below the hem of her black dress. Prudence read excruciating embarrassment and profound humiliation in the gesture.

"If you didn't steal the diamonds out of the Marie Antoinette necklace, did Leonard Abbott do it?" It was a gamble, because if Taylor denied having anything to do with the theft, there was no way to be sure she was telling the truth.

Taylor's head came up. "I honestly don't know, Miss MacKenzie." She sat stiffly in place, as though newly determined to save herself, even if it meant accusing someone else. "It's possible. There were times when the necklace was left on the dressing table with no one to guard it. Mrs. De Vries didn't see it as being careless; she trusted everyone in the house. But I know for a fact that others besides me had opportunities they shouldn't have had."

"How long would it take to pry a stone loose and put another in its place?"

"Seconds, if the thief knew what he was doing."

"Was Leonard Abbott skilled enough to be able to do it?"

"He had to polish the gentlemen's gold cuff links and cigar and cigarette cases. Tighten the prongs around stones set in their stickpins when they became loose. Any valet worth his salt trains himself to do whatever is necessary to keep his employer well turned out."

"Was that a *yes* or a *no*, Taylor?"

"He could have done it. Leonard was fast and smooth enough to have been able to do it."

"Not once, but several times?"

"As often as he had to. He was desperate to be out of livery."

By the time Prudence had dismissed Amelia Taylor and left the De Vries house, she was as convinced as she had once been skeptical that Leonard Abbott and Aubrey Canfield had managed to pull off one of the most cleverly planned thefts she had ever heard of.

But both of them were dead.

So where were the diamonds?

CHAPTER 25

"None of the stolen diamonds has shown up here," the head of Tiffany's security division told Geoffrey. "We purchase almost exclusively from reputable dealers we've used for years. In the case of the French Crown jewels, which was arguably one of our most talked about transactions, there was no doubt whatsoever that the gems we acquired matched their provenance."

"Is it possible for a stone to pass unremarked through a number of less than honest dealers and yet somehow end up in a setting designed by a firm such as Tiffany or perhaps a much smaller but still trustworthy firm?" Prudence asked. She was thinking of the pieces that James Carpenter had designed and sold from his shop. The jeweler had been murdered and his premises emptied of stock. There had to be a reason for that.

"Anything is possible, Miss MacKenzie, but we have so many safeguards in our system that we've made it highly unlikely for a thief to penetrate our defenses."

"It sounds like a military action," she said.

"We guard our clients against fraud of any kind."

"And you have a reputation to protect," Geoffrey added.

He hadn't expected anything less from the world's most well-known creator of fine jewelry, silver pieces, and stained glass, but to be thorough, he'd had to ask.

And to Prudence, the world of rare stones and one-of-a-kind designs had become unexpectedly fascinating. Appalled at her niece's ignorance, Lady Rotherton had insisted on pointing out the finer features of the jewels she had brought with her from England. A brief but intense introduction that had enthralled her niece. Prudence was far from being an expert, but she now had at least a glimmering of the kind of education her aunt considered essential for any lady considering marriage. Which was as much a business proposition as purchasing stocks or property, Lady Rotherton reminded her.

Or, as Prudence preferred to consider her newly acquired jewelry skills, a necessary part of her burgeoning career as a private detective.

"Where else can we find out about what might have happened to Lena's diamonds?" she asked when they had left Tiffany.

"I think it's time to bring Ned Hayes back into the picture," Geoffrey suggested. "Billy McGlory is laying low for the time being, but Ned has other contacts."

"It's hard to imagine Ned was ever a New York City police detective," Prudence said as they made their way to where Danny Dennis and Mr. Washington waited for them. "He seems more comfortable in what you always call the underworld than he does above ground."

"It's hard to explain," Geoffrey said. "I'm not sure even Ned himself understands all the whys of it, but you're right, Prudence. He does fit in better with a certain category of men who inhabit Billy McGlory's world. The difference is that Ned has principles he's never compromised. That type of criminal rarely comes across such stark honesty. It sets Ned apart from everyone else in his realm. McGlory values the quality and the man who personifies it."

*   *   *

They found Ned ensconced in his long dead father's easy chair, several packs of cards stacked on a writing table in front of him. Pallid and trembly, he was a man struggling to face daylight again after a bad bender.

It had been a month since he and Geoffrey had gone to Bellevue to view the body of the jeweler's assistant and bring his clothes back to the office to be examined, but Ned had a habit of disappearing without warning. He'd so far never failed to answer a summons from his friend, but he rarely appeared at Geoffrey's office without one. And he never answered questions about where he'd been or what he'd been doing.

"Pick a card, Prudence," Ned ordered, trying to fan out a deck where she could reach it.

His hands shook so badly the cards scattered over the tabletop.

Prudence turned over the queen of spades.

"It's not the death card," Ned told her, "but it's not good luck, either."

She had no idea what he was talking about. It sounded like a tarot reading without the special images that fortune-tellers used.

"We're here for a consultation," Geoffrey said, nimble fingers picking up the cards, shuffling them, fanning them out in a perfect arc. "Ace of hearts," he announced before he turned it over.

"I hate a show-off," Ned muttered.

"I think Mr. Ned could use some coffee, Tyrus," Prudence said.

The ancient body servant who had been taking care of the only Hayes child since the day he was born shook his head. "He's had all the coffee he's gonna hold, Miss Prudence. And he's right nearly sober. Pretty soon it'll be time to shovel in some food."

"I told you a hundred times I don't want anything," Ned declared.

"Cain't keep nothin' down yet," Tyrus explained. "Leastwise he don't think he can."

He didn't need to say more. Geoffrey and the aged ex-slave had gone out hunting Ned more times than they cared to remember, asking for him at bar after bar until they finally found where he'd collapsed and fallen asleep over what he always promised Tyrus would be the last drink he ever took. Ned could only stay dried out and sober for an indeterminate amount of time before the itch had to be scratched. He'd lasted longer these past few months than ever before; his friends had begun to believe he really had taken his final drink. They should have known better.

"What kind of consultation?" Ned asked, Geoffrey's question finally making sense enough to answer.

"We need to find whoever bought the De Vries diamonds we think were originally sold to James Carpenter."

"Carpenter's dead."

"That's why we're here, Ned," Prudence said. "Tiffany hasn't bought them and Billy McGlory's not around to send out feelers for us."

"Geoff knows where to look. There aren't that many fences who can handle quality diamonds without leaving a trail."

"I've exhausted my sources," Geoffrey said. "And so have the other ex-Pinks. Whoever took them off the thief's hands is buried deep."

"And you think I know who it might be?"

"I think you may be the only one." Geoffrey returned the deck of cards he'd been fanning to Ned's table. No more tricks.

"Mistuh Ned don't go nowhere by hisself," Tyrus said.

"You know we'd welcome you to come along," Prudence said. She had a particular fondness for the determined old man who never gave up on his charge.

"The fence I'm thinking of won't talk to either of you," Ned declared. "He'll disappear like smoke on a windy day if he so much as thinks I'm bringing you his way."

"Danny Dennis and Mr. Washington are waiting outside." It was as close to cajoling as Prudence could bring herself to get.

Ned looked up at her and nodded. "Only way I'm ever going to get some peace and quiet around here," he said, edging toward the front of his chair, a wave of ill-digested whiskey preceding him.

Geoffrey helped Ned to his feet and held him upright while Tyrus stuffed his arms into a coat, wound a wool scarf around his neck, and set a hat on his head. The January wind was fierce today and Ned wasn't in any condition to fight off a pneumonia.

"He'll be skating on the lake in Central Park." Ned's teeth chattered as he talked despite the hot bricks at his feet and the baked potato nestled in a wool sock that Tyrus had placed in his hands before climbing up to sit beside Danny Dennis atop the hansom cab.

"A fence who ice skates?" Prudence asked.

"He rides when the pond isn't iced over. And he goes to early morning mass at Saint Patrick's every day. That's how he's been able to do business for so long without getting caught."

"He buys stolen goods in the cathedral?"

"That's where he names a price and makes arrangements for delivery. The payoff doesn't happen until the goods are in his hands. And it's always done in a different place."

"Will he tell you what we want to find out?" Prudence had never known Ned Hayes to fail at working his contacts in New York's seedy criminal world, but this case had so far been nothing but dead ends.

"We go back a ways." Which meant whatever Ned needed it to mean. "Stay in the cab. Don't try to follow me to the pond. You'll only scare him off."

They watched Ned stomp and weave through the snow toward the frozen lake where dark-coated adults circled majestically and children in brightly colored mittens and knit hats
spun and chased each other, their laughter rising on puffs of
warm breath.

"Can you see anything?" Prudence asked, angling herself to
peer past Mr. Washington's large white rump without betraying
her presence.

"Mr. Hayes is talking to a little fellow who's sitting on a
bench taking off his skates," Danny said from his perch atop
the rear of the cab. "Standing up now. No bigger than an eight-
year-old, but thickset. He's like P.T. Barnum's General Tom
Thumb."

"A dwarf?" General Tom Thumb had been one of Barnum's
most famous attractions. Even though he'd been dead for more
than six years, Prudence still remembered being taken to see
him perform.

Geoffrey chuckled ruefully. "I should have known. None of
my men have heard anything about this fence for the last couple of years. We all thought he'd died or left the city. Nobody
knows his real name or where he lives, but everybody with a
stolen stone to sell would like to be able to deal with him. He
pays good money and there's never a trail for the police to follow. The man's as much a legend as Barnum's Tom Thumb,
Prudence, but for different reasons."

"Mr. Hayes is on his way back," Danny Dennis said. "But I
don't know where the little fellow has gotten to. I swear I haven't
taken my eyes off him. He just disappeared into thin air."

"That's another one of the legends he's created about himself," Geoffrey said. "He's as corporeal as the rest of us, but
he'd like you to believe he's as elusive as an elf. It's good cover."

"He says he hasn't laid eyes on a single one of the stones I
described," Ned Hayes reported as Tyrus bundled him in a
blanket, wedged him between Prudence and Geoffrey for extra
warmth, then climbed up to sit beside Danny Dennis again.

"I wouldn't have expected that," Geoffrey commented.

"He told me he knew there were some old, high quality stones being fenced, but he heard they were all recut before they appeared on the market. What he figures is they were too easily recognizable to do anything else with them. No professional would waste stones like that; he'd find some way to get rid of them without ruining them, even if he had to take them to Europe. It's the mark of an amateur to settle for wholesale cutting."

"Another useless lead," Prudence mourned. "I'm beginning to think we'll never get to the bottom of this, Geoffrey."

"There's one more thing we could try," Ned commented, breaking open the rapidly cooling baked potato he'd been given to warm his hands. Now that he was out and about with a case to solve, he'd shaken off his hangover and recovered his appetite.

"What's that?" Geoffrey asked.

"Is your aunt at home, Prudence?" Ned mumbled through a mouthful of floury potato.

"It's almost four o'clock. She'll be having her afternoon tea," Prudence said. The elaborate ritual had become as much a part of her household's routine as Josiah's brewing of imported leaves whenever Lady Rotherton graced the office with her presence.

"Let me work this out a moment." Ned scooped more potato flesh into his mouth. "Needs salt," he said.

"What we do is spread the word that there's an Englishwoman of means and social standing who's looking to purchase quality gems to take back to England with her. And that she'll buy what's on offer without provenance because she's planning to smuggle them past Customs to avoid paying duty. That should bring every twitchy rabbit out of his hole."

"How do we do it without revealing my identity?" Lady

Rotherton asked, eyes sparkling at the idea of pulling off what amounted to a nearly Pinkerton-like ruse. "And where do I meet your criminal rabbits?"

"We take a leaf from the book of New York's most successful fence," Geoffrey said. "You meet each one out in the open, at different locations. And we set up the meets through the want ads."

"It's done all the time," Ned explained, wolfing down cucumber-and-ham sandwiches with cup after cup of sugary tea. "Everybody reads the want ads; they're the best part of the newspaper."

"*Aristocratic British noblewoman wants to buy stolen diamonds?*" Lady Rotherton scoffed. "I think we need something a bit more discreet."

"There are certain code words and phrases our thief or his fence will recognize," Ned continued. "We'll write up the ad and Josiah can put it in all of tomorrow's papers. Morning, afternoon, and evening editions."

"Won't that attract too many of your dubious characters?" Lady Rotherton asked. She disliked not being in complete control of the plot Ned had sketched out.

"You won't be alone and there will never be more than one respondent at a time," Geoffrey promised. "Whoever answers the ad writes to a box number. We tackle them individually, and most of them we won't reply to at all."

"Trust me, my lady," Ned promised. "I can spot a likely suspect from a mile away."

"And you've done this type of thing successfully before?" she asked.

"More times than you can imagine," Ned lied. More often than not, the ploy had been a bust. But Lady Rotherton didn't need to know that.

"Where do we start?" Lady Rotherton asked, tugging on the bellpull for more tea and another plate of sandwiches.

"With the ad itself," Geoffrey replied.

He set his Pinkerton-style notebook and gold-nibbed fountain pen on the table, daring a conspiratorial wink at Prudence. She'd coached them in exactly how to seduce her aunt into agreeing to work the con. Adept as Prudence was at disguises, she knew she'd never manage as good an eccentric, titled English lady persona as her aunt Gillian.

Who was, after all, the real thing.

They settled on two responses to the ad that had only had to run for a single day to bring them what Ned called *the real deal.*

"They may not have the stones we're after," he said, eyes scanning a map of Manhattan, "but they'll know if they ever made it on to the market and probably how they were recut. And who did the job."

"What about the rest of these?" Josiah asked. He'd created a file for the letters that had quickly filled up the post office box they'd rented as being a safer and more efficient option than allowing answers to pile up at the various newspapers. The Hunter and MacKenzie secretary was loathe to let go of any scrap of paper pertaining to a case. You never knew when you might end up needing what at first glance had seemed irrelevant.

"Keep them if there's room in the cabinet," Geoffrey ordered, knowing that Josiah was likely to ignore any suggestion that he burn them in the fireplace or tear them into bits too tiny for anyone to piece together.

"We can take care of both of these tomorrow," Ned decided, pointing out the two locations he'd chosen, one in a small park near the Astor Hotel, the other in the enormous and always crowded waiting room of Grand Central Depot. Neither of their correspondents had identified himself by name, but both Ned and Josiah had agreed that one of them appeared far more cautious than the other.

"He'll be reassured by having a crowd around him," Ned had decided. "This other man sounds like the type not to want to be trapped in any kind of confined space. The park I'm directing him to doesn't have a fence or a gate to make him feel hemmed in."

It was Lady Rotherton's opinion that neither man would notice his surroundings once she mentioned the number of stones she wanted to purchase and the amount of cash money she was prepared to pay. She was also counting on the fact that even when she wasn't proposing an attractive business deal, most men found her irresistible.

The only thing they'd argued over was Prudence's determination to be somewhere nearby while her aunt was meeting with the presumed diamond thieves.

"If you're spotted, there won't be a second chance with either of these men," Geoffrey maintained. He didn't see how any red-blooded male could be unaware of Prudence's presence, even at a distance.

"Dress her as a nursemaid and give her a carriage to push through the park," Lady Rotherton suggested. "And at Grand Central Depot she can stand in one of the corners and sell flowers out of a bucket. No one will pay any attention to her."

It wasn't ideal, and she wouldn't be within hearing distance, but it was the best Prudence could get Geoffrey and Ned to agree to.

In the end, Prudence's elaborate disguises didn't matter at all.

The stones offered to the aristocratic English lady who planned to smuggle them through Customs weren't worth the risk or the money. Even recut, Lady Rotherton knew right away that what she was shown had never been intended to adorn the neck of Marie Antoinette. And when she leaned close enough so the Paris perfume blended especially for her enveloped the men she proceeded to question, neither of them could swear to ever having laid eyes on any of the famous stones Tiffany had brought back from France.

After Ned's nameless General Tom Thumb lookalike, they were the most talented fences in the city. But even they turned out to be dead ends.

It looked as though Lena's stolen diamonds had evaporated into thin air.

CHAPTER 26

William De Vries's condition took a sudden turn for the worse the day after Ned's scheme to locate the Marie Antoinette diamonds failed.

"She writes that the doctor has told her to prepare for the end," Prudence told Geoffrey, handing him Lena's note.

"*We have very little time left,*" he read aloud. "That's an odd way to phrase it. I wonder what she means by *we*."

"Lena's not a fool."

"Far from it," he agreed.

"William might not be able to speak, but it's possible he can answer yes or no questions by blinking his eyes," Prudence mused.

"What could he have to tell us that we don't already know?" Geoffrey asked. "He fired us and tried to end the investigation when he decided Morgan was the guilty party, and he never changed his mind. He believed his stepson was a drunken thief right up until the moment he collapsed."

"There's something else," Prudence insisted. "There has to be."

* * *

Straw had been laid in the street outside the De Vries home and in the alleyway behind it. All of the curtains and draperies were drawn tightly over the windows to muffle the sound of horse-drawn vehicles passing along this residential section of Fifth Avenue. Preparations for death, rituals to be observed as a life ended and a family girded itself for loss.

The feeling of opulent gloom that Prudence always experienced whenever she stepped inside the mansion was stronger than ever, the heavy silence more oppressive. The butler and the footman who took their wraps directed her and Lady Rotherton toward the staircase leading to the upper stories. Lena's lady's maid waited to escort them to the room where the vigil was being kept. Geoffrey had elected to remain at the office.

"I've done this more times than I care to think about," Lady Rotherton commented as they walked across the black and white tile floor. "It's never easy to watch someone die."

"You've known William for a very long time," Prudence said. She'd sat at her father's bedside during his final illness, straining her ears for the sound of a heartbeat, eyes glued to the diminishing rise and fall of his chest as his heart failed.

"William was a different man in his younger years. We all change as we age. Some of us more than others," Lady Rotherton said.

She lapsed into silence then, not another word spoken until Taylor opened the door to her employer's bedroom and Lena rose from her post at her husband's bedside to greet them. One hand drifted without conscious thought to her waist.

Lady Rotherton's slight but audible intake of breath broke the silence of the death vigil.

Everett Rinehart, standing at one of the windows facing onto Fifth Avenue, let fall the drape he had twitched aside and bowed in their direction. The nurse who had been attending William when the crisis began leaned over her patient to wipe a trail of spittle from his chin. The doctor who would pronounce him dead paused for a moment in the writing of his case notes.

The room was airless, close, overly warm with heat radiating from the fireplace and the registers of the gas furnace pumping away in the basement. Bowls of water stood on dresser and tabletops and in the corners of the room, moistening the dryness of the air to a nearly tropical mugginess.

The once bristling, vibrantly alive banker lay wasted, shriveled, and frighteningly still beneath neatly tucked white sheets and a down coverlet.

As she folded Lena into her arms, Prudence detected an unexpected hard roundness not unlike the protuberant belly older women sometimes developed when they no longer denied themselves the indulgences of the table. But Lena had always been so slender. After the death of her son and now with the final illness of her husband, Prudence wouldn't have been surprised to find her nearly as thin as the frail figure in the bed.

"I didn't know whom else to tell," Lena said, moving from Prudence's arms to embrace Lady Rotherton. "Neither William nor I have any remaining family." She blinked rapidly, then flushed. "Except Everett, of course. And he's already here."

"You must rest, my dear," Lady Rotherton said, leading Lena back to the chair where she had been sitting for who knew how long. "Young man?"

Everett moved quickly, opening the bedroom door to order the footman on duty outside to bring more chairs. Once Prudence and Lady Rotherton had settled in beside Lena, he went back to stand at the window, again tweaking aside the drape with one finger so he could look out at the world of the living.

The doctor spoke quietly to the nurse, leaned briefly over Lena, then left the room.

Prudence didn't have to be told that he would not be summoned back until William's last few moments, when the death rattle signaled that the end was imminent. She tried to banish from her mind the memory of her father's final moments. She had hoped never to have to relive them.

Lady Rotherton reached out with one hand, gripping Prudence's fingers firmly yet reassuringly. Her other hand lay quietly across Lena's upturned palm. "Courage, my dears," she whispered. "Courage."

It was only a murmur in the silent room, but William's eyelids fluttered and then opened. His unfocused gaze drifted past the three women to the figure at the window, then back again, as if he were trying to place all of them. Who were they? Why were they here? When his eyes came to rest on Lena, she inched her chair as close to the bed as she could, bending toward her husband's face, speaking softly and soothingly to him.

A spasm contorted the mouth William could not control, and again the nurse leaned in to wipe away spittle.

"I don't think he can understand what you're saying, Mrs. De Vries," she said, "but the sound of your voice may be comforting."

William looked anything but comforted. The muscles of his face contorted into a masklike rigidity, then collapsed as quickly as they had twisted out of normal shape. His eyes bulged from their sockets and a guttural, grating noise rose from the back of his throat, loud and hostile like the growl of an angry dog. Clearly he was trying and failing to speak, the last remnant of the man he had once been fighting with all his strength to pierce through the armored cage of paralysis.

When he lost consciousness again and the anger he had tried to express sank into blankness, the nurse nodded to Everett. There wasn't much time left.

"Does he know?" Lady Rotherton asked Lena as the door closed behind William's nephew.

Lena turned away in mute despair.

And then Prudence understood why Lena looked and felt so different, why her dying husband had erupted into frustrated fury at the sight of her.

"Not now," Lady Rotherton whispered.

The door opened. Everett entered first, followed by the doctor. Both men stood at the foot of the bed, listening. When the last breath was exhaled and William had been pronounced well and truly gone, her now late husband's nephew led Lena from the room, trailed by Lady Rotherton and Prudence.

"Brandy, I think," Everett suggested, helping Lena down the staircase to the smaller of the two parlors. He poured a tot of Courvoisier for each of them. "To Uncle William," he said, raising a toast to the dead man.

"To William." Lena touched her lips to the glass, but did not drink.

Lady Rotherton's eyes were bright with unshed tears.

Prudence wished Geoffrey had come. She felt empty and alone, yet William De Vries had been nothing more to her than her father's friend and a bothersome client.

"I'll leave you ladies now," Everett said, putting down his empty glass. "I must speak to the doctor, and there are other details to be worked out."

"He took over management of the household as soon as William was brought home," Lena said when Everett had disappeared and they could hear his footsteps ascending to the second floor. "I don't know what I would have done without him."

"Are you familiar with the provisions of your husband's will?" Lady Rotherton asked.

"Aunt Gillian!" Prudence exclaimed.

"Lena is a widow in a delicate condition. Which makes her doubly vulnerable, Prudence. Something you should think

about in case you ever find yourself in a similar situation. I repeat, Lena. Are you familiar with the provisions of your husband's will?"

"William said I would never have to be concerned about my
welfare." Her voice shook as she spoke, but there were still no
tears.

"When did he tell you that?" Lady Rotherton pressed.

"Shortly after we were married."

"That was a long time ago. Both of you probably still hoped
for children."

Lena said nothing.

"I know what it's like to disappoint a husband," Lady
Rotherton continued. "Viscount Rotherton married me for my
fortune and my assumed fertility. I married him for his title and
the adventure of living somewhere other than where I'd been
born and raised. Except for the fertility, each of us got what we
bargained for, albeit for a much shorter time than anticipated.
Not quite a year of wedded bliss, to be exact. My father wrote
the provisions of the marriage contract. He was a very canny
gentleman when it came to finances. Let's hope you are equally
well protected."

"There's nothing of mine left," Lena said dispassionately.
"Whatever remained after giving so much of it to Morgan over
the years was lost in the gold mine fiasco."

"You gave him access to your private fortune?" Lady Rotherton plainly thought Lena had made a serious and foolish mistake.

"He forged my name," Lena whispered. "He never intended
to steal the money. Morgan believed he'd be able to pay it back
with interest."

"He was swindled." Prudence remembered the whispers at
his funeral.

"Every dime he and I possessed went down the shaft of that

phony gold mine. That's why he got so drunk the night he died. He couldn't face having to tell me what had happened."

"How did you find out?"

"Everett told me. After he'd informed William. He said he had a hunch there might be something wrong, so he took a look at my account before the quarterly audit was due. He found the papers Morgan had forged that authorized him to withdraw funds. He didn't try to hide them because he didn't think anyone would ever examine them that closely. He never meant any harm. My son loved me, Prudence. We were everything to one another."

"Did Everett take over the business as well as the household?" Lady Rotherton asked. She poured herself and Prudence another Courvoisier.

"That same day. Banking and investment management is built on trust. Clients and employees alike have to believe that the institution handling their money is built on solid ground. The incapacitation of one man can't be allowed to disturb the smooth flow of business."

"Is that what Everett told you?"

"My husband believed it as well. He stepped into his father's shoes under much the same circumstances."

"Have you seen the documents giving Everett control of the business?" Lady Rotherton demanded. "Seen them, not just been told about them?"

"William promoted him to second-in-command around the time Morgan went to Illinois to take the Keeley Cure."

"Your husband obviously didn't have much faith in the good doctor's bichloride of gold injections."

"He called it quackery," Prudence remembered.

"But Morgan believed in them. That's what was important," Lena said.

"The documents? Have you read them?" Lady Rotherton persisted.

Lena's straight back sagged and her face fell. "I don't know anything about William's business," she confessed. "He was generous with the household allowances and with everything else. He paid the bills I put on his desk and never asked me to explain a single one."

"That doesn't answer my question."

"Does it really matter, Lady Rotherton?"

"Don't be ridiculous, girl. Of course it matters. Either you own De Vries Bank and Trust and De Vries Capital or you don't. Has Everett given you anything to sign?"

"In the library," Lena said. "He brought some documents home yesterday, but the doctor was here, so I put them in the desk drawer to sign as soon as he left. That was when William took his turn. From that moment on, I never left his side."

"Everett will lay them in front of you once we're gone," Lady Rotherton predicted.

Prudence made a beeline for the parlor door. "Is the library desk locked?" she asked just before she reached for the handle.

"No," Lena answered. "It's a large buff-colored envelope. In the middle drawer."

When Prudence returned she was carrying the packet Lena had described. "I haven't opened it," she said.

"Use this." Lady Rotherton handed her a wickedly sharp hat pin.

"Lena?"

"Please, Prudence. I'm not sure I could manage it."

By the time Prudence had extracted a sheaf of papers from the envelope, Lena had downed her small glass of Courvoisier, guided by Lady Rotherton's insistent hand. Her cheeks flushed from the liquor, she straightened her back and reached for the documents her husband's nephew had prepared for her. Lady Rotherton leaned in close enough to read them over her shoulder.

"I think that's rather self-evident," Lady Rotherton said

when they had skimmed the final page. "Everett must know the contents of your husband's will, Lena. Otherwise he wouldn't need you to sign the business over to him outright. *In recognition of his contributions to the firm and at the express wish of his uncle, William De Vries.* Nicely put. It makes it sound as though you and your husband were in agreement and that William was in the process of changing his will when he was suddenly and unexpectedly struck down."

"You can't sign this, Lena," Prudence said.

"Burn it." Lena's fingers trembled.

"No." Prudence placed the deed of gift back into the envelope before Lena could fling it into the fireplace. "Geoffrey will want to see this. It's evidence of an attempt to defraud."

"Perhaps more than that," Lady Rotherton said.

"What do you mean, Aunt Gillian?"

"Everett said he discovered Morgan's looting of your fortune because he became suspicious and thought to check your account. Didn't you once tell us that he had made substantial profits on behalf of the clients William entrusted to him?"

"More than any of the other brokers or account managers," Lena confirmed. "William was ecstatic. I don't think I ever heard him heap as much praise on any of the young men he'd hired. Each of them had to prove himself, you know. Morgan was no exception, even though he was my son. But there was no comparison to what Everett accomplished."

"Interesting," Lady Rotherton murmured.

"Don't tell him what we've discovered," Prudence cautioned. "When Everett asks what you've done with the papers he wanted you to sign, act confused. Burst into tears. Tell him you can't remember where you put them, but that you'll instruct your lady's maid to look for them. Whatever else you do, you must appear so overcome by grief that you can't possibly attend to business right away."

"You'll have to be careful though," Lady Rotherton cautioned. "You mustn't seem to be so distraught that you don't know what you're doing. Your husband's nephew could pounce on that as an indication you're not in your right mind. And that way lies a court order appointing him your legal guardian."

"I can't believe what I'm hearing," Lena said.

"Believe it," Prudence declared vehemently. After the death of her father, a greedy and vicious stepmother had plotted to have her declared mentally incompetent and locked up in an institution that administered regular doses of laudanum to women whose families wanted them out of the way. Lena was skirting perilously close to being also victimized by greed.

"Let him make the funeral arrangements," Lady Rotherton advised. "I'm sure he has something grand in mind, a service commensurate with William's importance to the city and the world of finance."

"You're already in mourning for Morgan, but there's no reason why you can't turn to Everett to support you in this hour of increased need," Prudence counseled. "Allow him to believe that you see him as stepping naturally into your husband's roles both at home and at the firm. Don't do or say anything to make him suspect you intend to take charge of your own affairs. You'll have to behave like a legal infant, Lena."

"What if he brings another set of those papers home for me to sign?"

"Faint," Lady Rotherton said. "That always confuses them. He'll call for the doctor, who will confine you to bed and tell you to take laudanum to soothe your nerves."

"Don't do that, either," Prudence said. "Tell him you're taking it, but pour it down the drain dose by dose. Act sleepy and supremely calm. Can you do that?"

"I've seen what laudanum can do to an otherwise intelligent woman," Lena said bitterly. "There was a time when William thought it would help me endure Morgan's many falls from grace. I didn't argue with him, but neither did I allow him to persuade me. One drunken member of the family was quite enough, thank you."

"It's not exactly the same as alcohol," Prudence told her.

"Close enough," Lady Rotherton snapped. "Whatever causes you to lose control of your senses and your willpower is to be avoided. Too much wine, laudanum, a lust for money or power, passionate love—they're all the same in the end."

An undertaker's van was pulling around the block toward the De Vries stables as Prudence and Lady Rotherton left.

Their next stop would be the offices of Hunter and MacKenzie, Investigative Law.

CHAPTER 27

Geoffrey's conclusion that there was nothing blatantly illegal in the papers Prudence and Lady Rotherton brought him to examine was soon eclipsed by the announcement of Everett Rinehart's engagement to Lorinda Bouwmeester.

"It's been coming for a long time," Prudence said. "No one should be the least surprised."

"The timing is what has everyone talking," Lady Rotherton declared. "It's too soon after William's death. The family will still be in deep mourning when the wedding takes place. I'm surprised the Bouwmeesters consented to so early a spring date, given the circumstances."

"Gossip has it that tickets to Europe for the honeymoon were already purchased and hotel reservations made before William's stroke threatened to knock everyone's plans into a cocked hat," Josiah contributed.

"Are you sure?" Prudence asked. Even Josiah's most outlandish statements usually turned out to be accurate, but this one seemed particularly speculative.

"According to Amos Lang's most recent report, copies of letters written to the various hotels were found in the Bouwmeester library wastebasket, as well as notes referring to the sailing. It would seem that much of the honeymoon is a gift from the bride's parents, and being old New York Knicker-bockers, they organized it to a fare-thee-well and negotiated favorable rates by booking well in advance. The groom's future father-in-law kept him informed of how the plans were proceeding."

"How convenient," Lady Rotherton sniffed. "What of Lena in all this?"

"She has apparently withdrawn into a proper widow's seclusion," Prudence reported. "I haven't heard a word from her in over two weeks."

"Nor have I," Lady Rotherton confirmed. "It's time we paid a call."

"She won't be receiving," Prudence objected.

"She wasn't welcoming callers after Morgan died, either," Lady Rotherton said. "That didn't stop us."

"As far as I know, we're still on the case," Geoffrey put in. "My ex-Pinks are picking up whatever tidbits they can, but it's not much."

"We're continuing to bill for their hours," Josiah said. His records were impeccably accurate.

"What I want to know is whether young Mr. Rinehart is aware of his aunt's interesting condition," Lady Rotherton said. "And what he makes of it."

"Has it been confirmed then? Do we know if Lena has seen a physician?" Geoffrey asked.

"She's in the family way, doctor or no doctor," Lady Rotherton stated firmly. "I've never known anyone to be able to hide the condition indefinitely. Too many women, especially maids, know exactly what to look for."

"Not a word from Amos Lang about Mrs. De Vries's expectations." Josiah phrased it as delicately as he could.

"Amos is a man," Lady Rotherton said dismissively.

* * *

Not even a man could be in any doubt about Lena De Vries's impending motherhood. She had lost the wasp waist affected by society women and grown a slight but definite abdominal protuberance. Her skin had the rich creaminess of a well-fed breeding woman, and her eyes reflected the deep calm of someone who looks toward the future with joyful anticipation. The child she carried was already taking the place of the child she had lost.

"I've decided to name him William if it's a boy, Wilhelmina if a girl," she told Prudence and Lady Rotherton.

"Leaving no doubt in anyone's mind about the infant's parentage," Lady Rotherton commented waspishly.

"None whatsoever," Lena agreed. She smiled complacently.

"Lena," Prudence began. She and Geoffrey had decided that it was time to be unapologetically honest with their client. "I'm afraid we haven't been successful in finding proof of Morgan's innocence. Both Geoffrey and I feel it would be deceptive for us to continue to keep up your hopes that we'll discover something we're afraid may never materialize."

"Are you telling me you want to withdraw from the case?"

"What I'm telling you is that there is no more case. Every lead we've followed has smacked us against a brick wall. As time passes, the trails get colder. There really is nothing we haven't tried. I'm so sorry."

"I thought if anyone could clear his name, it would be you two," Lena said. Heartbreak was on her face and in her voice.

"We thought it might be possible. At the beginning," Prudence admitted.

"What changed your minds?"

"Shall I tell you what we think happened? How the diamonds were stolen and who was responsible?"

Lena shrugged.

"This is all speculation, you understand," Prudence said, glancing at her aunt for support. "Those who could tell us the truth are dead. We've had to extrapolate the story from the few facts others have been able to supply and the clues we feel we can trust."

"It's logical, Lena," Lady Rotherton said. "And while it won't restore Morgan's reputation, it will give you some peace of mind. Listen to what Prudence has to say. Believe it." She reached for Lena's hands and held them lightly, comfortingly, in her own.

"It all started because of a need for money," Prudence began. "Aubrey Canfield and Morgan were in desperate straits. Neither of them knew how they were going to cover their debts. Both feared what would happen if they couldn't. It was almost an accident that they came up with the scheme to steal your diamonds. If you can take comfort in anything I'm about to tell you, it's that the idea didn't come from Morgan."

"My son would never have done anything to hurt or distress me."

"Except continue a lifestyle that brought you pain and suffering," Lady Rotherton said bluntly. "He loved you, Lena, as a son should love his mother. But he wasn't strong enough to choose you over liquor and gambling. Morgan was one of the weak ones for whom we can still feel affection, but for whose actions we cannot make excuses."

Lena slipped her hands from Lady Rotherton's. A mulish stubbornness settled onto the features of her face.

"He changed his mind as things got worse and there were threats from the people to whom he and Aubrey owed money. In the end, Aubrey persuaded him that they had no choice. They may even have agreed that both of them would eventually go back to the Keeley Institute and try once more to get and stay sober."

"They talked themselves into becoming thieves in pursuit of what they perceived to be a greater good," Lady Rotherton said. "One has to feel sorry for them."

"Aubrey had already begun a liaison with your footman cum valet, Leonard," Prudence continued. "There can be no doubt that it was sincerely felt on both sides. Taylor was an unwitting dupe in their plans. Leonard pretended to want her help in learning to care for a gentleman's diamond studs and cuff links. She showed him how to clean them, what to do if one of the prongs holding a stone in place needed tightening."

"Which also meant he learned how to bend a prong just enough to slip the diamond out and put a paste duplicate in its place," Lady Rotherton explained.

"We think Taylor wondered later if what she showed him had been put to a use she never intended."

"But you haven't asked her?"

"Not in so many words, Lena. We're convinced she had nothing to do with the actual theft." Prudence waited until Lena nodded her acceptance of Taylor's limited role in the drama of her diamonds. "Aubrey and Leonard were the ones who pried the stones out of the necklace, and not all at once. They got bolder after the first few imitations passed for real. We think the final extractions were done right before Lady Rotherton blew the lid off their scheme. Leonard had met Vincent Reynolds during his early days in the city, when he had run away from his father's farm on Long Island and was forced to earn his living on the street. Reynolds put him on to James Carpenter, who was open to buying stones that had no provenance, and offered to act as intermediary. Carpenter sold and recut the stones, Reynolds took his fee, and the rest of the money went to Aubrey and Morgan. If you look at the debts they paid off, it's obvious what was going on and where they found the money."

"We think Leonard killed both Carpenter and Reynolds," Lady Rotherton said. "There had to have been some sort of falling out among thieves. Either someone wanted a bigger cut or there was a threat to expose Aubrey and Morgan. Whichever it was, Leonard believed that the future he saw with Aubrey was slipping through his fingers. You have to remember that he didn't go directly from his family's farm into the servants' hall of a great house. We can only guess at what he did to survive during the interim, but we know it was in the Five Points, and there's no more dangerous or depraved place in New York City. He killed Carpenter to save Aubrey and then he eliminated the only link between himself and Carpenter. Which was Reynolds."

"A cold-blooded killer doesn't commit suicide when it looks as though he's gotten away with two murders," Lena protested.

"Leonard wasn't just a cold-blooded murderer," Prudence said. "He was a man in love. After he'd killed for Aubrey and for their future together, something happened to make him believe it had all been in vain. We'll never know what that was, but it thrust him into a despair from which he was convinced the only escape was to take his life."

"The rest of it we know," Lady Rotherton said. "Aubrey's death was a tragic accident, as was Morgan's."

"Aubrey was probably inebriated when the sailboat boom knocked him overboard, and Morgan was certainly far beyond sobriety the night he died," Lena said. "Everyone believes they bear some of the responsibility for their own deaths. Friends are too polite to say it within my hearing, but I can read it in their eyes."

"As you say . . ." Lady Rotherton was loath to whitewash the two young men she believed had led wasted, undisciplined lives, but neither did she wish to cause Lena further suffering. She let the subject drop.

"Everett continues to be my strong right arm in all of this," Lena offered. She appeared to have accepted Prudence's explanation of what had happened. Perhaps she just wanted to move on to what were bound to be happier days. "I'm content to allow him to continue to live here for as long as he and Lorinda wish, which I think will be only until they can construct a home of their own on Fifth Avenue. I understand he and her father are considering several building sites."

"And the businesses?" asked Lady Rotherton.

"We've agreed to postpone that discussion until after the baby is born," Lena said. "At the suggestion of William's attorney, who drew up the will originally. If it's another William, then we must take into consideration the fact that he may wish to take over his father's firm one day. If it's a girl, it might be to her advantage for Everett to buy her out of active management and invest the funds in a trust instrument."

"But, as William promised all those years ago, you yourself have nothing to worry about?" Prudence asked. It was always difficult and embarrassing to have to discuss money.

"Nothing," Lena confirmed. "Even with the disaster Morgan precipitated, William was generous to a fault. As I predicted he would be." She glanced sharply at Lady Rotherton, an unmistakable gleam of triumph in her eyes.

"Geoffrey will be relieved," Prudence said. "You had us worried for a while."

"I want you both to come to a small family dinner next week in honor of Everett and Lorinda's formal engagement," Lena said. "And you, too, of course, Lady Rotherton. It won't be anything splendid because we are all in mourning, and there won't be a mention in any of the newspapers, but we didn't want to let the occasion pass without something to mark our joy amid so much sorrow. You will come, won't you?"

"We shall be delighted," Prudence said.

"Wear the Marie Antoinette diamonds," Lady Rotherton suggested. "I can't think of a more appropriate occasion."

"The dinner should be at the young girl's home, not the young man's. What on earth is Lena thinking?" Lady Rotherton fussed. "William has been gone more than three weeks. It's entirely appropriate for us to wear gray, Prudence. He wasn't a relative."

"I'll wear black, Aunt Gillian. Out of respect for the very close friendship between Mr. De Vries and my father."

"Then you're forcing me to wear black, also," Lady Rotherton complained. "And it's not my best color." She stormed out of Prudence's dressing room, waving an impatient hand at her lady's maid. "The black pearls," she commanded. "I refuse to forgo the tiara, and I must also have a black ostrich plume. These Americans expect one to treat each of their functions as though it were a coronation."

"Will you want an ostrich plume, too, Miss Prudence?" Colleen Riordan asked. "Only I don't think you have one. Not in black, at any rate."

"I don't have a title either, so it's perfectly all right not to be grand. And it's only a family dinner to toast the newly engaged couple. There won't even be a line in the society columns tomorrow, so you needn't bother looking."

Prudence knew that Colleen kept an album of newspaper clippings in which Prudence's name appeared. In the months since Lady Rotherton's arrival, her maid had already added more articles to the pages than in the previous year altogether.

"Everything black, miss?" Colleen draped a pair of long silk evening gloves over one arm.

"Everything," Prudence confirmed. She wondered if the name cards at each place setting would be bordered in black, the way mourning stationery was, and made herself a mental note to check that arcane piece of etiquette.

Despite her protestations, Lady Rotherton looked regal and intimidating in her jet-embroidered black gown, ropes of black pearls, and sparkling diamond tiara. An enormous midnight ostrich feather added inches to her already formidable height for a woman.

Geoffrey paid her the compliment of a courtier's bow, then winked at Prudence behind her aunt's back as they climbed into the carriage that Kincaid had thoroughly warmed with hot bricks wrapped in woolen scarves.

"I have a feeling this is going to be one of those evenings when I find it difficult to stay awake," he whispered in Prudence's ear. "Kick me under the table if I seem to be dozing off." He often found the socially acceptable topics of conversation to be immensely boring, another of the reasons he begged off more than half the invitations littering his mantelpiece.

"We don't have to stay for very long after dinner is over," Lady Rotherton said, proving once again that her hearing was far too sharp for her age. "I for one will not linger over my brandy and coffee. I'll be quite happy to call it an early night. One can always offer the excuse of not wanting to impose on the hospitality of a house in mourning."

"Have you met the Bouwmeesters, Prudence?" Geoffrey asked.

"Lorinda, of course, at some debutante tea, I think. But not the parents."

"The name tells you everything you need to know, Mr. Hunter," Lady Rotherton told him. "Knickerbockers on both sides. Very prim and proper. They don't know quite what to make of the newcomers to New York society. If it's not old money it can't be respectable."

"Which would exclude half the people whose names regularly appear in the society columns."

"My point exactly," Lady Rotherton agreed. "I wonder if Lena will be wearing the Marie Antoinette diamonds tonight."

"She's too newly widowed," Prudence reminded her aunt.

"I know. But I'd like one last look at them."

"Why?"

"Just to be sure. I know what William said he had done. But that doesn't mean someone else hasn't been busy again."

Neither Prudence nor Geoffrey commented.

Lady Rotherton's assessment of the evening's guests was unerringly on target, except for one small disappointment. Lena De Vries did not wear the Marie Antoinette diamonds.

Lorinda Bouwmeester, dressed in black out of respect for the family she would soon be joining, was a small, pale blonde whose eyelashes were so light as to be nearly invisible, giving her an oddly startled look.

Prudence, smiling and murmuring polite nothings, finally remembered where they had been introduced. "It was at one of the Patriarchs Balls, wasn't it?" she asked.

"How good of you to remember," Lorinda said. "There were so many of us that night, all dressed in white, all probably wearing exactly the same anxious look. I'm so glad that's behind me. I know it's supposed to be a girl's finest hour, but I found it absolutely terrifying."

Which, Prudence decided, showed that Everett's bride-to-be had common sense and wasn't afraid to display it.

Mr. and Mrs. Bouwmeester were also very blond and lashless, two lookalike figures from New York's Dutch past, as rotund and devoid of pretense as a pair of wooden dolls. They clearly adored their only child and considered the handsome Everett Rinehart, since Lorinda had selected him, to be the perfect choice of son-in-law.

"They have a very old name and own half the Hudson River Valley," Lady Rotherton whispered.

"How do you know that, Aunt Gillian?"

"I ask the right questions of the right people, Prudence. How many times must I impress on you how important that is?" Lady Rotherton sipped a really fine champagne, silently thanking the departed William for stocking a decent cellar. Catching Mrs. Bouwmeester's eye lingering on Lena's slightly spherical waist and belly, she wondered what Everett's future mother-in-law was thinking.

"We're only eight this evening," Lena announced. "A small party but, I hope, a very happy one. I know I speak for my dear William when I say he would look upon Lorinda and Everett with great rejoicing and wish them a long, prosperous, and devoted life together."

It wasn't quite a formal toast, but in the absence of Everett's uncle, it would have to do. Mr. Bouwmeester came forward to escort Lena to the dining room, Everett claimed Mrs. Bouwmeester's arm, and Geoffrey conducted the blushing Lorinda to the table. Which left Lady Rotherton and Prudence following along behind.

"They certainly don't understand rank in this country," Lady Rotherton muttered.

"That's because we don't have it," Prudence reminded her.

"Of course you do. You just call it something else. I could definitely use another glass of that delicious champagne."

"Too late, Aunt Gillian. It's still wines from here on out."

"Lorinda is wearing an enormous engagement ring. I could see the size of it pushing against her glove."

"You're incorrigible."

"One of the small joys of life is comparing your jewels to everyone else's, especially when you know you'll come out on top."

Prudence read her aunt's face as they took their seats and knew there would be another few choice comments made in the carriage on the way home about the abysmal lack of correct formality at American dinner tables. Prudence would have to remind her that Lena had insisted on it being a very small family affair. In which case, Americans thought it perfectly fine to throw some of the rules of elegant dining out the window. She caught Geoffrey's eye across the table and guessed he was envisioning the same scene.

A beam of brilliant reflected candlelight flashed from Lorinda's engagement ring as she eased off her long black gloves and folded them neatly in her lap.

Prudence turned to ask Lorinda to extend her left hand so she could admire the ring Everett had given her—and then she froze. Lady Rotherton was holding Lorinda's hand in her own, one finger brushing across the top of the large diamond set in eighteen-karat gold. Back and forth, back and forth again, and then around the stone several times as if to memorize the shape and cut of it.

"It's definitely one of a kind," Lady Rotherton remarked. "A very special diamond."

"That's what Everett said." Lorinda blushed. "A very special diamond for a very special lady."

"I don't like being made a fool of," Lady Rotherton declared, thin-soled evening slippers drumming an angry tattoo on Kincaid's warm bricks.

"What on earth do you mean. Aunt Gillian?" Prudence asked. "It might have been a slightly boring evening, but everyone was excruciatingly polite."

"We've been made chumps of," Lady Rotherton insisted. "We've been conned, hoodwinked, duped, and misled. Had the wool well and truly pulled over our eyes. I don't like it one bit."

"Do you know what she's talking about, Geoffrey?"

"You can't mistake the eighteenth-century cut for anything else," Lady Rotherton said. "Every era thinks of some new way to enhance the brilliance of a stone. The court of Louis the Sixteenth was no exception. The diamonds cut for the necklace that was never made for Marie Antoinette are unmistakable. Lorinda is wearing one of them on the ring finger of her left hand."

"Are you certain? How can you tell?" Prudence felt as though the carriage were whirling through thin air.

"I told you I know my stones," Lady Rotherton said. "I've worn and studied Europe's finest gems all my life. I'd have to be some kind of an idiot not to recognize one of the Marie Antoinette diamonds when I see it."

"You're sure there's no mistaking it for another stone?" Geoffrey asked quietly. Not that he doubted Lady Rotherton's eye, but only that he had to ask one final time before committing them to as dangerous an action as any he'd ever undertaken for Allan Pinkerton.

"There's no doubt at all," Lady Rotherton said. "I saw you watching me, Mr. Hunter. Do you know what I was doing?"

He shook his head.

"Examining the facets. Feeling the shape and size of them. Making a mental picture I can sketch for you. Any decent gem expert would recognize it."

"What do we do, Geoffrey?" Prudence asked.

"I'm almost afraid to tell you," he answered.

CHAPTER 28

The burglary of the Bouwmeester home made all the morning editions of the city's newspapers. It was a shocking and deeply disturbing assault on New York society's privileged isolation safe from the depredations of a criminal element it largely ignored. Fifth Avenue mansions, seemingly impregnable in their solid bulk, were revealed to be as vulnerable to intrusion as the most ordinary citizen's much humbler dwelling. It was all anyone could talk about.

"It says here that Miss Bouwmeester had removed her engagement ring from her finger and deposited it in a Spode trinket dish on her dressing table for the night. That she was in the habit of doing so because of the size of the diamond. The household staff was questioned as soon as the piece of jewelry was discovered to be missing. In the course of the investigation, the police found that a window on the second floor had been forced open. The carpeting below it was dampened by the overnight inclement weather." Prudence folded the newspaper to the story she had been reading aloud, then tackled the next in the stack of papers Josiah had deposited on Geoffrey's desk.

"They're all about the same, miss," Josiah said. He had already skimmed the best and the worst of the accounts, most of which seemed to be nearly identical copies of what the first reporter to break the story had written. "They couldn't have gotten those details except from one of the servants."

"No doubt about it," Geoffrey said, sipping at the strong coffee Josiah had brewed as soon as he saw his employer's haggard face. "Half the gossip in the society columns comes from maids and footmen." He ran a hand over his chin and realized that his razor had missed a spot that morning. It had been a long and danger-fraught night.

"When will the Tiffany story break?" Prudence asked.

"A messenger delivered Miss Bouwmeester's ring and an anonymous note to the Tiffany appraisal department when the store opened. As soon as they've authenticated the diamond as being one of the Marie Antoinette stones previously set into Lena De Vries's necklace, Russell Coughlin will go to his editor with the story. The whole thing."

"I assume Mrs. De Vries hasn't been warned what to expect?" Josiah queried.

"We thought it best to keep her in the dark," Geoffrey said. "If what we suspect is true, she'll be safer if she can be seen not to have recognized the diamond Miss Bouwmeester was wearing at the dinner party."

"Will Everett try to bluff his way through?" Prudence asked.

Geoffrey shrugged. "There's no predicting what he'll do. We barely scratched the surface of who and what Everett Rinehart is."

"A thief and a murderer," Josiah contributed.

"Almost certainly," Geoffrey agreed.

"Almost?" Prudence questioned.

"We need proof," Geoffrey temporized. "We don't have it yet."

"Circumstantial evidence," Josiah concurred.

"I'm hypothesizing that if Everett did steal Lena's diamonds, it had to have been because he desperately needed large sums of cash that couldn't be traced back to him the way an ordinary loan would be," Geoffrey began.

"But the way he lives doesn't demonstrate any kind of extravagance," Prudence said, applying the same logic that had convinced them of Morgan's innocence. "We know he doesn't drink to excess or gamble, and the only hobby he seems to indulge is sailing. But the boat isn't anything near yacht size and he doesn't belong to a club with high membership fees."

"Something we were told about him has stuck with me ever since I heard it," Geoffrey mused. "No red flags popped up at the time, but they probably should have."

"What's that?" Prudence asked.

"Everett supposedly made more money for the investment clients whose portfolios he managed than any of the other agents working at the De Vries companies. William boasted about his performance and contrasted it with Morgan's. That's why he was promoted so quickly, why be became his uncle's second-in-command as fast as he did."

"And it could also be why no one questioned or challenged him when he took over the day-to-day operations after William had his stroke," Prudence said. "He's obviously a capable organizer. He ran the household for Lena so she could spend more time at her husband's bedside, and he continued to do so after William died. I don't recall anyone ever saying anything critical about him." She remembered the odd way Lena had seemed to brush Everett's casual kiss off her cheek, then decided not to mention what had only been a fleeting impression.

"Too perfect?" questioned Josiah.

"We need a look inside the portfolios he oversees," Geoffrey said. "If his clients aren't getting the returns he promised them, he might have taken the diamonds to cover their losses whenever someone wanted to pull out cash."

"And sold them to James Carpenter?" Prudence asked.

"Some of them," Geoffrey agreed. "But my guess is he's keeping most of them in reserve, hoping the stock market choices he's made will rebound in time for him to be able to hold on to them. He may be running the De Vries banking and investment businesses, but he doesn't own either company."

"Not yet," Prudence said. "Lena seems to trust him now, certainly more than she did when he first tried to have her sign away William's assets. I remember she was so angry that she told me to burn those papers. I wonder what made her change her mind."

"He's a snake oil salesman," Josiah said, tapping brusquely on his stenographer's pad. "Slick as can be and hardly ever makes a misstep."

"Giving his fiancée one of the Marie Antoinette diamonds was more than a misstep," Prudence said. "It was stupid."

"Greedy," Josiah concurred.

"It's always something simple that brings them down," Geoffrey said. "There's no way to prove it now, but I think he probably had James Carpenter create Lorinda's engagement ring. He's smart enough not to risk the stone being identified by a legitimate jeweler, but too arrogant to believe anyone would recognize it out of the context of the necklace from which he took it. And he must have known that Lorinda and her parents would expect solid proof of considerable wealth. As I said, something simple."

"It's a broad leap from embezzlement to murder," Prudence said.

"But in Everett's case, the potential rewards were dazzling. Think about it for a moment. He has a good, solid Knickerbocker name, but no money to speak of. He's raised in a small town by a widowed mother while other young men of less substantial background but more wealth lead a life that he can only envy among the cream of the New York elite."

"Jealousy must have eaten away at his soul every time he read one of the society columns," Josiah contributed.

"And then, seemingly out of the blue, his enormously wealthy uncle invites him into his business and his home."

"Two things had to happen to make that possible," Prudence speculated. "Morgan, the heir apparent, had to so profoundly disappoint his stepfather that William gave up on him. For Lena's sake, he might have pretended to believe that Morgan could reform, but he was already looking for a replacement. Then Everett's mother died; his filial responsibilities ended. William might never have reached out to his nephew while Everett played the dutiful son, but as soon as he was free, his uncle saw him as a possible surrogate for the stepson who had so grievously shattered his illusions."

"You don't suppose . . . ?" Josiah began.

"He might have begun to wish for his mother's death," Prudence said, "but I can't believe he would have hastened it. Not then. It wasn't until the floodgates of opportunity opened that he realized how simple it was to remove the obstacles that threatened his success. The first being James Carpenter."

"That may have been a crime of opportunity," Geoffrey said. "Unpremeditated, unplanned. Setting off an inevitable chain reaction once he'd gotten away with the first killing."

"How so?" asked Prudence.

"James Carpenter was a skilled jeweler, but he wasn't as good a businessman. We know from his accounts book that he was having trouble making the rental payments on his shop. So when Everett showed up with his stolen diamonds, it must have seemed the perfect answer to Carpenter's dilemma."

"Meaning that Aubrey and Morgan had nothing to do with the theft?"

"I think it was all Everett. Aubrey and Morgan were foils. Their obvious weaknesses made them natural suspects. We all bought into the deception Everett did everything in his power to concoct. I don't doubt that Aubrey and the footman were attracted to one another and perhaps were even planning a future together, but Leonard's suicide had everything to do with love gone wrong and nothing to do with Lena's diamonds."

"Then how did Mr. Canfield and Mr. Whitley manage to pay off their gambling debts?" Josiah asked.

"The way chronic gamblers always do," Geoffrey answered. "They went back to the tables over and over again, and sometimes, inevitably, they won. They would have paid off some of what they owed, but kept enough for another stake. It's a pattern of winning and losing that repeats until the gambler quits the game or dies, and it can play itself out at a fancy roulette table or over loaded dice in a back alley. The only thing that's sure and certain is that the gambler who can't walk away is as doomed as the drunkard who pours himself another whiskey."

"Back to James Carpenter's death," Prudence said.

"I think he got greedy after he made Lorinda's ring and realized how much more he could squeeze out of Everett. Carpenter was a small man who looked like he'd spent years hunched over a jeweler's bench."

"While Everett is well over six feet tall," Prudence said. "He likely played tennis and football at Harvard, and we know he sails whenever he has the opportunity. He's also much younger than Carpenter was."

"Carpenter probably locked the shop door and drew down the shades as soon as Everett walked in that final time," Geoffrey continued. "The last thing either of them wanted was to be interrupted by a casual customer. Carpenter may have threatened Everett with exposure if he didn't get a larger cut of the profits. We don't know whether Everett has an explosive temper when he's crossed or if he's simply a coldly calculating individual who makes quick decisions and acts on them immediately. In the end, it didn't matter for James Carpenter. He was a dead man as soon as he threatened his killer."

"Why cut his throat?" Josiah asked.

"To make it look like the type of violence that might have made its way up to Fifth Avenue from the Five Points," Geoffrey said. "A rogue criminal ignoring the police lines drawn around the Ladies' Mile. That's also why the shop was trashed.

A professional thief would have emptied out the premises at night. Neatly and very quietly. Everything we saw was a distraction, leading the investigation away from the direction in which it should have gone."

"And Carpenter's assistant?"

"Another obstacle to be removed. A link that had to be severed so nothing could be traced back to Everett. Aubrey was killed because we would have discovered eventually that his only connection to the De Vries home was his unfortunate flirtation with the footman who had the misfortune to fall in love with him. Morgan was a lucky accident for Everett, although we ought to assume that he was constantly and subtly poisoning William against his wife's son. As angry and disappointed as he was, I don't think William would have ordered his home locked against Morgan unless someone had pushed him beyond tolerance and forgiveness into implacability."

The door to the outer office opened and closed, letting in a draft of cold air from the hallway. Amos Lang had a newspaper in his hand and a triumphant look on his face.

"Here it is," he said, unfolding the paper so they could read the headline. "Special edition. I guess they figured the story was too big to wait for the regular afternoon print run. Russell Coughlin has his byline on it, and he hasn't pulled any punches."

"He names names?" Geoffrey asked.

"And openly asks how the Marie Antoinette stone in Lorinda Bouwmeester's engagement ring came into her possession."

"Does he mention Everett?"

"He identifies him as Miss Bouwmeester's fiancé, but stops short of accusing him of knowingly acquiring a stolen stone. The really scandalous part of the story is the hypothesis that William De Vries knew about the theft of the diamonds and conspired to keep that information from the police, thereby impeding the investigations of two murders."

"Only two?" Josiah asked. By his count Everett was guilty

of four killings, five if you counted his role in hardening William's heart against his stepson.

"Leonard Abbott's death is on the books as a suicide, and Aubrey Canfield's swim in the East River is officially an accident," Amos explained.

"I doubt we'll ever be able to prove any differently," Geoffrey said. He'd known from the beginning that even the intrepidly daring Russell Coughlin wouldn't go too far out on the limb of speculation. His reading public didn't want to hear about the heartaches of a man who loved other men and preferred to think that the shortening of Aubrey's life was probably a blessing in disguise for the young man and his family. Best leave those two stories in the dark where they belonged. Geoffrey had reluctantly agreed, well aware that Coughlin kept painstakingly accurate records of stories he or his editor considered too hot to print. Many a reporter planned to come out with a tell-all book once his newsprint days were over.

"What's not in any of the newspapers is that some of the De Vries clients have begun to pull their investments out of the company. And their cash funds out of the bank," Amos continued. "It's only a trickle as yet, but the flood is coming."

"It's what William feared from the beginning," Prudence recalled. "I remember him saying that a client had to trust the man and the institution that controlled his finances. And how could you be expected to trust someone who couldn't keep his own house in order?"

"He was right," Josiah said.

"Everett will have to make his move soon," Amos predicted. "If the rest of the investment moguls turn on him, he won't be able to escape financial ruin."

"He has to pull his assets together and get out of New York before anyone thinks to stop him," Geoffrey mused, reaching for one of the train schedules he kept in an upper desk drawer. "North to Canada or west to Chicago or California. There's no quick money to be made in the states of the former Confederacy right now and Florida is still a wilderness. Everett is a schemer. He'll want to be where the action is."

"And if he's smart, out of reach of the American authorities."

"Canada?" questioned Amos. "He could still reach California or Chicago eventually, if that's where he wants to end up, but he'd be a lot safer making the journey on the Canadian side of the border."

"His investors will likely send Pinkertons after him," Geoffrey said.

"That depends on how badly he's fleeced them," Amos said. "Pinkertons don't come cheap nowadays."

Geoffrey rose from behind his desk and removed the Colt .45 revolver and shoulder holster from the locked drawer to which he had the only key. He spun the cylinder and grinned at Prudence, who had also gotten to her feet and was checking the derringer in her reticule.

She fully intended to come with him, which meant there was an argument in the offing that he would probably lose.

But with Prudence, winning wasn't always the point.

CHAPTER 29

Everett Rinehart entered his late uncle's office and locked the door behind him.

He hadn't liked the chary looks cast in his direction as he crossed the bank lobby and made his way past tellers' cages and loan officers' desks. Everywhere he glanced he'd seen small groups of employees huddled together, reluctant to meet his gaze as they hastily whisked out of sight the newspapers over which they'd been clucking. Newsboys on Broadway had sold out of the special edition within minutes of its hitting the street, but that hadn't stopped them from shouting the headline and promising more papers as soon as the presses stopped rolling and the ink dried.

Damn the woman! He knew without a shadow of a doubt that the busybody Lady Rotherton, who should have stayed in London and out of his business, was responsible for what was happening. He could feel her coldly appraising look washing over him, finding him wanting, judging him inadequate. It had always been like that. Even before he'd managed to escape to Harvard he'd had to endure snide references to his father's failures that no amount of family influence had been able to hide. After Conrad Rinehart's death by his own hand, his mother's clinging dependence had chained Everett to her side and away from the vibrant New York City life he deserved to live. Those years had been the worst, so close to and yet so far from a world he could only read about in newspaper accounts.

Uncle William's summons had freed him. Within days of receiving the letter that changed his destiny, Everett had sold the miserable family home that had needed costly repairs for years. Then he paid a final, gloating visit to the graves of the parents who had nearly robbed him of a decent future, and left Wickelton forever, determined never to look back.

He hadn't counted on the fear that began to stalk him as soon as he was plunged into the world of investments whose worth rose and fell with dizzying, incomprehensible rapidity. Everett was handsome, intelligent, well-educated, and by birth a member of the Knickerbocker segment of New York society, but he had been marked from childhood by the specter of a spineless suicide father and a weeping, washed-out excuse for a mother.

Unable to believe that his struggles might really be over, he saw threats, competition, and conspiracy everywhere he looked. His uncle's stepson was a pitiful drunkard who blithely gambled away a fortune larger than anything Everett had ever possessed. Everett's facial muscles ached from the effort of smiling all the time and his jaws pained him every morning from the hours of frustrating grinding that made sleep an ordeal.

The possibility of failure haunted his every waking hour, never more so than when his uncle entrusted him with the investment portfolios of some of the firm's oldest clients.

"You can cut your teeth on these," William De Vries had said, depositing a stack of fat folders on Everett's desk. "I put them in safe securities years ago. Nothing glamorous or daring, but the returns are steady and the risk is minimal. As long as they can continue to live the way they always have, these clients will leave everything in your capable hands."

And so they had.

If Everett had been content with monitoring his uncle's successes and learning from them, all might have been well. But he was ambitious and impatient, two qualities that warred against steadiness of purpose and maintaining the status quo. He dipped into the portfolios with greedy fingers that swiftly became adept at hiding what he was doing. A stock sold here and there, inflated or entirely falsified figures on a balance sheet, funds shifted from one account into another when a payment had to be made. He became expert at satisfying the unsuspecting clientele whose wealth he was gradually depleting. William, concentrating for Lena's sake on the worthless and unreformable Morgan, became blind to what was going on. For the first time in his business life he let down his guard and trusted someone absolutely. Everett was his deceased sister's only child and the closest he'd ever come to having a son of his own.

William's office boasted a concealed safe that was nearly as secure as the bank vaults in which coffers of cash and client records were kept. The first thing Everett had done on taking over the day-to-day management of the business had been to move the diamonds he'd pried out of Lena's necklace from their vulnerable hiding places into the safe to which no one but he had access. Many of the stones had been recut and readied for resale by James Carpenter before Everett had had to eliminate him. Everett had nevertheless held on to as many of them as he could, unwilling to part with the stones for far less than what he knew Tiffany and other society jewelers charged their customers. There had to be a way of maximizing his profit, given the risks he'd run to acquire the diamonds in the first place.

Things changed again when William died. Lena stubbornly

refused to sign the papers Everett put in front of her, but he'd steeled himself to remain even-tempered and imperturbable. He saw to the smooth running of the household and the continued efficiency of the businesses. His transition from second-in-command to unquestioned successor to his uncle seemed assured. It was just a matter of time, he reminded himself. And meanwhile, there was the immensely wealthy heiress Lorinda Bouwmeester to ensnare securely in the web he was weaving.

It had been almost too easy. Everett was bored with the conquest even before she consented to marry him. The timing might have been thrown off by his uncle's death, but he hadn't allowed it to postpone the wedding plans. They were simply scaled back from grand social event to a suitably intimate family occasion. Which was actually something of a relief to the publicity shy Bouwmeester parents. They might have been richer than Croesus, but they were Knickerbocker enough to instinctively dislike and distrust any vulgar flaunting of wealth.

The single concession Everett made to an almost insane desire to shout his new prospects to the world was the engagement ring he placed on Lorinda's finger. He'd gloried in the shock on her face when she saw it, and the way her hand trembled at its weight. Whatever else he'd been, James Carpenter had known how to show off a stone to its best advantage. He'd wanted to recut it, but Everett had vetoed that suggestion. Every time he looked at the fourth finger of his wife-to-be's left hand, he wanted to see a stone that had been meant for a queen. And know that he was the only person in the world who recognized the truth of it.

And that was what brought him down. Not having grown up among people who were almost as expert as professional jewelers in the consideration and evaluation of the stones with which they bedecked themselves, he didn't recognize the subtle ways one diamond differed from another, how a cut defined the era, the country, and even the master craftsman who had effected it. Lady Rotherton had known what she was looking at within moments of Lorinda's taking off her glove at that damned dinner celebrating the engagement. He remembered the way the viscountess's fingers had caressed the stone, rubbing against the facets as though reacquainting themselves with a long lost friend.

Damn the woman!

Everett spun the combination lock of his uncle's safe with a steady hand. All his life he'd planned and schemed, instinctively preparing escape routes from even the safest, most perfectly executed stratagem. His present life was no exception.

The Marie Antoinette diamonds went into a banker's briefcase, along with bundles of cash and bags of gold coins he'd been accumulating for months. An untraceable fortune no one would know was missing until the next time an investment client had to be paid his quarterly dividends and an accountant discovered the portfolio had been looted. By then Everett Rinehart would have become someone else. Someplace far away from New York City. He'd miss the adulation he'd come to enjoy here, but he had no doubt that he'd find it again. Under a different name and with facial hair to disguise his features.

The secretary sitting outside his office heard Mr. Rinehart laugh aloud and wondered what a man on the brink of ruin could find to rejoice over.

"We have to catch him with the diamonds," Geoffrey insisted, "otherwise we have no case against him."

"Embezzlement?" Prudence suggested. "Surely he's cooked the books?"

"Where on earth did you pick up that phrase?" Geoffrey asked. He never ceased to be surprised by the things she came out with sometimes.

Josiah blinked and concentrated on keeping his mouth closed. He wanted to be in on the discussion he knew was going to turn into an argument as soon as Miss Prudence reached for her coat. There was no way Mr. Hunter would want her involved in Everett Rinehart's capture. Josiah was certain the man would be armed. And he'd seen the familiar Colt .45 disappear beneath Mr. Hunter's jacket into its leather shoulder holster. Amos Lang, he knew, never went anywhere without protection. They were expecting trouble, which was no place for Miss Prudence to be.

"I'm coming with you," Prudence said quietly.

Here it comes, Josiah thought, sidling back toward his desk, out of the way of the fireworks about to explode.

"No, you're not."

"Yes, I am."

Amos Lang slipped out of the office to wait in the hallway. Nobody noticed he'd left.

"I'll need you here to coordinate with the police when the time comes," Geoffrey began.

"Josiah can do that," Prudence said, perfectly aware that Geoffrey had no intention of bringing the police in on the operation. If there was anything a Pinkerton gloried in, it was circumventing the cumbersome apparatus of official law enforcement. Ex-Pinkertons were even more determined to sidestep officialdom.

"Your aunt would never forgive me if anything happened to you."

"And I'll never forgive you if you shut me out of this. I've been in on it from the beginning, Geoffrey, and I have a right to see it through," Prudence insisted. She felt the tiny derringer concealed in her reticule as she shoved her arms into her coat and secured her hat with a wickedly long, sharp pin. Gloves on against the February cold, and she was ready. If she knew anything about Josiah, he'd already summoned Danny Dennis. The hansom cab drawn by the enormous Mr. Washington was probably waiting at the curb downstairs.

"Stay behind me and out of sight," Geoffrey temporized.

"Of course," Prudence promised, having no intention of keeping her pledge.

Josiah picked up the telephone to inform Her Ladyship of where her niece was going, reflecting as he waited for the operator to respond to his impatient clicks that the argument he'd been looking forward to witnessing had turned out to be a bust. Miss Prudence and Mr. Hunter were definitely getting along better since they'd come back from that murderous wedding in Georgia.

Hardly a really angry spark between them.

He thought he knew why and wondered when they'd figure it out for themselves.

"That's him," Prudence said, pointing toward a bearded gentleman in slightly shabby clothing who emerged from the De Vries building carrying a square leather banker's bag. "He's wearing a really awful beard and a suit off a secondhand rack, but it's definitely Everett Rinehart."

"I wonder how he got past his secretary without attracting attention," Geoffrey said, taking in the changes in Everett's appearance that hadn't fooled his sharp-eyed partner.

"Sent him on an errand, then slipped away as soon as the outer office was empty," Prudence decided. "He's hailing a cab."

"Grand Central Depot," Danny Dennis called down through the trapdoor in the hansom's ceiling. Drivers had a system of hand signals that allowed them to tell each other where they were going without a word being spoken.

"Don't get too close," Geoffrey instructed. "We don't want him to spot us."

"Do you think he's heading for Canada?" Prudence asked.

"I'd be surprised if he weren't. He'll get a compartment so he can lock himself in and not have to speak to anyone but the porter. Everett is carrying a fortune in that case. He won't feel safe until he's across the border."

"Poor Miss Bouwmeester," Prudence sighed.

"Her parents will take her on a European tour," Geoffrey prophesized. "By the time they get back the scandal will have been forgotten. Or at least been replaced by something more outrageous."

"I don't see any sign that the police were watching him," Prudence said. She'd looked for a telltale presence lingering outside the De Vries building or hailing a cab after Everett came out, but no one on the sidewalk or across the street had seemed interested in the scruffy man hurrying toward New York's most important train station. "Surely they've put two and two together after reading Russell Coughlin's story."

"William paid them off to stay out of his family's affairs," Geoffrey reminded her. "They'll be slow to react, especially if Everett has kept up his uncle's bribes."

"There will be an outcry if it's thought the police deliberately let him get away."

"No worse than the other public condemnations they've survived," Geoffrey said. Someday a reformer would come along to clean up the New York City Police Department, but until then it was a grab bag of bribes, payoffs, intimidations, and outright thievery. Nothing of value remained in the property rooms longer than it took someone to decide to lift it.

The hansom cab taking Everett Rinehart to Grand Central Depot slowed down at an intersection to edge its way around two other cabs whose drivers were determined not to give an inch. One of Danny Dennis's street urchins ran out of nowhere to attach himself crablike to the back of the cab, signaling with a thumbs-up that the man he was being sent to follow into the train station wouldn't get away from him.

"I wonder how old he is," Prudence said, watching the boy find precarious handholds where it seemed none existed.

"Probably ten or eleven," Geoffrey said. Too many of the city's abandoned and orphaned children froze or starved to death in doorways and alleys. Every now and then one of the newspapers ran a story about their short, miserable lives, but no one seemed to know how to solve the problem. Or perhaps no one cared enough to bother.

"I'll remind Josiah to make sure we always have plenty of clothes and shoes in the storage closet," Prudence said. "And a jar full of nickels." Flashing larger coins meant their ragged possessors would be beaten up or robbed.

"We'll wait until he's bought his ticket and found the right platform," Geoffrey said as the boy riding on the back of Everett's cab jumped off and blended into the crowd making its way through the doors of Grand Central.

Amos Lang climbed down from his seat beside Danny Dennis and ambled his way after the newly bearded Everett.

"You haven't told me when you're planning to pick him up," Prudence said, itching to be out of the close confines of the hansom cab.

"On the train," Geoffrey said. "Between Grand Central and one of the next stations. We have to be able to prove that he was taking the diamonds out of the city."

"Of course he is," Prudence snapped.

"We have to be able to prove it," Geoffrey repeated. Telling her to be patient would make his partner edgier than she already was. "He'll be trapped in his compartment once he's aboard the train. No crowd to lose himself in. No well-intentioned on-looker to come to his defense. No chance he'll shoot an innocent bystander."

"I'll pull into the hansom stand," Danny Dennis said as they climbed out of the cab. Mr. Washington snorted and tossed his huge white head.

Prudence slipped a nickel into the grimy hand of the boy who guided them to a platform where they stood behind a pillar and watched Everett Rinehart approach the Chicago-bound train scheduled to leave in less than fifteen minutes.

"What's he doing?" Prudence hissed. "I thought you said

he'd make a run for Canada." The train for Montreal steamed on the other track of the same platform.

"Like I told Mr. Lang, the man bought a ticket for Chicago," the boy said, slipping his nickel into his pants pocket. "Look, there he is."

Amos Lang was already aboard the Chicago train, a newspaper held casually before him as other passengers found their seats in the car where they would sleep sitting up all night.

"Good man," Geoffrey said.

"If Everett doesn't hurry up and get on, the train will pull out without him," Prudence fussed.

"Not a chance," Geoffrey assured her. "He's just waiting until the last possible moment."

"Why?"

"To make sure he hasn't been followed."

To the *all-aboard* bellows of its conductor, the Montreal train began to move out of the station, its mighty wheels striking sparks from the track as they gathered momentum.

For a moment, Geoffrey and Prudence lost sight of their prey as friends and relatives strode along the platform, waving farewell and keeping pace with the slow-rolling cars.

"Where is he?" Prudence called out, a lick of panic forcing her voice above the clatter of the departing train.

She didn't hear Geoffrey's answer.

One second he was beside her, the next he was lunging toward the Montreal train, reaching out for a handhold, leaping aboard as it gathered speed.

Prudence didn't hesitate.

Picking up her skirts, she followed Geoffrey at the fastest run she'd ever managed.

One hand clutching an iron handhold, the other in a porter's tight clasp, her booted feet slipping on the steps of the last passenger car, she was unceremoniously hauled aboard.

"What the hell did you think you were doing?" a voice boomed in her ear as she settled her hat and smoothed down her skirts. The porter who had saved her from falling onto the tracks melted into the background.

"I'm either your partner or I'm not, Geoffrey. Make up your mind!"

CHAPTER 30

Thanks to an enormous bribe and Geoffrey's habit of carrying considerable amounts of cash, they were able to buy a private compartment in the same car where Everett Rinehart was hiding out. Without Amos Lang to assist with the takedown, Geoffrey was forced to consider his options, none of which he liked.

"There's no reason why I can't take Amos's place," Prudence argued.

"You don't have a decent gun with you," Geoffrey pointed out.

"Whose fault is that?" The tiny, nearly useless derringer was the only weapon that would fit into a lady's reticule. The rest of her was so tightly laced that anything wider than a whalebone stay would ruin her silhouette. Fashion was Prudence's greatest enemy and frustration.

"I'm not blaming you for anything," Geoffrey said, attempting to soothe his partner's ruffled feathers. He really wasn't. When he took a moment to think about it, he had nothing but commiseration for the plight of intelligent, ambitious women. There just didn't seem any way around it. Society was an implacable ruler. "I don't know that in your place I would have attempted that leap onto the train." He'd caught only a glimpse of Prudence's mad scramble and effort to catch her breath, but it had been enough to leave him with his heart in his mouth. Fear, not anger, had caused him to berate her.

"I accept your apology," Prudence said. She'd had her own moment of panic when she felt her boots sliding off the train car steps before her scrabbling feet finally found a purchase and the porter hauled her to safety. "But what do you propose we do?"

It was already turning dark outside. The scenery flashing by their compartment window was a series of dusky shapes lit here and there by flickering candles or dim lantern light. They were nearing the outskirts of the city, miles of open farmland lying ahead of them before the next station.

"I think we have to wait," Geoffrey said. "Allow Everett to feel safe. He probably won't go to the dining car; he'll order the porter to bring something to the compartment. He may allow the berth to be let down and made up as the night progresses."

"I don't think I'd sleep a wink if I were on the run." Prudence peeled off her leather gloves and removed the wide-brimmed hat she was wearing. It had almost defeated her, catching the departing train's rush of air as the porter pulled her onto the car's rear platform. Why did every garment she wore have to be uncomfortable or get in the way of easy movement?

"The porter has agreed to keep us informed."

"What excuse did you give?"

"I said Everett was an adulterous husband deserting his wife and children," Geoffrey explained.

"And he believed you?"

"Turns out our porter doesn't have much sympathy for men who abandon their responsibilities. It didn't hurt that I was able to pay him as much as he makes in a month of riding the train back and forth between New York City and Montreal."

"I could use a sandwich," Prudence decided. "We missed tea and who knows when we'll be able to eat a decent meal again." If they weren't to do anything about William's nephew right away, they might as well see to their own well-being.

"There's an element of danger to this, Prudence," Geoffrey warned. He didn't expect to run into a problem he couldn't surmount, but his partner's blithe disregard of the possible complications made him uneasy. He'd disarmed and handcuffed more criminals than he could remember, but he never relaxed his guard until he heard the final click of the steel bracelets and felt the sag of a defeated prisoner's body. Even then, there was always the chance you'd run into the one in a hundred crooks who knew how to disengage the lock immobilizing him.

"What's the porter's name?" Prudence asked, moving toward the door of the compartment.

"Henry," Geoffrey answered.

"I'll ask for sandwiches, cake, and tea," Prudence said. "Or do you want coffee? Either one should keep us awake."

It was no use trying to corral her. Prudence simply bulled her way through barriers. She reminded Geoffrey of her English aunt in moments like that. He didn't know whether to smile or groan.

"He let me make up his berth," Henry told Geoffrey and Prudence when he came to pick up their cups and dishes. "Quiet gentleman. Wouldn't never tag him for runnin' out on his family."

"Did you hear him lock the compartment door behind you?" Geoffrey asked.

Henry paused a moment and cocked his head, as if listening

for the sound of a bolt sliding into a door frame. "Yessir, I believe he did. Most folks like a little privacy of a night."

"Can you open it?" Prudence asked, knowing this was the information Geoffrey needed.

"All us porters got keys to the compartments. Have to, in case somebody needs help." Henry stiffened his back, not liking the direction this conversation was going.

"Henry, what if I told you that the man in that locked compartment was responsible for taking the lives of at least two people?" Geoffrey fastened his eyes on Henry's face, willing him to believe what must seem far-fetched at best. "He's a dangerous person I'm following until I can take him into custody."

"You a policeman?"

"I used to be a Pinkerton. Now I work for myself. As a private detective."

"You got papers?" Henry asked. "I got to see some papers. Got to talk to my conductor, too."

Prudence laid a placating hand on Henry's uniform sleeve. "We may not have time for that," she said persuasively. "I think you're just going to have to trust us."

For a long few moments the porter stared at the two well-dressed and well-spoken white people who, he sensed, were about to involve him in a situation he'd be lucky to get out of with his job and skin intact. Then he thought about the shabbily dressed man whose clothes didn't quite fit and whose hands never left the expensive leather briefcase that didn't match the rest of him. He remembered thinking that something wasn't right about the passenger's beard when he'd inched open the compartment door to accept the tray containing the dinner he'd ordered. As if it had somehow slipped a little. Which wasn't possible unless it was pasted on instead of grown hair. And the eyes. Cold blue and without a hint of real interest in anything but himself. Henry had served hundreds of passengers. Sizing

up a man or a woman was second nature; he did it without conscious intent.

"We'll need that door unfastened," Geoffrey urged. "But our
man can't hear the sound of the key turning in the lock. Can
you manage that, Henry?"

"Yessir, I can." Mind made up, Henry touched the master
key hanging from the watch chain looped across his chest. He
wouldn't mention the number of times he'd performed exactly
that service for a man in his dressing gown or a slippered
woman swathed in fur. Folks felt free to do things aboard trains
that they'd never consider chancing at home.

"In about an hour then," Geoffrey instructed.

"Midnight it is, sir," Henry agreed. He backed out of the
compartment, tray of dirty dishes in hand, wondering when to
broach the topic of an additional tip for extra services rendered.

"I'll take him in his sleep," Geoffrey told Prudence. "A lot
safer that way." He smiled reassuringly at her, noting the worried frown gradually fade from her forehead.

"I'll be right behind you," she said. "Your backup." She'd
heard Geoffrey and other ex-Pinkertons use that term dozens
of times. The prudent investigator never stepped into a dangerous situation without being sure there'd be someone he could
count on if things went wrong.

"I'd rather you stayed in the corridor," Geoffrey said, making it sound like a suggestion instead of an order. Prudence
never responded well to direct commands.

"In the corridor then," she agreed. "But I'll have my derringer out, just in case."

She pictured the operation in her mind's eye, looking for unlikely happenstances they might fail to anticipate. Geoffrey's
broad back in front of her, his Colt .45 trained at Everett asleep
in his berth. Shaking the man awake with the same hand that
slipped on the handcuffs in one smooth movement. Tugging

him to his feet. Shoving him into the seat Henry created by folding up the sleeping berth. Sitting opposite him, weapons at the ready, until the train reached a station where she and Geoffrey could hustle him onto the platform and turn him over to a policeman. Or arrange to take him back to the scene of his crimes themselves. Telegrams winging their way to and from Metropolitan Police Headquarters in New York City. The end of a very messy case.

She thought they'd foreseen every eventuality. And to predict was to forestall. Confident about what was to happen, sleepy from the late hour and the sandwiches she'd eaten, Prudence leaned back against the white-linened headrest. She pictured the astonishment on Lena's face when they told her the whole story of Everett's cruel deception. And smiled.

Geoffrey let her rest. He went over the plan he'd sketched out until he was sure he'd thought of every incidental development that might scupper it. In the end, everything depended on being able to unlock Everett's compartment without waking him up. The only moment of real danger would be as the door from the dimly lit corridor opened into the darkness of the sleeping compartment. For a few seconds Geoffrey would be outlined in the doorway, as tempting a target as any shooter could wish for. But Everett would be dead to the world, lulled into complacency by the rhythmic clack of the train wheels and his own arrogance.

Get past those initial seconds and Geoffrey would be home free.

He wouldn't fall asleep either, but he closed his eyes to run through the plan again.

"It's time," Geoffrey whispered, nudging Prudence lightly. He'd considered slipping past her to capture Everett Rinehart by himself if she dozed off, questioning the idea as soon as he'd had it. She'd never forgive him for shutting her out of the resolution of a case she'd worked on as hard as he had. And she'd be right, he acknowledged, grateful that she hadn't fallen asleep and put him to the test. What was it she'd said? *I'm either your partner or I'm not. Make up your mind!*

For better or worse, he'd made his decision.

Prudence sat up as cleanly and neatly as she did most things. She blinked once or twice, and then she was all business, all focus, the potentially deadly but undependably inaccurate derringer in her hand. Her skirts rustled as she stood up. "He won't hear that with the compartment door closed. I'll stand very still while you're unlocking it."

But Henry the porter wouldn't turn over his key. "No sir," he said, fingering the chain from which it hung. "Nobody takes holt of this 'cept me."

"I don't want to put you in danger," Geoffrey whispered. They were huddled together at the end of the train car.

"Tell you what I'm gonna do," Henry said. "Gonna turn that key as sweet and soft as you please. Then I'm gonna step on down to the other end of the car. What you do after that ain't no bidness of mine."

It was, Geoffrey thought, exactly what he had been about to suggest. Henry was a slender, agile man, but he had years on him, and Geoffrey wasn't sure the porter would be able to get to safety quickly enough if something went wrong. There was one less thing to worry about if he was out of gunshot range when the door opened.

He nodded his agreement, then he and Prudence stood rigidly alert and silent, watching Henry slip his master key into the lock of Everett Rinehart's stateroom. True to his promise, they heard not a sound, not even the snick of the bolt being withdrawn from the door frame. Henry returned the long chain to its place across his chest, touched one crooked finger to his cap, then disappeared as stealthily as a cat down the narrow corridor toward the next car.

Not even a whisper to break the midnight stillness against which the clack of the wheels was the only noise to be heard. So steady, so monotonous that any competing sound would be as out of place and alarming as the clang of a bell.

With Prudence behind him, Geoffrey inched his way closer to Everett's door, their shadows falling on the wall beside them. Henry had shaken his head when asked if the lights could be turned off. They'd been dimmed for sleeping, but that was the best the porter could do.

One last glance at his partner's pale, strained face, then Geoffrey curled his fingers around Everett's brass doorknob, registering its cold smoothness, tightening the palm of his hand so it wouldn't slip.

The bullet caught him in the vulnerable spot between chest and shoulder. Simultaneous with the echoing boom of the shot bloomed a starburst of red blood that spattered Prudence's face. Geoffrey raised an arm to fire, but a second bullet tore the gun from his hand and sprayed more blood over his partner. She caught his body as it fell, bracing herself to lower him to the floor, holding on to the derringer for dear life, staring into the darkness of the compartment to find her target.

Nothing. She could see nothing, though she was sure Everett Rinehart had to be mere feet away from her. She could smell his hair oil and the heavy scent of the expensive cologne he wore.

Another shot, and Geoffrey's body in her arms jerked spasmodically. A third bullet had bitten into his flesh, knocking the derringer from her hand as it did so.

A heavy boot kicked the minuscule weapon aside, sending it spinning.

For a moment Everett Rinehart loomed over Prudence, gun aimed at Geoffrey's head. Then he seemed to think better of wasting ammunition on a dying man. Heavy banker's briefcase in hand, he tore off down the corridor, slamming against Henry and sending the porter crashing to the floor. Voices called from behind closed doors as groggy sleepers tried to figure out what had awakened them, what was happening just outside the small, enclosed spaces where they had thought they were safe.

A rush of cold air swept over Prudence as she pressed Geoffrey's coat against the wound that was bubbling blood into her hand. She reached out for Henry, who was crawling along the corridor, trying to get to her, gasping as he fought to catch his breath.

"He's jumpin', miss. We're slowing down to take a curve. He'll be gone by the time we get around it." Henry hauled himself painfully to his feet, lurching toward the emergency pull that would bring the roaring train to a halt.

"No," Prudence shouted. "Let him go. We've got to get to a doctor, to a hospital. How far to the next station?"

"Twenty minutes. Mebbe a little more. You sure you don't want me to pull this here cord?"

"I'm sure. Don't do it!" she said angrily, despairingly. "The bastard isn't worth it."

Prudence bent over Geoffrey, whispering encouraging words while she continued to hold him, pressing as hard as she could on the wound that wouldn't stop bleeding. His face was a pallid, bloodless gray, eyes closed, spasms of pain furrowing the skin. She could barely feel a faint whisper of breath against her cheek. An icy chill crept across his body, as if warmth and life were leeching out with the rivers of blood.

A clean white handkerchief fluttered down from Henry's pocket, turning dark gray in the dimness as blood that would be red in daylight saturated its folds.

"I'm gonna go callin' for a doctor," the porter muttered. "Might be we got us one somewhere." He hauled blankets from Everett's compartment and draped them over Prudence's shoulders and around Geoffrey's legs, gathered pillows and another blanket to make a nest in which to cradle the injured man. Heaped towels where Prudence could reach them.

Then he set off down the car, calling for a doctor as he went.

Compartment doors were opening, men and women in long white nightgowns peering out, exclaiming at what they saw, the men enveloping the women in protective embraces, then gently pushing them back toward their berths so they wouldn't have to watch a stranger take his last breath.

"Please, God," Prudence whispered, "please don't let him die."

CHAPTER 31

In what was perhaps the only unplanned event in Everett Rinehart's life, he leaped from the Montreal-bound train on which he had been fleeing New York City into the Adirondack wilderness. No time for second thoughts. Behind him Geoffrey Hunter lay hemorrhaging out his heart's blood while his partner tried frantically to staunch the flow and keep him alive. Ahead lay darkness and a forest so thickly overgrown that ordinary humans seldom ventured into it.

Safety. He had to find a deserted cabin in which to shelter long enough to plan what needed to happen next.

He couldn't remember how many shots he'd fired at the figure outlined against the ill-lit train corridor. Enough to take him down. And then the moment when he'd realized that another bullet into the ex-Pinkerton's brain might be the very one he needed to defend himself against one of the Adirondack black bears who should be hibernating at this time of year. But you never knew. And if he found an isolated cabin, would he need to rid himself of its hermit occupant? Whatever ammunition remained in the cylinder of his Smith & Wesson .38 and a handful of bullets in his jacket pocket was all he had.

So Geoffrey Hunter continued to bleed out his life and Everett Rinehart jumped into the next phase of his.

The luck that had always brought him out on top of every situation ensured that he broke no bones and didn't lose consciousness when he landed on a deep bed of pine needles as the train slowed to take the sharpest curve of its run. He never lost his hold on the banker's case into which he'd packed bundles of cash, a fortune in loose diamonds, and a sack of gold coins under whose weight he struggled to get to his feet. He was a rich man, albeit at the moment a disoriented one lost in the wilds of the back of beyond.

He stumbled over and then picked up a stout limb blown to the ground in one of the frequent storms that swept across the mountains. Holding it out in front of him like a blind man's white cane, Everett began his long trek to freedom and the full enjoyment of the wealth he'd taken so many chances to acquire.

He deserved his new life.

God knows, it had cost him dearly.

Geoffrey was carried from the train on a hastily put together canvas stretcher, loaded into a horse-drawn ambulance barely large enough for Prudence to squeeze in next to him. The attendant sat across from her, one hand on his patient's thready pulse, the other holding a compress against the chest wound that would have killed a weaker man outright.

As a young soldier, Robert Carmichael had been well taught in the terrible war that had trained him to sit beside the dying and ease their passage into the next world. Though he tried to keep the foreboding from his face, he wasn't sure this newest victim of man's brutality against his own kind would make it to the small country hospital where there was a doctor who had performed miracles in battlefield hospital tents. Older now, and committed to spending half his life in the oblivion of a prodigious whiskey thirst, Dr. McNulty was still steady of hand when he was sober. He was this casualty's only hope. Carmichael prayed it was one of the doctor's good days.

Halfway between midnight and sunrise, Everett pitched to the ground in exhaustion. The heavy bag in which lay his future had ground the flesh from the palm of his right hand. He would have given one of the precious stones within for the pair of workman's leather gloves he'd left behind him on the train. And the heavy overcoat that might have protected him against the night's biting cold. He was pouring sweat within his clothing and shaking with freezing chills at the same time. How was that possible?

He'd acted so quickly, not yet asleep when the brush of the porter's sleeve against his compartment door alerted him to danger. Lying fully dressed on his berth, weapon in hand, Everett had prepared for trouble while not quite believing it would happen. He hadn't seen Geoffrey Hunter and Prudence MacKenzie board the train; he'd thought his clever ruse of purchasing a ticket to Chicago would thwart anyone who might be following him. And then that dance on the quay as he stayed closer to the western-bound train than the northern-bound one. The burst of speed at the last moment that carried him across the platform and into the moving car where he'd gone to ground in a hastily purchased compartment. The train was no more than half full. Proof that destiny was on his side. Who wanted to travel to Canada in February?

He'd fired more as a reflex action than anything else, but once his trigger finger sent the first bullet on its way, he hadn't been able to stop it from launching another. And a third. At least three, perhaps four. He couldn't remember. But the smell of blood had stayed in his nostrils, that and the angry, frightened shriek that had burst from Prudence MacKenzie's throat as she caught Hunter's body in its backward fall. Her face had been illuminated just enough to make out the set of her features as he'd stood over the two of them in those brief moments when their lives were entirely at his mercy. A determination that knew no bounds. And a steely loathing that was both contempt and revulsion. He was less than nothing to her. And she would track him down. Make no mistake about it.

Too late now. He should have killed her while he had the chance.

Dr. McNulty's hospital was four beds in what had once been the parlor of his family home on the outskirts of Waupaxit, New York. He had retreated there at the end of the war, battered, disillusioned, and more than ready to withdraw from most human contact. Into the depths of a whiskey bottle. But he remained a doctor. Over the ensuing years, as the desperately ill sought him out, he treated them as best he could, sometimes with such unexpected success that his reputation spread beyond the confines of the small village that lay five miles from the nearest railroad station.

The ex-Union medical officer had been passed out and dead asleep when Geoffrey Hunter was unloaded from the horse-drawn wagon that had jostled him over dirt roads little better than shallow wagon tracks. Alarmingly pale and unresponsive, the patient had already been pronounced a goner by the town doctor hastily summoned to the train station to evaluate him. Only the ambulance attendant's insistence on the curative powers of the reclusive Dr. McNulty had persuaded Prudence to agree to transport him to where a miracle might be worked. The town physician who had declared him beyond treatment wished her luck, agreed to lend the war surplus ambulance that was the best this rural region could provide, and waved them into the darkness. He expected to see the body brought to his makeshift morgue by the end of the day.

"Bring him inside," Dr. McNulty said gruffly, taking a pull from the whiskey bottle he then shoved back into the pocket of a dirty white coat that passed in this wilderness for proper medical attire. The veteran climbing down from the ambulance was a thorn in his side and a pain in his ass. Carmichael had been nearly as good a wound treater as any doctor during the war, but he'd refused to leave McNulty alone after they'd both made their way home again. It was the cases this ex-orderly brought to his front door that roused McNulty from his despair and vaulted him into periodic stabs at sobriety.

And now this ex-Pinkerton with bullet holes in him.

"I know he's been shot before," Prudence explained as she helped cut off Geoffrey's clothing. "Not this badly, and it was a number of years ago. He was still working for the Pinkerton Agency at the time." She was babbling, pulling out odd bits about Geoffrey's past that probably had nothing to do with his present, but her hands were caked with his blood and she was terrified that when they got his shirt off she wouldn't see the rise and fall of his chest that meant he was still alive.

"If you don't have any medical experience, you'd better get out of the way, young lady," Dr. McNulty said, motioning to Carmichael to join him at the kitchen table where he'd pushed aside the night's dirty dishes to make room for surgery. "Boil these, if you want to make yourself useful." He put a pan full of instruments into her outstretched hand and nodded toward the stove and the wood box standing next to it. "Build up the fire. The pump is outside. Right by the door. There's a bucket hanging on the spigot."

Geoffrey had insisted that Prudence, as part of her training to be a detective, familiarize herself with what could be done to keep an injured colleague or prisoner alive until he could be gotten to the nearest doctor or hospital. On her own she'd read articles claiming that the relatively new idea of boiling everything connected with a surgery achieved better results than Joseph Lister's carbolic spray. She shoved pieces of wood into the stove, jabbing them into flame with a poker, ignoring splinters and skittering bugs. Then she grabbed a bar of laundry soap from the tin sink where more dirty dishes had been piled and sped outside to wash her hands and fetch water to boil on the now stoked up stove.

By the time she got back inside, Geoffrey lay naked on the table, his genitals modestly covered with a dish towel. A strong smell of carbolic permeated the air; the doctor hadn't waited for his instruments to be boiled before beginning to probe for the bullets that were draining away his patient's life.

"He'll stay unconscious," Dr. McNulty predicted. "No need to use ether or laudanum. I'm not sure he'd survive either of them." His fingers and a long, curved instrument disappeared into the hole he'd just cut in Geoffrey's chest. "If we're lucky, the bullet will have missed the breastbone."

"And the lung," commented his former orderly, wiping at the pooling blood with what appeared to be his own handkerchief.

"Too late for that. Be ready to pound on him if he stops breathing."

Prudence placed the shallow pan of instruments on the hot stove, adding just enough water to cover them. She didn't know how many minutes it took for water to come to a boil.

"How long?" she asked. "How long should I cook them?"

"It's called sterilizing, and it usually takes thirty minutes, but this young man doesn't have that kind of time. Five minutes from when you see the water simmering will have to be enough. Start another pot and throw some cloths into it. Whatever looks clean."

Nothing in the doctor's kitchen appeared to be anything but used up or dirty. Lifting her skirt, Prudence began to rip at the linen underskirt she was wearing, tearing off long strips that looked enough like bandages to pass muster.

"I've got it," Doctor McNulty said.

Nobody moved or breathed as his forceps pulled out a slightly flattened piece of rounded metal. "This is what's been causing most of the damage." He dropped it onto the uneven tabletop, where it rolled unnoticed to the floor beneath.

"Did it go through the lung?" the attendant asked.

"Missed it by a hair. But it's made a mess of his pectoralis major. Throw some thread and a needle into that hot water, miss. I've got some fine sewing to do if he's to regain use of his left arm."

Two hours later Geoffrey was bullet free. And still alive. Barely.

Doctor McNulty had probed and stitched additional wounds in his right arm, right leg, and between two broken ribs, dropping each bullet onto the table, where it promptly rolled off. The kitchen was as steamy as a laundry room. Beads of moisture dripped down Prudence's face; her bodice was as soaked as the skirts she'd used to protect her hands against the boiling hot instruments. Dr. McNulty and his orderly had worked in rolled up shirtsleeves, tight collars torn off, blood and water drenching their thick wool trousers.

"He can't be moved," Dr. McNulty decreed when they'd carried Geoffrey to one of the empty beds in the former parlor. "If he makes it through the next twenty-four hours, he stands a chance of surviving." He held out a small brown bottle of laudanum to Prudence. "You need something, young lady. For a job well done." He thought she looked almost as spent as the patient over whom he'd labored.

Prudence pushed away the laudanum. "I can't," she murmured, not offering any further explanation, sinking down onto a chair beside Geoffrey's bed to begin what she knew would be a long vigil.

McNulty used what was left of the hot water to steep tea leaves in a pot that looked as though it had never been used. Three heaping teaspoons of sugar for its restorative powers. He stood over her while she drank it, and only left her side when the cup was empty.

"Is there a law enforcement officer in town?" she asked, smoothing Geoffrey's hair back from his forehead and temples.

"The shooting took place on the train, miss. Unless you know exactly where he was when your friend was wounded, my guess is nobody's going to want to touch it. Jurisdictional problem. And I think the railroads have their own police." Robert Carmichael had little or no faith that justice was ever done without a hefty bribe. People who wanted satisfaction for a wrong done to them generally took matters into their own hands. That was the way the town officials preferred it.

"I need to send a telegram." Josiah had to be informed of what had happened. And Ned Hayes. Between them they'd know what needed to be done.

"You write it out and I'll carry it back to town," Carmichael promised. "We've got a telegraph operator at the station. I'll get him out of bed if I have to."

Dawn woke Everett Rinehart from the stupor into which he had fallen. He felt half frozen, the ground beneath him rocky hard, the sparse winter grass beaded with tiny icicles. He struggled to a sitting position, rubbing his hands together to get some circulation going, shaking his head from side to side to dispel the fog that seemed to be everywhere. He couldn't see an arm's reach in front of him, but he didn't know whether that was nature or something he'd done to himself when exhaustion had taken him down. His mouth tasted like blood, but he had no saliva to spit out. It took him almost half an hour to make it onto his feet, every moment a fight against pain, undependable shaky muscles, and fear.

Fear was what he most needed to beat back. Fear was what could defeat him if he let it. He kept before him the vision of an abandoned cabin somewhere in the early dawn grayness out ahead of him, a sturdily built single room refuge with a pile of last year's wood on the covered porch. And a box of safety matches sitting on the stove top next to a battered tin coffeepot.

He could smell the coffee he'd brew from grounds left forgotten in a pantry. Maybe cornmeal, too, which he could fashion into cakes with a little melted snow. No fat to fry them in, but that didn't matter. It was heat that counted, dry logs burning brightly in a fireplace and a stove. He could almost taste the coffee and see the corn cakes turning brown in the iron skillet.

He stepped off the edge of a high cliff before he knew it was there. One foot scrabbling atop thin air while the other tried and failed to stay on solid ground. He heard himself scream as he hurtled headlong down the rocky precipice, arms and legs windmilling but desperate fingers never letting go of the precious banker's briefcase. It seemed to take forever, but when the ending came, it was sudden.

Everett's head hit a moss-covered boulder, splitting open with a cracking sound that was swallowed up by the fog. The banker's briefcase burst open, bundles of cash breaking out of their ribbons, scattering into the early morning breeze. Heavy gold coins rained down on the fragile paper. The velvet pouch containing the stolen Marie Antoinette diamonds rolled beneath his lifeless hands, spilling its contents. When the sun burned away the fog the precious stones would sparkle like drops of frozen dew.

Until the pack of wolves who had heard his cries loped near to gather round the dead man, waiting patiently for a sign of life before they moved in to feast on him. Then blood spattered the ground and the gems meant to adorn the neck of a doomed queen. Flesh nourished flesh, and eventually what had once been a man was carried away bone by bone.

The stones for which he'd died would sink into the ground and be covered over by leaves and dirt. The gold coins would lose their luster in the mud. The fortune in paper currency blowing across the mountainside would melt under winter snow and spring rain until nothing remained.

Everett Rinehart, once so promising a young man, was no more.

*   *   *

Amos Lang had caught the next Canada-bound train out of Grand Central Depot. At every stop he grilled the stationmaster, demanding to know if anyone answering to Geoffrey or Everett or Prudence's description had gotten off. When he finally showed up at Dr. McNulty's makeshift hospital, he had cabled Josiah and was driving a hired carriage fitted out with half a dozen mattresses and every pillow and blanket he'd been able to buy.

By the time they got him back to New York City, Geoffrey had regained and relost consciousness more times than anyone could count. But against Dr. McNulty's dire predictions and all odds, he was still alive. A doctor from the Bellevue Emergency Pavilion who was said to be the city's foremost expert on gunshot wounds visited him in his suite at the Fifth Avenue Hotel. He declared he couldn't have done a better job on the wounds had he probed and stitched them up himself, then said the words that drove a chill into Prudence's heart.

"He's in God's hands now."

EPILOGUE

"They never did find the exact spot where Everett leaped from the train," Prudence told Geoffrey a few weeks later. "No body, no diamonds. Amos Lang says the locals believe he made it to Canada with the help of one of the mountain men living on the land back where it's too steep to farm and too remote to attract anyone else." She'd held off talking about what happened that night for as long as she could, but now that Geoffrey was no longer delirious with fever, he was demanding answers.

It would be months before he could walk without crutches on the shattered leg, and odds were good that he would always need a cane. But at least he hadn't lost the limb to amputation or his life to gangrene.

Josiah had seen to it that his employer's suite at the Fifth Avenue Hotel was as medically well-equipped and staffed as a Bellevue Hospital ward. He'd hired the best help to be found in the city, relying on the contacts he had made during Senator Roscoe Conkling's losing battle with exposure after the Great Blizzard. And every day, as regularly as he appeared at the offices of Hunter and MacKenzie, Investigative Law, he checked to make sure that Geoffrey Hunter's continuing care met the high standards he had set.

Today, for the first time since the shooting, Geoffrey had hobbled from his bed into the suite's parlor without the assistance of one of the nurses whose care had brought him back from the brink. For hours and days on end, as he thrashed in febrile delirium, they had bathed his fiery skin with cool cloths soaked in a mixture of alcohol, water, and tincture of willow bark. Forced beef broth and strengthening sips of diluted whiskey down his swollen throat, changed his dressings with exquisite tenderness, and replaced his linen as soon as it became soiled.

Even Tyrus, standing behind Ned Hayes as they waited for the doctor's verdict every time he visited his patient, had no complaints.

"They know they bidness, them nurses," he reassured a pale, exhausted Prudence. "He gonna be all right, Miss P. Take my word on it."

"Tyrus knows what he's talking about," Ned promised. "Lord knows I should have died half a dozen times, but he was just too stubborn to let me go."

"More like a couple dozen, Mistuh Ned. You never have learned to count proper. That's why I beat you at cards ever' time we deal 'em out."

"He cheats," Ned confided. "I can't catch him at it, but I know he cheats."

Their bickering lightened the burden of concern that interfered with Prudence's sleep, robbed her of appetite, and turned her thoughts toward the solace of laudanum. Whenever she felt herself begin to weaken, she only had to envision the look on Geoffrey's face if he were to see dullness in her eyes or smell a telltale bitterness on her breath. The prospect of his disappointment and the need to prove to herself that she was stronger than her addiction strengthened her resolve against the temptation of giving in. Her step had faltered more than once when she passed the apothecary's shop two doors down from the hotel, but then she'd picked up the pace and swept by as though the demons of hell were on her heels. Which they were—in the form of cork-stoppered little brown bottles.

Glancing toward where Geoffrey sat in a cushioned armchair, the bad leg stretched out in front of him on a hassock, she breathed a sigh of relief.

"You're smiling, Prudence," Geoffrey said. He thought the tightness of her lips was a little too grim to be expressing pleasure, but even the hint of a smile was better than some of the looks he'd caught on her face when she didn't think he was watching. He'd been close to death before, but it was different this time. He hadn't had much to lose then; now he had everything.

"We'll be on our way," Ned Hayes said, stooping to kiss Prudence's hand in his exaggerated gentlemanly way. He cuffed Geoffrey lightly on the shoulder, as close as he could come to the loving gesture of a brother, then nodded to Tyrus, who was already getting to his feet.

"I'll have the kitchen send up some tea," Josiah offered.

He could have placed the order by phone, but that wouldn't have left Geoffrey and Prudence alone for the first time since his bullet-ridden body had fallen into her arms. And they needed to be on their own for a change. No nurses, no friends, no witnesses to whatever they had to say to one another. Whatever had been held back for so long.

Josiah wasn't sure that Mr. Hunter and Miss Prudence realized how close they had come, how near they still were to losing what neither of them seemed bold enough to claim, but he and everyone else around them understood.

Especially Lady Rotherton. Beautiful, powerful, British, and rich she might be, but Josiah suspected she'd step on her niece's chance at happiness without a second thought. He wouldn't go back to the office right away. He'd stop by the MacKenzie mansion for tea and the kind of chat that could go on for hours.

And keep Prudence's aunt from deciding to drop by the Fifth Avenue Hotel to poke her long, aristocratic nose in where it had no business being.

When Josiah slipped from the parlor into the corridor, he paused for a moment, the door open just wide enough to hear what Mr. Hunter and Miss Prudence might be saying to one another.

Nothing. A silence so profound he shook his head in as close to despair as he ever allowed himself to get.

A waiter had set the laden tea tray on the low table in front of them, then withdrawn when Prudence signaled that she would pour.

The door clicked shut behind him. The suffocating silence descended again.

One of them would have to say something. What had happened to the easy camaraderie they'd found at the end of the Bradford Island experience?

"You almost died, Geoffrey."

"But I didn't. Anyway, it comes with the territory." He shrugged, then grimaced. His shoulder and chest muscles were knitting back together too slowly to suit him. Every time he moved he pulled something tender and still sore. "I accepted a long time ago that it's the price I may have to pay for the way I choose to live my life."

She poured tea into two cups, held one out to him. Seemed not to have heard what he had said. Kept her eyes lowered, refused to scale the wall he had flung up between them.

He thought he knew why she had withdrawn into a protective shell of her own creation. Hearing a truth put into words almost always brought with it a choice to be made. And that was something he feared Prudence was not ready to do. She had already lost too many people she loved. And now there was no guarantee he would heal into wholeness, no matter what the doctors optimistically promised. Was she strong enough to walk with eyes wide open into a future that seemed to promise more pain? More death?

Geoffrey had thought of nothing else in the long days and nights when he'd fought his way toward recovery, when it seemed to those caring for him that his mind was lost in incoherent nightmares. In reality, it had seldom been far from the young woman who had sat for hours at a stretch beside his bed, always there when a flicker of consciousness broke through the fever, never absent when he longed to call out for her but did not.

When the fever finally broke and he had longer periods of awareness, he had forced himself to study her through lowered lashes. If she believed him to be sleeping, she allowed herself to doze, and that was when she was at her most vulnerable. Revealed to his hungry gaze as she never was when on her guard against him. Or against feelings she would or could not acknowledge? He wished he knew for certain which it was.

He'd chastised himself for unforgiveable carelessness at the idiocy of standing backlit in a doorway and believing it would not bring him grave harm. It was the kind of thing a fledgling detective did—only once. A tough and sometimes mortal lesson to have to learn. Of the shots themselves or the pain of bullets piercing flesh, he remembered almost nothing. Just the first one. The first shot and the instantly humiliating realization that he'd bungled. Very, very badly. But then, what choice had he had?

Between studying a sleeping Prudence and steeling himself not to wince against pain that tore through him every time he took a deep breath, he had replayed the moments leading up to Everett Rinehart's escape. And found there were gaps in his memory that he would probably never be able to fill. Gradually, he would come to accept those empty spaces, as he had had to do in the past when a case invaded his mind in ways against which he had no defense. It was something other Pinkertons hinted at over one too many drinks. Everyone in the business feared the black dogs and the emptiness; nobody talked about them.

Would it be fair to Prudence to ask her to spend her life with a man injured in both body and memory? Sometimes the mental balance shifted. For reasons no one could ever articulate, a detective or private operative took his own life. By rope or gunshot, liquor or opium. It didn't matter the method. The end result was the same.

Society made outcasts of self-killers. Their loved ones might as well have died with them, forever sharing the burden of guilt. His inner eye shifted to the memory of Leonard Abbott's body dangling from an attic beam. The ugly, desperate waste of it.

Geoffrey could not do that to Prudence. But nor could he give her up.

Had he realized what he'd said?
I accepted a long time ago that it's the price I may have to pay for the way I choose to live my life. I accepted . . . It's the price I may have to pay.

Over and over until Prudence despaired of ever getting Geoffrey's words out of her head. To give one's life in the service of one's country or to risk death to save another was understandable. Laudatory. Commendable even. But to be willing to embrace death in pursuit of a criminal who contributed nothing to society was . . . stupid. Senseless. Irresponsible. Cruel to those who loved you. All of the things Prudence knew Geoffrey was not.

How could she love a man who would risk breaking her heart for the allure of heroic balderdash? How could she love a man . . . ?

How could she not love Geoffrey, no matter who and what he was?

All those hours by his bedside had taught her nothing if she could not accept the truth of the feelings that had been growing for who knew how long inside her. In her fragile, wounded heart, in her stubborn head, in every fiber of the body that had nearly betrayed her so many times.

She had only to close her eyes to remember what it felt like to whirl around the dance floor at Delmonico's in his embrace, one muscled arm tightly clasped around her waist, his gloved hand holding hers. Flesh never touched flesh, but it might as well have. The fire that burned her had not come from candle flames or too many bodies pressed too tightly together in a small space. It could only have come from a hidden place where some hitherto untapped hunger had erupted at the sound of Geoffrey's voice, the look in his dark eyes, the animal strength of a man in his prime.

One of them had to speak first. One of them had to open the floodgates.

"Aunt Gillian is sailing back to England."

That wasn't what she'd meant to say. Wasn't what she wanted to tell him.

"She's insisting that I go with her."

Prudence waited. He had clasped her hand in the civility of a dance. Would he reach out to her now?

The silence stretched on. Excruciating. Unbroken.

Until finally Geoffrey forced himself to speak.

"Will you go?"

Slowly, Prudence raised her head from the cup she held in a hand that now trembled uncontrollably.

She needed to read her answer in his eyes.

AUTHOR'S NOTE

The diamond necklace worn by Lena De Vries at the Assembly Ball held at Delmonico's on December 12, 1889, is, alas, imaginary. No doubt King Louis XVI must have been overjoyed at the birth of the Dauphin in 1781, but whether he planned to celebrate the arrival of an heir by bestowing a spectacular waterfall of diamonds on Queen Marie Antoinette is pure speculation on my part.

We do know that what was left of the French Crown jewels after the looting of the royal treasury in 1792 was auctioned off by the government of the French Third Republic from May 12 to May 23, 1887. The sales were attended by representatives of many of the royal houses then in existence, as well as famous jewelers from throughout the world. Including Tiffany.

Many of the jewels that had been stolen during the Revolution had been recovered over the years since Madame La Guillotine reigned, although some of the most famous among them had disappeared. For readers who are interested in a description of what was auctioned, and especially the Tiffany purchases, there are many articles available on the Internet, including some that contain citations from the sales catalogue. The pictures of individual pieces are breathtaking, as is the mental image of handfuls of diamonds, sapphires, rubies, emeralds, and pearls spilling through the fingers of the successful buyers.

The Keeley Institute was established in Dwight, Illinois, in 1879 by Dr. Leslie E. Keeley, a former Union Army surgeon who believed that alcoholism was a disease that could be cured. Specifically, that he alone possessed the secret recipe whose ingredients would eradicate an individual's addiction to both alcohol and opium, including laudanum. Patients agreed to a four- to six-week stay at the institute he founded, lining up four times daily to receive injections of what Keeley claimed to be bichloride of gold. The treatment could only be obtained through residency at the institute, where patients also followed a prescribed regimen of exercise and healthy diet, including a tonic that had to be drunk every few hours throughout the day. The tonic was more than 25 percent alcohol and the injections contained atropine, boric acid, strychnine, and other dubious ingredients—but no bichloride of gold.

Despite skepticism and opposition by many in the medical field, Keeley's Gold Cure was immensely popular, especially in the 1890s, not least because patients were lodged in the pleasant, relaxed surroundings of local hotels and boardinghouses where they were made to feel comfortable and always reassured that freedom from addiction was not only possible, but well within their grasp. Women who took the Gold Cure were not required to line up to receive their injections; they were treated in the privacy of their rooms. At the height of its popularity, the Keeley Institute numbered more than two hundred branch clinics and had treated hundreds of thousands of patients. Those who relapsed into alcohol or opium addiction were considered to have been cured at one time, their regression a matter of individual choice.

As always, thanks go to my editor, John Scognamiglio, and to my literary agent, Jessica Faust. Their belief in my writing and commitment to the stories I spin is a constant source of encouragement.

My Tuesday morning critique group knows how much I value their input. They keep the intrigue moving in the right direction and always let me know when a character tries to step outside his purview.

And last but never least, it would be much harder to do this without the support of my husband, who never interrupts me when the Joker is face up on the piano.